MISSING LINK

STEVEN DABNEY

Copyright © 2022 by Steven Dabney.

All rights reserved. No part of this publication may be reproduced, distributed, or transmitted in any form or by any means, including photocopying, recording, or other electronic or mechanical methods, without the prior written permission of the author, except in the case of brief quotations embodied in critical reviews and certain other noncommercial uses permitted by copyright law.

Printed in the United States of America.

Library of Congress Control Number: 2022939807

ISBN	Paperback	978-1-68536-618-6
	Hardback	978-1-68536-619-3
	eBook	978-1-68536-620-9

Westwood Books Publishing LLC
Atlanta Financial Center
3343 Peachtree Rd NE Ste 145-725
Atlanta, GA 30326

www.westwoodbookspublishing.com

PROLOGUE

THE BEGINNING OF THE END

Lemuria the lost continent
before recorded history

    The migration of the birds, discordant, was the first sign. What normally were harmonious patterns of flight, the flocks had abandoned their symmetric shapes. Gone were the flying wedges, only to be replaced by chaos, as if they were trying to run away from something, but there was nowhere to escape. All were flying in different directions, turning around, then trying another way as if attempting to flee from something unseen.

    Their screeching was another hint. No sing-song chirping, only the sounds of utter panic as if they were being chased by some form of predator, yet there was nothing, just a feeling.... A paranoid wail as if their lives were in danger from some unseen force which was yet to appear.

    It's not that very odd things hadn't been happening lately, since the 'Higher Ones' had arrived and bestowed upon the Lemurian inhabitants what they called 'the gift'. Everything had been changing rapidly. It was possible that the birds actions were the result of one of the new air machines passing somewhere close by, or perhaps the rumors were true that the Elders were using their newfound energy source to control the weather. Things certainly were very different. The 'Higher

Ones' had come and gone. 'The Gift', as the Elders had called it, had brought about seemingly endless technological advances to what before then was a peaceful agrarian society which now was all too quickly being replaced by previously unheard of inventions. Until a few years ago such inventions were thought of as dreams by the most advanced minds. Flying machines, hovercraft, robotics, and most importantly, weapons had appeared almost overnight. The potential for much more aggressive phenomenon was limitless. These changes had also created a wider gap in their caste system that had been set, up to this point, a successful coexistence for generations. 'The Gift' created a totally new industrial class that was filled by mostly upper class inhabitants, and these newer inventions were replacing the lower class' means of existence, thus giving them no way to support themselves and too much free time on their hands leaving themselves open to corruption.

These Elders were representatives of each of the class or caste systems. They were in effect the Constables of their society, the decision makers and final judges of the laws that had successfully brought advancements up until now. Now they had become fiercely divided, torn between the benefits 'the gift' had brought and the breakdown of the society that had successfully worked for generations. The Elders were to meet this very day, hopefully to agree upon a path to remedy the expanding differences between them.

"It appears that our feathered friends are severely disturbed, Argon," remarked Hagar, his bespectacled and normally humorous eyes showing a trace of concern. The portly and jovial elder of the Farmers caste was the second elder to enter the meeting hall. His usual perpetually happy personality was beginning to show wear and tear from the pressures of his status.

"It's just another example of how out of control our brothers in the 'New Energy' caste are getting." replied Argon. The chief elder of the Arts caste, his lean and aquiline features showing his years watched out the window.

"The birds know something we don't. Too bad they can't speak so they could talk some sense into our friends that are attempting to control our new found power- we really need to be careful."

"True, however, I've just received this year's crop predictions. At this rate we'll have doubled our harvests' thanks to the advances in our technology." Hagar, was trying to sound supportive; even though he wasn't really clear as to how to appraise this new situation.

Not really a pessimist, Argon simply affixed his friend of many years with a smile. He knew his friend in reality was as baffled as he and all the other Elders were, about their unfathomable advances and how to control them. He had dedicated his life for the betterment of the people. But now that the 'higher ones' had come and gone leaving them 'the gift', he couldn't help but become worried about the changes it had caused. True, if used correctly and conscientiously the evolution of their species could advance by leaps and bounds. If not...

"Greetings brethren," roared Ulric as he entered the chamber. "It's another fine day for our New Age."

"Have you noticed the birds?" quizzed Andar, although apparently he was talking to himself.

"I have brought the crowning jewel of our development." Ignoring Andar, pride almost oozing from every orifice of his considerable frame, Ulric was the 'New Technology' elder and to say the least these rapid accomplishments had gone to his head. His voice boomed out of his large muscular frame and his full head of his flaming red hair. His mere presence had demanded attention and there wasn't a bigger Ego in all of Lemuria. "I hope we don't have to contend with any whining, especially today after I reveal our latest accomplishments." His loud voice echoing off the walls of the chamber portrayed strength rather than rationality.

Soon the chamber was filled with the Elders of all the classes. They were seated around the round table designed for these occasions. Each Elder, chosen not by where they were born, but by success gained in their fields. All were much respected, and the pressures of their position were handled proficiently.

Unable to contain his exuberance, Ulric started his palaver again, even before everyone had the time to sit down. "We're becoming like the gods themselves," he spewed proudly. "This," as he pulled out a folder from inside his robe, "will secure us all a spot in the heavens." He slammed down the folder upon the round table. There was a quiet murmur of astonishment around the table and misgivings as each elder stared at the folder.

"By the gods, Ulric, what have you done now?" pleaded Andar as he broke out in a cold sweat. "We are all required to agree with what you do with our new power source," he choked. "The 'Higher Ones' were explicit about this when they showed us the magnitudes' far reaching potential of energy control! We must tread lightly into the unknown one step at a time with all caution and respect."

"Nonsense," retorted Ulric, a far off glazed expression on his face. "With this," he picked up and shook the folder, "we will be like the Gods themselves!" he almost chanted. He was totally overwhelmed by his lately exalted position within the group. Without waiting for a reply, he went on: "Brothers, what we have here is the answer to all our problems. No doubt you've all heard rumors about weather control. Well what we have done is one step bigger and better." A grim foreboding manifested in the chamber. Clearly, the knowledge from the 'Higher Ones' turned a once humble elder into one drunk with a power of maniacal proportions. He's gone over the edge, thought Andar, what now could he possibly have done, the lines of sincere concern etched on his features.

Ulric charged on: "Instead of attempting to control the weather, what we have done is built the biggest magnets here and a twin on our sister continent Atlantis, that when turned on opposite poles will have enough pull as gravity itself, thus being able to control the tilt of the whole planet at will… Brothers, we will control the seasons, the day and night, snow fall, sunshine, and…" Ulrics words were lost in a haze of apprehension. Andar stood up, his normally cheerful countenance completely gone.

"Ulric you are totally and unequivocally out of your mind!" he bellowed, frothing at the mouth. "Don't you realize what a delicate balance Mother Nature is in, not to mention your total disregard for our limited knowledge of the magnetic field that regulates our whole planet; and gravity itself? The slightest change in this balance could prove catastrophic!"

"That's exactly how I thought you'd react, Andar." Ulric retorted. "Your limited scope of what we can do with this gift has shown what a lily-livered conservative you are. So therefore I planned ahead. Today is the day of days we become like gods, rulers of the entire world! And there's nothing you spineless cowards can do about it." Ulric's palms were spread and arms raised as if he was talking to the creator himself.

At that moment, a very sizable Condor, at least a six to eight foot wingspan, crashed through the window shattering glass over the entire group and coming to a quick landing on the round table, a mass of feathers and bloody gore, the remains splattering the Elders white robes with the excrement of the Continents' most revered bird. It's entrails covering each elder as they gaped in awe at the suicidal bird. A moment of stunned silence enveloped all, before the real show began.

Then, like countless fingernails screeching across a chalkboard, it began, all body hair standing on end and an overpowering hum that was more felt than heard permeated the entire group, gradually building to a crescendo of unfathomable proportions.

Suddenly, all of the elemental forces of nature came to a standstill; in a state of suspended animation, similar to being at the top of a roller coaster heading down into the abyssal depths of hell on earth, no spot yet to be unscathed from the inner core to the surface.

The results of Ulric's 'brainstorm' didn't occur according to plan. What he didn't know was that the asthenosphere under the earth's crust was eternally in a very delicate balance. This is a malleable lair of molten rock heated by radioactive decay of the elements such as Uranium, Thorium, and Potassium, it's fluid atmosphere circulating as convection currents underneath the Lithosphere which is up to sixty miles thick and made up of earth's crustal plates. These plates are constantly moving because of the currents. They are the source of volcanoes, hot springs, geysers, and raw material that pushes up mid-ocean ridges producing currents of magma. They flow in opposite directions until they eventually come into contact with the continental plates. The ocean floor is constantly moving, spreading from the center and sinking at the edges. This constantly regenerating source is radioactive. It lays deep in the earth's mantle and affects its magnetic field. Ulric failed to foresee what tampering with this delicate balance would cause. By attempting to control the gravitational force from the surface instead of it occurring naturally in earth's core, all inner forces reversed as soon as he powered up his surface magnets on both Atlantis and Lemuria. After the initial shock and standstill, this reversal instantly changed the direction of the movement of the continental plates and mid-ocean ridges.

"It looks like your urge to become a god has finished us all, Ulric." Andar's remark sounded like barely a whisper amidst the growing tumult, it's intensity growing by the second.

"The gift! We must preserve the gift, nothing else is as important compared to the gift! Quickly! We must get it into the casing it was delivered in. Brothers," Ulric pleaded, "I didn't expect…" VZHT! The tumult was quickly changing into an involuntary global shiver, increasing in magnitude to a preposterous proportion.

Andar, chief elder, took what little control that there was left as they all scrambled trying to maintain any resemblance of balance in the ever increasing chaos that was just beginning.

Thankfully 'the gift' was the most revered and protected item on each continent, it's concealment was known only to the Elders of the round table. Andar was at least blessed with the forethought of how to deal with a worst-case scenario, and it looked as if this one was definitely going to take the cake. He previously pondered night after night what could or might possibly happen if it was to fall into the wrong hands. Too late for that now. 'The gift' was hidden in their latest flying machine that could reach altitudes not yet conceived. Never in Andar's wildest nightmare did he ever think it would come to this. But all the choices in this matter were now out of the question. "Wait Andar," Ulric blustered "we need to fix…"

"Close that hole in your face you pompous amoeba! This has already gone beyond anything we could possibly imagine. The 'higher ones' warned us to use the utmost caution with 'the gift' and now you've, oh, forget it." Andar reached into his blood spattered robe and produced one of the new laser light ray weapons and sliced Ulric in half from the head to the crotch, each slide slithering to the floor in a mass of blood and innards. "If I had only done that sooner."

Andar's composure completely disintegrated and in his last act of sanity, he managed to get to the launch button and send 'the gift' back to the heavens from whence it came.

Throwing caution to the wind, Ulric and his caste of power hungry maniacs had built these two gargantuan magnets and concealed them both on each continent of Lemuria, located in the Pacific Ocean and on Atlantis in the Atlantic. The idea sounded good enough on paper, but without a conscientious application of forethought and discretion there was no way to tell if they were sealing their fate and dooming the human race to almost total extinction. When they 'powered on', instead of enhancing mother nature, they reversed it's natural process and turned the primal forces against each other, from deep inside the earth's mantle causing a chain reaction that would reach to the surface and beyond. Something had to give and it did.

What they originally wanted to do was have control of the tilt of the axis so the earth's climates would be more beneficial to crop production, thus giving everyone more work and food on the table. What they did not realize was how perpetually precarious a state of inner forces the earth was in. In a matter of minutes, the planet overcompensated up to forty five degrees and set off every type of upheaval and major cataclysm known to man. What saved the earth from total annihilation was that the mountain ranges concealing the magnets instantaneously turned into raging volcanoes and disintegrated the magnets. Had this not happened, there's no telling how far destruction would have gone.

The first repercussion was the change in the axis had put the polar ice caps in a seriously detrimental imbalance that started causing a wobble in the gyroscopic spin of the planet. This caused continental-sized icebergs to immediately break off into the oceans. Not mere pebbles in a pond that cause little ripples, but tidal waves up to thousands of feet high coming and going in all directions at once which would eventually meet at the 'new' equator, smash into each other, and then cause them to reach outwards in every direction simultaneously; concussion and repercussion over and over, again and again. No coastline was spared. Some land ceased to exist. The rushing waters reached miles inland erasing any trace of humanity inhabited there.

What were previously thought of as mountain ranges immediately turned into cauldrons of fire spewing molten lava. Furnaces regurgitating the earth's innards of such a magnitude that there was no square inch of the planet safe from damage, as the waters vented their wrath upon the surface that was changing rapidly. Blue skies were replaced by black fire breathing clouds containing flaming rock bombs flying in every direction, destruction of anything and everything in their path, inevitable. The noise was so all-enveloping that there was no way to tell the difference between the eruptions and the subsequent earthquakes that were simultaneously changing the face of the earth. All this, combined with the wobble effect left absolutely nothing spared. The chaos was complete.

But this was just the opening act. The real dance was about to begin. The cow patties were about to hit the windmill.

"Say yer prayers. Say yer prayers." Andar resembled an automaton zombie walking while chanting in endless monotone. Being the intellectual he was, there was still plenty of room for reverence: Not that it would do any good… His once steadfast confident demeanor had been replaced by this trancelike state. His face was devoid of expression. The remaining Elders, who had usually looked to him for simplistic answers to complex problems stood dumbfounded hoping Andar had yet another solution, but it just didn't exist. Their screams and pleadings went unheard. Andar, the once pillar of their society was oblivious to all the goings on around him except perhaps the deep growling underneath his feet. The footing became next to impossible. The tides had receded almost to the horizon leaving sea creatures exposed to dry land. Deep fissures, cracks miles long replaced the sea floor. Then the horizon seemed to lift from both the new south and new north and the roaring from the incoming water became equal to that which was emanating from the earth. By the time these colossal mountains of water met, these fissures were in upheaval, growing from the ocean bottoms to become fire belching mountaintops.

Conversely, both continents were the epicenters of the cataclysm. They were surrounded by boiling oceans; a river of water that never seemed to diminish. The waves that had battered into each of them went into opposite directions only to eventually hit the bigger continents and return, over and over, time and time again. The earth's core had regurgitated so much magma at once that there was a void created therein that had to be filled. The tectonic plates were affected so vigorously that on one side more void was created and on the other side they overlapped causing mountain ranges to rise up and come into existence almost instantaneously.

Although these two flowers of civilization appeared to be continents because of their large land mass, they were in reality islands surrounded by oceans. Between the battering on the surface and the altering of the tectonic plates, combined with the imbalance the axis shift had caused, maybe throw in some flaming rock bombs and something had to give. It did.

Atlantis, which is more of a plateau, sank less than gracefully under the sea and left no trace of its existence. Lemuria, by contrast, was more mountainous and stubborn. Its geophysical makeup was made of sterner rock and in some places refused to sink so easily. All that was left of the two most advanced civilizations on earth was a relatively small island chain in the middle of the Pacific Ocean.

As the bigger continents had to adjust themselves to the new magnetic poles, no spot on the entire planet was left untouched. As the earth finally started to settle itself, its face was completely rearranged. Civilizations had vanished, replaced by shell shocked tribal formations. It took generations for them to finally start adjusting to their new topography. Complete climate changes ensured that only the strong would survive. Any histories compiled to this point vanished, leaving questions still unanswered.

Andar's attempt to save 'the gift' was only partially successful. When the Atlantean and Lemurian magnets were instantaneously destroyed, there just wasn't enough 'oomph' in their airship to completely leave the atmosphere. Add the gravitational pull of the planet in its ultimate tantrum, as irony would have it the ship came down to almost exactly where it had been launched; into what was now a dormant volcano in the new island chain, all traces of its existence completely forgotten: for the time being.

SPACE PATROL

SOMEWHERE ABOVE THE EARTH

"Yes oh yes the bet lives" chortled Rawar as he gleefully bounced around the flight deck.

"Close, real close, as close as it can get" retorted Oxomoxo, "they didn't completely destroy themselves." His tone was not quite as confident as when the wager was made. They were using speech now, their outdated vocal chords hadn't been used in a while. Thought transference was coming along a lot easier. "I've got to admit though, that is about as close as it can get" he replied grudgingly as if it was just a matter of time before they would have to clean up yet another mess. Rawar and Oxomoxo, a part of the Space Patrol, were intergalactic debris collectors/planet planters who looked down at the third sphere from the star and were actually both relieved they did not have to clean up another space debris this time. Their function was to attempt to elevate the lower-consciousness species to a level equivalent to join with theirs in the Planetary Consortium that had evolved enough to realize the basic inner truths; then and only then would said planet be made aware of them and be able to apply. If any given sphere didn't realize these truths as they evolved, eventually they would blow themselves to oblivion and then these two would have to get to work. Keeping space relatively free of flying chunks of previously unsuccessful projects was not an easy task.

"They had potential though. So close yet so far. When that rock we missed before hit their surface it caused so much havoc. Even their dinosaurs became extinct. I thought they'd had it. But it seems they're gradually and quite possibly going to make it," replied Rawar.

"Maybe, but after what they've done this time, it's obviously going to be up to them. Just look at that mess."

They both gazed at another one of their projects gone awry, both relieved the wager was still on. But judging from the wobbling sphere there was no way to tell, just yet. Their percentage ratio of success/failure of the evolutionary process was jeopardized, and as usual the last step of consciousness again proved that at this time this planet was just not ready.

"With what we gave them this last time you would think that they finally had gotten it right," Oxomoxo surmised. He was responsible for bringing human beings and their unborn to this sphere. This one particularly had potential to grow and take the last crucial step toward evolution, but once again 'the gift' had been this planet's demise.

"They even tried to get rid of our gift after almost totally ruining their home, but ha, it fell back down and it is there somewhere. I am going to win this bet, just when is the question," Rawar retorted confidently.

"True, and that is exactly why you may have to eat your words. They are eventually going to find our gift again, so the bet is still ongoing," Oxomoxo replied, hoping that what he was saying would eventually be true.

"The beacon is faint, but it's still down there somewhere. It is probably lost in the aftermath. So I'll have to admit, our bet is still on." Rawar did like to win, but playing the game was still the most fun of all. They both agreed even though it was give and take, their dedication to the evolutionary process was first and foremost. After all, their project seemed to have the most intense results of all. Although sometimes it seemed silly to say it, this particular planet deserved just a little more TLC and gave it a gentle nudge now and then; it was as though it was their personal little baby.

"Well after what they had just done to themselves, we at least can both agree that it's going to be awhile before anything happens. Look at that. Two continents gone, new mountain ranges and what few humans remain left are definitely back to the basics. Got to admit though, that is one tough planet," Oxomoxo remarked, torn between disappointment and admiration, he still felt that somehow they would bounce back again.

"Agreed. Well there is nothing that we can do about it at this point. When the gift does get found, the beacon will get stronger so we'll know it's time to come back for a look-see. We still have a lot of projects to check on so let's go."

To the surviving inhabitants coherent enough to notice, Oxomoxo and Rawar looked just like another shooting star passing across the heavens. Little did these survivors know it was their guardians who always had kept a close look from afar that had just been by to see if they had made it through this cataclysm, and also thus concluded their bet. But for now only time would tell.

THE SANDWICH ISLANDS

LATE 19TH CENTURY

A rainbow spray feathered lightly off the translucent blue green wave that gently lapped upon the heavily steaming lava which was forming yet another new coastline of the island Mowee of the then called 'Sandwich Islands', the waves symmetry enhanced by the light offshore breeze.

Haleakala, house of the sun had regurgitated once again, this time venting its fury upon the southern shore of the island chain's most sheltered island. Another giant swath of smoldering rock melted into the sea, covering the garden of Eden like quality of this gem of the ocean. A befitting example of the constant inner turmoil that still existed in the depths of the earth.

The predatory birds were having a field day. The plentiful fish of the sea were either dead or stunned by the meeting of the lava that had reached the shoreline, producing an abundant bounty for both man and bird alike.

On this particular and soon to be auspicious day the hunt was on. The best catch for the upcoming festival would be rewarded with the much coveted prize of paddling canoe with 'the ripe fruit of the vine', the eligible females to the yearly island wide gathering that was about to commence. Not only prestigious was this prize, but the benefits included therein spoke for themselves. The pungent aroma of the flowers they wore and the ladies themselves were the stuff that dreams were made of, not to mention the fact that to become the winners of this most coveted prize throughout the land was becoming a reality; fame and fortune realized.

This festival was not an ordinary gathering. At this time of year all grudges and differences were set aside as fleets of canoes from each island and its inhabitants would head for Mowee's west shore for an island wide meeting with a mutual understanding that there was only one reason for doing so: sex. There were always minor skirmishes and sometimes even major wars between island tribes, but on this particular occasion all spears and stone clubs were set aside so as to achieve the desired effect for everyone in attendance. The reason and/or excuse was to prevent or at least kept to a bare minimum the in-breeding of each island tribe. This was a sound idea and was enthusiastically agreed upon by each island king; a meeting for the sole purpose of one giant gathering for making love not war.

The rules were simple: no rules. Anyone who was lusty or horny enough and had a seaworthy canoe could attend. Anyone in their right mind would be a fool not to go to this week- long orgy on the beach, in the jungle, in the rivers and ponds, waterfalls or just basically anywhere two (or more) could find a vacant spot to couple. Why not? Instead of bludgeoning each other to death, the primary objective was to drink as much awa root tea as it took to remove any inhibitions whatsoever and rut, rut, rut.

And just by the whim of the oceanic currents combined with a small belch of Loihi, a submerged pre-cataclysmic mountain top twenty miles southeast of the big island (Hawaii) that this could and would support the theory that mother nature truly does have a sense of humor.

As fate would have it this small burp from the earth sent a long forgotten cylinder once known as 'the gift' towards the surface, the currents carrying it in the direction of two unsuspecting natives throwing net on the steaming shores of Mowee.

"I think we were right to come here Meliko, just look at all those fish" observed Kawika, better known as Bully to his friends. His towering frame was abnormal enough to almost be called odd. What he lacked in brains was replaced by an ample supply of muscle and girth. "Even a blind fisherman could catch here."

"That's the general idea, even a blind mongoose gets a mouse sometimes" as Meliko gazed out at the multitude of sea creatures floating beyond the surf. He always used the mongoose parody because if anyone on the island more resembled one it was he, his ferret like qualities were often joked about, but not to his face. His keen intelligence easily replaced what he lacked in size, and it was this intelligence that had brought them here, to this obscure spot on the island to vie for the prized catch that would win them the award of paddling with the women.

Meliko and Kawika were the recipients of most of the unique situations that occurred. If something out of the ordinary happened, it was odds on that they were somewhere at the bottom of it all. Their misadventures were legendary. It seemed that Murphy had a special law just for them. What could go wrong usually did. But it just did not faze them. They were a very good natured pair and figured no matter what was said about them at least it caused a reaction. At this point in their lives they had managed to cause every disturbance known to the tribe and carry it to the point of precariousness but still managed to survive unscathed. Only this mismatch pair would have the audacity to go netting right next to a still smouldering volcano; why? Probably just because it hadn't been done before. The lava was flowing down, but it still had enough momentum to hit the ocean and stun enough sea life to fill their nets.

"What is this?" stammered Bully as he was dragging his last 'net throw' back through the surf. At first he had thought it was one of the deep sea fish that had been turning up on the shoreline lately, as if something was going on down below that was forcing them to the surface. But no, it wasn't shaped like a fish at all, nor anything else he had seen for that matter. "Hey Meliko, you better get over here and see what's in my net. I don't know…"

"Now what have you managed to do, catch another piece of driftwood?" Meliko sauntered over to take a look at his friend's latest blunder. "How you manage to do what you do I'll never know" his remarks were quickly caught in his throat as he came up to the net of floundering fish, he stopped in his tracks. He finally managed to stammer "That is not driftwood".

The two stood in silence staring at the cylindrical type sphere that had got tangled in the net. It seemed to be made of a foreign substance they had never seen before. But it wasn't the substance that was the object of their bewildered state. It was a small blinking light that seemed to emanate a sort of vibratory pulse that could be felt but not heard.

Meliko broke the stunned silence, "I have no idea what it is, but whatever it is, I think the king is definitely going to like it" surmised Meliko. "And it's probably going to land us a spot paddling with the girls" his mind already in overdrive racing ahead to the upcoming event, and there was a distinct tingling in between his legs that seemed to be predicting the outcome of the contest. "But since we did come all the way out here, we might as well load up on fish, being that they're all over the place." Oh boy, now he thought. The pair continued on throughout the day netting a combination of surface and deep sea variety fish yet to be seen by their tribe. As the violet pink and orange clouds announced sunset, the two gathered their catch and started the long trek back to their village, knowing that this event would be the crowning achievement of their escapades so far in life. Little did they know the chain reaction that was about to start again.

King Kamanawanalaya awoke with a start to the murmur of the tribe that gathered outside his bamboo hut. Something had caused them to gather outside his personal shelter. This was odd because at this time of day everyone usually took their midday siesta. As much as he disliked to do it, he grudgingly rolled off his coconut husk mattress to see what was amiss. This was not an easy task, with his three hundred plus pounds body he was almost as wide as he was tall.

He was a benevolent dictator, a cross me once- shame on you, cross me twice- shame on me kind of King. Therefore he was beloved by almost all that came under his reign. He had been in a very good mood lately, knowing the upcoming festival would bring a substantial amount of new wives to his bed. Being one of the fiercer supporters of the gathering, he dove into it with real gusto. It would be a welcome relief after having to deal with that bothersome volcano. Dealing with the chaos and destruction it caused had not been easy. Oh well, approaching his entranceway, might as well see what's causing all this noise.

When he came outside he saw almost the whole village gathered in a circle around Meliko and Bully. Oh wonderful, he thought. Now what has this pair of characters gotten themselves into. Whenever they were involved, it was a good bet something wrong had occurred, but by the confident look on their faces and the quizzical stares on those around them, he wasn't so sure.

The murmuring stopped abruptly as heads bowed and a path cleared to the middle of the circle when the King appeared. No one moved until he sat his bulky frame upon his throne. His weight caused it to creak and bend as he settled in; a cup of awa root tea immediately appeared in his hand.

As he settled in, Meliko and Kawika cautiously approached the throne. Usually when they did this they had managed to get themselves in one form of trouble or another, so they tread lightly as if walking on eggshells.

"Greetings oh most benevolent one" they chorused in unison.

Meliko, being the natural born comedian he was, took center stage.

"We have thrown net today and became extremely lucky," he said nervously. He wasn't used to not being in some form of hot seat or another. Bully stood next to him not uttering a sound. This was a make or break their already precarious standing within the tribe. "Our catch is both plentiful and curious, your highness, this time we have truly outdone ourselves" he beamed. Oh gods thought the king, why me? These two bumbling idiots could be the ruin of us all. If their misadventures weren't so funny I'd have had them sacrificed long ago. But then again sacrificing them might not get the desired results, all things considered.

"Well now, could it possibly be that you two have done something right? Finally? For a change? This I've got to see" he rumbled.

"Oh yes your highness, we have been where no one had thought to go and retrieved a catch of a lifetime" replied Meliko as Bully retreated to pick up the unusual bulging net behind them. Only he could pick up such a mass of fish by himself. Meliko went on, "we have been to the new shoreline by the lava flow and have come back with this" he said proudly.

Bully dumped the net at the king's feet and began unwrapping it. When he was done there was the largest pile of diversified types of fish anyone had ever seen. But they seemed insignificant compared to the 'other thing' in the net. As it was exposed, goosebumps appeared on all those around it. Never had anyone seen or felt anything even remotely like it.

"From the gods of the sea, your highness, delivered to us, to give to you, a true omen. The festival will be the most memorable of all" Meliko spoke eloquently, taking center stage naturally. He picked up the object and laid it at the king's feet.

Immediately the goosebumps spread over his entire mammoth body. The hairs on his neck coming to attention. Not usually superstitious in nature, the king had to admit to himself that this unknown object seemed to have a life of its own. Throw in the fire that was no fire coming from the inside of the object convinced him that this truly did come from the gods. Little did he know how close to the truth he really was. At last he managed to whisper "you two have definitely made up for all the trouble you've caused and I'm sure that there will be no argument that you two are the winners of our contest, hands down." A raucous cheer as Meliko was easily lifted and Bully was not so easily lifted upon shoulders, the normal buffoons of the tribe were instantly raised to heroic status. Now that the contest was over it was time to get down to business and get ready for the festival. Bundles of awa root and provisions gathered, the canoes would be launched at the next sunrise for the paddle across the channel. In the lead would be good king Kamanawanalaya, closely followed by the women folk and that pair of dubious distinction, Meliko and Kawika fully elevated to their new status within the tribe; and rightfully so, the 'omen' as they called it, was to be the center of attention at the festival, its goosebump causing qualities raising the emotions to a higher state of frenzy than ever before.

The voyage to Ukumehame canyon on the west shore was extraordinary in itself. The schools of porpoise and hundreds of humpback whales down from Alaska for their mating season seemed to 'know' about the mysterious object aboard the king's canoe. They acted as though they were chaperones as they escorted the entourage toward its destination, much to the delight of all. Their acrobatics brought screams of delight from the women as the creatures jumped, flipped, spun, and splashed their way around the canoes. This caused an air of excitement that stirred up the general mood so it seemed that the gathering had started even before they had gotten there.

Even today Ukumehame is one of the most picturesque places on the island. It's narrow entrance opens up into a vast mile wide natural amphitheater surrounded by cliffs hundreds of feet high. Within this canyon, there are a multitude of mini-canyon off-shoots that have waterfalls, streams and ponds unmatched in their beauty. Today, the only way to see this is taking one of the many helicopter tours offered to those who visit. It is no surprise why the Sandwich Islanders picked this spot to have their lovefest.

When Kamanawanalaya's troops showed up they were the immediate center of attention because of the curious object they had brought with them. The effect it caused combined with the vast quantities of awa root tea sent spirits even higher than ever before.

The rolling hills of grass seemed like waves of the sea because of the light breezes as they shimmered in the light of the full moon. All this punctuated by light mist from the sky that caused moonbows to appear throughout the night's festivities. A more romantic environment couldn't be made. It was perfect.

Some attachments were made quickly as the males and females sized each other up. Others took a little more time. Eventually the cliffs echoed with wails of pleasures and grunts of satisfaction. Naked bodies glistened in the moonlight contorted in every conceivable position. On through the night this would continue until about sunrise, when things would slow down and the participants would regroup, take stock and shop around for their next adventure. This was how it was for most, but not all; some of the more robust would continue on in a nonstop pleasure marathon and in the forefront of this contingent was the good king Kamanawanalaya.

The king's fornication capabilities were legendary and as constant as the tides. He moved through the festival as a scythe does through wheat. Being a king certainly didn't hurt either, for the possibility of becoming a queen was ever present in the minds of the ladies. All one would have to do is look for the biggest pile up of bodies, day or night, and right there in the middle of it would be the good king in all of inhibitionless splendor.

"Looks kinda like an octopus doesn't he?" remarked Bully. It was the third morning and it was the time for most to take a breather. He sought out and found Meliko who was laid out under a coconut palm, looking like he just might die of heart failure, a smile of complete contentment on his face.

"I bet ya he wishes he was one" replied Meliko. "I've never ever seen anything like that before. He can be in so many orifices at the same time, and hasn't stopped since we got here. Unbelievable."

These two hadn't done too bad for themselves either. After word had spread that they were the finders of now what was called 'the omen' their popularity skyrocketed immediately. But after three days in a row, their endurance was at an ebb. They couldn't help but gape in wonderment at their ruler. He hadn't let up yet, and it didn't look like he was going to. Being the king did have its advantages and it would be awful hard to say 'no' to beauties such as these chasing him, but every man does have his limit, or should. But in the king's case, he certainly was in another dimension.

"By the way, how've you been doing, Bully?" asked Meliko, a cheshire cat type grin on his face.

"I lost count. As soon as the word got out that we found that thing, it's been nonstop. I've got to hide for a while, I'm completely drained" replied Bully.

"Me too. I never thought I'd see the day that this would happen. I need a serious break. But then again, life is not a rehearsal." Meliko's statement was interrupted by the screech of a dozen absolutely beautiful ladies.

"There they are" the ladies screamed with delight, "let's get them!"

"Quick! Run for your life!" Meliko was running down towards the beach in an instant, closely followed by Bully, and in hot pursuit were the ladies. They were like outlaws being chased by a posse but this was different- they wouldn't get far, and probably didn't know if they wanted to, for that matter.

On and on it went, day and night, until the evening of the fourth day which was the peak of the festival. So far it had been a colossal success in the attempt to eradicate in-breeding. New inter-island bonds were made which more often than not kept the warlike natures of the tribes to a minimum. It wasn't that easy to crack open your lover's brother's skull or toss a spear through your sister's new husband. So in actuality the gathering was threefold; lessen inbreeding, keep wars to a minimum, and increase family bonds throughout the island chain. All in all they could not pick a better week to do it.

"Coca! Coca! Coca!" the chant reverberated throughout the canyons. Tonight was the night, midway, when the much coveted leaf was distributed to the participants. It was from somewhere called Amerika was all that the natives knew. Every once in a while the yellow men from the east would stop by en route to or from trading with the hairy ones on the wooden ships. Then all the leaf traded for would be hoarded all year, only to be used on this special night. When masticated, all the wear and tear from the previous nights would evaporate and the leaf-chewer's senses would be raised to a new level of awareness and endurance. It was good they only did this once a year for one could only imagine what would happen if it was available to them year round. The portents were not good; once was dangerous enough. To everyone that had experienced these leaves before, all they wanted was one thing: more.

And so it went; the intensity level was magnified, the pace multiplied, and the debauchery intensified to new highs and/or lows depending on how one looked at it. Like rolling waves in a sea of bodies, couples danced, gyrated, and contorted throughout the night, a full moon smiling down on them all.

"Meliko! Meliko, get up we're in serious trouble" Bully yelled pleadingly as he approached the pile of bodies Meliko had passed out in. He was completely coated in the juices of the ladies' lusty behavior.

"Whaaat? Go away. Can't you see I'm busy?" Meliko was in similar shape, the pile of bodies so thick it was hard to tell whose limb belonged to who or whom. "Trouble? what trouble?"

"The king is dead, is what trouble. Not only that, he squashed the king of Oahu's niece in doing so, and her brother is threatening war on all islands. Some kid named K-something. And some of them are trying to lay the blame on us" choked Bully. "How could we possibly… uh oh, 'the omen'". Meliko's vision quickly turned into grim foreboding as he disentangled from the pile of females. "What a way to go" he chuckled, trying to make light of a bad situation.

"Oh yeah. The story going around is said when he went, he had his hands, toes, face, and tool buried in one orifice or another, but the niece couldn't get out from under him and got smothered- it's not good. Brother, we've got to move fast." Bully wasn't one to stand around and think about what should be done; he was a mover.

"We've got to get a grip on this situation before things get out of hand. For us the party's over, it could get ugly" Melikos' face betrayed his emotion.

"Truth. Rumors are already flying that 'our find' is actually a bad omen and it's our fault that all this has happened. If there's blame to fall on anyone it's going to be us. We've got to gather the body, the omen, our people, and get into the canoes before something really bad happens. That K-something kid isn't helping things out one bit." Bully was talking as he was moving. There was no time to sit around and ponder the situation. "Besides, moods after a coca leaf night were scattered enough as it is, without this mess."

The two took control quickly and as formally as they could in this situation, used their manners and courtesies like a defense weapon. In a few hours they managed to wrap up the king in his stately robes and semi- ceremoniously dump him into his canoe. The omen was a different matter, but Meliko and Kawika handled a delicate situation like true ambassadors, offering praise and apologies like a machine gun as they removed the 'omen' from its pedestal. The sandwich islanders were a superstitious lot and by this time nobody wanted to touch it or even get near it. The fear of ill luck had replaced the party atmosphere. By mid day all was packed and the Mowee contingents' party canoes had turned funeral barges, left for home without any further incident. It was just in time too, as Meliko and Kawika looked back towards shore for one final farewell they saw that the prince K-something had already successfully agitated the others into a warlike frenzy. But for now the Mowee folk were safely on their way. They had other ceremonies to attend to as they solemnly paddled towards home.

    The fury of the rain was enhanced by the gusty winds as it relentlessly pummeled the procession. It was as if the gods themselves wept. It seemed like mother nature itself was taking part in this particular funeral ceremony. The normally lucid blue sky was replaced by a staccato of unforgiving rain as the line of mourners trudged onwards and upwards to the chosen burial chamber.

    Upon their return from the festival, the once usually cheerful villagers were struck dumb by news of the fate of their king. Lost in the moment were the regaling of tales that normally accompanied the festival goers' return. This once happy time was not to be. Mixed emotions such as shock, disbelief, horror, and abject misery spread like wildfire; add the undercurrent of superstition therein is found a complete picture of the tribes reaction.

    In spite of all this, there was still much work and preparation to be done. All in all, the king's reign had been beneficial to almost everyone and a befitting burial was usually supposed to accompany it. But there was 'the omen'. The village was fiercely divided, about what part it had played in the king's demise. It would be easy to use it as a scapegoat, but since it was such a foreign object none had a fitting answer. Arguments surged back and forth about what was to be done with it, but by being generally superstitious in nature, it was eventually agreed upon that the 'omen' would accompany the king to his place in the hereafter.

Meliko and Kawika hadn't fared that well either. They had been more or less ostracized overnight, their status as heroes quickly replaced by superstitious dread. It was as if they were responsible for the king fornicating himself to death. Shunned by most and talked about behind their back, it seemed like they were strangers in their own home village. There were even rumors that some thought they should be buried with the king and the omen. Either way it was definitely time for them to move on, if they could that is.

But first things first. The search for the deepest burial cave was complete. The search was extensive and one had been found at the top of the smoking mountain. It seemed to have no end; none had been found, anyhow. So it was there that the king and the omen would be laid to rest. In reality the superstitious dread had overwhelmed the villagers and they wanted the omen as far away from them as possible for the luck it had brought could be contagious. Out of sight out of mind was the desired effect.

All preparations complete, the procession and its retinue of priests, mourners and casket bearers began their multi-day trek up the volcano to the summit, when the storm hit. The combination of the king's weight and casket combined with the slippery conditions the rain was causing, turned a formal solemn occasion into a living nightmare. By the time they reached the summit, only a ten thousand foot plus horrendous trek, the normally richly clad procession had turned into a mud and blood spattered bunch of miserable mud balls with eye sockets. The deep desire to be rid of this other-worldly totem of ill luck and superstitious dread had taken its toll.

"Well here's another fine mess we've gotten ourselves into" puffed Bully. Dead on his feet, he slithered down the face of the giant rock to sit by his friend and partner in chaos. They were the only ones each other had. Almost all the tribe members treated them like they were contagious. He also wanted to temporarily escape the driving torrent of wind and rain.

"Yeah, out of all the troubles we've stirred up and situations we've managed to get into, this is by far the…" he stopped mid-sentence for the lack of an appropriate word that would describe this. "And look at them, it looks like they would like to kill us."

"They're definitely looking for something or someone to blame. And face it, out of all the people that could possibly bear the brunt of this situation, it's us, again. And that cursed whatever it is that we fished from the sea. Oh well, it's just another episode that has backfired against us, and it's not that it hasn't happened before. The weight of this though, it's off the charts" replied Meliko wiping yet another droplet of mud from his eye. "And if it wasn't for you helping carry that million pound casket all the way up here they probably wouldn't have made it" he added.

"My size comes in handy sometimes and it's downhill from here" remarked Bully. They both gazed down into the dormant volcano, it's rim sloping downward a half a mile to the floor. "We could ride it like a sled from here."

"Fat chance cousin, wishful thinking. Those priests aren't much for informality." Just then came the all too familiar far away glint in Meliko's eyes, and usually what followed was some form of audacious chain of events. "What we could do is 'accidentally' slip at the right moment and ride it down and act as if we're trying to save it. That might even change the way they've been thinking about us lately since our popularity level is about zero" chuckled Meliko.

"Sounds good to me. Sometimes I think you are smarter than all those priests put together. Anyway it's too damn cold up here. Let's get this over with, the sooner the better" responded Bully as he gathered his huge frame up and prepared for their next caper.

So off they went, with torrential rain, mud-splattered priests, casket bearers and their paraphernalia carriers following the dubious pair on what could best be described as a sled ride, straight down the inside of the now dormant volcano, only to land unceremoniously at the bottom. The casket survived miraculously intact as did Bully and Meliko less worse for wear than the others. I suspect Murphy and his law had a hand in this, even so, when they all finally gathered at the bottom there were surprisingly no complaints nor recriminations because in actuality everyone was too exhausted and cold to do so.

When the priests and casket bearers disappeared into the burial cave, some thought they had gotten lost or possibly had some kind of accident, it took them so long. But eventually they reappeared and the rocks were stacked until the entrance was well hidden, and final prayers were said. But the usual markers of small pyramids were not built because it was mutually agreed upon and as yet unspoken that nobody ever wanted to see that cursed object again.

As for Kawika and Meliko, they managed to disappear on the return trip, which was good because the priests had made some secret plans for them that were seriously detrimental to their health. Rumors filtered back now and then that the pair made their way to the valley of Honokohau on the northside of the island. This was good because they fit right in. Honokohau Valley was notorious for their eccentric behavior. Good riddance.

As generations passed, stories of the curious object that was fished from the sea became a myth. At each telling the story became more outrageous and unbelievable until it became ravings of were thought of as crazy people. Eventually it was lost in the word-of-mouth history of the Island and completely forgotten by the time writing was introduced. There were none left to testify about the numerous shooting star sightings that seemed to pass back and forth across the sky.

CHAPTER 1

HALEAKALA OBSERVATORY AT THE TURN OF THE 21ST CENTURY

A pastel pink complemented the clouds that had gathered, their hues announcing the upcoming sunset on Haleakala, house of the sun. By the time the sun had slipped into the sea between the two islands of Kahoolawe and Lanai the clouds would travel the spectrum from light pink to a deep velvety violet in a symphony of silence, a befitting end to another day atop the dormant volcano.

Haleakala. It was here that Maui, a hero of Polynesian mythology, threw his fishnet into the sky and caught the sun to slow down its travel across the heavens so the people of Hawaii would have more sunshine to enjoy each day.

However there is nothing mythical about this sleeping giant that rises out of the Pacific to a height of ten thousand twenty three feet. Haleakala volcano is thirty three miles long and twenty four wide, topped by a crater twenty miles in circumference; one of the bigger pimples on the face of Earth. If measured from the ocean floor it would be twenty five thousand miles plus high, only four thousand less than Mount Everest, and this is a dormant volcano.

Perched atop the rim in an area known as Kolekole is the Haleakala High Altitude Observatory, better known as 'science city', which houses the MEES zodiacal light and Lure observatories. Lure, built in nineteen seventy four was built by the University of Hawaii Institute for astronomy purposes, under contract with NASA Goddard space flight center. It is a double domed building and housing a lunar receiver telescope in a nine meter north dome and a laser transmit and satellite receiver in the seven meter south dome; both doing double duty as a laser transmitter and a laser reflection detector with a fixed forty centimeter diameter objective lens and a flat sixty five centimeter pointing mirror which makes the 'time of flight' measurements of short laser pulses between them and five reflectors on the moon. The reflectors were established by three Apollo missions and two Russian federation robot spacecraft; with accuracy within less than two centimeters. This data is used to measure the movement of the tectonic plates and also for determining the accuracy of orbiting artificial earth satellites; there are sixteen satellites in all, ranging from four hundred to twenty thousand kilometers high that monitor the earth's resources, climate parameters, ocean levels, and temperatures. They also determine the polar motion and also allowed scientists to test Einstein's theory of relativity. In short, Lure has its hands on the pulse of the Earth and beyond. It is not a lightweight facility. On with the story.

"Not too many of us earthlings get to see sunsets such as these, Mr. Mallory" remarked Dr. Harold Bloomfield, taking a quick coffee break from his duties at science city. "Quite remarkable are they not?"

"That they are doctor, absolutely spectacular" retorted Connor Mallory, veteran speleologist, traces of his Irish heritage showing in his speech. "Have you ever seen the 'green flash' from up here? If so, how many?" Connor Mallory, graduate from MIT with a doctorate in geology, a man of medium build with a sandy complexion, his most compelling features were his penetrating green eyes which had a combination of a 'devil may care' attitude and a stoic determination. His lineage was obvious; if he was only a few feet high, he could easily have passed as a leprechaun. In his circle of endeavors he was regarded as a free spirit and a rebel, always managing to stray from the beaten path of normalcy, his projects were considered eccentric by most, and it was for these reasons that had brought him here to this obscure part of the planet.

"Yes, quite a few times actually, on a clear afternoon when the sun ducks behind the horizon, you briefly see a green tint that sometimes reflects off the mist in the sky. I wouldn't have believed it unless I saw it myself. Most everyone thinks it's a fairy tale" replied Dr. Bloomfield, enjoying the break from the tedious job of sky watching.

"I've seen it too. I believe it's a sign of good luck."

"I certainly hope so, considering what you are planning to attempt. There's no hard facts that what you are looking for even exists."

Their conversation was interrupted by the flap flap of rotor blades from the helicopter that was bringing Mallory's new partner in on his latest caper. They had only communicated on the internet but their mutual interest and disdain for the status quo had formed a bond between them, even before meeting each other in person. That meeting was just about to happen. Each of their exploits in subterranean crawls were well known worldwide and were mutually admired by both. To attempt this project would require a sense of humor and a temperament that bordered on lunacy. Their compatibility had been established via email and their equally eccentric natures found them in agreement upon meeting in these abnormal surroundings. Of course one never knew the whole picture until meeting face to face, thought Mallory as the helicopter settled down on the pad, its blades slowly coming to a halt. His curiosity was mounting with each passing second.

The door opened and out stepped a heavily bundled hourglass figure, blond hair tightly pulled back and concealed by goggles and a hat with earmuffs, her stride easily giving away the fact that this was an epitome of female species. As Mallory approached he could discern a twinkling behind the sky blue eyes and a smirk on the full bodied pouty mouth of Victoria Barbie, his new 'partner in crime'.

"Dr. Livingstone I presume, I'm Stanley" she gave him a courtesy chuckle. They clasped hands and an immediate electrical charge was felt by both. They each knew it was a match a long time coming, and an easy going companionship to be nurtured, not abused.

"Oh my, stammered Mallory, the pleasure is mine" unusually at a loss for words. He was not only struck dumb by the aura of her presence but by the obvious beauty that lay underneath the mass of cold weather gear she wore. This was truly a fortuitous occasion. "Please step inside this dome of warmth. It's a much more comfortable spot to get acquainted" said Mallory, regrouping his composure after the initial shock of their first meeting. He almost tripped over his jaw as he followed her womanly gait into the building. Upon entering the dome, Victoria disrobed from her foul weather gear. What lay underneath was a sight to behold for all mankind. First she took off her hat and shook her head and out flowed a mass of naturally curly long blond locks that flowed etherically to the small of her back. Next came off the baggy overcoat and there stood a feline frame encased in a skin tight black leather jumpsuit that complemented her every curve, the most heavenly curves Mallory could ever remember seeing. She looked as though she might belong more appropriately on a model runway instead of an astronomy laboratory on the top of a dormant volcano. A side glance at Dr. Bloomfield showed that his reaction was having the same effect. They were both like two kids gaping at the ninth wonder of the world. Connor concluded that this was going to be one of the most enjoyable undertakings of his not too short life.

"Well now, that's much better," she said, stretching out the kinks from the helicopter ride. The two men just stood there unable to pick their jaws up off the floor. "Is everything alright gentlemen?" she mock-innocently asked. In her twenty seven years she had become accustomed to her effect on the members of the opposite sex. If you got it, flaunt it, was her code of ethics. She had it.

"Perfectly, perfectly, please have a seat and get comfortable" stammered Dr. Bloomfield, breaking the spell. Can I get you something to drink?"

"Coffee, black with a shot of brandy would do nicely if you please" answered Victoria as she settled down on the overstuffed couch. Every move seemed to be choreographed; a calculated pose. Whether she was doing this either naturally or on purpose, it most definitely was working.

She's a fucking cat woman come to life thought Mallory in his feeble attempt to gain composure. It's going to be hard keeping focused on the project he quickly surmised. Oh but what a heavenly and monumental distraction, he mentally rejoiced.

"Here you are folks, this should do the trick" commented Dr. Bloomfield as he returned, breaking the spell. Upon the tray he carried was an insulated pot, cups, and a decanter with a brownish liquid. "Sorry Ms. Barbie, no brandy, but will Jack Daniels black label do?"

"Miss, but will you please call me Vicky? And Jack Black will do quite nicely" returned 'Miss' Barbie as she poured a generous double shot for all and topped it off with coffee. "Okole maluna" she toasted. "Which is Hawaiian for bottoms up" and down went the elixir.

Bottoms up. Boy will I have to leave that one alone, pondered Connor Mallory. His mind couldn't help but form a mental picture of his new partner's 'bottoms up'. That, plus Victoria's recipe for coffee was loosening up their first meeting proficiently.

"Your eyes are quite penetrating Mister Mallory, Irish, aren't they?"

"They're X-rated," blurted Connor. The answer shot out automatically before he could catch himself. "And please call me Connor" in his feeble attempt to whitewash the previous remark. "Uhh, excuse me I…"

"Cut the crap Connor I've got five brothers and I've heard it all, or almost all I think, but that was a good one; I'll have to file it in my memory bank. Mind if I borrow it? I promise I'll put it to good use." Victoria was quickly breaking the non-existent ice and it was easy to see that compatibility was inevitable.

"By all means, but still please excuse me, it's just that you are so stunningly beautiful. And yes I'm Irish through and through. My ancestors were knee deep in the I.R.A. from the get-go, but my granddad detested violence, so here we are. When my dad read Leon Uris' <u>Trinity</u>, he named me after the book's hero Connor Larkin."

"Oh I love that book! I also personally avoid violence of any kind at all costs but when Connor blew up that castle…"

And on it went, shots of Jack Black and swapping stories. It was as if they had been lifelong friends. Each tentatively feeling each other out, but sooner than later they all could tell that this project was not only going to be a great adventure, but good fun also.

They shot the breeze until about midnight with no talk about tomorrow's venture. Just philosophical small talk to get to know each other, both in mutual agreement that they could work quite comfortably together. Eventually Dr. Bloomfield showed them to their sleeping quarters and they bade each other good night and knocked out. Tomorrow was time to get down to business. It would take two eccentric characters such as these to attempt the unusual project they were about to undertake. Little did they know just how unusual it would turn out to be.

Haleakala, as well as every other mountain in the island chain has innumerable catacombs of lava tubes throughout each island. They're formed by a long volcanic eruption when flows tend to become channeled. The overflows solidify quickly creating levies and good thermal insulators so that the lava that runs through them remains hot and fluid longer than on the surface. This allows the lava to travel longer distances. The 1969/74 Kilauea eruptions created lava tubes as long as seven miles that finally ended up in the ocean; this constantly making the 'big' island bigger. It is basically the same as a stream traveling under winter ice, just the opposite spectrum in temperature. The longest tube known as "Ape Cave" is twelve thousand eight hundred ten feet or three point nine kilometers and is located in Mount Saint Helens. Connor Mallory and Victoria Barbie were going to attempt to change that.

Legends handed down through generations of pre-recorded Hawaiian history told of a long lost lava tube that led between the islands of Maui and Hawaii- the big island. Although only a myth, it was their mutual curiosity that originally had brought Connor and Victoria together. There was no proof of its existence, but perseverance combined with a mere whim of the earth's turbulence and a minor earthquake had revealed the opening of a possible colossal tube yet unknown. It had been stumbled upon by park rangers hunting the numerous goats that inhabited the crater. Rocks had fallen only to reveal a small crack, but it's conflagration showed the possibility of it being the opening of a cave or maybe an unknown tube. Further excavation showed that it was definitely one or the other. Both speleologists were the first to jump at the chance to explore this new discovery, and it was this expedition that had led them to their meeting the night before.

"Tis a wee bit chilly up here in the morning, lass" Mallory's irish brogue evident in his speech. Victoria suspected it was on purpose. Mallory approached the table and placed a steaming cup of coffee in front of a large picture window that overlooked the crater. "An awe inspiring sunrise, a beautiful woman, and a good strong blast of go- juice, who could ask for more?"

"Good morning Mr. Mallory, yes it's hard to believe we're in Hawaii. It is even known to snow up here a few times a year; now I know why" returned Victoria. She had shed her jump- suit and replaced it with standard camouflage army wear with thermal underwear, a rational choice for the working conditions that lie ahead. But even these clothes couldn't conceal the curves that were hidden underneath. "Even so, people come from all around the world to view this sunrise; it's very famous and supposed to be worth the drive and the wait" she added, nodding toward the group of tourists huddled atop the rim.

"They look fairly miserable and bewildered to me. It's cold out there. It's been said that learning the hard way has never been easy. Maybe we should invite them in for…"

"Sorry against the rules" interjected Harold Bloomfield. "Plus it would be like trying to plug a dam with your finger. Let one in and it's all over" he added as he entered the room, followed by two grizzly old rangers that looked like they would be more at home as prospectors during the California gold rush or perhaps on the deck of a square rigger in the Caribees flying the Jolly Roger. Either way, they definitely were two pieces of work. "Connor Mallory and Victoria Barbie, let me introduce your guides; Raymond Souza and Richard Townsend. This unlikely pair are responsible for this discovery of the cave, or tube as it were."

"Pleez ta meetcha" they growled in unison. Then Souza added "Hey doc how bout some coffee, and uh little shot of Jack?" Both men limped over to empty seats and settled in. "So you folks plannin to take a hike into that hole we found, huh? Looks pretty deep."

Townsend finally spoke "yeah if it weren't for that stupid goat fallin' thru the crack we'd a never seen it. He just kept runnin 'n bleatin until the noise was lost in the distance." Long pause; "It's big."

Bloomfield returned with the goods and remarked mock chastisingly "you two clowns know it's against the regulations to drink on duty, but what the heck, it's before your shifts anyway, besides, I know all about those hip flasks you carry."

In unison: "aww doc we didn't do nothin."

"That's right you didn't do nothin, which means you definitely did something." Bloomfield had their number "you're the picture of innocence."

The two guides cringed as if they were about to be struck by a bullwhip, they looked at each other, then at the trio watching the show, and simultaneously broke out in contagious gut laughter that soon infected all.

Connor and Victoria took to the two guides immediately. It was easy to tell by their craggy features and deeply etched laugh lines that these two amicable and jovial gentlemen had seen and done quite a lot in their lives and enjoyed it all. It was also easy to see it would be much better to have them with you rather than against.

"How did you fellas get your limps? They're almost identical" asked Connor, trying to steer the conversation away from the flasks. He had one himself, and unbeknownst to him, so did Victoria.

Townsend, usually the silent one, spoke up first. "Well, back in our earlier years we used to hunt buffalo and it gets mighty lonely out there, and a man has certain (pause) needs. When you mount a buffalo from behind you have to quickly twist the tail or you can get kicked in the legs. Souza here was so horny that he completely forgot to do so. And me, well, my hand slipped and the rest is history; so now we each call each other buffalofucks. Or any other duerogatory term that comes in handy.

"Don't believe half of what comes out of his mouth. Actually we used to dive for black coral; it's three hundred feet plus underwater and we both managed to get a slight case of the bends. After a while it catches up to you." Souza's answer was much more feasible Connor surmised, but with these two, well, you just never could really tell.

Victoria had almost fallen out of her chair in sheer delight, Bloomfield turned a little 'pinkish' from the actions of his 'park rangers' and Connor quickly deduced that the fates couldn't have delivered a better set of people to round out the crew. Peas in a pod was all he could come up with. Their expedition would be anything but boring.

As the dark night sky started to show traces of gray, the four began to get acquainted by swapping stories of previous adventures. Dr. Bloomfield quickly faded away and went back to his routine. As he closed the door behind him, he could hear guffaws and shrieks of laughter reverberating around the dome in a cyclone of mirth. The 'coffee' was forming a strong bond in the new alliance. Oh well, since there was no telling how long the expedition was going to take, they might as well enjoy each other's company.

As expected, there was much more to Souza and Townsend than met the eye. They both had spent more than half a century on Maui, and partly on the other islands and their stories of the party zone in the sixties and the seventies and well into the eighties and nineties left Mallory and Victoria mesmerized throughout the sunrise. By the time the rim of the sun peeked out over the horizon each were convinced that they couldn't be in better hands. If there was a speck of truth in their outrageous stories, these two were very resourceful and competent characters the likes of which in this day and age were becoming a rare breed and quite possibly candidates for the endangered species list.

Sunrise atop Haleakala is a memorable event, in one way or another. Over a million people come yearly here from all over the globe to experience it. The temperature average is thirty six to forty degrees fahrenheit during the event, add the wind chill factor and it can reach zero and below. Almost everyone that braves this experience comes totally unprepared, expecting Hawaii to be warm and temperate. On this particular morning the crater was hit by a rain squall adding more misery to the tourists huddled atop the rim waiting to witness this world renowned event. Most scattered to the heaters in their vehicles or the shelter of the information center. Those left had either been there before or wisely heeded the warnings on the brochure or the warnings from previous attendants. One by one the stars blinked out and the sky turned from black to gray to blue. The clouds appeared first turning a deep violet into a reddish pink and finally a golden yellow when the sun came blindingly bursting from behind the crater wall to announce another day.

"Wow, I'm sure glad we're in here instead of out there" observed Victoria, her cup of steaming hot coffee and Jack in her hand. They had all taken a break from getting acquainted to witness the spectacular event from the warmth of the dome.

"Yeah, well the visitors bureau encourages the sunrise visits. So when by the time the tourists go back down the mountain, the stores will be opening and they can buy something. Sunsets are the true prize though, because it's still relatively warm. But by then the tourist traps are closed" returned Raymond Souza.

"It's said that learning the hard way's never been easy" added Townsend, slipping another shot into his cup.

"Ha! I just said that a while ago" added Connor.

"That he did," added Victoria.

They all had yet another chuckle together before the inevitable seriousness of the trip set in.

"Shall we get down to business?" suggested Townsend. He was a man of few words, but they were usually well placed.

They scattered to gather all their respective material that pertained to the expedition; the rangers for the map of the trails and the list of supplies and provisions needed for overnight stays, Mallory for his equipment list for exploration and spelunking. But it was Victoria that brought the most enlightening and curious information of all. She let the men go over the essential details needed to complete a thorough investigation of the project. After all, there weren't any stores nearby to pick up something they had forgotten. When they were finished and satisfied, she laid her contribution on the table.

"I have an ex uncle-in-law that has connections very high up. He's retired now but still has connections and enough clout to ask NASA to take a few photos for me using geophysical imaging systems with transmitting instrument packages. On one of our satellites he managed to get me this" This was a map of the crater taken from miles up that was more of an X-ray than a photo, and it showed what was underneath the surface of the crater. The photo distinctively showed lava tubes already known and some yet undiscovered. But it was the one that they were about to explore that grabbed everyone's attention.

"As you can see, except for the various twists and turns it seems to reach all the way down to the ocean. The satellite couldn't penetrate the ocean to get more, but it certainly does appear that we have hit the jackpot."

"What's this?" asked Connor, pointing to a large blur that appeared to be a mile or so inside the entrance.

"An astute question. That's just it, we don't know. At first we thought it might be a glitch in the system or bum film. So after a few successive revolutions of the satellite we took more pictures and this 'blur' as you call it showed up on every one of them. Whatever it is, it shouldn't be there. Not even NASA could explain what would cause such a reaction. What they could tell us is that it's definitely not a natural geological formation. In short, somebody has been there at some time and has left behind something that no one can explain." Victoria's revelation left everyone in stunned silence.

"The plot thickens and we haven't even started yet" said Mallory, breaking the spell. "This definitely shines new light on things."

Townsend and Souza simply looked at each other and shrugged their shoulders. "What's new?" they chorused. Then Souza added: "I guess we'll have to bring along an extra pack mule to bring back whatever it is, if you choose to, that is."

"Well one thing is for sure, we won't know till we get there, shall we?" Connor motivated.

At that they once again parted to prepare for the journey, little did they know what kind of Pandora's Box they were about to open.

As Mallory and Victoria packed their personal items, the rangers loaded the pack mules to cover for any possible contingency. Since the speleologists were entering unknown territory, everything was doubled. The sun rose, warming everything up considerably. When the sunlight descended into the crater it revealed a sight few people see in a lifetime. A total of 14 cinder cones spread throughout the inside of the crater. They vary in size, but it's their color that is the attention grabber. In direct sunlight, they are more red than brown, with black streaks that make them look like they dried yesterday. The general feeling by all who visit is that the mountain is still very much alive, which it is.

"Are we still on earth?" asked Victoria, approaching Connor who was staring as if in a trance towards the intended direction of their expedition.

"What? Ah, oh yeah I think so. Just look at that, I've never, it's so ummm…"

"Take it easy Connor, this place has the same effect on almost everyone.

"It's so alive! And we're going inside! We must be absolutely certifiable! It seems like this whole place is humming" Mallory stammered, truly moved by the surroundings.

After the initial shock, Connor regained his composure just as Souza and Townsend approached with the pack team and horses.

"Still want to crawl inside Mr. Mallory? You're looking a little peekid" ribbed Souza jovialy. He was used to peoples' reactions, but he could see he was gonna have to handle these scientists with kid gloves, for now.

"Well we've come this far, it's just that this place is so… alive."

"That it is, Ms. Barbie. You okay?" Souza asked.

"Magnificent. Will you please be our tour guide? This is much different than looking at pictures."

"Comes with the job, maam. Anything I leave out, just ask. First, we are going down this long sweeping trail called sliding sands. It descends to about three thousand feet and is three point eight miles to the first fork. Then we could either take the scenic route or the direct route which is about a mile shorter. It's an eight plus mile trip to Paliku cabin, our headquarters."

"Sliding sands, that's appropriate" muttered Mallory. "Sure hope these beasts of yours are sure footed. One slip and it looks like you'd go all the way down."

"Not to worry. They're used to it. But it has happened before" Townsend interjected. He wanted them to feel as calm as possible, but not to the point of being lackadaisical.

"I'd have opted for a sled, but what the hell, let's go" Mallory preferred to make light of sticky situations. It had saved his skin and that of lots of others before, and he figured why attempt fix it if it's not broken.

They proceeded down the trail, each lost in their own thoughts. After a slow careful journey, they reached the bottom unscathed to the unspoken relief of all.

"Kalu'u o ka o o, kamoali'i and Pu'u o pele straight ahead. Three miles to go to get to the fork, then it's your choice" Souza's sing- song Hawaiian accent rolled easily off his tongue. The pronunciation of the Hawaiian words were expressed correctly; from the gut. By the time they reached the first fork it was mutually agreed upon to go the direct route. They could take the other route upon their return. The energy of the crater was contagious and the excitement of the pending exploration was mounting.

During the trek to Paliku cabin, not much was said except for minor tidbits of information Souza would interject from time to time regarding known lava tubes and names of cinder cones. They gradually left the moonscape until vegetation began to appear. By the time they reached their objective the environment was covered by rich grasslands and fruit trees and resembled ranch lands here in the U. S. of A.

"Just when I think I've heard and seen it all" remarked Mallory, pulling up to the hitching post at the cabin. "This trip so far is an experience in itself."

"I just love it" answered Victoria like a kid in a candy store.

"Did you know that all of this vegetation and all of these birds are only found in Hawaii?"

"Why doesn't that surprise me?" countered Mallory. "It's definitely an experience to remember."

While Townsend and Souza unpacked the mule team and set up headquarters, Mallory and Victoria went exploring.

"What are these? Are they edible?" asked Mallory.

"Guava and Lilikoi, better known as passion fruit. Try some, they're a bit seedy but very tasty" answered Victoria.

"Passion fruit? Mmmmm."

"As if you need any of that, Mr. Testosterone" quipped Victoria as they taste- tested the bounty surrounding the canyon.

Their expedition over, the speleologists returned to the canyon and found Townsend chopping wood. Upon entering they found the amenities were close to nil. A wood burning stove surrounded by six bunk beds and a picnic table. Souza had already smartly distributed their personal items to the beds closest to the cast iron stove, and the expedition gear was piled on the table ready to be sorted out. He was busy building a fire in the stove.

"This is our heater and cooking facilities" informed Souza pointing to the small stove. "We must keep it going at all times, especially during the night. Anyone who wakes up should put on another log or two in here." Souza pointed to the swinging entrance of the stove. "Trust me, you do not want this to go out."

"Judging from how those tourists were acting at sunrise I'll take your word for it. A five star resort it's not, but I like it. It's rather bohemian, so where's the jacuzzi and the sauna by the way?" joked Mallory as he pulled out his hip flask from inside his jacket pocket. The sun had slipped beyond the rim and a distinct chill was rapidly descending upon the area. "Anyone care for a nip?"

Townsend had just brought in a pile of wood, enough to last until morning, when it would be someone else's turn to chop. All three chorused "no thanks" as each reached for their own flask which brought yet another mutual chuckle from all. They toasted and each set about their own business. No words were needed, a camaraderie had been established in less than a day that would last a lifetime. Soon the shop was set up and the smell of chili permeated the air. Food was shared, good nights were said and all turned in early, wishing it was morning already so they could get down to business. Besides an occasional log getting thrown in the stove, it wasn't long before they were woken by a symphony of bird calls.

"Now that's the most beautiful alarm clock I've ever heard" commented Victoria as she approached the table. She was the last to rise and much to the delight of the men, her yawns and stretches were poetry in motion. It was as if they got up earlier on purpose to get a front row seat while trying not to be obvious.

"Oh yes, now that's a cup of coffee" she added congenially. It was a good sign to all that no one woke up with a 'don't bother me yet' attitude.

"That would be the Apapane I'iwi, Amakihi, and Alauahio, better known as honeycreepers. The Nene goose, the Pueo short eared owl, and the üaü the dark rumped petrel. They're all Native Hawaiian and even though our islands make up .02% of the United States' land mass, twenty percent of the endangered species are from here. The coffee you can blame on Townsend" Souza replied, always ever ready to enlighten others with appropriate information. "There's also Chuckers and Ring Neck pheasant.

"Well there's certainly an abundance here, it's such a delightful sound" Victoria replied. When looking at the two rangers, she had to leave the 'endangered' part alone.

"I soak the grounds in Jack Black before adding the water. It's a recipe my mother taught me" interjected Townsend, his few words naturally right on the money.

"I thought that recipe came from County Cork, from my mother's mother" added Connor Mallory, throwing fuel on the fire. He was always ready to give the Irish credit where it was due. "It seems me mother added quite a bit more on the grounds though."

On it went throughout the morning, exchanging culinary tidbits about coffee recipes and their medicinal value. There was no telling where the line was crossed between serious and out and out B.S. and in no time at all they were once again sharing a mutual chuckle, a great way to start the day; until eventually the maps and the plans were laid out on the table.

"The entrance to whatever it is lies here, just below the mist-maker mountain out towards the Kaupo Gap. It's not that hard to get to, but we are all going to have to remove quite a lot of volcano before you get safely inside. It should take a better part of the day to set up shop there, so it depends on how long it takes to do this before you can go in" informed Souza.

"We'll probably go in for a little peek if we have enough time. Safety first. After all, it's been there for quite a long time and it isn't going anywhere" replied Connor. In actuality he was like a horse chomping at the bit to get inside. But then again he was no fool; going in was easy. But getting out safely required taking the utmost precautionary measures that they could think of.

All the necessary provisions and equipment were loaded up including pick and shovel and the dreaded 'oh oh'. The column set out led by ranger Souza, followed by Victoria then Mallory and bringing up the rear were the appropriate team of Townsend and the mules.

In a little over an hour they reached the spot where they had to leave the trail.

"It's up there," Souza pointed. "From here we get to hand carry the equipment to the entrance. What fun, huh?"

"My god, are you sure we don't need climbing equipment?" asked Victoria.

"It's not as bad as it looks. Actually there's a goat trail not far from here, you just can't see it yet" replied Souza, pulling out a machete to cut a path to the trail. "From there it's just a little climb," he added reassuringly.

"A little climb… humph" Connor muttered, grabbing his machete. "Want to join the fun, Vicki? Just kidding."

It wasn't long before they were following a barely discernible goat trail up the mountain. "We've managed to eradicate seventeen thousand goats since 1958 and they stopped counting in 1993. "It helps prevent erosion and endangered plants," Souza commented. Anything to break the monotony of this back breaking part of the excursion. We found this cave of yours totally by accident." After two jack black 'breathers' they finally reached their destination. "I hope this is what you're looking for, it's a hell of a lot easier toting a rifle than all of this stuff."

"The bare necessities, my good man" replied Connor in his best Irish brogue. "Mostly safety precautions. We have a compass, naturally, a magnetometer, infrared night vision equipment, geophysical imaging system, video cameras, and rope, plenty of it. It's all necessary; actually if we want to do this correctly that is. Okole Maluna." Connor raised his flask partly in thirst and a celebratory gesture for reaching their destination.

After a few more 'toasts' the crew set about their business. Townsend set up a lean-to with a tarp and tree branches he had whittled the night before. Souza unpacked the mule team, and the speleologists organized their tools of the trade. After hacking away the vegetation around the 'crack' Victoria took a reading with her equipment.

"Gentlemen, this appears to be a cave opening, much bigger than the 'crack' as you call it. It's only a few feet thick and appears to be a good sized opening. It's almost round as though it was shaped. Very curious" Victoria announced.

"There's only one way to find out" muttered Townsend dryly. "Boys, man your weapons."

Surprisingly, the earth moved easily from around the entrance. It was met with little resistance. Townsend and Souza alternated between pick and Oh Oh. Mallory's using a shovel and bare hands to remove debris.

"Ho! What's this?" asked Souza as he lifted a rock for all to see. "This is coral from sea level. It's not supposed to be here. Well well...."

As Mallory and Victoria exchanged glances, Townsend was quick to explain. "Coral of this nature that is found in places like these points to a Hawaiian burial chamber. But way up here it's totally abnormal. They've been discovered in very out of the way places but it's unheard of all the way up here."

"It's either a practical joke or somebody went out of their way to plant someone up here for some reason." Souza was thinking out loud.

He wasn't of a superstitious nature but living in Hawaii for so long had ingrained respect and reverence for Hawaiian mythology. "Mr. Mallory and Miss Barbie, you might get more than you bargained for, much more."

As rocks and dirt fell away the team found more pieces of coral amongst the rocks. After a few hours there was an opening one could drive a compact car through. Satisfied, the excavators relinquished their tools and looked in awe at what they had found. This definitely gave a whole new perspective on the project.

"It seems like whoever it was that found this existing hole made it bigger and went out of their way to cover it up again. This has crypt written all over it" Souza announced.

"Maybe it ties in with the glitch in the satellite photos your 'uncle outlaw' got you, Vicki" Mallory quizzed.

"Outlaw?" Victoria asked.

"It's a lot easier to say than ex-uncle-in-law and more appropriate, plus it puts things on the lighter side" Connor answered.

"Actually, I like it- very much. And if you knew him, you would know how right on the money you are. Okole Maluna." She raised her flask in delight and elation about the new twist in their project.

In their concentration the crew didn't notice how much time had passed. A slight chill broke the mesmerized speleologists as reality set in.

"Looks like we might have to call it a day folks" suggested Souza. "If you are going in for a peek, we won't get back until after dark. It's up to you though."

"That's quite all right. We'll just set up so we can go in bright and early tomorrow" said Mallory. "Besides, we have a little more to think about, considering what we have found" he added.

"I'd say that's a pretty big understatement" added Townsend, his reverence for Hawaiian ways was as deep as Souza's. "Shall we? Somebody's got wood to chop and it ain't me." With that he led the column down; horses were mounted, mules were drawn, the trip back was laced with more than a few "Okole Malunas".

After dark, when chores were done, the team gathered around the table to eat and discuss their new finding. Somehow a new bottle of Jack Daniels mysteriously appeared and even a few cans of beer. Nothing was said about it, but all correctly guessed that Townsend was the culprit and they were equally delighted and impressed with his resourcefulness.

"O.K. It's a given that coral is not supposed to be up here. Whether it's a practical joke or not remains to be seen" Souza suggested. "If it's a burial chamber, then whoever it was that was put in there was a very big cheese or…"

"Someone who was a higher up and got themselves in so much trouble that they were brought up here to be completely cut off from history" interrupted Townsend.

"Oh both" interjected Victoria.

"One thing's for sure, our lava tube search could be put on the back burner if what you're saying is true" added Mallory. "What baffles me is what could anyone possibly have done to deserve such a fate as this?"

"There's absolutely no parallel here. All known burial chambers found so far are nowhere near as inaccessible as this" replied Souza.

"It must be your great great grandfather; it's the only answer" ribbed Townsend. Even though Souza's name didn't give it away, his heritage went far back before recorded history. It actually was a possibility.

"Funny! I was just thinking the same about you, except your ancestors wound up behind bars" countered Souza.

"Or in them" countered Townsend. "Okole Maluna". The atmosphere permeated glee as barbs were exchanged and friendships continued to be cemented, but tomorrow's business remained to be the priority, so they stoked up the cast iron stove and turned in early, wishing again that tomorrow was already here.

The natural alarm clock got everyone up in a quick muster that would have made a drill sergeant proud. The team was away from the mist maker mountain even before it started making clouds. They reached their destination in half the time, ready to go to work.

"O.K. no more than seven hours in before you stop. That'll give you time to get back. Agreed?" Souza more than less commanded. Souza became deadly serious. "Try not to disturb anything you might find. The laws pertaining to this are as strict as they can get."

"Absolutely. We'll lay line as we go so it will be easier to return or if worse comes to worse we can be found. If we run into a snag we'll blow the air horn. Sound has nowhere else to travel but out, so we should be easy to hear. Also with lava tubes you never know how porous they are and there probably would be numerous offshoots that would soak up sound. You just never know." Mallory calculated.

"Let's hope it doesn't come to that. Plus it seems you know your way around these things," replied Souza.

"Self preservation," said Connor. "Well, partner, are you about ready?"

"One more minute. I want to double check," answered Victoria. She had the video equipment and wanted to make absolutely sure there were enough cartridges to record their journey.

Much to his disappointment, Mallory would have to lead. It would have been much more entertaining to follow Victoria's curves throughout the expedition. Oh well, he thought. There's always the way back.

Upon entering, they put on night vision glasses and a helmet with a lamp. After they moved a few paces in, just far enough to get away from the outside daylight, they turned off their lamps to adjust their eyes. They were now enveloped by a complete stygian darkness that few people see in their entire lifetime.

"This never ceases to amaze me" remarked Mallory. "Compared to this, a starless night on a new moon is like Broadway on new years eve."

"Ummmm." Victoria had no remark. She preferred to add silence to their sense deprivation to enhance their perception even more. Mallory picked up on this quickly and made no further comment. He smiled to himself wondering if the response Victoria made was a sign she preferred silence, or a "ohm" used in meditation.

"Umph" was his only response. The next few minutes passed in a comfortable silence that was comparable to a married couple after so many years.

"Time to go," Connor whispered. He might as well have spoken through a rock group's P.A. system, his whisper sounded so loud.

Helmet lamps were lit and the cave lit up like a stage. Both speleologists were awed by the natural splendor they were seeing. By looking inward it was easy to deduce that this was truly a lava tube, but someone at some time had excavated it for an unknown reason because there was a barely discernible foot path on the floor. The walls and ceiling however had all the marks of a lava tube complete with reflectatory composition in the rock. Everything sparkled. After a few yards, the first signs of previous exploration appeared on the floor. Palm frond coconut husk torch remains immediately told them they were not the first people to travel through here. It had, however, been a mighty long time since.

"First traces of previous travelers appear in ancient Hawaiian torches," spoke Victoria softly. She was not speaking to Connor, but narrating the video she was taking, and zeroed in on Connor pointing to the torch remains.

Slowly and cautiously they proceeded forward through the twists and turns, rises and drops only a volcano in a temper tantrum could make. There were occasional minor offshoots but it didn't take a rocket scientist to tell that this was by far the most gigantic tube ever discovered. At between fifteen twenty minute intervals other torch remains were found and duly recorded.

"The Hawaiians used the oil from the Kukui nut for their torches. It is known that it was sometimes used as a natural stomach pump, otherwise it is poisonous if too much is ingested. The nuts themselves today are used to make leis to sell to tourists," more narrative by Victoria. "Ah, Connor the magetometer is acting up and the readings are much higher than they should be," her tone was much different than the narrative.

Mallory turned around to look and was shocked to see that the needles were rising and falling in rhythm instead of gauging a measurement.

"Either this thing is broken or there is something really weird going on," responded Mallory in a shocked whisper. Magnetometers just didn't work like this. Either it was on or off; not recording a pulse-like measurement. "This is really spooky," he added.

Victoria felt the hairs on the nape of her neck raise, as well as goosebumps completely up and down on her arms. Not since childhood did she have this sensation. It was just like it was directly off the script of a horror thriller, but she was in it, not watching it.

"Agreed. But curiosity killed the cat. Lets move on," said Mallory in his sincerest attempt to sound cheerful.

"Oh great analogy Mr. Mallory, just wonderful," retorted Victoria. But in reality there was no stopping now. This was just too surreal.

With each twist and turn the magnetometer reading got stronger. After a while a faint glow began to appear ahead, with a pulse that corresponded to the rise and fall of the needles on the gauge. Victoria and Connor were way beyond speech and with each step, their up to now superstitious dread became more viable and penetrating.

"Whatever this is, it's right around the corner in that big chamber." Like kids peeking around a door looking for Santa Claus, they peeked around the last bend and received the shock of their lives. They both gasped their intake of breath and Victoria came as close to fainting as she ever had before. Mallory's jaw dropped and went slack and both speleologists stood shock still as they stared in wonderment at what they stumbled on to.

"Shh.. shh.. shh.. shall we blow the horn?" stuttered Victoria barely able to speak.

Mallory still couldn't talk. He was completely dumbfounded, bewildered, and immobile. All they could do is feebeley attempt to gather their wits, total and undeniable shock complete.

Perched upon an ancient bamboo dias was one of the biggest skeletons clad in full kingly regalia they had ever seen. But that wasn't the real shocker. Wrapped in the skeleton's arms was the source of the magnometer's readings. Both speleologists legs gave out and they fell butt first onto the floor. They could actually feel what they were seeing, even if they couldn't believe what they saw. The object in the king's arms was completely out of context. It was impossible; yet there it was, made of some unknown metallic substance that didn't belong in the historical time frame commonly understood by mankind. Not only that, but there was a small pulsating pinprick of a light that had a life of its own emanating from within.

"May the saints preserve us," Mallory finally uttered. "This can't be happening!" Yet it was.

When they finally found their legs, they crept slowly up to the giant skeleton perched on the dias, that set upon a Hawaiian outrigger canoe that looked like it was built yesterday. They were way beyond any coherent answer, so they just shuffled forward totally stupefied. In her trancelike state, Victoria neglected to notice the various gourds encased in a wax-like substance that were strewn about the floor. She finally noticed them when she tripped over one and Connor had to grab her to keep her from falling, getting a cheap thrill in the process.

Mallory cautiously reached out a fingertip to touch it. No shocks, neither cold nor warm, yet there it was; a rectangularish sphere with curved edges, something that defied any previous knowledge. Completely illogical.

"I believe this most likely takes the cake," whispered Mallory. "Do you have any idea what this is?"

"Not in the slightest," replied Victoria, finally able to speak. "From the looks of it, I doubt anyone else can answer that either."

"You're probably correct in that assumption. Just look at that guy. He must have weighed close to four hundred pounds. And to bring him, this canoe, and those gourd-like thingies way up here? What a piece of work that must have been," Connor surmised.

"I bet that 'thing' had something to do with it," Victoria stammered.

"Also probably correct. But what is it?" queried Mallory.

"No idea. I've never seen any material like it. But then again that's not my field. Maybe Dr. Bloomfield has got a clue. The question is, what shall we do now?" she pondered.

"Good question, I know we shouldn't disturb the burial site. It is probably the greater if not the greatest find in Hawaiian history. But this object, however, is a different story. Did you get it on video?" asked Connor.

"Not yet. I was just in too much shock to do anything. It stopped me cold," answered Victoria.

"I think maybe we should remove the object. Because of its scientific value. And since it has nothing to do with any historical context, we take it; and perhaps one or two of these gourds you tripped over as proof of our find. Let's remove whatever it is out of the skeletons arms first, then proceed to record it on video. Out of sight out of mind so to speak," suggested Mallory.

"Oh that's devious Mr. Mallory, yet I can't help but tend to agree with your idea, but since this is so weird anyway, let's do it." replied Victoria Barbie, speleologist, not quite sure of what she was getting herself into. If she only knew…

So, ever so carefully they removed the find, then recorded the burial chamber as if the object never existed. This move, as unconventional as it could be, and unbeknownst to them at the time, would later prove to be a savior and benefit to all mankind. The can of worms was open once again.

"Raymond, wake up. I think I hear them comin" said Townsend, shaking Souza out of his afternoon siesta. His dream had been interrupted. He had been somewhere in a jungle surrounded by members of the opposite sex, but he was carrying a throw- net, which made no sense. His bewilderment instantly changed back to reality as the echo of the calls from the speleologists brought him back to a cognizant state.

"Huh, already? They're back early. I wonder if something happened," quizzed Souza in his waking moments.

"Obviously," muttered Townsend. He had the 'sixth sense' that at the moment was in high gear.

As the noise of their approach grew louder, they got prepared for any contingency; worst to best case scenario, the possibilities limitless. Much to their relief, Mallory and Victoria emerged from the abyss unscathed. But the look on their faces told a different tale. Apprehension filled the air as no word was said upon their emergence. The cave crawlers looked a touch pale, as if they had seen a ghost. All premonitions aside, they couldn't have been more correct.

"Hello and Aloha, how goes it?" smiled Souza soothingly, there was something about this picture he couldn't put a finger on, but he let it ride until the explorers adjusted themselves back to the land of the here and now. They seemed to be acting very peculiar considering the circumstances, but then again he wasn't a cave dweller.

The speleologists took their time to answer, as if there was one. "I don't know where to start, it's all just too bizarre, Victoria, finally able to come up with a word to describe, replied, "Look."

As the speleologists dumped their packs on the ground, the Rangers noticed two extra bundles. When they were unwrapped, their reaction was totally unexpected.

"There must be a god!" Townsend almost shouted, his eyes riveted on the gourds. Souza said nothing, but they started dancing in place, crooked arm with crooked arm around in circles, much to the bewilderment of the speleologists. "Uh, what's that?" asked Townsend, noticing the peculiar object next to the gourds.

"If I had an answer, I'd give you one," replied Mallory. "Whatever has happened, we hit the jackpot."

"You have no clue," retorted the Rangers almost in unison. Immediately they both went straight to the gourds to make sure their wildest dreams had come true. Reverently they picked up each one and shook them to substantiate their opinions.

"Yeeaaah!" they yelled like two punk rockers in a mosh pit. It was all they could say.

As if it wasn't strange enough, the Rangers reaction was icing on the cake to the speleologists. Absolutely nothing more could be done to make this day more surreal than it already was- or so they thought.

As emotions settled, Townsend gave Souza a sly glance and they both nodded to each other, then he said: "We're going to make this a big surprise. Just wait until we get back to the cabin." The speleologists' concentration showed they appeared to be oblivious to the 'other' discovery, which was true, for the time being. After a few 'okole malunas' they quickly broke camp and headed for Paliku cabin, the Rangers giddy as merry pranksters, the speleologists completely overcome by a combination of all the above and more. There were just no words to describe the situation, and it wasn't going to get any better for a long while.

As the column headed home, the speleologists settled into a complacent passivity, a result of the day's adventure. They were unaware of the Ranger's knowledge pertaining to the gourds. If things were as they appeared to be, Souza and Townsend's 'surprise' would be a welcome relief from the rigors of the expedition. Their mirth they kept to themselves until they were ready to spring the trap.

"It seems this thing has an effect on the horses and mules" observed Victoria upon their arrival. "Did you notice their ears perk up when we got close to them?" she asked.

"Yes. Their ears appeared to be like antennae. All of them too. Not just one. And the mule isn't supposed to be the sharpest pencil in the pack either. This is really something," answered Mallory. "On top of this, the Ranger's reaction to the gourds beats all. Whatever they know that we don't seems to have made their day. Speaking of which, I don't believe I'll ever forget this day either."

"That's the understatement of the year. Those two are acting like kids at Disneyland," replied Victoria. "They're inside now with the gourds. We better get in there to make sure they don't destroy the evidence."

It was too late for that. Upon entering the cabin, they found Souza and Townsend breaking the wax seal of one of the gourds. When they opened the top, they cheered and started dancing arm in arm around again, in a circle as if they were attending a ho-down. By this time the day's occurrences had put the speleologists in a numb state of shock. Even the Ranger's strange behavior didn't seem to phase them.

"My friends," announced Souza, "what we have here is a gourd full of aged Awa Root tea. Probably put there to help that King on his travel to eternity. Awa root is still used today, but aged like this, it should probably kick our asses."

Townsend gathered four cups and set them on the table. Reverently, Souza poured a shot of the dark brownish liquid in each of them, chanting in Hawaiian all the while as if it was some type of ceremony, which it was. At the end of his prayer he gestured towards the cups and added "okole maluna." At that, they threw down the shots like cowfolk at a whiskey bar.

"Aggh. That's terrible," cried Victoria. "That has to be the most bitter substance I've ever tasted in my life."

"It'll grow on you. Trust me," replied Souza, grimacing himself from the taste of it. "Just you wait, little lady." Earlier he had sampled a meager dosage to test the strength of it and wasn't surprised. And it was good that he did.

In a matter of minutes all of their limbs seemed to grow in weight and they found it increasingly harder to move them. Souza thought it appropriate to have only four shots after appraising its strength.

"I can't feel my body," chuckled Victoria.

"I will," chorused the men in unison.

"I've been kicked in the head by one of the mules," slurred Mallory.

"It's fairly concentrated. Must be the aging," Souza garbled.

"Fairly? This is ass-kicking stuff," Townsend barely discernible.

Slowly but surely they slithered off their chairs and on to the floor. All they were capable of was crawling. Balancing on only two limbs was out of the question, and the intensity did not stop. After around an hour they were still glued to the floor, incapable of mobility.

"Say, this stuff is delightful," slurred Victoria. "Will I ever be able to move again?" Giddy. "I really don't care."

"It's going to take a while," answered Souza. "It's by far the strongest batch I've ever experienced. Kick back and enjoy. You don't find shit like this on any shelf in any store. Eh, how many of these gourds are down there, by the way?" He was the picture of innocence.

"We didn't count. It should be on the video. I know there is a dozen at least," replied Mallory, trying his best to make the noise coming out of his mouth sound like words. "Let's check it out."

It took some time, but as immobilized as they were, they managed to set up the camera and view the recorded excursion. Even Townsend and Souza gasped when they saw the burial chamber. They would have danced again if they could, after counting the gourds. But at that moment it was way beyond the realm of possibility. While in their state of euphoric immobility, another round was passed around. Victoria muffled a polite decline and Mallory managed a feeble attempt, but his arms didn't work that well, nor could he hold a cup.

"Tilt your head back," ordered Townsend in barely discernible mumblings. The Rangers were tough old birds and their stern constitutions permitted them to successfully find the orifice in their face to throw down one more shot. As if they needed it.

Time passed like a slo motion cartoon. Speech consisted of garbled incoherencies, and movement, what little there was, was limited to a bare minimum. At least they all had the common sense enough to go with the flow and not fight the effects of the Awa Root tea. When the tea finally started to wear off, Mallory found himself in his bunk, Victoria was draped halfway across hers and the Rangers seemed to have not moved at all. Mallory, a life-long prankster managed to turn on the video to record the event for posterity. Although it wouldn't win an Oscar for action thriller, it did however convey to the viewer the highs and/or depths that were reached during the occasion. They recorded until the tape ran out, which was long before the participants started coming around. It wasn't all, but it was enough.

"Is that stuff legal?" Victoria finally managed to enunciate. "If it is, it shouldn't be."

"If the F.D.A. got their hands on this stuff it would be put on the controlled substance list immediately. Shit, they would probably either bottle it up and tax it and sell it, or use it for lab experiments or maybe even warfare; imagine giving that to an enemy," Mallory surmised.

"If everybody had that shit there wouldn't be any enemies," answered Souza. "And no, it's not illegal. Actually it's not that well known. It is mostly known by the natives of the Pacific Rim, usually used in ceremonies regarding weddings and canoe races and such. If word did get out, it could reach epidemic proportions; so we keep a lid on it. Also, the aging process concentrates it quite a lot. In all my years I've never come across a batch so potent."

"It kicked our butts and we hardly even dented it," added Townsend. He picked up the gourd and shook it for all to hear. Sure enough the level of liquid had hardly dropped at all. "This here is a year's supply at least."

They were all rapidly coming back to the world of clarity, the effects of the tea leaving as fast as they had come. The only difference was that hours had passed and no one could account for what happened. No one had moved very far and no one got hurt and much to the astonishment of all, there was no hangover.

"I can safely say I've never had anything quite like it," said Victoria, actually I wouldn't mind a little for myself on occasion, plus I have a few friends I'd like to slip a 'mickey' to."

I've tried angel dust, P.C.P. which is bull tranquilizer, once. That's the only drug I could compare it to, but that lasted only a few minutes, not hours like that concoction," added Mallory. "I wouldn't mind having a little stash of my own."

"That's settled then. It's a good thing we brought out two, otherwise we'd have to go back. Besides, there's a bunch of it, probably enough to immobilize an army," from Souza.

As the group gathered their wits Mallory went over to the camera and hit rewind. "I have a little surprise for you," he chuckled. "I got it all on tape."

"You devious S.O.B."

"What for, evidence?"

"Blackmail."

Mallory pressed start and they watched the expedition all over again. Then, when it abruptly ended, it was replaced by a picture of what appeared to be dead bodies, except they occasionally moved. But in the top left-hand corner on the screen was that all too familiar blur.

"That's the same as your satellite photos," remarked an astonished Mallory. "And the camera is only pointed in the vicinity of that 'thing'. What the hell is going on?" Their attention had been temporarily diverted by their Awa root experiment, but this brought everyone back to focus on their curious discovery.

"And look, the blur seems to fade in and out, corresponding to the blinking light," observed Victoria.

"I've got an idea." Mallory went to his backpack and extracted his compass. "Isn't this something," pointing to the needle. "It's magnetic. It's emanating a magnetic pulse, and a mighty strong one at that. Even a satellite could pick it up. What's it for though, is the question." The needle was also dancing to the pulse of the light. "If I didn't know any better, I'd say it's a beacon of some sort."

"For whom or what?" asked Victoria.

"That, my dear, is a question I'm not sure I want to know the answer to" returned Mallory, "or find out".

The next morning they broke camp. The four- legged animals took a serious dislike to the discovery even when covered and put in a pack. They still knew it was there. When Mallory approached the lead horse it shied back on its two hind legs causing a domino effect on the rest, scattering everything that had been loaded on the pack horses back on the ground. After packing everything twice the party proceeded on their prearranged course through the middle of the crater, passing through some of the most unique landscape that went by almost totally unnoticed. Each member was preoccupied with their own thoughts. Even the hip flasks went untouched. Eventually they reached Holua cabin and the two-mile switchback trail that would lead them back out. After endless zigs and zags they finally reached Halemau (Ha lay mau ew) Which was located at the eight thousand foot level where Dr. Bloomfield was waiting.

"Greetings. You're back so early. Is everything alright? Did something go wrong? What happened?" Dr. Bloomfield was on them like white on the moon. Hello. Yes. No. Yes. I don't know yet, thought Mallory to himself. Christ what a dork! "Hello Doc. Yes I think we may have stumbled onto something," was what he really said.

Townsend and Souza simply glanced at each other. Victoria was bursting at the seams, and Mallory had gone into a semi-catatonic state for the trip back. The past few days had taken its toll on him. He was ill-tempered and suffering a trauma over what had happened and what could happen, his uneasiness overwhelming. By now doctor Bloomfield's curiosity was red-lining.

Souza broke the ice. "Hey doc, how's this for starters?" He reached into the pack of the lead horse and pulled out the unopened gourd. They had all thought it best to claim only one. It was agreed upon and brought out with a what-they-don't-know-can't-hurt-them pretext. Souza carried the gourd over to Dr. Bloomfield. Bloomfield glanced at the gourd, then at the explorers and back again, twice, a look of utter disbelief on his face.

"Impossible! That can't be what I think it is," stammered Bloomfield. "What's inside?"

"Maybe we should open it and find out?" suggested Townsend, winking at Victoria.

"How? Where? What happened? Oh I get it, very funny. Good joke. It is a joke, isn't it?"

"It's no joke, doctor," said Victoria soothingly. "Although I must add that these two 'Rangers' you appointed us could be quite capable of it."

"Ah, miss Barbie, would we do anything like that maam?" mocked Souza.

"That and more, you pirates," interjected Mallory, coming out of his daze.

Bloomfield could see that the four of them had turned into close friends. His focus though, was on the gourd. He wanted answers. Although he was a telescope technician, he had gathered enough bits and pieces of Hawaiian lore to correctly assume what it was. "This must be hundreds of years old," he judged just by the look and feel of it. "Is this the only one?"

"No, actually there are quite a few more. It's on video. We counted at least over a dozen, and there's lots more to this. But let's just have the video do the talking.

"Shall we crack this one open to find out what's inside?" Townsend a picture of innocence. "If you shake it, you'll find it's some sort of liquid."

Mallory stifled a smile. Victoria's eyes rolled up as the Rangers led the doctor back to the car with their prize.

"Oh no you two, we'll have to photograph and catalog this first before we do anything. Besides, don't you two have some animals to tend to first?" scolded Bloomfield. He had the feeling that he was the brunt of some sort of practical joke, but that wasn't new, when dealing with these characters, so he let it slide.

"Miss Barbie and Mr. Mallory, why don't you join me in my automobile and let these two earn their pay," suggested Dr. Bloomfield as he shot a glance at the Rangers which resembled that of a school principal sending class rowdies to detention.

"Thanks but no, doctor," answered Mallory. "You can take the lady as she would probably like to freshen up. We'll follow and see you shortly." He grabbed the other pack to put it in Bloomfield's vehicle. As he passed the line of animals, they each shied and some winnied and hee-hawed. He set the pack in the back seat with the gourd, a cheshire cat with a feather-in-his-mouth look on his face. "See you there," he added.

"That was odd," observed Bloomfield.

"It certainly is," smirked Victoria, barely able to contain herself.

As the pair drove away, the trio reached for their hip flasks. One 'okole maluna' and they were off.

"Shall we open it and find out," mocked an amused Mallory. "Ranger Townsend, you are deplorable."

"That's his middle name," replied Souza. "Let's be on our way. I don't want to miss the fun when the doc opens the other pack."

The horses and mules had settled down the more distance that was put between them and Bloomfield's car which made the final leg of their journey much easier. But as they neared the dome, they could hear the wail of sirens and the screaming of alarms. They quickened their pace and upon arrival there stood Dr. Bloomfield and Victoria at the entrance, Victoria holding the gourd and the good doctor holding the backpack, a quizzical look of bewilderment on his face.

"Your backpack set off the alarm system. What on earth is inside?"

"Good question, doctor," answered Mallory. "We were hoping you could tell us. Shall we?" Mallory, the eternal gentleman opened the door for the lady and with a bow and flourish that would have befitted a kings court, he gestured her inside.

"Thank you sir," Victoria over emphasized loudly, "Cornball" out of the side of her mouth as she passed by.

"The pleasure is mine your highness," he mocked, barely able to contain himself as she passed by, her fabulous bottom resembled a pendulum of a clock, only much more curvaceous.

She shot him a mock-stern glance trying to sound convincingly uptight. She wasn't doing very well.

After resetting the alarm system, they again went off immediately. In exasperation the doctor finally shut them down. He approached the table where Mallory and Victoria were setting up the video equipment. Souza and Townsend took care of the animals that had calmed down after the removal of the object from their vicinity. Soon the Rangers joined the trio at the table, setting themselves close to the gourd in anticipation, like kids on Christmas morning. Bloomfield's barrage of questions went unanswered by the repeated "just watch and see." The backpack remained closed for the grand finale.

"As you have probably guessed we didn't find what we were looking for, yet." lectured Mallory. "Eventually it might prove out to be we will, but we got kind of sidetracked." At that, he let the video run its course which had all the makings of a documentary. Bloomfield had to grab the table for balance when they reached the King's tomb. The look of incomprehensible astonishment on his face. After the scene in the cabin depicting the 'dead' bodies he was completely baffled.

"This is a find of incalculable importance," said Bloomfield, gathering his composure. "However, a burial chamber housing one of the Ali'i, or Kings remains which includes a canoe, gourds, weapons accompanying him, portrays his importance within his tribe," he observed. "Also by the looks of you all in the cabin, it appears that our ranger Townsend here, smuggled in at least half a case of Jack Black for the trip."

"But doc, I'm innocent this time. It's..." acknowledged Townsend.

"Ahem," interrupted Souza, to cut him off from a needless confession and also giving him a stiff elbow in the ribs.

The cat was out of the bag thought Victoria, so she took the floor.

"Doctor as you can see we found the chamber with numerous gourds. So we brought out two and tested one, which we have the remains of, in our personal possession. Ranger Souza, if you please."

Like a kid caught with his hand in the cookie jar, Souza reluctantly provided the opened gourd that had the remains of the solution encased inside. Bloomfield sauntered over to the Rangers giving them a withering glare, opened the top and sniffed its contents. He wrinkled his nose and stared around the table.

"That's the most god awful stench of Awa Root I've ever encountered. It has fermented successfully, and you tested this and that's what happened?" he asked pointing to the freeze frame on the screen. "What's this blur in the corner?"

"It's the same thing that's on the satellite photo, and is also where the real mystery begins," answered Mallory as he opened the backpack and provided the object. "This was in the kings arms, we removed it because…"

"Save your breath Connor," interrupted Townsend, "and find some smelling salts. The doctor just fainted and is out cold."

Upon revival the doctor was set in a chair and all he could do was stare at the object for a few moments until he started babbling. "Impossible! It's some kind of joke. It's completely out of historical context. Technology of their time couldn't possibly have built it even if they had the material for it, whatever that is. It was before electricity was discovered yet it has a blinking light in it. Impossible." Bloomfield rattled on as if in a state of shock, which he probably was. "Well, one thing we can do is take this to the lab and find out what it's made of. Bloomfield gave them a mischievous glance and added, "I noticed you eliminated it from your video recording."

"Precautionary measures doc," replied Mallory. "These two finds are completely out of context. To be honest, I'll tell you it was wrapped in the kings arms so there's a connection somewhere. It probably has something to do with why he was put so far away from any known burial sites. As a matter of fact I'd bet on it. The point is, that since it's so unusual we thought it best to keep both discoveries disconnected for the time being, until we have more answers, if we can find any."

Bloomfield was quiet for a moment debating within himself. When he finally looked up at them he smiled. "Sound idea," he said conspiratorially then added, "for now."

"Hey doc, wanna try some tea?" asked Townend, hoping to smooth out the situation.

"Thanks but no. Judging by the looks of what it did to you it's counterproductive. I'll take a rain check. Besides, after analyzing whatever this is, I just might need to take you up on your offer," replied the good doctor. "Let me go ahead and clear out the laboratory. Obviously you want to keep this temporarily a secret. Give me five minutes. The lab is down the corridor, third door on the right. I'll have to invent a story to get my colleagues to leave. Try to look as innocent as you can until you see them go. Then we can get down to business." Then he was off.

"Connor, are you sure about this?" asked Victoria, a look of genuine concern on her face.

"Absolutely not Miss Barbie. The one thing I do know is if we include it in with the burial chamber find, somebody's going to want to claim it, and we will get lost in a quagmire of bureaucratic bullshit," answered Mallory. "Let's try to find some answers first." Then he added pointing to the Rangers, "and you two: stay out of the gourd. We have to stay on our toes."

"Yessah massah." chorused the Rangers, a look of minor disappointment on their features. But in actuality they had been around the block way too many times not to agree. "We'll guard it with our lives," added Souza.

"I bet you will," thought Dr. Bloomfield. "The other scientists are leaving. Lets go," observed Victoria.

The men stood aside for the lady in a gentlemanly fashion. There were no dummies in that department. Besides, who in their right mind wouldn't want to follow behind such a womanly gait as hers.

They entered the laboratory and were taken aback by the myriad of scientific machinery. They were also utterly lost as to the functions of each piece. Dr. Bloomfield however, was in his element. He was busy over in a corner where a table was encased in a plexiglass room, the object already inside. Bloomfield was engrossed in setting up equipment and twisting various dials and flipping numerous switches.

"This will analyze its composition. Then we can go from there. It's going to take a few minutes so pardon me while I ignore you," said the doctor.

The minutes passed by while the spectators became increasingly impressed with the doctors competence. Apparently his expertise was much wider than just the field of stargazing. After various adjustments he finally announced, "for better or worse, we're ready."

"What is this thing?" asked the ever quizzical Victoria. She had always been an information sponge, during her formative years. It started when she was a baby- at first trying to eat anything that wasn't nailed down. Her curiosity compounded as she grew up and with her parents financial and moral support, wound up with a degree in geophysics and anthropology at Stanford university during the years of the sexual revolution. The area and the era had molded a well rounded worldly personality which combined with her looks made her a force to be reckoned with.

"It's the mechanical equivalent to a human M.R.I. machine. Not only does it give us a peek inside but it can also tell us what it's made of… Whoa, what's this?" responded Bloomfield, his discourse interrupted by the readings on the screen.

They all followed his glance to the blank screen. All it showed was the outline of the object. "This is supposed to act like an X-ray to see what's inside, but the exterior of your discovery seems to be blocking the probe. Most unusual," said Bloomfield answering his own question. He checked his settings, then added "No, not unusual, impossible."

"Maybe it's broke," interjected Souza. He was standing on the side in an attempt to stay out of the way of the scientist, allowing him to do 'his thing'. The crusty old Ranger in the clinically clean laboratory was the equivalent to a prostitute in a confessional.

"Unfortunately no. Everything is in order. There is some type of shielding preventing us from seeing what's inside, and this machine is supposed to see through anything, including lead," answered the doctor. Souza was actually surprised to even get a response from him. Bloomfield's focus seemed to be entirely on his work, as if no one else was even present in the room with him.

"There's nothing wrong with the machine, but there's definitely something wrong with this picture." He turned to his conspirators, "cheer up though, if we cannot get to its components, we can at least find out why. But that's going to take some time. The machine does it on its own, so how about some coffee?" The doctor was visibly shaken. The scientist was acting like a child when his toys were broken. His scientific world consists of finding answers and this was not a good start, nor a good omen. "And maybe a little Jack."

The others looked at each other in complete bewilderment. The normally confident doctor was acting like the rug had been pulled out from under him, his demeanor totally altered. Victoria was the first to act. She put her arm around the scientist and led him to a seat. It was obvious that whatever was going on rarely happened, if ever. The ever-ready Townsend quickly appeared with the coffee and 'condiments' and Bloomfield poured himself a generous shot of the nerve calming potion into his coffee; a look that convinced the onlookers that something definitely was amiss.

Nothing was said. There was nothing to say. Each of them were in their own particular world of bewilderment. The only sound was the whirring of the analyzer and the slurping of coffee. Finally a buzzer sounded announcing the end of the analytical process. Apprehension filled the air as no one was quick to move to see the results. All inherently thought it best to let the good doctor regain his composure as perhaps it was a sixth sense or maybe even superstition that had immobilized them. Either/or, nobody moved.

"Hey doc, want me to get this for you?" asked Mallory lightly as he moved towards the sheet of paper coming out of the machine.

"What? Oh, yes, that would be nice Mr. Mallory, if you please," answered Bloomfield. Apparently the potion was doing the trick. "This at least should give us some answers. Aghhh!" The doctor unconsciously attempted to jump out of his chair and slumped back down out cold; the paper slipping from his clenched fist to the floor.

After a split second the others burst into action.

"Smelling salts!" barked Mallory.

"Pillow and blankets" ordered Victoria.

Souza quickly appeared with a first aid kit, opened it and pulled out an amyl nitrate capsule. "Popper" He prescribed. "Oops. amyl nitrate I mean."

"We know what you mean," chuckled Mallory as he broke the vial under the doctor's nose. "We weren't born yesterday. And Ranger Townsend, I believe a small cup of Awa root just might be in order at the moment, if you please."

Townsend didn't need to be told twice. Magically appearing out of nowhere, a cup of tea was quickly produced as Dr. Bloomfield began to come around. Mallory gave the Ranger a quick glance and a wry smile.

"Hip flask," Townsend quickly explained, just a little embarrassed. "So? I'm guilty. Sue me," he added reassuringly. He wasn't very convincing.

"No matter Ranger Townsend, it seems to be working," was Mallory's only rebuttal. To each his own he thought, thinking of glass houses.

And indeed it was working. The doctor's instant panic was quickly transforming into a euphoric passivity. As the doctor's eyes began to focus, his giddiness had a Jeckyl/Hyde ish twist to it. "ah ha ha ha, you're not going to believe it, but you're going to like it, ah ha ha."

The bewildered group let the doctor have his way. They certainly didn't want to make anything stranger than it was already. Townsend put the flask away without touching a drop. Victoria cradled the doctor's head in her lap and he was perfectly content to be there. Mallory went to retrieve the paper, and Souza didn't move, he observed, ready to deal with any surreal contingency that might yet appear.

"Well well; why doesn't this surprise me?" remarked Connor as he read the paper containing the results. "Except for some form of titanium alloy, all other ingredients are labeled unknown origin."

Later that afternoon, when Dr. Bloomfield had regained his composure and the speleologists had recovered from the initial shock, they all gathered around the object on the table. Unremarkably, the scenario didn't seem to phase the Rangers much, to them it was just another day in the park. All had followed suit in the doctor's Awa root prescription; this time in a meager dosage, just enough to settle an unsettling situation.

"This is another fine mess we've got ourselves into," remarked Mallory, trying his best to mimic Oliver Hardy addressing Stan Laurel. "Now what are we supposed to do?"

"I believe I just might have the answer to that one," replied Victoria. "Remember the 'uncle outlaw' I mentioned? Well he's actually a retired brigadier general in the U.S. Air Force. Quite a colorful character actually. To put him in perspective, I'd say he would fit in quite nicely with our Rangers here. Tyrone 'Bull' Exley is his name. As chance would have it, his tour of duty was mostly centered around Roswell, New Mexico during the years everyone asks questions about. He's a lovable old guy and kind of a pirate in his own way. During his enlistment, his rumored exploits were known to be monumental. As a matter of fact he was forced into early retirement because he got himself into so much trouble, the harmless kind for the most part, but nevertheless he might possibly be able to help. Whenever I quizzed him before, he'd automatically claim "national security" no matter what the question was about. But in the light of this discovery here, he might just change his tune. One thing's for sure, he'd fit right in."

"Sounds plausible," agreed Mallory. "Where can we find him?"

"When he 'retired,' he moved to Florida and opened a retirement home that's more like a resort. He's an acute fun lover. It's somewhere around Key West and he calls it 'Sons of the Beach' or 'Sun of a Beach'; something like that. I'm sure you recognize the correlation," answered Victoria.

"I sure do and I like him already. What a name! Mallory guffawed thinking 'Bull' Exley would add to this cast of characters quite nicely. "Florida, though. Considering what this thing does to alarm systems etcetera, getting there undetected could be a problem."

"Maybe not," interjected Townsend with a twinkle in his eye. He glanced toward Souza for an unspoken approval. Souza smiled and nodded affirmatively. "We have high friends in places." He then added: "who just might be your ticket outta here." His confidence and tone suggested a no 'questions/no lies' mode of operandi.

Souza broke in, "of course we will have to check with them first. A quick cell phone call should do it. Their occupational hazards require, ah, discretion. And our mutual desire for secrecy makes the trust factor mandatory. In other words, I'll have to partially let them know what's going on. We've known them for decades and they are totally trustworthy. Honor among thieves so to speak."

"Sounds cryptic, but good"

"How soon can you…"

"Just trust me. I'll be back shortly," answered Souza. He grabbed the cell phone and was out the door. Then he turned around: "just how much can I tell them?"

"I'll leave that up to you. Your friends are my friends, right?"

"For life, bruddah." Then he was gone.

Townsend then added "with friends like this it's like hitting the jackpot. You could do no better."

Souza soon returned announcing "they're on their way."

"And just what am I supposed to do? interrupted Dr. Bloomfield. "I feel like I'm left holding the bag, literally. I'm supposed to act like nothing happened?" Exasperation was clearly in his voice.

Victoria came to the rescue soothingly. "Doctor, first of all we are taking 'the bag' with us and we really don't have a choice. Once the burial chamber news gets out it's going to be chaos, so can you please keep a lid on it until we get back? There's no telling what might happen at this point. Besides, if the news leaks out, it's a circus you're going to have to handle yourself. And we wouldn't want to saddle you with all that responsibility. This should only take a few days, a week at the most," she pleaded.

The good doctor pondered this for a moment, then looked at them and smiled, "see no evil, speak no evil, hear no evil," he responded.

A short while later the sounds of un-muffled engines were heard far off in the distance completely destroying the peaceful environment of Haleakala at sunset as they approached.

"Good god, what is that?" stammered Mallory as the sounds of the approaching engines turned into a thunderous roar. When he had at first heard them, it sounded like they were already at the top of the mountain; when in actuality they were still over a mile away. But now, it seemed like the foundations of the dome itself were shaking.

"Bored out Harley Hogs with Glass Pax mufflers," explained Townsend. "They live down below on the mountain in Kula and never take their Hogs into public; they'd be arrested on the spot. They prefer to have their presence known, and felt before being seen." He almost had to yell.

As the rumbling grew into a crescendo, around the corner came a sight that should have belonged in a comedy movie instead of atop a dormant volcano. A combination of Hells Angels, The Wild Ones, and Easy Rider approached the dumbstruck group in a cloud of noise that could have woken the dead. They were dressed in a variety of costumes that would have made Spielberg or Mel Brooks proud of their work. Adding to the scenario were a combination of long ponytails and shaved heads accentuated by various illustrated and pierced body parts, each dressed from the cut-off t-shirt and jeans to black leather everything, a sight suited more for either the Barnum and Bailey circus or the cuckoo's nest.

Bloomfield, Mallory, and Victoria were beyond speech. They kept glancing from the Rangers to the motorcycle pack and back again in total astonishment and disbelief. Townsend and Souza were aware of this and were doing their best to hold a straight face and thus accentuate the situation by acting nonchalant, as if this was an everyday occurrence. The bikers surrounded them, circling like Indians around a wagon train, complete with hoots and hollers and gunning their engines and causing backfires for, well, just for the hell of it. If intimidation was their intent, they were completely successful.

Victoria looked ready to faint. Bloomfield was ghost white again and Mallory was as close to strangling the Rangers as he possibly could get. As if on cue, the pack came to a halt in a circle around them and the first one to step off his bike was a man dressed only in a sleeveless t-shirt and trunks, perfect anti-clothing for the plummeting temperatures, that revealed a body almost completely covered in tattoos.

"Good evening folks, fine weather for an evening cruise, wouldn't you say?" His speech intonation was totally contradictory to his appearance, and had an amiable quality to it that couldn't be ignored. "I'm pleased to make your acquaintance. My name is, Captain Magic, and my friends here would rather remain anonymous, for now. Although Raymond's description was brief, I gathered you are in a little bit of hot water. How can we help?" As if the last few days weren't enough, this was just more icing on the proverbial cake.

The speleologists almost jumped back expecting a mugging when Captain Magic reached into his pocket, pulled out a pouch and proceeded to quickly roll a very large cigarette, light it with a snap of his zippo, and inhaled deeply. "Would you care for some of Maui's finest? It goes quite well with Haleakala's sunsets," he offered.

Mallory was about ready to decline when a wonderfully sweet chocolatey licorice aroma filled the air. In a style befitting an indian ceremony Mallory gratefully accepted. "Why thank you Captain Magic, don't mind if I do." He had smoked herb before, but never had he encountered any that had such a beautifully pungent aroma as this.

"Call me Captain Magic if you will. We're not big on formality, as you probably can tell." He then broke into an ear to ear grin that was so contagious it would have made Davy Crockett envious, and his infamous bear as well. "Will somebody introduce me to this gorgeous creature before I stick a foot in my mouth?"

The doctor took the floor since Mallory had slipped into a fit of coughing spasms, a direct result of the peace offering he had just received.

"Miss Barbie, let me introduce you to the members of 'Old Coots on Scoots'. Captain Magic you've met. May I present…"

"Nicknames Doc," interrupted Captain Magic. "All things considered."

"Ah, er yes. I believe you're right. Let me see if I can get them right at that. Here we have Amoeba Man, Funk Dog, Cue Ball, Sea Hawk, and The Colonel. The Rangers you already know."

At that, the bikers and the Rangers broke out in laughter accompanied by a lot of back-slapping. It was easy to tell their friendship had gone back a long way. As each member was introduced, they would either wave or tip their hat. All accept Amoeba Man, who kissed Victoria's hand in gentlemanly fashion. He was a small man with age old wizened eyes. Funk Dog was another piece of work. He had scars of various shapes and sizes, but his main distinctive feature was his skin. It was perpetually red from being a fisherman most of his life. He had other nicknames as well, such as Lobster Man, Mr. Magenta, and others of more of the lewd variety. He was less congenial than the rest on the surface, but it was easy to tell he had a heart of gold. Cue Ball added a different flair to the variety pack. Well dressed with a permanent smile, cynical at best, he might have been the brains of the outfit, but at this point it was impossible to tell. His nickname was apt because of his head that was prematurely bald and would have made any skinhead green with envy. Sea Hawk was an enigma because he never stopped moving or tinkering with something, or anything for that matter. At that point in time the group was interrupted by the sound of another motorcycle coming up the mountain. Captain Magic smiled, "oh, and here comes Slo Mo Blair bringing up the rear." His pace was slower than the rest. He was the image of an over-the-hill professional wrestler, but the twinkle in his sky-blue eyes suggested a younger version of Santa Claus. The Colonel rounded out the group by appearing almost normal, except for his nose. It had definitely been on the receiving end of many objects and the multitude of scars in various stages of healing suggested a recent altercation of some sort. On top of this, his nose was a modern version of W.C. Fields, except maybe even bigger and redder. He also had a limp similar to the Rangers' which prompted Victoria to ask "Mr. Colonel, are you a buffalo hunter like the Rangers?"

One would have thought they were on a studio set with cue cards stating laugh or applause. The entire gang, plus the Rangers laughed so hard at this, some were on the ground holding their guts while others leaned on anything available. Some even shed tears of glee at the question. She couldn't have said anything better to win the hearts of the club members, as if her looks hadn't done so already.

After minutes of uncontrollable laughter the men finally started calming down. Then one would chuckle ever so slightly and it would start all over again. They finally had to split up for a while to keep it from happening again as mere eye contact would light the fuse again.

"Yes and no ma'am," The Colonel finally managed to answer. "Actually, originally I got this by loading up musical equipment. I was a harmonica player in a blues band and we got a gig in Watts, during the Watts riots, and while we were loading up our equipment in the back of our van it was rear ended by a drunk. The buffalos came later." He then shot Souza and Townsend a mock evil glance and added, "can't you leave our private lives out of this?" which started the contagious laughter all over again. Mallory had quietly observed this whole show from the sidelines. His impression when they had first arrived was apprehensive. But after watching all this, he concluded that they couldn't have been in better hands. These characters in the club seemed to be some type of brotherhood; and it didn't take a genius to figure out they were very capable of achieving any form of underhanded shenanigans required. Besides, they looked like a hell of a lot of fun to be with. "Gentlemen, my name is Connor Mallory, very pleased to meet you." Short and sweet. "I believe we have some business to discuss that is probably in your field of endeavor." Then, like an instant brainstorm he added, "we've found, among other things, an ancient gourd filled with something called Awa Root tea."

This stopped them in their tracks. Mallory had their complete rapt attention. The group looked towards the Rangers who simply smiled and gave an affirmative nod.

Christ, they looked like salivating Pavlov dogs Connor thought. "We happen to have a little extra after business is discussed, I thought you might like to sample some." He might as well have been a drill sergeant calling basic trainees to attention. Amongst whoops of delight and murmurs of "tea," the group filed into the dome. Mallory's remark had focused their attention to the business at hand. They were ready to grind out the details and then move on to bigger and better things, namely the Awa Root tea.

As Mallory led the motorcyclists and Rangers into the dome, Victoria approached the doctor who was absently staring down into the crater apparently in a mental world of his own. When she was near, he came out of his reverie and gave her a weak smile. "I bet you don't see too much action up here often, doctor." The soothing remark was more of a statement than a question. The past few hours had taken its toll on doctor Bloomfield and it showed.

"Actually no Vitoria. It's usually totally quiet up here. We value our silence. It actually helps our concentration level. Occasionally someone puts on some music, a symphony or such, and sometimes we'll be adventurous and put on some big band swing to really rock the place, but this? Never." Talking to a lady as beautiful as Victoria seemed to be medicinal. The doctor hadn't been accustomed to change in his routine in a while. He was becoming his normal self again.

"Your Ranger's friends are certainly something else. They're old friends, are they not?" quizzed Victoria. She had noticed the conversation was having a calming effect on the doctor.

"And then some. In reality the one to take the credit, or blame, depends on how you see it, is me. I got the Rangers their jobs originally. You see, many years ago we all used to run around together in Lahaina, over on the west side. We were all black coral divers and sort of ran the town. This was before the tourist invasion and Lahaina was a party town where many people of unscrupulous backgrounds gathered there to hide from the law or just plain get away from the mainland during the sixties. Maui was very lax back then and it was a perfect place to drop out from public scrutiny. What we didn't realize was that so many people had the same idea. Black coral was plentiful at that time and it was a legal way to make a buck. However it's a highly hazardous profession because you have to dive down three hundred plus feet to get to it and risk the bends. Nitrogen narcosis comes with the territory, so when we were either on land or in the water we were in a higher state of consciousness." A completely different look came on the good doctor's face as he was reminiscing. Victoria could see there was much more to the scientist that met the eye.

"Sounds like you could write a book."

"Ah yes, well, it's all pretty much of a blur now and most everyone left feel the same way; It was a ten to fifteen year party. Fifth amendment stuff. Besides, it would implicate too many people like me who have re-joined society. Anyway, the feds got wind of this and we were way too notorious for our own good, so I went back to school and managed to get my doctorate with the brain cells I had left, and upon return managed to get Ray and Richard jobs as Rangers, which was a magic act in itself. The 'gentlemen' and I use the term loosely, you have met were the band, the bouncers, and the bartenders of the nightclubs we partied at. We chalk it up to experience, and what an experience it was. Speaking of which, we better get in there before they destroy the place."

Victoria, much more impressed than she was minutes ago, allowed Dr. Bloomfield to escort her back into the dome. The gang had just finished viewing the video and they were having words over it.

"Sorry Mr. Mallory, we do not partake in smuggling Hawaiian artifacts. They belong to the Hawaiians and that's that," insisted Captain Magic. "You really picked the wrong crew because we're on their side. We will however give you a chance to reconsider or leave, real fast." Nods of agreement went around the table.

"You've got the wrong idea!" stammered Mallory. This could turn real ugly, he thought. "We have no intention of anything of the kind. We need to…"

"Hold it!" Souza raised his voice for the first time Mallory had seen and it had the right effect. "Guys, you got it all wrong. That's not their game, take my word for it. It's something like, 'if you don't know about it won't hurt you.' They just want to get something to the mainland without anyone finding out, and that's what you're good at. It's not Hawaiian artifacts" Souza's commanding voice settled the disagreement immediately. "It has nothing to do with taking anything from the Islands. In fact, it doesn't even belong here." Souza grinned at Townsend who grinned back, the inside joke between them.

"In that case, we're your team. We have dirt bikes, a helicopter and a sailboat. It's how we do ah, our business." Captain Magic seemed to be their spokesman and there was no dissension in the ranks. "our fee is contingent on the bulkiness of your cargo. Hell, we might even settle for a gourd or two of your tea, if there's enough that is."

"Speaking of which, Ranger Souza, if you please," announced Mallory. These were just the right kind of people he thought to himself. Luck and fate certainly seemed to be on their side, so far. The Rangers produced the remains of the gourd amongst ooo's and ahh's from the gang. A round was quickly passed around which produced a cheer from the participants. Two 'okole malunas' and they were there, wherever 'there' was.

Details were worked out over transport. They were ready to leave the next morning. The speleologists would get a ride to the gang's 'ranch' where they were to be transferred to dirt bikes. Then routes through the sugar cane fields would be taken to Maalaea Harbor where they would grab the White Wings catamaran to Honolulu where their schooner was moored, then a two to three week sail across the Pacific to California. This would be the first leg of their journey, eventually winding up in Florida. When found out the size of their cargo they were even more pleased. They were used to a cargo of the more bulky and pungent variety. To the 'Old Coots on Scoots' it was like a paid vacation.

Victoria made the call to her 'uncle outlaw' and he was tickled over the visit. She was extremely vague about the reason, but Exley, being the worldly man he was, didn't press the issue. This was the good news. The bad news was that since the retired brigadier general had been stationed at Nellis Air Force base and had top secret national security clearance, he was certainly under scrutiny; his phones were tapped since his retirement and the conversations recorded and duly noted. Unbeknownst to those atop Haleakala, a security alert had been sent out to find out just what it was that was being taken from an offshoot of N.A.S.A. and being delivered to a retired air force general with a very colorful and checkered background without official authorization. This move would later prove to be the reason behind the possible downfall of civilization- once again.

CHAPTER 2

THE SPACE PATROL SOMEWHERE ABOVE EARTH

To anyone on earth who noticed the shooting star that passed across the heavens and disappeared behind the moon, it wouldn't have been that abnormal. Except for the fact that once behind the moon, it didn't reappear.

"Looks like the bet stands Oxomoxo. The beacon has surfaced again. Right from where it disappeared before," observed Rawar, surprise etched over his humanoid features. "Yes, about 200 revolutions around their star. That brief period of time when the signal was full again only to disappear shortly thereafter. We did not even have the time to get back here to see what was happening before it was gone again."

"Face the facts. We are here now and the pulse is strong. We should stay closer to our routes to keep a sharper lookout this time. I'll have to admit that it's quite a productive planet. Look how much they have evolved since our last visit." Rawar had a grudging admiration for the inhabitants of their project. "Ever since they had almost ruined themselves and destroyed their planet in the process." He really didn't think they would possibly evolve this far again. Even though he would have won the bet, it would have been a meagre victory at best.

"Yes they definitely have come a long way, but look at that mess. Their air is so polluted we cannot see the population areas, and look; they have even managed to bore a hole in the ozone layer. It's probably just a matter of time before you win." Oxomoxo's confidence was on the wane.

"It looks that way, but since they have our gift back, it might get them over the last crucial step this time," countered Rawar. He was trying to reassure his co-pilot even though things looked grim. He wasn't sure he even wanted to win, which was partially the truth.

"Their technology has come even further than before. It's what they do with it now that matters. They're about as close as they can get to reaching the next level, or complete annihilation. This will require closer scrutiny." Oxomoxo's hopes brightened at the idea. "Since they've managed to figure out satellites, we can put some monitors behind them to keep a closer eye on their progress. A few wouldn't be noticed, then we can patch in during our travels and see what's happening. It can't hurt," he added hopefully.

Reluctantly, Rawar pondered the suggestion. The Space Patrol's job requirements didn't include tampering with the evolutionary process. But then again, this was their pet project and it certainly wouldn't hurt their percentage ratio if this one was a success. This planet had come so far, again, which usually didn't happen and they were on the verge of pass/fail, it was the deciding factor.

"Alright. I know this has gone beyond a bet and I want you to know I am pulling for them too. But we can't get too close or get any more involved than we are already, because judging from what we see from up here, it does not look that promising. Let's do it."

"We can monitor the pulse. That way we can keep track where it's going and what they're doing with it. If they use our gift correctly this time, they can join the Planetary Consortium." Oxomoxo's hopes brightened. After all, when planets evolve this far, it's a make or break situation.

As the planet revolved, the planet planters/debris collectors placed enough monitors to keep tabs on their gift, no matter where it was located on the globe. Now they were more involved than ever before. Even though neither would admit it, their curiosity level was at an all time high concerning this project. The time ahead would be crucial to the planet's survival.

"Perhaps we should call off the bet since we are both pulling for them. You don't want me to win and I don't want you to lose, so what's the point?" Rawar had finally laid his cards on the table.

"That's alright, besides, it's not the only project we have going. This one is just the most interesting. We can always go down and grab a few and plant them somewhere else, if they don't destroy themselves first, that is. I vote for the bet stands." Oxomoxo was pleased with his co-pilot's suggestion, but to call off the bet at this point could possibly cause disinterest in their participation. They had known each other too long for that. And besides there also was a possibility they might have to intercede even though it was stretching the rules to the limit. But now they knew if it came to that, it would be an easier decision. Only time would tell.

"It would be a shame if they didn't make it this time. The last few times we have passed by they have come so far each time. That is usually the first sign of doom for the entire project. But yet here they are still. Most interesting, and puzzling."

"The inhabitants are so different from each other in each region. They are evolving at different levels, mostly depending on how much weaponry they can build. They appear not to have equal living standards, worship different gods, and always seem to be at war somewhere: what a mess." Oxomoxo felt he had to point out, "They are not sharing: a very bad sign."

"Some develop in different ways at a different pace. Some lands are more fertile than others. If they do figure out that sharing instead of warfare is the key, they still might have a chance."

"It also depends on what type of people found our gift. It is still on what is left on the earlier continent Lemuria. No telling what will happen once they figure out what it is and does. If it's in the wrong hands we'll have a lot of debris to clean up, soon."

"We have done what we can do here. Let's move on. There's probably a mess to clean up somewhere, at least it's not here. We can go."

After one last look at the pulse that had again resurfaced, the Space Patrol set off once again on their rounds. Their pet project was still on-going, that much they knew. They also knew that since civilization had advanced once again, it would depend entirely on who did what with the information they had in their possession. It was make it or break it time, they both knew. As they were leaving, they didn't realize they were being watched.

HALEAKALA

The clear crisp morning air had a golden hue from the sun that had just peeked over the clouds on the horizon. The speleologists had been up early and had just finished packing, watching this stellar sunrise as the doctor approached with a cheery "good morning." The pair reciprocated in kind as they all refilled their cups with 100% Kona coffee, the preferred 'go juice' of the L.U.R.E. settlement. "We had a most unusual occurrence last night," began Bloomfield. "One of our telescopes caught the track of a shooting star, and as it approached the vicinity of the moon, it just disappeared. But that's not the odd part. A few minutes later, another came from the very same area and shot away in a completely different direction."

"That's odd, does that happen often?" asked Victoria.

"I'm really not at liberty to say, national security and all. But let's just say much stranger things have happened that we're not allowed to talk about," answered the doctor. "This could be categorized as an annual or bi-annual occurrence. It's just strange that it coincides with your discovery." Bloomfield was already spooked from the last few days' occurrences. He certainly didn't need anything more to think about. He had appeared to age a few years in the last forty eight hours. The speleologists dismissed it as stress. At that moment the doctor's cell phone came alive. He pulled it out from his smock and answered, "yes?" As he listened, his eyes widened and he didn't say a word. Although he did glance at Mallory and Victoria with a look of terror in his eyes. "Thanks" was all he said as he disconnected. Without a word he quickly punched in another number that answered immediately. Before he could say anything, he was listening intently with a "you did? Good! Right", when he could get an edge in word-wise. He was moving before he disconnected. "That first call was the Rangers station. Apparently three government cars just pulled in flashing F.B.I. badges asking for your whereabouts. We are supposed to detain you until their arrival. Not only that, but a helicopter is on its way from Kahului airport to transport you out of here under their supervision. The second call was to Captain Magic. They had a police band radio and had heard it all. They're on their way up now, ahead of them just by minutes. They are on their dirt bikes this time. We'll be able to hear them coming even more than yesterday. In other words, it's the moment of truth. Whatever you want to do, it's up to you." Bloomfield was clear, concise, and acting like he had just woke up from a deep sleep.

Something deeply inherent, a sixth sense, galvanized Mallory into action, albeit without the slightest pretense of indecisiveness, it might have been as if that forces unseen, yet felt, had shaped themselves into gut instinct, and at that point in time, hesitation was not even an option.

Victoria was on the same wavelength. Without words they were moving. In the distance came a rumble of high RPM engines. Mallory grabbed the backpack containing their discovery. Victoria picked the one of hers that had the bare necessities and they were out the door, Bloomfield closely behind. Around the corner and into the parking lot came Captain Magic and the Old Coots on Scoots skidding to a halt in front of the trio, giant shit-eating grins plastered on their faces like bulls in a china shoppe. Mallory leaped behind Captain Magic's bike. Victoria latched on to Slo Mo, quickly surmising his weight would counteract her lithe frame during the ride ahead.

"I'll stall them as long as I can," shouted doctor Bloomfield. "Keep me posted," he added as the entire entourage burned rubber out of the parking lot.

The Rangers magically appeared out of nowhere leading a team of mules designed to discourage pursuit. An "okole maluna" in sign language as the pack sped by. As soon as they were gone, the Rangers transformed themselves into a picture of illiterate muleskinners to aptly disorientate the government vehicles that were about to arrive. To confound things further, were the sunrise spectators that hadn't left yet, who had been temporarily immobilized by the scene that had just passed.

As the three 'non-descript' government vehicles attempted to enter the already jammed parking lot, the Rangers unerringly lost control of the mule pack. They innocently feigned ignorance of the vehement protestations of the 'G' men's attempt to enter, an act that would have made a vaudevillian choreographer proud. The ranger-made catastrophe was succinct, and a whopping success.

During the confusion; Bloomfield quickly got himself lost in the catacombs of science city. By the time the government officials had found him, their patience level had gone from frayed to tatters. Their government issue suits were rumpled and their G.Q. plastered down hair-do's were disheveled. One had the distinct odor as if he had stepped in muleshit.

"Oh there you are gentlemen, I just was going to…" Bloomfields' attempt at appearing innocent was a trifle transparent.

"Cut the crap, Dr. Bloomfield. We are agents, Persons and Fife and you know why we're here. Where are they?" The 'plainclothesmen' quickly flashed their badges and it was agent Fife who did the talking. Agent Persons seemed to be preoccupied with something on his shoe.

"What? Oh, you mean Mr. Mallory and Miss Barbie? I'm afraid you just missed them. You see they had some friends visiting them. Quite a bunch of ruffians, actually. Mr. Mallory explained to me that they no longer needed a ride because they were going to take a tour with them. You might have seen them on your way up. They were on motorcycles." Dr. Bloomfield's filibuster bought them a few extra precious seconds.

At that, agent Fife reached into his coat pocket and retrieved a communication device. "Code red. Targets on motorcycles going down crater road. Helicopter pursuit. Apprehend and hold. Will follow. Out." The agents about-faced and were heading towards the entrance, "you are going to be in hot water for this, doctor," yelled Fife over his shoulder. "We will be back for further questioning." Then they were out the door.

"Nice meeting you too," chuckled Bloomfield. He couldn't remember a day when he had ever had so much fun at work. "Good luck, friends," he muttered to himself while following the agents out. He had to go for a look-see to observe what the Rangers had cooked up for them. He was glad he did.

Somehow the mules had escaped their tethers and were kicking and hee-hawing all around the parking lot. 'Unfortunately' their packs hadn't been properly secured tight and they were strewn all across the entrance, causing a first rate traffic jam. Bloomfield wanted to dance with glee until he heard the rotors of a helicopter approaching in the distance. The Rangers were currently being yelled at by the other government officials. They appeared dumbfounded as if they didn't understand English. With a rush of wind the helicopter landed as the agents scrambled towards it. They piled in, all except for Persons, agent Fife pushing him back and holding his nose. It was a scene reminiscent of an old Keystone Cops movie, thought Bloomfield. As the helicopter took off, the Rangers had magically gotten ahold of the mules and were the new centers of attention for the tourists with their cameras. Amidst laughter and wisecracks, the Rangers posed as the tourists clicked away, this probably being, if not the highlight, of their entire trip. Certainly the most unforgettable. The Rangers waved Bloomfield over for a few quick poses as the tourists fired away. The ever-ready Townsend produced his own camera from his pocket and had a curvaceous young teenage girl take one last shot for posterity. As the flashbulb fired, Bloomfield muttered out the side of his mouth, "Absolutely beautiful." When Townsend later got the picture developed, the results proved they had captured the essence of the moment and it would eventually be the centerpiece on the wall in the good doctor's office.'

Meanwhile, Mallory and Victoria were hanging on for dear life as the motorcycle pack sped down the highway. From sea level, Haleakala Highway is a thirty eight mile stretch, but the last twenty to the top is one hairpin turn after another. The state roads division, in their supreme intelligence had carved the roads off-camber from a normal banking turn. This counter productive idea might be successful for rain, but at the same time traveling on the road required intense concentration. Instead of being able to lean into turns with the help of a correct bank in the road, each curve fell away which discouraged any form of safe driving. At each hairpin, Mallory was convinced that they were either going to lay the bike down, or hurtle off into space; neither of which happened. Victoria on the other hand, was clinging on to Slo Mo like a baby monkey does its mother, her eyes clenched tightly shut. What probably saved their lives was the familiarity factor of the bikers to the roads, as they attacked each turn proficiently, barely keeping their wheels on the tarmac. What Mallory didn't know was that Captain Magic was born and raised here, and had been traveling these roads all his life, from Flexi Flyers to Soap Box Derby racers, to skateboards and bicycles, and then to Harley hogs, where he was a master of the game and nobody could touch him; he was the premier talent on the Island. On the last few turns before a straightaway, there was a barely discernible dirt track that went straight down the mountain in which the two bikers and their charges took instead of following the road. The rest of the pack stayed on the road to keep the pursuers following them, and thus gave time for the pair to make a break for the sugar cane fields ahead. On the last curve there was a sort of ski jump on the straightaway dirt path that required full throttle to leap over the road to get into the cane field. Both Captain Magic/Mallory and Slo Mo/Victoria got airborne on this maneuver and both speleologists were convinced they were going to die. But upon landing they were still breathing and had made the cane field dirt road which cushioned the fall back to earth. A quick ninety degree turn straight into the eight foot sugar cane and engines momentarily turned off. The totality of the maneuver would have made Evil Kanevil proud. In the distance they could hear the sirens of the three government vehicles in hot pursuit of the rest of the pack, and the clap-clap of the helicopter following the sirens.

"Phase one a total success. Want to go again?" remarked Captain Magic as he removed his goggles. Mallory was sitting in the dirt leaning on a cane stalk, trying to catch his breath. Slo Mo was unsuccessfully trying to pry Victoria off his back. She was clearly in a state of shock and was using him as her security blanket. After a few seconds she relaxed and slithered down to the ground in complete surprise that she was still in one piece.

"Thanks, no. Who built those roads anyway? The crown prince of reverse logic? You could have warned us," stuttered Mallory as he gathered his senses.

"There was no time for hesitation. Besides, if you knew, you probably wouldn't have gone," he answered. "I built that last little jump myself years ago. Pretty intense, huh? We do this all the time," he added, trying to comfort the passengers.

Mallory, hands shaking, reached into his pocket and produced his hip flask. He took a healthy pull then passed it around. By the time this is over I'll have nerves of steel, he thought.

"Thanks, a man after mine own heart," Captain Magic declared. "The going is slow from here on, we don't want to raise any dust. Once the bureaucrats catch on, we might have to put the pedal to the metal again. After we lose the G-men, we'll gather at the ranch in the afternoon. The rest are splitting up as soon as they can, get belongings and make sure they're not followed. Then it's to Honolulu at sunrise with Pickle and Moonpie aboard 'The White Wings," he answered. "Shall we?"

"Pickle and Moonpie, I'm curious as to how you all earned your nicknames," said Mallory as he jumped on behind Captain Magic.

"The trip to the mainland is two to three weeks, depending on winds. I'm sure you'll hear it all and then some. One short stop at the bottom of the mountain to change vehicles. We're too notorious for these." He was interrupted by the familiar clap clap of their nemesis. "Slo Mo, silent running."

Slowly, methodically, they traversed one cane field after another. Mallory noticed Captain Magic seemed to know his way around the inside of cane fields. With engines on low idle, the party slid through the eight to ten foot cane shoots almost totally undetectable. Once the helicopter got as close as fifty feet away, so they simply just stopped and pulled the leaves over their heads as the bird went by.

Captain Magic stopped and shut off his engine, a quizzical look on his face. The northeast trade winds had picked up slightly, causing the sugar cane stalks to rustle with the gusts, occasionally blocking out the sky, which made taking bearings off the position of the sun next to impossible. "Let me use your compass, mine has gone haywire." Mallory peeked over his shoulder. The needle was pointing at him instead of magnetic north and then back again in that same familiar pulse.

"Hey mine's on the blink too. What gives?"

The speleologists exchanged knowing looks. Mallory shrugged his shoulders palms up and she returned with a pair of raised eyebrows and smiled guiltily. "We have the answer but we don't have the answer," she answered. This time it was the bikers' turn to exchange looks. They did, then both looked at Mallory, "huh?"

"Well, it has something to do with our cargo. We found it in a cave up there along with the burial chamber. We don't know what it is, but we do know what it isn't.

"Huh?"

Victoria attempted, "it isn't anything we know. All we know is that we don't know."

"Huh?"

"What we're trying to explain is that it is not made with any material we have knowledge about. What little data we've gathered terms it as 'unknown origin.' In other words it might not be from Earth. Whatever it is, it's affecting your compass."

Captain Magic stood poker faced for a minute, then broke out with one of his infectious grins. "Oh, that explains it. I like that. This just keeps getting better by the minute. Just when I thought I'd heard and seen it all. Eh, you're not joking, are you?"

"Fortunately or most unfortunately, no," answered Victoria. "The reason behind this escapade is to get some answers, if there are any."

Captain Magic saw that they were serious. He considered himself as a keen judge of character, and could see that the speleologists were being genuine with him. He was always ready for something new, but this certainly had a new twist. "Well we won't find any answers out here.

We'll just have to make do without a compass. Lets go," he suggested, and they were off.

Mallory was relieved at their reaction. He was glad they were in on the secret, and had taken it with a grain of salt. Oh, they seemed worldly enough; by a long shot, actually. But with this kind of information one never knew. His relief turned into confidence as they rode on. He definitely had the feeling he had hit the jackpot with this crew. At this point he didn't know just how right he was.

An Island wide security alert was sent out for the speleologists under the pretense of mugging and robbing tourists of their belongings. In cooperation with the Maui police department, all roads leading off Haleakala crater had roadblocks set up on every conceivable exit down the mountain. The sugar company sent out a dispatch to all workers and drivers to keep an eye out for these fugitives from justice.

The G-men had little or no luck in pursuit other than the destruction of two out of three vehicles. One had missed a hairpin turn at the top and went off the road sideways, which began a roll that lasted close to a mile and a half down the side of the steep mountain. By the time it came to a halt, it had become a barely discernible mass of metal that left a trail of broken glass and auto parts in its wake. The other mishap was caused by a road crew in which the driver had to dodge, causing him to fly off the road into a pasture of curious on-looking cows. The driver in the third car, although unsuccessful in pursuit, made it down the mountain safely. He did however have with him a distinct aroma of muleshit.

Rudi Balingbong, a truck driver for the sugar company for twenty years was sitting in his truck having a lunch hour siesta when the alert came through dispatch. What caught his attention was the reward offered for any information leading to the arrest (and conviction) of the fugitives. He hadn't had much luck lately at the chicken fights, so the money had aroused his interest. A few minutes later he was awoken by two dirt bikers carrying two passengers that were emerging out of one of his cane fields. Rudy greedily reached for his microphone, but he stopped only inches from his mouth when he saw who was riding. Rudi had been a steady customer of Captain Magic's for the last two decades. A quick blast of his airhorn caught their attention.

"Hey Rudi, how goes it?" asked a smiling Captain Magic as he pulled up.

"De ah po po stay louking por yer priends," said Rudy in barely discernible english. "Eh, dese no louk like bad guy to me."

"They're not. They're on our side," was all he had to say. Captain Magic's word was gold on the island.

"I call in, tell em dey way ovah uddah side. You go," said Rudi, his dreams of reward money sailing off into the distance. "I geeve dem big kine meex up."

"Thanks. I owe you one," Rudi's eyes lit up because he knew what 'one' was. The speleologists were clueless. They could barely understand a word Rudi said. Captain Magic let them steep in curiosity as they took off towards their destination.

The 'ranch' took the speleologists completely by surprise. In reality it was an old World War II ammunition dump that had been built in the middle of the flatlands between east and west Maui. It was smack dab in the middle of one of the largest cane fields on the island and avoided scrutiny from the public eye. From the outside it looked like a typical old cement 'pill box'. That was where the facade ended. After uncountable twists and turns the bikers silently dismounted. Slo Mo, in sign language, silently explained to Mallory he was to cover the tire tracks by brushing the dirt with cane leaves. Once done, it looked like they were never there. Captain Magic put a finger to his lips and led them through the last leg of their journey walking their bikes, stopping only once to point out a trip wire from their alarm system. A length of a football field later, they arrived at the cement edifice only to find the rest of the pack waiting for them. After stashing their bikes, the speleologists were led inside.

Inside was a whole nest of surprises. Once inside the doors, they were immediately greeted by another one. Once opened it was easy to see why. The inside walls were completely surrounded, like a house within a house. "We have a friend in the recording business," was he said. The interior could have been a penthouse in upstate New York; wall to wall shag carpet, easy chairs and giant couch-beds, complete with state of the art sound system and big screen T.V.. A microwave kitchen with a four burner propane stove, gas refrigerator and freezer. The 'pill box' was self sufficiency personified. Mallory was busy picking up his jaw off the floor as Victoria fell into an easy chair, once again the look of astonishment on her face. The 'old coots' let their shock take some time to settle in before making a sweeping gesture explaining "the hazards of our profession."

"How?" was the only thing Mallory could utter.

"Helicopter at night. One of our tricks of the trade so to speak," he answered. "We excavated and have an underground generator system that also facilitates the grow lighting system for our business. Care for a tour?"

"Maybe in a few minutes. I've got to get over this first," answered Mallory. He had thought he was impressed with these people before, but now it went way beyond words.

"Well then, how about something cold to drink?" The motorcycle club was certainly getting a kick out of the speleologists reaction. Up to then it had been a secret just kept between themselves, but considering the circumstances, they deemed the speleologists trustworthy.

Mallory agreed to a cold beer, Victoria a glass of chilled wine as they allowed the essence of their surroundings to sink in. The guys went about their business of preparing for their 'vacation'. It seemed that an unspoken law had once been established, because everyone knew their role. They were a well-oiled machine thought Mallory, good to have them around when the chips were down.

About an hour later, the Rangers appeared with the remains of the gourd.

"We got time off for good behavior," explained Souza. "Plus the doctor wanted to make sure you were still in one piece."

"We wanted to bring you a little going away present," added Townsend, picking up the gourd. "For passing the long hours at sea. By the way, did you enjoy your trip down the mountain?"

"Unforgettable, and we lived to tell the tale," answered Mallory. Although there were times I wasn't quite sure we would."

Victoria got up and wrapped her arms around each Ranger and planted a giant kiss on both of their cheeks. "We couldn't have done it without you. Your suggestion and introduction to these 'gentlemen' here, have certainly saved the day. If it wasn't for them we would probably be guests of the United States Government. We owe you a debt of gratitude."

Back slaps and handshakes were again exchanged between the Rangers and the Old Coots, then Captain Magic suggested a tour. The Rangers only smiled. They knew already what was in store for the speleologists. He led them to a back corner and lifted a throw rug which revealed a trap door. A blinding light came through the cracks as the door was lifted that made the speleologists wince as their eyes adjusted. Everyone proceeded down the steps and once again Mallory and Victoria were met with yet another surprise. A long tunnel spread outwardly in both directions as far as the eye could see. It was obvious it had been built in the W.W.II. era. Probably as a bomb shelter and/or ammunition dump. It was completely encased in cement and the lighting system had been changed into grow lights designed for indoor propagation. Although the speleologists could smell it before they saw it, it was still a sight to behold.

Perched on top of the tables were hundreds of potted plants of cannabis. From inch high baby starts to ten foot hedges, the underground facility was packed wall to wall with each in various stages of maturity. On the wall in each section, were charts depicting the dates of planting, fertilization tables, type of seed and its genealogy from the first generation on.

"Different seeds from each generation are crossbred to bring out different effects from each plant. Red Colombian, for example, will put you on your ass. But if it's crossbred with an Afgani strain, it will lighten the load for a more introspective high. We have been experimenting for over twenty generations of the growth cycle and have the desired effect for any given situation," Captain Magic explained. "Then over here we have our cloning procedure which guarantees a female plant, which is, of course, more potent.

"Very informative," returned Victoria. Mallory was speechless.

"Then down there," pointed off in the distance, "is our seed producing male/female area. It's amazing how far a spore will travel to impregnate a female." He then pointed in the other direction; "Drying rooms. Quite a place, yes?"

"I wouldn't believe it unless I saw it with my own two eyes," remarked Mallory. "How is this even possible? It's illegal!"

"Our clientele reaches all the way to the Governor's office, and there are rumors that are probably true that it goes further than that. Hell, even one of our last Presidents was a sax player. Adding a little grease in a few palms doesn't do any harm either. Want some?" Once again, Captain Magic 's infectious grin came to life like a merry prankster from the sixties which was exactly who he was.

"Huh? No thanks.... Well, maybe." Mallory was quickly approaching the line one goes over from time to time, but considering the circumstances, he was holding up well.

"Maybe we should go back to your 'pill box' announced Victoria, as she grabbed Mallory's arm to lead him towards the way out. "It seems Connor here has gotten a contact high." She was looking at the Rangers with her eyebrows raised and a glare that suggested they hop to it, which was exactly what they did.

Once situated in the comfort of the sitting room, Townsend produced a disk and announced, "you might get a kick out of this. One of the tourists at the parking lot captured this whole fiasco. It's good," he smirked.

The shenanigans proved true to form. Uproarious laughter bounced off the soundproof walls as the show progressed. It also managed to bring Mallory out of his stupor. The last scene showed the good Doctor Bloomfield in the center, flanked by the Rangers with the mules behind and the other tourists who were caught up in the fray either crouched or on their knees in front, smiles all around.

The good doctor was in a world of his own when the phone rang.

"Yes. Oh, hello Miss Barbie. I'm glad you made it safely. Listen, these agents up here were very nosey. They mentioned your uncle's name more than once when they questioned me. Exley, isn't it? If and when you call again use the cell. Landlines are probably tapped." He was beaming. The shock and excitement the past few days had brought him out of his day to day routine and it was like it had breathed new life into him, although he was also happy that it was back to relatively normal: even though it was only temporary.

"Yes you're right doctor. My mistake. Didn't somebody say learning the hard way was never easy?" Victoria was attempting to lighten the situation. "Yes, and I'll tell them. Goodbye. He sends good luck and commends everyone for a job well done. He also wants the Rangers to know that a certain gourd was misplaced."

Victoria's last statement was met with a cheer and they responded by passing around a round for all. That, plus one of the Old Coots' cigars of Maui's Finest made the afternoon pass nicely. Conversation almost totally disappeared as each participant was in their own world of euphoria. From the little that was said, the speleologists learned that it was the Rangers who had originally stumbled upon this facility. Townsend in particular. He was surfing on his computer about Maui's part in W.W.II. and came upon a part that needed a federal clearance to get to. Since he was a National Park Ranger it was no problem. And since the Old Coots and the Rangers had been partners in hi-jinks for three decades, the rest was history.

"Uh, now that you know about us, how about a little show and tell? We'd like to know why we're risking all this for," requested Cue Ball. A man of few words but straight to the point.

"Okay, but I don't know if it will do you any good," announced a rejuvenated Mallory. At that he rose out of the easy chair he had been planted in for the last few hours and went to his backpack and put it on the table. "We have no idea what it is or what it is used for. If you have any ideas, we'd love to hear them." He pulled out the object and laid it on the table. A stunned silence filled the room, except for a few oohs and ahhs.

Captain Magic finally broke the silence saying, "you know, I've lived here all my life and have seen some pretty weird shit in the sky. But this here confirms everything." A mutter of agreement went around the table. "Even though the burial chamber is a major mystery, it doesn't even come close to this. We asked for a show and tell and we got it. Boys and girls it's show time. Let's move."

The sea that slipped by the hull shimmered in the moonlight as the waves danced to the gentle northeast trade winds that pushed the 'White Wings' catamaran along the way towards Honolulu.

The flight from the 'pill box' had gone without a hitch. Once away from the general vicinity of their hideaway, the group mounted their motorcycles and fled in the opposite direction they were later going to take, which made no difference to the speleologists since they had no idea where they were going anyway. Taking back roads, they wound up in an out of the way industrial section in Puunene where they stashed their bikes and had two cabs waiting for them upon their arrival. Nothing was said and it was obvious that these cabbies and old coots were old acquaintances and had done this many times before. They were then taken to the boat harbor at Maalaea Bay. One of the island's smaller harbors was centrally located on the peninsula that separates east and west Maui and caters mostly to sport fishing and whale watching. They arrived at the slip that housed the 'White Wings' and were met by a gregarious and congenial pair named Pickle and Moonpie. After high fives, back slapping, and a brief "pleezed to meetcha," they were instantly about their business loading travel gear, essentials and amenities for the trip across the Molokai channel. First mate Moonpie took the time to explain to the speleologists that they wanted to blend in with the boats leaving the harbor for their sunset cruises. Mallory could detect the distinct aroma of rum in the air upon their explanation. Even so, it didn't seem to hamper their capabilities of performing their duties in the slightest. After a few minutes, Moonpie announced "Captain Pickle, ready to cast lines," with a flourish that befitted a comedy routine in a live-act play.

The White Wings, an old yet well kept catamaran motored out of the harbor in line with all of the sunset cruisers. Mai Tais were passed around by first mate Moonpie with a brief explanation of "Keeping with the decor of a sunset cruise," which all in all wasn't a bad idea anyway.

The only distinction between White Wings and the other boats was instead of mellow Hawaiian music to accompany the sunset cruise, an old Rolling Stones album came blaring out of their sound system, "It's a gas gas gas," and more. Eventually the White Wings veered out of the pack towards Honolulu as the sun sank over the horizon of an azure sea.

The sky had turned from a crimson gold to a silvery gray as the moon rose over Haleakala. Sails were unfurled as the White Wings reached the windline and she was off like a child's skimmer rock across the waves. The excitement of the past few days wore down when Captain Pickle turned off the sound system and then the only sound was the lapping of the ocean against the hull and the wind in the sails. Except for an occasional wisecrack and a return chortle, a comfortable silence was enjoyed by all as they soaked up mother nature's bounty like a sponge. The rocking notion of the boat, plus the blissful silence and serenity of the moment allowed a lethargy to set in that caused the speleologists to sink into a welcome deep slumber like babes in their mother's arms.

"Well top of the mornin to ya," announced an affable captain Pickle. He had just stuck a steaming mug of one hundred percent Kona coffee under the nose of a sleeping Mallory and he woke with a start to a crisp glittering sunshiny morning in the middle of the Molokai Channel, halfway to their destination. Mallory gratefully accepted the cup and noticed he had fallen asleep cuddled with Victoria, which he had to admit to himself wasn't a bad way to wake up. There was also a particular tingling between his legs he had to mentally acknowledge. Not bad either. Pickle's smile was twinned to Captain Magic's, Mallory noticed as he muttered a sleepy "hello." They had fallen asleep in the netting that separates the twin hulls on the fore end of the boat, and it had a distinct resemblance to a giant rocking hammock which explained the great night's sleep they'd just had. Mallory carefully removed himself and Victoria, who merely groaned as she rolled over, was still dead to the world. "Care for a little grog with your coffee?" asked Pickle as he lifted a bottle of Ron Rico 151 rum out from under the captain's chair.

"Ah, well yes. Don't mind if I do," answered Mallory. What a way to start the day he thought, as Pickle started pouring with a "say when."

"When" came after about a shot and a half entered his cup. No slouch in the amenities department he thought as he returned the captain's morning smile. Pickle and Moonpie obviously had been up all night sailing the boat but had no discernible adverse effects. Mallory quickly surmised the mixture of 151 and the rolling motion of the boat made a compatible combination. One by one everyone woke to a generous portion of eye opener until Victoria was the last to rise into an already engaged celebration of life aboard the White Wings. The sail proceeded smoothly downwind all the way to Honolulu except for a remark made by Pickle that he was having trouble with his compass. They arrived at Ala Wai Yacht Harbor docking area without a problem, then unloaded everyone's personal items, gave the crew of the White Wings a package containing the 'fruits of their labor' for their payment and they were off again amidst "goodlucks" and "goodbyes."

"That's quite a pair of friends you have Captain Magic," observed Mallory as the 'White Wings' headed out of the harbor towards home. "That's some nicknames," he added.

"Oh yes. Well, the captain adheres to the 'Pickle Principle' of 'you have to be a pickle to pickle someone, and Moonpie, well, there is no explanation for his label. Their hulls come in quite handy sometimes. They're excellent in the water, but sometimes on land it's a toss up," laughed the Captain. "Our other little watercraft is across the harbor, so it's a small hike. Our caretakers should have everything ready to go when we arrive. I made a call before we left and they are really good at keeping things ready to go at any given moment, which in our profession is obviously a good thing," he explained.

The 'hike' took about twenty minutes. The Old Coots weren't exactly the epitome of the yachting class. Their appearance acquired more than a few surprised glances from the 'hoi polloi' of the yachting world, only to be met with "alohas" and "howzits" along the way. Finally they reached their destination and Captain Magic proudly announced, "Folks, this is the Flying Cloud." The speleologists were taken aback by the majesty and symmetry of the sight that filled their eyes. The Flying Cloud was an antique, completely restored one hundred ten foot schooner that dreams were made of. Built in the twenties in Belfast, she was originally a plaything for the earl of something or another, then sold to the mob for rum running during prohibition. Her sleek lines and beauty caught the eye of a Hollywood producer and she was then brought to L.A. for various movie appearances, then finally wound up in Honolulu in the hands of one of the many uncles who simply passed it onto the capable hands of Captain Magic when he was too old to sail. Much of his profits were well spent in the complete painstaking restoration of the all-wood boat that looked as if she came out of the dockyard yesterday. There wasn't a more beautiful boat in the harbor. That wasn't all. The 'caretakers' turned out to be a pair of gorgeous suntanned goddesses that could have been or probably were out of a bikini advertisement. When they spotted the Old Coots, there were shrieks of joy as they came running to welcome their benefactors with flower leis for all. They were introduced to the speleologists as Sunshine and Surfer Sue. Both were scantily clad and seemed to have no inhibitions whatsoever, as leis and kisses were planted on each and everyone. Captain Magic winked at Mallory receiving his lei and kisses and remarked out of the side of his mouth "good for morale." Victoria was temporarily stunned, but the ladies were so outgoing and friendly, it wasn't long before they were acting like life-long friends and/or members of a sorority. There was just plain nothing not to like.

 This is just too good to be true, thought Mallory. The Captain shot him a conspiratorial glance with an affirmative nod and a smile, which caused Mallory's eyes to roll up thinking he had died and gone to heaven, which was partially true except for the dying part. The ladies started busying themselves with the galley area as provisions were brought on board. Their conversation they kept to themselves, amidst giggles and sultry glances towards members of the crew.

 The speleologists were shown their berth which was a neat little affair that included a double futon, fan, and porthole. Captain Magic explained, "hope you don't mind, but we have to double up on this voyage. There's usually just us and our cargo. Sunshine and Surfer Sue, they ah, move around."

"Just don't get any wild ideas, Mr. Mallory," said Victoria. Not quite sure just how she felt about the arrangement, which was a surprise in itself.

Before Mallory could reply, Captain Magic interrupted, "thank you for understanding Miss Barbie, it's just that the guys don't feel like sleeping together."

Mallory was delighted by it all, especially the fact that the caretakers were going along on the trip. He merely smiled and said "I'll be on my best behavior." (Right…)

"It's all settled then. You'll both be getting your night watch shift and your turn at the wheel. By the way, have either of you ever done any sailing before?"

"I've sailed cats around Newport harbor, but never such a grand boat as this," said Mallory. Victoria shook her head negatively but was more than eager to learn.

"Ah she's a fine tub at that. It's not that hard to sail at all and in the ocean there's not that much to bump into, if you keep your eyes open that is. Actually I think you'll find it quite enjoyable."

"No doubt about that, captain," returned Mallory. "Will the artifact's effect on your compass be a problem?"

"Not at all. We have a Loran and a G.P.S. on board. Global Positioning Satellite. It shouldn't be a problem. Why don't you get settled in now. We'll be on our way shortly…" They were interrupted by a cacophony of laughter coming from the main cabin.

Sunshine came down the ladder and motioned to them, "come. I think you should see this," she said as she turned around and wiggled back up, closely followed by the trio.

When they arrived topside, the speleologists were shocked to see their faces on T.V. "Any information leading to their arrest and conviction, call Crime Stoppers," the T.V. droned.

"You're famous, you criminals, can I have your autograph?" among other cat calls went merrily around the cabin. "Not only that," broke in the colonel, "but according to the news flash, they were being spirited away by some motorcycle thugs," which brought on another round of laughter.

"That does it. Since we're on the lam, we better move," suggested Captain Magic in a mock jittery voice Nixon style and also feigned terror on his face to go along with it.

Lines were hauled in as they cast off and slowly motored out of the boat slip. In a few minutes they reached the breakwall relatively unnoticed except for looks of admiration as they passed by. The schooner slid by the harbor master's office like a hot knife through butter. The 'criminals' had made their escape. Just to make sure, they headed back towards Maui until they rounded the infamous Diamond Head crater, attempting to appear to be a pleasure cruise, which they did successfully. The day proceeded in haphazard tacks until they reached the north shore of Oahu, stopping briefly at Waimea Bay to complete their tourist facade. They lingered around until dusk, then Captain Magic ordered anchors up. "Boys and girls, it's time to lay on some canvas and break out the colors which brought about cheers from those in the know. It came as no surprise to the speleologists when 'the colors' turned out to be a Jolly Roger. Soon the flying cloud was under full sail as they headed out towards the sea like a thief in the night.

CHAPTER 3

MIDDLE OF THE PACIFIC

On the first night out a festive spirit filled the air and the speleologists were caught up in it like Dorothy and Toto towards OZ. The Flying Cloud was set on a northeasterly track that would last through the night, so there wasn't much left to do but enjoy. The atmosphere was gleeful and was helped along by the contents of the gourd, Jack Black, Maui's finest, and whatever other particular chaser was desired. The ladies opted for a bottle of thick Cabernet and the guys were happy with cold beer. To add to the merriment, Cue Ball broke out an old Martin acoustic guitar, The Colonel, a set of well used harmonicas. The harps were so worn down that the colonel had to soak them in a glass of gin before playing them. "It loosens the reeds plus they taste good," he explained. The speleologists were pleasantly surprised to find that these were competent musicians. Slo Mo and Funk Dog made a couple of drum sets out of pots and pans and soon there was concert level music filling the air. They dug into their 'bag of tricks' and pulled out originals such as 'Born in Lahaina'; similar to Paul Butterfield's 'Born in Chicago' and their personal favorite 'Hot Boilin' Water: Ode to a Lobster feeling blue.' Hysteria was running rampant during 'Dog Love' because during the chorus everyone joined in singing "bow wow wow, bow wow wow, ahoooo," and new impromptu lyrics were added depending what kind of dog it was. Tears of uncontrollable laughter fell to the deck as musical requests were filled, the musicians having a seemingly bottomless pit of talent to spare. After hours of pure unadulterated fun, one by one the crew fell out and headed towards prone position. The speleologists found their way to their futon with the aid of the walls. The rolling motion of the boat plus what they had consumed made this not so easy of a task. Both had thought this moment might be awkward, but the fun of the evening combined with the excitement of the past few days caused them both to simply just fall over and pass out. Victoria managed a kiss on the cheek and a "good night Connor," and Mallory's last thought before falling into a deep sleep was that he didn't mind it one bit.

The next morning however, was a little bit different. The residue and lingering effects from the night before had taken its toll. Mallory woke up with a throbbing in his temples and managed to sleep-walk to the galley where he was met by members of the crew with the same affliction. Sunshine passed him a cup she described as 'the cure' and Mallory was pleasantly surprised that it didn't contain coffee, but instead was one of the tastiest Bloody Mary's he'd ever had. Within minutes his hangover evaporated. He found his way topside to the greetings of a smiling Captain Magic at the helm, and much to his surprise an overcast sky. "It seems that the gods are with us," explained the wheelmaster, "It's hurricane season and there's a pair of low pressure systems forming down south that should bring us some favorable winds. It might not be pretty, but we're going to fly." The sails were maximum full and the wooden masts were already creaking. "It's usually northeast trades at this time of year, but we are blessed with some uncommonly strong southerlies." Captain Magic seemed to be at home wherever he went, and he was definitely in his element now. Hurricane season. Oh that's just wonderful thought Mallory. He had to admit though, that the Flying Cloud was running at a nice clip and he could certainly see how the schooner got her name. The weather might not be ideal, but the elements were a true sailor's delight. His temporary paranoia quickly passed and it was easy to see that they were going to be in for quite a ride. As if on cue, the sky lit up with a lightning bolt followed closely by a thunderclap heard in the distance. "Oh boy" was all Mallory could think of to say.

Victoria appeared on deck, also looking a little worse for wear and took a look around. The captain asked "do you like roller coasters?" Victoria managed a weak smile and without a word went back down below. "Try a cup of the cure," he yelled after her.

"Captain, you mentioned earlier about seeing strange things in the sky, like what?" asked Mallory.

He was introspective for a minute, then finally answered, "oh not much really, but things I don't have an answer for I've seen not just once, but a number of times. I've seen stars shoot across the sky, then stop. They'd look just like any other star, but then take off in another direction. I'll never forget the first time it happened. I was hiking in the crater. We had a cabin for the night, so I was laying outside on the ground with a girlfriend stargazing when it happened. We both saw it, but still couldn't believe our eyes, but we were so curious we did the same thing the next night and it happened again. Naturally nobody believed us, but for me it was my own personal sighting. Epiphany as it were."

"Funny you should mention that," returned Mallory. "The night before we left one of doctor Bloomfield's telescopes picked up the same thing. It went something like disappearing behind the Moon then reappearing later. He was pretty hush-hush about it though, claiming national security and such."

"That doesn't surprise me, apparently there's strange shit happening all the time over Hawaii. There have been some that have been so blatant that the government has put notices in the newspapers claiming satellite launches and/or weather balloons. Bloomfield doesn't talk because he wants to keep his job. Can't say as I blame him."

"Well I think our discovery will shine some new light on that subject, if it is what we are thinking it is, that is."

Captain Magic gave him a quizzical look then smiled. "You know, that's not all. There are some that believe the islands are mountain tops of an ancient civilization that flourished here before recorded history that even might have had contact with extraterrestrials. It's rumored that they abused their power which caused them and their sister continent called Atlantis to sink. Pretty far-fetched, but you never know…"

"Yeah. Crop circles, landing pads, and cave paintings depicting space travelers, it certainly does make one wonder," answered Mallory.

Although neither of them said it, they were both thinking about the object in the backpack. Little did they know just how really close they were.

At that moment a very large raindrop fell from the sky and landed right on the tip of Mallory's nose which caused him to blink. The captain thought that it was quite funny until more started sporadically falling around them. The winds were gathering momentum and the sky was quickly becoming darker with intermittent flashes of lightning and rumbles of thunder.

"Looks like it's time to break out the foul weather gear, It seems the weather is going to turn a touch inclement." He was clearly putting it lightly and trying to sound convincing, but the look in his eyes told it was time to do just exactly what the captain said. To fortify his 'suggestion', a gust of wind hit them causing the boat to jump and the masts to groan. Mallory was instantly down the causeway to alert the rest of the crew.

In the next few hours the gusts had turned into steady sixty to eighty mile per hour gale force winds. The low pressure system had turned into a tropical storm that soon was turning into borderline hurricane status. The good news was they were running ahead of the storm, the bad news is they weren't running fast enough. Off the stern of the Flying Cloud was an angry black mass of clouds spewing bolts of lightning and growling claps of thunder. At first the lightning was just like far-off flashbulbs in the sky, but as the storm got closer the electricity in the air compounded. Bolts of lightning cracked followed by what sounded like the roll of a kettledrum that turned into an explosion in the distance. The intermittent raindrops became a constant cascade of water that most resembled a full blast shower head.

Captain Magic's analogy of a roller coaster turned out to be right on the money. One of these tropical storms reached hurricane status and was aptly named Elvira. Elvira was twelve hundred miles further to the south which allowed her to create fetch, the distance between water and winds that made the waves in the ocean. Elvira was steadily pumping eighteen to twenty foot ground swells of machine-like quality that by the time they reached the Flying Cloud they seemed like endless mountains of moving water. To compound the issue, the closer storm was also creating waves. Although smaller, they were coming from a different direction, thus creating a cross-section ripple effect on the bigger ground swells, as if two giant stones were dropped in a calm pool at the same time from opposite sides. The results would be the same, only on a much smaller scale. Mother Nature's elements we're having a field day and had converged on this particular spot in the Pacific Ocean. And the Flying Cloud was right in the middle of it all.

Although the ocean and sky was a moving mass of chaos, it seemed to have no adverse effect on the crew at all. To them it was just another day in the park. Mallory's alert jump-started everyone into action, not the kind born from panic, but of a cool, calm, and calculative nature. The ladies produced rolls of duct tape and began securing anything that wasn't nailed down. The Old Coots passed out rain slickers and harnesses to strap themselves in for when the shit hit the fan. It was obvious they had been through this drill before. As the storm gathered, hangovers were forgotten and survival was the order of the day. Mallory and Victoria we're at first puzzled as to why there seemed to be no panic, but the competence of the crew's actions answered their question for them. By the time the full fury of the storm hit, they were as prepared as they could possibly get.

Hell, they're even having fun, thought Mallory, as the Flying Cloud pitched and rolled over another wave. One glance at Victoria told him she was holding up nicely, although a little green around the gills. Funk Dog and The Colonel joined Captain Magic topside to reef the sails halfway for riding close to gale force winds and waves from trough to whitecaps were forty to sixty, maybe eighty feet high. The rest of the crew appeared to be going with the rolling seemingly unconcerned about the chaos around them. Mallory deduced that these were true veterans of many ocean crossings before. He decided to brave the topside to see what it was all about. He knew enough to know he had to have a grip on something at all times. When he slid back the hatch he was greeted by

Mother Nature at her best. Inside a minute he was soaked head to toe. This was definitely something he wouldn't forget for a lifetime, if there was one.

The Flying Cloud at that moment was deep in a trough, just starting to climb another mountain of water. Captain Magic was at the helm, his familiar infectious grin totally lit up. He signaled to Mallory to stay put and hold on with both hands as the Flying Cloud climbed the mountain. When she reached the pinnacle she unweighted and almost got airborne. Right then, Captain Magic spun the wheel starboard and tacked in mid maneuver only to land proficiently on the back side. Sheer poetry in motion. He signaled Mallory to join him at the wheel. "Hey Connor enjoying the fun? It doesn't get much better than this." They were clearly enjoying themselves and they were like kids at an amusement park, except the stakes were a lot higher.

"Actually it's a bit much. But I'm getting used to it," answered Mallory. That was as far as he got before the Flying Cloud jumped yet another monster. The captain then jammed the wheel portside and the Cloud responded by cutting diagonally down the backside of the wave and grabbing more wind for a little extra push. This brought about a cheer from everyone. They were definitely in their element.

"We've been in worse, but this is definitely top drawer." Captain Magic was beaming. "Here, take the wheel for a moment."

Before he could decline, Captain Magic grabbed Mallory's sleeve and slid him over to the wheel. Mallory had no choice but to comply, much to his astonishment. The captain reached inside his rain slicker and pulled out a cigar-shaped torpedo, quickly lit it, then took back over before Mallory could panic.

"Thanks," he said as he flashed yet another conspiratorial grin at the speleologist. "Boys, break time," he yelled to the others top side. They quickly huddled together and when the cigar was passed to Mallory he automatically decided to partake. Considering the circumstances, it was a 'when in Rome' situation. As it turned out it was a good move on Mallory's part for it enhanced the goings-on around him allowing his faculties to adjust to the situation at hand. He started to feel one with the ocean and the vessel, which contributed profusely to his comfortability factor. The next time span went in a succession of wave jumps, tacks, pitches, and roles as the crew cheered at every twist and turn Mother Nature was dealing them. Mallory eventually found he was actually enjoying himself along with the others.

Then, as fast as the storm had gathered, it disappeared. The sun broke through the clouds and except for the groundswell, the sea calmed down. "We're in the eye of the storm," the Captain explained. It was true. In a three hundred and sixty degree panorama, they were completely surrounded by the angry black mass. "You don't see this every day," he remarked as the rest of the crew came topside to enjoy the temporary respite. Rain slickers and harnesses were removed and a round of 'the cure' was passed around. The enjoyable relief was short-lived, but it was just enough time for the relief crew to take over duties on deck. Colonel Natural took the wheel and was joined by Seahawk, Cue Ball, and Slo Mo. The ladies stayed below to keep things festive. As the wind started to pick up, the exhausted sailors went below. "Did you enjoy the ride?" he asked Mallory once below.

"It took a little getting used to, but it is something I don't think I'll ever forget," answered Mallory. "That cigar of yours helped out quite a lot, I must admit. You sure seemed to be enjoying yourself," he added.

"Yeah. Well that was the easy part. We were on what is called the 'reach', going with the winds. Now they are going to come straight back at us after we are through the eye," explained the Captain. "The next part is called 'beating,' and believe me it's an appropriate term."

Which indeed it was. When the winds returned, they hit the Flying Cloud head-on. This caused the new team to meet them at forty five degree angles to make any headway and stay afloat. Besides the open groundswell, the ripples from the winds were like everlasting speed bumps. It reminded Mallory of an old washboard and it didn't help the Flying Cloud's wave riding capabilities either. The wave top's weren't as bad, but when they would reach the crest the boat would keel over in the opposite direction they were traveling causing an even more severe rocking motion upon each landing. Captain Magic, the eternal optimist, could not help himself; he had to join the boys top side. It was as if the storm had plugged him into an electric socket. He reminded Mallory of the Energizer Bunny which was an apt analogy. Mallory noticed Victoria looked a little peekid, so he joined her at the galley table. He asked her how she was holding up and a "eghhhh" was her only response. He patted her shoulder then decided to join the fun topside. When he slid open the hatch he was greeted by a full blast of rain in his face. If it was even possible, the elements seem to have taken a turn for the worse. Mallory, being no fool, crawled to the steering compartment where the crew was cheerfully huddling to take the brunt of the storm. The rain and wind had become so fierce it was bending the brims of the foul weather hats everyone was wearing. This part of the storm was definitely no joyride. Captain Magic signalled to strap on harnesses and it was good that he did because it saved Mallory's life. Almost every time the Flying Cloud hit the water after a jump, a wall of water would come flying off the bow sometimes covering the whole deck. The rain, plus the waves left no dry spot, rain slicker or not. A true test of his endurance, Mallory's first experience at this jolted him into an awareness of the precarious position they were actually in. The onslaught of water off the bow caused his harness to strain at the maximum. Without it he would have been easily washed off the deck like a child's toy. Captain Magic spelled The Colonel about every half hour at the wheel. The job had turned from a joyride to a workout. At each tack, ropes were released on one side and cinched up on the other; every time a life-and-death situation for the crew. Mallory marveled at their expertise and the Flying Cloud proved to be all her name portrayed. There wasn't a more seaworthy old lady on the ocean. Eventually the storm began to abate and by dawn the next day it was gone as quickly as it had come. The crew again changed shifts and Mallory wearily went down his cabin to fall over into the sleep of the dead.

  He woke up a little after midday. His muscles he didn't even know he had, we're screaming in protest. He felt like he had been on a medieval torture rack. As he lay there groaning he heard the door open and much to his surprise it wasn't Victoria, But Sunshine clad only in an extra large wet t-shirt that revealed Gorgeous curves barely hidden underneath.

"Ah, good morning" he managed to say, wondering if he was still dreaming, which wasn't even close to the truth as his muscles testified to that fact.

Sunshine merely smiled and held up bottles of camphor and aloe lotion and said, "Captain's orders, roll over." Mallory did as he was told, and felt first his shoes and then everything else being removed. When naked, he heard the wet t-shirt fall to the floor and then a squirt from the bottles upon the small of his back, moving upwards to his shoulders. Sunshine dexterously manipulated the goop into his overworked shoulders and by the time she was through he was putty in her hands. She then told him to roll over. When he did so, he found himself face to face with a pair of some of the most beautiful breasts he had ever seen in his entire life. This time, Sunshine squirted the goop upon herself and lowered down upon an astonished Mallory in a writhing motion that spread the goop between them. She passionately whispered in his ear "rewards to the hero of the sea," then replaced the words with her tongue which immediately caused Mallory to spring to attention, and the rest they let nature take its course.

About an hour later Mallory was laying there feeling he had been through a complete overhaul. Then the door opened, Surfer Sue peeked in, appraised a naked Mallory like a cat would a mouse, smiled and without a word closed the door. He didn't need to be a mind reader to tell what she was thinking. Sunshine slipped her t-shirt on and told Mallory to leave so she could replace the sheets. Mallory did what he was told and managed a grateful "thank you" as he put back on his clothes. She then explained to him that the cruise would last two weeks, the undertone meaning being obvious.

Mallory reached the galley and the sweet aroma of good strong Kona coffee and pungent smell of Maui's finest. He felt like a kid caught with his hands in the cookie jar, but a chorus of "good mornings" from the crew changed all that. Only a knowing smile from Captain Magic and a partially disgruntled look from Victoria gave away the fact the Flying

Cloud was in a small world of its own. He accepted a cup of the strong brew, but politely declined on Maui's finest and guiltily went topside for some fresh air.

Funk Dog was at the wheel and Slo Mo was working the rigging. The rest of the crew was either recuperating or rejuvenating and the caretakers were nowhere to be seen. Funk dog decided to good naturedly 'twist the knife' by asking, "did you enjoy your wake up call?" an all knowing smirk on his face. Mallory smiled and left it at that.

The Pacific Ocean had turned into a completely different personality. Besides a slight gray hue in the distance, there was no trace of the storm from the day before. A brilliant light blue cloudless dome complemented the deep blue of the sea and the Flying Cloud was easily cutting through a slight five foot groundswell. The day was picture perfect. The only trace of the storm that remained was in the form of a light southerly breeze that pushed the schooner along its course.

"This is a little more like it," observed Mallory. "Is it going to stay like this for a while?"

Funk Dog was being stoic and merely nodded, but behind him was Captain Magic coming topside with the appropriate answer. "It should be like this the whole way. We were either just in the wrong place at the right time or the right place at the wrong time, depending on how you look at it. One thing's for sure, I can safely say we weren't followed."

One by one the crew appeared topside to enjoy the gift of the sun, all wearing bathing suits or less except for Funk Dog, who had to protect his bright red skin from the ultraviolet rays. Later in the day Sea Hawk shimmied up the foremast and rigged a dunking rope off a pulley on the yardarm. Captain Magic was the first to partake as he donned his birthday suit and took a running leap off the port side deck attached to the rope that held a customized swing-type seat at the bottom. After dragging alongside for a minute, the rope was raised just enough to skim the surface and get dunked by the passing ground swells, with mock sputters and "yahoos" along with cheers from the crew. Each took their turn with their self made toy. A special cheer went up as Victoria came up from a dunk minus her top. Her inhibitions were quickly fading away while the merriment became infectious as the day progressed.

"Your 'partner in crime' seems to be loosening up a touch," observed Captain Magic as he sat next to a tearful from laughing Mallory. Victoria had taken a second turn on the swing and was enjoying every minute of it. Her bottoms had disappeared also.(yay)

"Well I wasn't quite sure when I came out this morning, she actually looked maybe, ah, jealous," returned Mallory. "You'd think we were married or something."

"We asked her first if she would do the honors. When she declined, the girls almost jumped out of their seats to volunteer. They had to settle for drawing straws. You see, you're the new meat on board and our lifestyle out here is a little, ah, loose."

"You'll get no complaints from me. Shit, it was a dream come true. Besides, the 'massage' actually worked."

"The fruits of hazardous duty, my friend," returned Captain Magic, his infectious grin appearing once again.

Even though Mallory was convinced already, it was now beyond a shadow of doubt that the Ranger's suggestion of their "high friends in places" was a gift from the fickle hand of fate. Here he was, in the middle of the Pacific Ocean, on one of the finest schooners ever built, with a cast of characters that was as fun to be with as humanly possible, a partner that was beautiful as she was compatible, and on a mission that might just quite possibly be beneficial for all mankind. Even though a worst case scenario was also entirely possible, the way things were going so far, it seemed like a fairytale come true. The entirety of the situation was the elixir of life.

CHAPTER 4

NEWPORT BEACH, CALIFORNIA

Fog. Damp, cold, gray with a tinge of internal combustion fumes, permeated the atmosphere. After seventeen days of only what could be best described as bliss, the west coast of the United States carried with it an aura of pessimistic gloom. In reality, it actually wasn't quite as bad as it seemed, but to the crew, after a cruise of pure unadulterated enjoyment, the approach to their destination was like an overwhelming slap in the face of grim reality. The hard facts were that this leg of the tour was almost over. Even though the first few days were touch and go, the remainder of the cruise was storybook material.

Shimmering moonlit nights, contrasted by cloudless sunlit days where complemented by a gentle southerly breeze that pushed the Flying Cloud along her course. The days passed with minimal physical exertion, just an occasional tack to stay on course. Mallory's premonition proved to be true as the schooner's compass pointed to his cargo instead of magnetic north, so they relied on celestial navigation for positioning which worked proficiently. After the seas calmed down, they set out fishing lines and on the fourth day they latched onto a Marlin. Funk Dog, the fisherman of the group, brought it in just under a half hour. During the battle between man and fish, theory and wisecracks flew until the Marlin was brought on board. The marlin was probably so sick of the B.S. flying around, it just wanted to jump into the boat and get it over with… It turned out to be too small, a little baby, so they threw it back, in hopes of meeting another day. Almost immediately after, Funky snagged an Ahi tuna, big enough to feed everyone for a week. The ladies usually did all the cooking, but when it came to fresh fish, especially Ahi, each member's private recipe was tried much to the delight of all. Funk Dogs recipe called 'masochistic tendency' turned out to be the most popular because he used the famous Hawaiian chili pepper which required extra amounts of beer to wash it down with. Musical sing alongs became a regularity after dinner as did the massage sessions by the caretakers. Mallory found himself looking forward to his turn that came every few days. He also found that Victoria became a little 'Huffy' after each one and he didn't know if that was a good thing or not. The night before they were to reach the west coast he found out.

Earlier that day, the remainder of the gourd was passed around along with a chaser of Jack Black. Mallory noticed that Victoria wasn't taking her usual ladylike sips. Whenever a torpedo of Maui's finest was passed around she would partake in that also. Then in celebration of a successful Voyage, Captain Magic broke out bottles of Dom Perignon for the occasion. Mallory had also noticed that during the day the ladies would huddle together in discussion which included giggles and lewd stares. At one point he caught them all looking at him like they were sizing up a slave on an auction block. The enormity of the situation didn't really set in, because during the cruise this had been normal, except for participation on Victoria's part. Everyone continued celebrating all throughout the afternoon, into the evening dinner, and the musical get-together thereafter. Victoria's participation became more raucous as the day progressed. She particularly stole the show when a rendition of 'Louie Louie' was played, looking more like she belonged more at the Animal House fraternity party then aboard the schooner. Her inhibitions completely evaporated, she got various members of the crew to dance to the tune, then fell back into her chair to a round of applause, not to move again; the possibility of her being able to was debatable. Mallory had received more than a few mock startled glances throughout the festivities, he being the most surprised of all.

"Connor Mallory, I think I need a little help," slurred Victoria. She had attempted to get out of her chair but fell directly back in, a number of times. Mallory gently as possible, lifted her out of her chair. She wrapped her arms around his neck and laid her head on his chest. He had to walk sideways down the companionway to reach their berth where he dumped her as ceremoniously as he could on the bed. Much to his surprise she didn't let go but held on tighter. They fell together in a clump of intertwined legs and arms and oh yes, torsos. Victoria's breathing turned into panting as she said "take my clothes off, slowly." Mallory got the picture quickly and did as he was told. He undid button after button until her blouse fell open revealing a black lace front opening bra that held a set of breasts that rivaled no other. "Kiss them. Hard." She ordered. Mallory obliged as his hands moved down toward the zipper of her skirt. He removed the skirt as his tongue found its way down to her belly button, then to her thighs and then to her… "ERRRAGHHHHHAGHHHHHH!." Victoria had sat up and most unceremoniously the Awa, the Jack Black, the champagne, and her dinner came flying out like a full blast hose, only to land on the back of Mallory's head and down his back. Needless to say this put a damper on the situation. "Oh Connor, I'm soooo sorry. ERAGGHAHAHHH" once again, this time all over the front. Mallory, being a worldly veteran in his own right, quickly rallied. He grabbed a towel for the lady and a washbowl that was handy. After making sure she had finished and wiping up as much as he could, he headed towards the galley. "Yes" was the response from the crew as he entered. Everyone had been pulling for the pair to cement their relationship, but the cheers turned into groans judging from the looks, and smell, of Mallory's appearance.

Mallory turned to the caretakers and pleaded, "my partner needs a little looking after and some ah, clean sheets. I need to go topside for a few buckets of water." The girls rallied and quickly went into action bringing a sponge, clean towels, clean water and disinfectant to the rescue. Mallory went topside and after more than a few buckets of seawater, himself and the cabin were once again clean. Upon returning, he found a new set of clean clothes and a towel outside his door, which he immediately changed into and returned to the galley. Amongst smiles, snickers, and occasional wisecracks he accepted the mock condolences. When the ladies returned they announced that all was fixed and Victoria was sleeping soundly. After verbalizing his sincere appreciation he attempted to return to his cabin but was held firmly in place by both Sunshine and Surfer Sue.

"Oh no you don't, Mr. Speleologist, she needs all the rest she can get. Judging by what she told us she was going to do with you, you shouldn't be anywhere near her," they explained, a sparkle in their eyes. "That means, sir, that your cabin is off-limits for now. So you'll have to deal with us." At that, they grabbed each arm and led him to their private sanctuary at the bow of the boat; a place rarely seen by mortal man. At this point, the speleologist was so stunned he was like a lamb led to slaughter. Oh well, what a way to go, he thought, what could a poor boy do?

The next morning, a rubber legged Mallory joined Captain Magic at the wheel topside. The Flying Cloud was slowly motoring through the fog bank that left visibility close to zero.

"Good morning," said the Captain, "notice the smell? The Santa Ana winds have blown all of the smog out of the LA basin and also tells us we're getting close."

"My God, that smells horrible. And look, the fog is brown." Mallory was relieved he wasn't going to have to take a ribbing from last night's fiasco, yet.

"Santa Ana's blow a few times a year. Most of the time the smog from all the cars and whatnot stays bottled up in the basin. But when these winds blow they clear it out. It's good for the city folk, but for the inhabitants of the coastline it's the short end of the stick." Captain Magic continued as if nothing had happened the night before. "Listen. I've been giving this some thought. Do you have plans once we reach land?"

Mallory looked up. Although he had kept it to himself, he secretly hoped this question would be asked. "No, not really, every once in a while the thought would pop into my head, but the cruise was so enjoyable I didn't want to spoil the fun. Your help getting thus far has been immeasurable, I hope someday I can find some way to repay you."

Captain Magic's eyes lit up. "Actually there is. I've been at the wheel here for some time now and I've been considering your situation. As you probably can tell, we have been fairly anti-establishment most all of our lives. So while you were being taken care of by the gals and your partner was sleeping it off, we took a vote."

The mention of last night's activities caused Mallory to blush; there was no getting around it. But he managed to keep the conversation to the business at hand. "I'm all ears," he replied.

"Well, it's a given that your 'discovery' can't pass inspection at airports, trains are a maybe, and buses are just plain uncomfortable. Also there's definitely a strong possibility that you already have an A.P.B. out on you…, considering what went down on the mountain. Shit, for that matter maybe there's one out on us too. We can deny everything and demand proof. Besides, we are not strangers to situations like these. Anyway, renting anything in your name is out. They'd be on you like flies on you know what." The Captain had a penchant for cutting to the quick. "Our vote was unanimous. Since the hands of fate have delivered us together, and your mission has portents of incalculable magnitude, we intend to stick it out until you reach your destination. Florida, wasn't it?"

"Yeah. Her ex-uncle in law runs a resort there called Sonofabitch or Suns of the Beach or something like that. Apparently he's quite a character and also a retired Air Force General at that," returned Mallory.

After a good gut laugh, they got back to business. "Well, our business requires us to have trustworthy friends in various areas, and we have a network that pretty much spans the globe, or the pertinent places anyhow. Here in California we have a few partners that decided to move back here to filter their funds into aboveboard enterprises, and are quite successful I might add. Anyway, with your permission I can give them a cell call and all your transportation needs will be taken care of. Also, if you deem it necessary, we can supply you with complete new identities; passports, birth certificates, socials and driver's licenses. The whole sheebang as it were. Just give me the nod and it's done."

Mallory felt like the weight of the world had been lifted from his shoulders. Every time he had given it thought, he drew a blank. The burial chamber, the discovery, the flight down the crater, the pill box, the White Wings, the Flying Cloud, the hurricane, the massage sessions, and especially the close encounter with Victoria had all happened so fast he felt as if he was caught up in a whirlwind of circumstances beyond his control. And on top of that, it was far from over. He breathed a deep sigh of relief and answered, "normally, I would consult my partner on this, but I really don't think she'll be in that good of shape to make decisions such as this. Besides, I don't think we could have been any luckier to have met you all. Even though it's been an adventure of a lifetime already, I couldn't think of anyone better I'd rather entrust our discoveries safety to. Let's do it."

A cheer went up behind Mallory. Unbeknownst to him the entire crew had been eavesdropping. They had every right; being just as much a part of it as anyone. Amidst back slaps and handshakes the 'well oiled machine' went into action furling sails and cleaning up the deck. Captain Magic reached first for the cell phone and then to yet another torpedo to cement the deal.

"Okay. We have a mooring in Newport Harbor we can use on occasion. It's right in the middle of lah-de-dah-land. All the boats there are multi-bucks so we won't be that conspicuous," announced Captain Magic. He punched in a number on his phone, "Hey Loaf. It's us and we're here. Yep, it's true, I wouldn't believe it either, if I didn't see it for myself… It was? They are? You're shitting me. Okay. I guess we better go into full clandestine mode. Yeah, I'll break it to them gently. Right. See you at Woods." He signed off and gave Mallory another conspiratorial grin.

At that moment, Victoria's face appeared out of the hatch. "What's all the noise about? Don't you people ever stop?" It was a meager attempt at best, but it did show that she was a real trooper. Her face was pale green from the night before, but even so, she came out shooting from the hip. "Ugh. Nevermind. Tell me later." She gave Mallory a sad puppy look, then disappeared below.

"It seems you are going to be in for a little surprise," Captain Magic announced happily. "You're famous. Apparently you are ring leaders of an island-wide robbery ring. TV and radio. Can I have your autograph?"

To Mallory this came as no surprise, all things considered. Anything was possible. But this was not a time to flinch. "Oh, is that all?" he responded with a poker face. But inside he knew the situation was precarious, to say the least.

"Not to worry. We can change your looks. We've had to from time to time. You won't recognize yourself. That's not all. I have a surprise I'll save for later". Captain Magic was clearly enjoying himself. He was a grand master of his game, and the games we're about to begin. Again.

The noxious fogbank, though detrimental to everyone's respiratory system, proved to be the perfect cover for entry into Newport Harbor. Not only was the visibility close to non-existent but the fumes in the air kept mostly all the coastal residents' indoors. The Flying Cloud glided silently through the sheet glass water of the harbor to it's mooring where it's lines were set, fore-and-aft, in close to complete silence. Once this task was completed, Captain Magic remarked, "perfect weather for Jack the Ripper." Just as his witty retort escaped his mouth, a familiar approaching sound of an outboard engine came within earshot. Out of the mists appeared not one, but two Zodiacs piloted by the all too familiar silhouettes of Rangers Raymond Souza and Richard Townsend, their ear to ear grins being the first distinguishable features on their approaching faces.

"Oh. Yes, that reminds me," he said with an all-too-familiar grin on his face. "You mentioned the fact of how you might ever be able to repay us? I believe our Federal Caretakers of the largest dormant volcano on the planet, managed to pilfer a gourd or two of Ava Root tea out of a certain burial chamber that has yet to be 'discovered.' Rumor has it there's quite a few to go around. So we didn't think one would be missed. To the victors go the spoils," he chuckled.

Torn somewhere between shock and delight, the speleologists were speechless. At the moment, the only thing they were capable of was mutual nods of agreement.

"Fancy meeting you here," said Souza, the picture of innocence. "I trust the voyage over here was enjoyable." Townsend just smiled and waved, then began catching the personal belongings being tossed overboard.

Victoria was the first to speak. "You scoundrels! Why didn't you tell us? Or better yet, how come you didn't just come with us?"

"Three reasons," answered Sousa. "First, we weren't sure we could finagle time off, second we wanted to see what those asshole FBI agents were going to do, and third, we get seasick."

"Actually doc Bloomfield had the original idea. He figured our Federal status being part of the law enforcement branch, might come in handy in a pinch", answered Townsend. And besides, knowing these characters the way we do, anything is possible, or more precisely, probable."

Souza added, "we brought our uniforms to look official if need be. By the way, Loaf, T-Boy, Z and HT are at Woods Wharf where they brought you your new faces", looking at the speleologists. "You're mighty popular these days. We better move."

The crew locked everything down and loaded into the zodiacs. A quick run and they were dockside at their Newport Beach hangout. "This place should be a city monument, it's so old. You can moor your crafts here, dock, and go in. Besides, we know the owner."

"Nothing surprises me anymore when it comes to you characters," observed Mallory. He was getting used to the fact that they were capable of almost anything.

Woods was everything they had described and more. From a distance, it appeared to be an old ramshackle building amidst the glitter dome of the 'nouveau riche' Newport Beach district. But on closer inspection, the wood was purposely designed to give it an aged appearance. From afar, it could actually be qualified as an eyesore; because it was surrounded by fancy buildings that were frequented by the hoi-polloi that had taken over as land values skyrocketed there. The Wharf was by far the most popular hangout for the die hard locals that refused to give up their homestead. The grizzly appearance kept most of the snobby away, which was the desired effect.

They docked The Zodiacs at the outside pier that led into the establishment. Once back on land, the speleologists found that their equilibrium was completely unused to solid land. It was as if the solid ground under their feet was rolling like they were still out on the ocean. Unfamiliar with this new situation, Victoria had to grab the Rangers arms to keep her footing. Mallory had experienced this before so he was ready for it, but the last time this happened it hadn't been as intense as this. He found himself holding onto walls until his balance had acclimated. Of course this was another source of enjoyment from the rest of the crew, but they let the ribbing and jokes slide because they had also been there before and knew what it was like. The fact that they were experiencing this also, was a contributing factor.

The interior of the establishment was also a surprise. The ambiance of Woods was as comfortable as one's own living room. The bar itself stood in front of a giant picture window that overlooked the harbor which gave the customer a front row seat view of the many boats passing by. The bar itself was made of what must have come off the deck of an old sea going vessel, that had been covered with countless coats of resin to give it a glass-like sheen unmatched anywhere. This allowed the bartender to slide drinks across its surface to their intended target, in which he was in the process of doing, as they entered. He must have been doing this for years because he was right on the money every time, much to the delight of the customers. The seats around the counter were not just mere bar stools, but overstuffed deep dish easy chairs with armrests covered with well used red leather that looked like it might have been next to impossible to get out of once sat in, which of course was the intended idea. In the corner was a wood burning cast iron pipe stove that added to the warmth and amiability of the room. On the walls were pictures of famous celebrities from the movie industry, politics, and even the underworld, most of which were autographed by the same, spanning decades of patronage. In most of the pictures each celebrity was standing with none other than the bartender himself, with the inscription, to

Woody from so and so, best wishes, etc etc. One of the more popular sets that hung side by side was a picture of then cowboy actor Ronald Reagan, and by him, mobster Bugsy Segal. Whoever had hung these pictures definitely had a sense of humor. Towards the rear of the establishment were booths big enough to hold parties of six to ten people, and in the back corner was the largest one of all: where raucous laughter was coming from and it was there that they were headed.

As they approached, the four that were seated rose to greet them like lifelong friends which was exactly what they were. The four appeared to be in direct contrast to the Old Coots; but it was the smile behind their eyes that gave them away.

"Doctors Mallory and Barbie, may I introduce Loaf, T-Boy, HT and Z," announced Captain Magic. "They are very old friends. And also, they are in cahoots with the Old Coots which brought even more of the same laughter.

Even though different in appearance, it was easy to tell their chameleon-like qualities were required to blend in with the surroundings. Each one in them was clean cut and well dressed, but that's where the diversity stopped. Their warm personalities matched those of the Maui contingent, and it was easy to tell they had been through quite a lot together in the past. Stories were swapped about the hurricane, golf tourneys, California surfing, pro baseball, football, basketball, ski slopes, and of course women and amidst everything else in between that was fun to do. HT, T-Boy and Z were the surfers and Loaf was the golf fanatic.

The bartender had come from around the bar and approached the party. "Hello Randall, back again? So soon? How's your dad?" he said.

"Oh hi, uncle Woody. We had to return because we missed you so much. Dad's as long in the tooth as you are, and he's as ornery as ever. He sends his regards too," answered 'Randall'.

"Great. Give him my best. And don't even think about trying to pay for these rounds, young man, they're on me. Are these the 'fugitives from justice' you're harboring? They don't look that threatening to me," said Woody good-naturedly. "Don't worry folks you're in the safest hands in the safest place in all of L.A. I ah, have a few connections."

"Thanks and thanks again, the pleasure is ours," returned the speleologists as Woody headed back towards his kingdom. Mallory turned to Captain Magic smiling, "Randall?"

"Don't rub it in. Woody and my Dad were fighter pilots during World War II. Their escapades were legendary; in and out of their pilot seats back then. Silver stars at Midway and what-not. They don't talk about the war part much, but their adventures on Hotel Street in Honolulu would leave you in tears. I'll leave it at that." 'Randall' was clearly proud of his uncle Woody, but his given name would get a blush out of him every time. He then turned to his partners and said, "well T, what's the best bet?"

T-Boy looked around the table, a cat-with-a-feather in his mouth look on his face. Then he glanced at Loaf who merely smiled and nodded affirmative. "We've given it some thought, and you have some options. But first we must factor in the variables and prioritize them. Distance, weight, time, travel, route, invisibility and Oysters."

"Oysters?"

"Yeah. Let's talk about this later. I'm hungry." T-Boy always enjoyed slipping in a curveball to see if everyone was paying attention. "Unless time is of the essence of course, we can think on our feet. Besides, I'd rather enjoy a meal with the ladies here, instead of talking to you clowns."

Mallory had come far enough to realize that every duerrogatory statement was made in jest. To anybody on the outside looking in, it might appear they took one another seriously, each being an actor in their own right. But insults and barbs were constantly being traded continuously throughout each and every day. When considering the source they were actually compliments. What surprised Mallory is he actually felt a slight tinge of jealousy when Victoria was included. But that didn't last long, especially when Woody showed up with a banquet fit for kings (and queens). Buckets of steamed clams with garlic bread, raw oysters in the half shell and oysters Rockefeller, king crabs with ramekins of melted clarified butter and finally some of Woody's private stash of abalone. The aroma of each dish wafted through the lounge, and the business at hand was put on hold. Between each savory mouthful were sighs and groans of ecstasy with an occasional pertinent remark concerning the task ahead. If these speleologists didn't realize the camaraderie involved, it might have appeared to be just gibberish.

But this was not to be; that day anyway, because by the time the meal was over, hours had passed and Woody was locking the front door. "Consider yourselves kidnapped. You are now my hostages." Woody's glare was semi-deadly serious to the point of having a slight resemblance to FBI agent Fife. The speleologists plans were finished even before they began. Or so they thought. The click of the lock accentuated Woody's statement. For a moment they could have heard a pin drop until Woody, a master of clowns-manship in his own right, broke into a grin when he stated, "nobody leaves until I find out what I can do to help. I believe an explanation is due, Randall."

The table was cleared and then the group moved to the now empty bar. The many colored lights in the harbor and on the boats reflected off the water of the canal, causing a light show that was a beautiful sight to see. The water had a glassiness to it that caused a mirror effect, except when a late night cruiser passed by, its weight causing ripples in the reflection of the lights, making them dance.

Woody, a seasoned old salt, listened patiently as the speleologists gave him a rundown on the original idea of their expedition, the subsequent finding of the burial chamber and the strange object, their flight from the law down Haleakala and the voyage across the Pacific. His eyes lit up at the mention of Tyrone 'Bull' Exley, otherwise he sat patiently as if he was hearing just another story from one of the many patrons of his establishment.

"You know, I've been behind this bar for so many years now and I've heard just about every kind of story imaginable, sober or not. But I've got to tell you, this one ranks somewhere at the top. Brigadier General Exley though, is another matter. You see, I had the privilege to serve under him in the Great War. And if there's anybody I'd trust to get things done, whether appropriate or not, it would be the Bull. He's more resourceful than all of us put together. If it's him you're going to see, I wouldn't worry one bit." Woody spoke reverently.

Victoria, although pleased to hear compliments about her uncle, wasn't used to being taken so lightly. She got up out of her chair and went over to her belongings and retrieved her video equipment and without a word hooked it up to the TV usually used for watching 'sports' programs. Mallory, sensing her determination, followed suit. Mallory grabbed his backpack and set it on the bar unopened. Captain Magic produced the gourd while Victoria set up glasses all around. Woody's amused eyes widened at the sight of the gourd: his "heard it all" attitude turning to surprise. "Uncle Woody," Victoria said, "no disrespect, but I believe you need proof." A shot was poured for all and the video was turned on. Surprise turned into disbelief as Woody took his medicine. He then watched with rapt attention as the video backed up their story. Then to ice the cake, Mallory pulled out the object from the backpack. Woody's demeanor had gone full circle and wound up somewhere between shock and reverence.

"I believe I owe you an apology." Woody said when he could find words. "I've heard and seen quite a lot, but this is by far, the capper. I hear so many whoppers here they usually go in one ear and out the other. But this here..." he pointed to the object. He was beyond words. He quickly turned serious as a judge. "Okay. My offer stands. You are headed in the right direction because 'The Bull' can be as devious as need be. But at any time you find that you might need my help, count me in." His features began to soften, "and this" he held up his glass, I haven't tasted in half a century that reminds me of a story..."

As the Ava root took effect, stories, some too outrageous to be on the level were swapped. Most of Woody's were centered around his then commander, General Tyrone 'Bull' Exley. If any of them were even close to the truth, Victoria's 'uncle outlaw' was the man for the next step in their journey. Woody continued: "Apparently before the Battle of Midway, all leaves were canceled for security purposes. Although the Bull could see the military logic behind this, it didn't make sense to him that the boys risking their lives, again, for their country, couldn't have one last night on the town before possibly checking out. During the preceding month he had blazed a trail through Honolulu that legends were made of, and his popularity level was at an all time high. So, to him the answer was simple: If the boys couldn't come to town, the Bull would bring the town to the boys."

"I've had a lot of memorable moments in that goddamn war, but next to VJ day, that was the highlight of them all." Woody spoke reverently as if he were living it once again.

"You see, we had just gotten back from the battle of the Coral Sea, on the aircraft carrier Yorktown. We had gotten the shit kicked out of us but managed to make it back to Pearl along with what was left of the aircraft from the Lexington which was sunk. Our boss, Admiral Fletcher was caught in the crossfire between commander-in-chief Chester A. Nimitz and General Douglas MacArthur. Both were giving conflicting orders throughout the battle. Neither side won although both claimed victories. Nevertheless we took a major hit and had to limp home. And as soon as we docked we were hit by a swarm of repair crews and rumors were flying that we were to turn right back around and head for Midway." Woody then turned to Victoria and gave her a penetrating stare that would have gotten the attention of a deaf mute, then broke into a huge grin. "Your uncle had gotten wind of this the night before liberties were canceled, and no way was he going to let his boys go out and risk their lives again without having a little fun beforehand. So, by using his devious expertise he managed to convince almost all the ladies of the night in Honolulu to attend a little party he was throwing aboard the Yorktown the next night. He then conscripted every type of hard liquor available from the Fort DeRussy Commissary, and also managed to convince the fort's dance band that they were going to play for some hoity-toity officers shindig aboard the same. How he did this is still unknown, but it happened all the same. And through some sort of barter system with the motor pool, he absconded with a dozen buses to get the ladies, booze and band to arrive dockside at the same time." Woody had to stop and take a deep breath. He then chuckled to himself while getting a round of beer from the cooler. "Needless to say, we were all moping around confined to quarters, waiting to step into the next pile of shit we were about to face, when around the dockside corner comes a Jeep flying generals colors with none other than the Bull himself in the lead followed by a parade of buses containing the loveliest site known to mankind. The chaos and confusion of the repair crews helped in creating a diversion which allowed the Bull to get through security. Hell, he even got a squad of MPs to help load the party favors and band equipment. At this point Woody had to stop because 'Randall' had laughed so hard while taking a pull off his beer, it had gone up and out his nose and he was gasping to contain himself. This started a chain reaction of howls and laughter that took a few minutes to subside. "The Bull then imperiously strode up to the radio room and through the PA system said these words I'll never forget. "Attention all air corps personnel: this is a surprise inspection. All hands on deck. And what the hell, all you swabbies too, for that matter." The next few hours is lost in a haze of frolicking dancers and boozing it up. To the boys on the Yorktown the Bull had become a national treasure overnight. Admiral Fletcher had been ashore going through last minute details with Admirals Nimitz, Spruance, and Halsey. When he returned the party was in full swing. I happened to be nearby and saw the whole thing. He got out of his Jeep and marched up the gangway stone faced.

At the top he was met by the Bull himself. They exchanged salutes and Fletcher said, "you're going to catch a lot of hell for this one Bull, carry on." And that was it. Fletcher went directly to his quarters without missing a beat. "I found out later that he could be heard laughing through the steel door of his cabin and rumor has it he was also visited by one of 'Honolulu's Finest' with a bottle of champagne; but that's only hearsay. Then, about two or three in the morning, the Bull went up to the band leader and used his microphone to announce something like "okay that's it. The better we make this disappear, the less crap I'm going to have to take. Don't forget to tip the band and the ladies," which was all he had to say. Those who could still function made a valiant attempt to do so. By dawn it looked like nothing had ever happened. "The next day we took off for Midway hungover as hell, but morale was at an all-time high. Shit, that's probably why we kicked ass so well. You see, the ladies left their dainties, sort of like the chivalry of knights in shining armor of old, to wear into battle. There were bras, panties, stockings and garter belts worn around the arm of every pilot and most of the crew during the Battle of Midway." Woody got up and went to his office. When he returned he was holding a frame which included a silver star surrounded by a pair of black lace panties, stocking and bra. "You see, I earned my share. Your dad and I got these medals for direct hits on the Soryu, Kaga and Akagi. So your uncle is partially responsible for the turning point of the war in the Pacific Theater. And for those on the Yorktown who didn't make it back, including the boat itself, at least they died with their boots, and/or panties on. The Yorktown got hit by three torpedoes on the way back. But at least it went to its watery grave with the distinction of having thrown the best party of the war before she was lost. We had to hitch a ride on the Hornet." He glanced at Captain Magic, "ask your dad about it sometime, when your mom's not around of course." No one could top that story, so the after hours party broke up. All agreed that it would be better to finish preparations in the morning. Much to their surprise, Woody's booths also turned out to be fold out beds. "For emergency," he explained. So T-Boy, Loaf, HT and Z, the Rangers and speleologists didn't have to go anywhere. Woody produced a 'closed for renovation' sign to hang outside the door. "Ignore this when you come in the morning. Consider this as your headquarters until you're ready to leave. I've got this gut-feeling that it's more than fairly important. Besides, I could use the day off."

Back on the Flying Cloud, Mallory courteously let Victoria go down below first, sensing it was the right thing to do. He had mentally put himself in her place and decided to let things come as they may. Besides, they all could use a good night's sleep after crossing the Pacific, plus the road ahead wasn't going to be easy. He quietly sat there for a few minutes enjoying the reflecting lights off the harbor. By the time he went below all was still. He tiptoed into his cabin and peeked inside to see that Victoria was sound asleep. As gently as he could he slid next to her and was out as soon as his head hit the pillow. What Mallory didn't know was that Victoria wasn't as out as she appeared. Her embarrassment had weighed heavily on her the whole day and wasn't quite sure how to handle it. But no one had rubbed it in nor made any snide remarks to make it worse, especially Connor. His courtesy and gentlemanly manner, especially this night, had eased the situation. Although he didn't know it, his actions had scored more points than anything he could have said or done. She sighed deeply and smiled inwardly and then matched his rhythm of breathing and was soon fast asleep, relieved of conscience.

It was mid-morning before all members of the crew came to life. They woke to a stunning crystal clear Southern California morning; the kind that only comes after a brisk few days of Santa Ana winds. The smog could be seen far out on the horizon, a brown bank of noxious fumes and filthy air. So Newport was completely free of the usual fumes that spilled out from inland. In short, it was an epic Newport Harbor morning, and it reflected on everyone's dispositions. The crew boarded the zodiacs and docked at Wood's to the heavenly smell of bacon, fried potatoes and onions and the sweet aroma of good strong coffee. They did as they were told and ignored Woody's 'closed' sign, and stepped inside to the wall of heavenly aromas. Woody and the Rangers were spreading a banquet buffet breakfast fit for royalty. And that's exactly how it made them feel.

Loaf, T-Boy, HT and Z, a.k.a. The Raiders, were huddled together with the Rangers, working out the kinks of their 'foolproof' plan of attack, coinciding with the look of a sort of detached amusement on their faces. Their confidence emanated success. "Good Mornings" were exchanged and coffee was poured when Woody appeared from the kitchen with a stainless steel tray of his specialty, Huevos Rancheros. By this time, salivation levels matched the aromas attacking the mucous membranes. When Woody announced, "don't be shy," it was all he had to say.

The pack attacked like ravenous wolves until every crumb had disappeared. Each crewmember partook in clean-up duty and soon it looked like breakfast never happened. Woody then motioned everyone to the Bar for his house specialty, Woody's Irish Coffee, which contained coffee, a generous shot of Christian Brothers brandy, and a floater of Baileys Irish Cream: a perfect capper to a perfect breakfast.

As the meal was digested and Woody's Specialty settled in, the players went about their business. The Raiders huddled for one last confirmation, then Z disappeared only to return just as fast holding a small suitcase in his hand. He motioned to the caretakers to join him in the booth. Amidst shrieks and giggles coming from the trio in the back corner, Loaf and T-Boy approached the speleologists. T-Boy took the floor. "After viewing your video and seeing you on the Boob-Tube we've fine tuned your itinerary according to the needs at hand. The invisibility factor is priority one and Loaf and the ladies will take care of that shortly. Time seems to be secondary and getting to Florida unnoticed can be easily accomplished by taking this route." T-Boy exchanged smiles with Loaf, HT and Z. They were clearly veterans of unscrupulous behavior involving clandestine acts of, let's leave it at that… Loaf produced a hand drawn map of the lower half of the United States and Northern Mexico. It was crude but effective. "To facilitate our business and vacations, we've acquired a few 'toys', and it appears that they could coincide with your needs. Our latest acquisition is a small seaplane we have over at the Isthmus of Catalina Island. So no airports are needed. If the Flying Cloud can get us there which is obvious, we can get you to Guaymas, Mexico on the mainland side of the Sea of Cortez. Loaf has a travelall tucked away there that we use occasionally. Usually to get to the Guadalajara Mariachi Festival and parts south. Z is our pilot and HT co-pilot and have done this a number of times. Their first water landings were a bit sketchy, but that's another story. They're better now and that's all that matters. So it's basically simple; Catalina, Guaymas, Guadalajara, El Paso, Louisiana, Florida and you're there." As T-Boy hopped his pencil across the map, any concern that the speleologists might have had, evaporated. They were in the hands of capable veterans of discretion. "So, that's it," T-Boy said proudly. "Now all we have to do is make you disappear."

That was HT and the ladies' cue. HT grabbed the suitcase and went to the men's room and soon returned then passed it to Sunshine and Surfer Sue. The speleologists were escorted to their respected restrooms for their makeover. Captain Magic turned to T-Boy and asked, "are they getting the full treatment?" T-Boy merely smiled.

"Oh yeah."

About a half an hour later, two completely different people emerged into the uproarious laughter from the entire contingent. Connor Mallory and Victoria Barbie no longer existed.

HT had used buzz clippers on Mallory's head to give him a boot camp quality flat top, then to accentuate this, he added a pair of coke bottle glasses and a pencil mustache. His wardrobe resembled that of a tourist from Hell: loud obnoxious shirt, plaid shorts with knee socks and loafers. Victoria clearly appeared to be his partner from the same area. Gone were her long blonde curly locks only to be replaced by bright red/orange headgear, accompanied by an extra thick application of plaster makeup. Her womanly curves were no longer visible. A below-the-knee flowered dress had a breast-flattener inside and around her belly was extra padding that made her look like a younger version of a Mrs. Doubtfire or maybe even Tootsie. A matching set of spectacles complimented the picture. When they turned and looked at each other they almost fainted. A round of applause was given to HT and the caretakers as they took their bows.

T-Boy took control once again. "Okay stage one complete. Sit down here and let me take your pictures. Victoria, you are going to be Raydene Souza and Mr. Mallory you are now Richard Townsend Junior." Then he pointed at the Rangers and said, "that's uncle Ray and dad. The Rangers had been in on the situation for sometime and blew them kisses. The razzing would come later. Their pictures were taken and Loaf was immediately out the door. "You see, we've given this a little extra thought. Since 'Uncle Ray' and 'Dad' are Federal Government Forest Rangers and they're in the computers as such, we thought it would be a good idea to have you two take their place, Raymond to Raydene and throw in a jr. for Richard. Z has a penchant for hacking, so, we just replace your new beautiful faces on the current IDs, change the spelling, so when you get to Roswell you'll have clearance along with your uncle. Last night we were inspired by Woody's story and we think your uncle will appreciate our work.

"What have I done to deserve a son like this? complained Townsend. "Anybody want a mail order bride?" quizzed Souza. "Hey Raydene, why don't you come over and sit on uncle Ray's lap and I'll tell you a story."

The speleologists just stood there gaping at everyone without speaking. Then with a brainstorm, suddenly Victoria hit Mallory with her purse and the whole place fell to pieces. To anyone within earshot they might have thought that Wood's wharf had turned into a Loony Bin.

Shortly after midday Loaf returned with the paperwork. Passports, Ranger IDs and even Hawaii state driver's licenses. The speleologists were getting used to one miracle after another, but still managed to acknowledge their appreciation. They had been getting into their new appearances by experimenting with voice timbres. Victoria settled for one resembling Granny Clampett while Mallory zeroed in on Gomer Pyle. The Raiders had taken this route to El Paso before, so a list of correct low-profile roads were included. By late afternoon they were ready to move. Goodbyes were traded and both Woody and the Raiders refused any payment. They did however point out the fact that if a couple more gourds were left, a happy home could be found for them. Both Townsend and Souza gave them an omniscient wink and the issue was settled.

"One more thing," said Woody as they were leaving, "about your Uncle. After we returned from Midway he was never brought up on any charges, but he did vanish. Rumors flew that he was sent stateside into obscurity. Roswell, don't it just figure. Please tell him he is still held in the highest esteem and regard by those who crossed his path." There was a hint of moisture in Woody's eye.

"I'll relay the message Uncle Woody," answered Victoria as she planted a giant wet kiss on the old salt's cheek. Z and HT joined the crew headed for the Flying Cloud much to the caretakers delight, then they parted ways. Woody yanked the 'closed' sign down and as the schooner was drifting out from Newport harbor the crowds were filling in as if on some sort of a sabbatical, which wasn't that far from the truth.

A bright red orange dominated the sky as the Flying Cloud motored towards Catalina Island. The wind was non-existent and the only movement was a pack of seagulls that chose to escort the schooner, their calls issuing back and forth sounding like echoes.

"At least that god-forsaken smog is good for one thing," remarked Captain Magic. "Sunsets like these are spectacular, even though they are man made."

"I'd much rather settle for natural although I do agree," returned Mallory. "I suppose one has to look for the good in all things."

"Sounds pretty philosophical for such an Okie," ribbed Captain Magic. He glanced at the speleologist and chuckled, "you really are a piece of work. They did quite a number on you, and Victoria, what a babe".

"I thought I was going to die laughing when she hit me with her purse. It was a perfect acknowledgement of a job well done," said Mallory. "How long is it to Catalina?"

"Well, there's no wind so we'll have to motor the whole way. It's twenty six miles, like the song. So probably sometime in the A.M. We can't do anything until daylight, so you might as well kick back and enjoy. Care for a smoke?" The merry prankster was at it again.

"No thanks. It's been fun, but now I'd prefer to stay sharp. We're heading into unknown territory," answered Mallory. "I'm going to turn in while I can." He headed below and when he opened the door to his berth, Victoria was herself again. She was just finishing off the layer of makeup from her face. The wig, thankfully, was on the shelf.

She turned and without a word rushed into his arms. "Oh Connor, this is all just too surreal." A tear had formed in the corner of her eye and it was clear that she was finally overly overwhelmed. A lump formed in Mallory's throat; (and pants). He felt the same way. It had all been so much of an experience and it was only just the beginning. They held each other for a few seconds then fell back upon the bed. Then they let nature take its course.

When Mallory woke it was to the sound of tiny waves lapping against the hull. Sometime in the night they had reached their destination and all was still; like a calm before the storm. He smiled to himself thinking this was an apt analogy and decided to take advantage of the situation by not moving an inch. He lay there snuggled against Victoria's naked body. Her breathing was even and deep. She stirred slightly and did a partial roll, with an "Ummmm" coming from somewhere within. My sentiments exactly he thought. Her roll had exposed a generous portion of her god given gift of medium sized breasts, a real novelty in this day in age of implants. Oh God could I get accustomed to this if only she'll let me. Last night had been a combination of gentle intimacy and raw unbridled carnal ecstasy. He had started slowly by covering every inch of her body with kisses, and then wound up like a cowboy breaking in a wild horse. They climaxed together and fell back in each other's arms feeling like they consummated a ritual, then slipped into a well deserved deep sleep. But it hadn't been just her breasts that had caught his attention, it was also the combination of those glorious curves she had kept well hidden until now. He had seen her naked during the cruise, but up close and personal he found that her skin was soft, creamy and pliable on the surface and well conditioned underneath. She reminded him of a theory his Dad once related to him: the bigger the nipples, the hotter in the package. And God, she had Silver Dollars! In this case Dad's theory was right on the money. She must have sensed this because at that moment her eyes opened and stared directly into his. She gave him a ravenous smile and said, "oh yeah, cum here." And that's exactly what he did.

About an hour later he rolled out and went topside. "What gives," asked Captain Magic. "You trying to sink my boat? It's been rocking around like a rubber ducky in the bathtub." Then he flashed one of those grins of his and handed him a mug of Joe. "Good morning, you might need this." His eyebrows raised thricely, adding to his cocksure smile. "Check out the Raiders toy." The 'toy', which was moored at a small dock in the Isthmus was not a toy at all. It was a pure example of aviation perfection right out of a corporate executives' dream. Bobbing dockside was a sky blue twin hulled seaplane. Their 'toy' was a nine passenger Beech 18 with an eighteen hundred pound payload. It sported two 450 Pratt & Whitney 985 radial engines on the wings and was supported by Edo 7850 floats, the biggest in the business. It was the Rolls-Royce of air, sea, and land. On the side painted white was the name 'Bluebird Travel'.

"There's even wheels underneath the floats. This thing can go anywhere, almost" he added.

"Wow"

"The Raiders had just arrived back via Zodiac from pre-flight check up and baggage handling. The Rangers turned into kids at a candy store. HT had a confident smile. "She's ready" was all he had to say. The entire crew was admiring the seaplane while he explained, "our 'Front' is a passenger service. We're actually busy. Bluebird also parks at John Wayne airport in Orange County. sometimes we actually do this, but for the most part is purely, ah, recreational."

"Nothing surprises me when it comes to you clowns," remarked Captain Magic. He was backed up by a chorus of "umhums."

"We want to go with you," said the caretakers, wily smiles on their faces. It was obvious where HT had spent the night.

"Please?"

"I don't see why not. Besides, we could use the company on the way back." That brought shrieks of glee from the girls as they scattered to grab a few of their belongings. "We also have a sport fishing boat at Cabo San Lucas. Maybe we'll stop there on the way back." Z was a pig in the proverbial shit.

"What about us?" protested Captain Magic. "We sailed across the Pacific Ocean and now you want to escape with the girls? I don't think so." Sunshine and Surfer Sue stopped in their tracks, disappointment clearly evident. "Ah, what the hell, we'll just meet you there. Cabo's on the way home anyway. Is the boat still named 'Only Fun'?

"Yep. Same boat, same place and there's also a few senioritas you might want to meet," stated HT happily. He was thinking he might be able to pay back the hospitality from the night before.

"Sounds good. If we move soon we can catch the windline and meet you there by sunset." Captain Magic's words were more of an order than a statement. The rest of the Old Coots were not ignorant of the delicacies of Cabo San Lucas.

Captain Magic turned to Mallory, "you should probably wake up Miss Souza. It's time to roll. Besides, there's something I want to discuss with you both before we leave. It might be important." His look was serious this time so Mallory went into action.

"Victoria, we…"

"I heard. We're almost ready. I packed for you. Good morning you Stud." She gave him a peck on the cheek and kept moving. Mallory grabbed what was packed and left the room.

When the speleologists were topside Captain Magic motioned them for a conference. As they approached he pulled out two packages from behind his back. "Here's a little going away present for you two, open them now." The speleologists complied and inside were brand new cell phones. "They're untraceable. Globestar satellite. They'll probably help in correspondence with your uncle. Also I'd like to know what your plans are after Roswell. We took a consensus and agreed to stick around and help you if you need it. We're going down to Mexico for a week or two, but we're not going to return home until we've heard from you. Face it. You're on the run from the law, you're carrying something of unknown origin and you're going into the jaws of probably the tightest security in the U S of A. You're going to need all the help you can get." He was uncharacteristically serious. The stakes were higher than they knew and the trail was going to be so very precarious from then on. "As you have probably figured out already we're pretty damn good at these types of situations, but in actuality you don't even know the half of it. We have safety spots all over and considering what you folks are doing, we just might come in handy again, real soon. Enough promotional bullshit. What I'm saying is we'll be here if you need us, just stay in touch."

"What have we done to deserve you people I seriously don't know, but we sure are grateful for it." answered Mallory. "Our gratitude is beyond calculation anyhow already, but this…" He was beyond words.

Victoria didn't say anything, but just wrapped her arms around him and planted a slobbery kiss on his cheek. If that wasn't confirmation, nothing was.

"Okay. That's settled, "Your uncle and daddy have the numbers and the codes. We use different words for different meanings if we think someone might be listening in. That way the conversation sounds harmless. Your object from now on will be called 'The Missing Link,' which it quite possibly might as well be anyway. We will be in constant contact and can probably bail you out of any given situation except Roswell. Any other explaining will be handled by then. Good luck and happy trails." Captain Magic wasn't much for goodbyes, so he turned and started getting ready to make way. He also didn't want anyone to see the moisture accumulated around his eyes.

Behind them the Bluebird came to life. Z being pilot and HT co-pilot. Last minute farewells and well wishes were exchanged then the speleologists loaded themselves into the zodiac that would take them over to the seaplane. The caretakers and Rangers had already boarded as to give time for the speleologists to have their last minute conversation with Captain Magic. All were aware of what the meeting was about, but didn't want to interfere with any decision the speleologists needed to make. While they were loading themselves into the Bluebird, Captain Magic gave the crew a thumbs up which was all he had to do. He then yelled across the water, "say hello to Hannibal for me." A cheer rose from all; knowing they were still in on the caper. As the seaplane made its last pass, various forms of goodbye gestures could be seen on the Flying Cloud. All of a sudden the speleologists felt like newborn birds that had just gotten kicked out of the nest. The enormity of the road ahead was now a reality.

CHAPTER 5

SOUTHWEST USA

The flight south of the border and across Baja California went smoothly. The drone of the engines kept conversation to a minimum. Only the occasional landmark description by HT was about the only thing said. The Santa Ana, also referred to as Santana winds, had cleared the coastline all the way to the San Bernardino mountains eastward and was quite a sight to see. The population explosion of the Southern California coast had grown to grotesque proportions. The cement jungle spread as far as the eye could see. But in direct contrast, the quality of life once across the border was appalling. Spread around the cities of Tijuana and Ensenada lay the squalor of what could best be described as slum districts. In recent years ramshackle houses built from cardboard, plywood and corrugated tin or anything else handy had spread like a plague. But as soon as they turned east they went over the beautiful coastal mountains of Baja California which eventually gave way to the unpopulated desert panorama on the way to the Sea of Cortez. In almost no time they were across the narrow strip of land and were once again flying over an emerald sea. It was here that the smooth ride stopped.

"Want to have a little fun?" asked Z with a twinkle in his eye. HT just rolled his eyes. Z's was more of a statement than a question. HT, in the co-pilot seat and behind him were Mallory, the ladies with the Rangers bringing up the rear. The Rangers looked at each other and shook their heads negatively as if they knew what was about to happen....

"Uh, sure, why not?" Mallory wasn't quite sure if that should be the correct response.

"Good. Let me show you what 'weightlessness' feels like. Mister Mallory, you can take the controls." This got everyone's attention except for the Rangers who seemed to be bracing themselves for what was to be coming next. Mallory grudgingly did as he was told. "Okay, you pull the wheel back slowly while I ease the throttle." Mallory complied and Bluebird nosed up as it slowed down. Soon this combination had Bluebird floating in the air not going forward, nor up or down. They were floating weightlessly in the air. Mallory looked around, a big smile on his face, the girls squeaked with delight and the Rangers for some reason didn't look all that too happy with the situation. "This is about as close to floating weightless as you can get, except for this"! Z pulled for full throttle and jammed the wheel all the way forward. The bluebird abruptly changed direction and went into a dive that would have made a WWII Kamikaze pilot proud. The passengers strained at the seatbelts as their stomachs entered their mouths. The seaplane proceeded into a three thousand foot dive-bomb run that made the world's scariest roller coaster drop seem like strolling with a baby carriage. Mallory was in too much shock to utter a sound while the ladies were making up for that and then some, shrieks of terror filling the cabin. The Rangers stoically braced themselves because they had been through this before. After about a minute of full anti G-Force, Z began to ease back on the wheel still at full throttle. They came out of their kamikaze run and Z complemented it with a 360 degree roll. Soon they were back on course as if nothing had happened, except for the fact they were three thousand feet lower. The only witnesses were a few disgruntled birds and some fishermen wondering what these crazy gringos were up to now. "Welcome to Z Air. You have just been christened." Mallory sat back in stunned disbelief as the girls pummeled Z with mock savage blows. The Rangers just sat there like nothing out of the ordinary had happened. Soon the sea town of Guaymas filled the horizon.

The town of Guaymas came as a complete surprise. The speleologists expected a sleepy little fishing town but it was quite the opposite. The town had blossomed into a miniature Riviera complete with a recently built Club Med. Besides being ideal for fishing, scuba diving and sailing, there were now speedboats complete with water skiers, sail boards and even amateur mining expeditions cannibalizing the hills for remnants of artifacts from previous civilizations. To top things off was a sight from a bygone era. A steam-powered paddle-wheeler was slowly plugging along through the vast array of every type of nautical gimmickry known to man. Construction on the shoreline was at epidemic proportions to facilitate the population explosion that infected the area.

HT had once again become tour guide to explain the situation. The passengers listened attentively as they made a few passes around the area. Z circled the paddlewheeler twice and wagged his wings and got a double blast from its whistle in return. "We know the Captain" was all he had to say. No surprise there. On his last pass he came in low as to signal the populace in the water that they were coming in for a landing. The dockside harbormaster announced through his public address system the same, for those not bright enough to figure it out. Z's improving landing capabilities proved out to be true as he came in on a one bounce landing, then skidded across the chop from the slight winds of the area, the sounds like a snare drum roll reverberating through the pontoons into the cockpit. They came to a halt in front of a buoy marked 'Bluebird Travel' fifty yards from dockside, the paddlewheeler giving another blast from its powerful whistle as if complimenting the pilot for a job well done. Z's response was a less than complimentary gesture as he stuck his arm out the window and used the universal finger gesture as a salute.

"Ladies and gentlemen, thank you for flying Bluebird travel," announced Z in a mock formal tone which brought yet another barrage of pummeling from the girls. Mallory was just happy to be at sea level again after surviving the kamikaze run. The Rangers were already up and out the door securing the lines to the buoy and waving to the paddlewheeler going by.

"Don't tell me," Mallory remarked sarcastically, "the Captain's part of your world-wide-web also." HT merely shrugged and smiled with his palms raised. "Is there any resort or area you don't have covered?" Z repeated the gesture. Then the sound of an outboard engine came within earshot. Mallory turned and saw the approaching watercraft, a Boston Whaler with the same markings as the paddlewheeler heading towards them. At the wheel was a sight completely out of context from this modern day and age. The boat's pilot was dressed in a mid nineteenth century powder blue suit complete with black silk vest, pocket watch and chain with matching top hat. As he got closer Mallory noticed he was dressed to resemble a Riverboat Gambler. As the craft got closer he noticed a silver silk ascot with a single diamond stickpin in the middle and a silver tipped walking cane to complete the wardrobe. The most striking feature was a perfectly trimmed snow white Van Dyke mustache and goatee that was definitely not an attachment and which probably had taken years to fine tune. He was grinning and the angle of the sun caused a brief flash of the gold of one of his eye teeth, a sight to make any Hollywood costume designer proud.

"Greetings travelers. Ah, yall hea foa the theatah tonight, My name is…'

"Cut the crap Grabbo these are friends of ours," interrupted Z. "You've got to work on that southern drawl of yours, it sucks."

"Oh hello there folks, I thought Z here had finally gotten a job. Come aboard I'll get you ashore." Grabbo spoke perfect English as soon as the facade wasn't required. "You folks hit the jackpot. Tonight's vaudeville night. Turtle sent me out to take a headcount for a ringside seat."

"They're on a mission. I don't know, it's up to them. First we're going to set them up with the Winnebago, then we'll see what's up."

"It's gassed and ready to rumble. We did a tune-up last week or so and she's purring like a kitten." Grabbo turned to the speleologists and added, "my real name is Jackson by the way. I was tagged in the band days. Myself, Cue Ball, Slo Mo, Seahawk and the Colonel had a way with the ladies, hence Grabbo. They're just jealous. Now I'm a card shark." He turned to Z, "your timing is perfect. Turtle will be in just about the time you get back. If it's in the realm of possibility, you really ought to stay for the show. First things first as they say," with that, he gunned the engine towards the dock, with the sound of the whistle blasting in the distance.

THE SPACE PATROL
SOMEWHERE IN THE HEAVENS

The vibrating beam of light sparkled momentarily as it shattered yet another chunk of spinning rock into micro-pieces, spreading what was left of a project away in all directions throughout the heavens, thus increasing the possibility of the bacteria left within, to land somewhere suitable for the propagation of the evolutionary process of life. This also reduced the chances of a bigger piece running into an existing project.

"Goodbye Ra, better luck next time," muttered Oxomoxo, as the last chunk of another failed project flew into pieces. He really hadn't had that much confidence in this project anyway. The species that had evolved there were somewhat at a negative consciousness level that based their civilization around violence, which usually proved to be the most dominating factor in the destruction of any given planet. Oh well, that wasn't their problem. It was their job to clean up the mess, salvage what they could, then destroy the rest so as not to contaminate any nearby projects. Any piece of debris that was missed could possibly some day run into another planet containing life forms, which could reduce their success/fail ratio that was precarious enough as is already. "Rawar, it's beyond me why they always blow it at the last crucial step. I really wish we could do more or have some more influence. Which reminds me, how is our pet project coming along?"

Rawar was just finishing up disintegrating the last pieces of 'Ra' that were possibly dangerous to other existing projects. They never got them all, nor did they want to. It made their work more interesting, and left things up to chance. Otherwise it would be a bit too boring. He shut down his equipment, the sound vibration ray, then checked the screen and nodded satisfactorily at a job well done. It was quite possible that any of the life-giving properties that were left could eventually land on a sphere containing conditions for propagation and thus start the evolutionary process over again. Once a sphere was suitable for a higher-consciousness life form, they would gather a pair or pairs of male and female subjects, move them across the galaxies and put them on the surface. The rest was left up to them, except for maybe an occasional 'nudge' as it was for their pet project.

"Let me take a look," project Earth was a source of entertainment. It had come so close to complete annihilation before, but it had managed to make comebacks without completely destroying itself, and on top of that, their gift had surfaced again. "Hmmm, interesting. It has left the Lemurian Mountain tops and crossed one of their oceans and is now in one of their densely populated areas, still on the move. That was a good sign. For a while there I thought it was on its way to… no! That's impossible!"

"Nothing is impossible, just improbable. They still have the scout ship that crashed there, although it's pretty beat up, although it's still capable of functioning. Imagine if they figured that out. Chances are against it, but you must admit, with this species, anything is possible."

"That would definitely speed up the process, in one direction or another," agreed Rawar. "For now our gift is headed away from the crash site. But for a moment I thought they might have figured it out. Their level of technology is at least capable of finding out what it isn't. But if they eventually put it together and figure what it is, we will be either having another member of the consortium or another mess to clean up."

"Our bet still stands. I just hope that if I do lose I can grab a pair or two of their species to put somewhere else before total destruction. You've got to admit; they're tenacious," replied Oxomoxo.

"For now they definitely deserve closer observation. We should stop by soon for a closer look." Rawar watched his partner's eyes light up. He had known for a long time that Oxomoxo was hoping these words would be said.

"Agreed. I would like to see how their personalities have developed. They're probably more diverse now." He had been hoping for this. Even though they had an ongoing bet, they both agreed that they enjoyed playing the game most of all.

BAJA CALIFORNIA

The sleepy town of Guaymas wasn't so sleepy at all anymore. In fact that it had turned from a small fishing village into a resort getaway tourist trap borderlining on circus material. Gringos from all walks of life were constantly fleeing from the north to converge on this community to 'let it all hang out' without the paranoia of getting busted for some minor infraction of what little law there was. With a little 'greasing' of the palm, the Federales would look the other way which was the desirable condition that had turned it into a boomtown. It had first become infamous for its week long spring break party, but now it seemed it went year round. Being the first coastal town to hit on mainland Mexico going south didn't hurt either. Add a few watersport amenities, a Club Med and a Riverboat Gambler and it was organized chaos complete. People came here to party, and party they did. Except for an occasional hurricane, the conditions were suitable the whole year around.

Once the entourage from the Bluebird reached the shore, Z quickly flagged a cab and disappeared. Mallory and the Rangers found a table under an umbrella at a bar and ordered three Cerveza Pacificos. And the ladies, well, they went shopping of course.

"What a Zoo. And all in the name of progress," muttered Townsend dryly. "We came through here in 1968 headed for the Olympics in Mexico City and this place was relatively nothing then." He almost had to yell to be heard because they were surrounded by party animals all under age testing the waters of oblivion. A beer and a half later Z pulled up in a Winnebago Chieftain, customed to allow its travelers to go in style. Ordinarily it would comfortably fit four, but the Raiders had modified it to fit twice as many. The cupboards had been removed and replaced by fold-away bunk beds which could also be used as shelves. The kitchen area had been reduced to a two-burner propane stove and small refrigerator. Under the sink had been refurbished into a storage area, the economy of space total. The sound system had been enhanced to that of a disco and the master bedroom was wall to wall futons and pillows. It was a penthouse on wheels. There was one curiosity however, right in the middle of the floor was a trap door leading outside. Its function was unquestionable, so nothing needed was to be explained. Z gave them a brief tour, showing them the 'emergency exit for contingencies' area and a false-backed toilet for putting things that didn't want to be found. "You can stash your Missing Link in here, and I hope you don't have to use the trapdoor," he explained. Nods of agreement went around then they proceeded to load the luggage. "One stop at the mercado and you are ready for action," he added.

Just then the ladies showed up with armloads of knick-knacks to make the trip enjoyable. They giggled with delight at seeing the bedroom area, Victoria giving Mallory a cat-eyeing-a-mouse look that made her intent obvious. The 'knick knacks' turned out to be a bottle of Mezcal, complete with the worm at the bottom, a couple of cases of Cerveza Pacificos and a small bottle containing pills resembling little pink hearts. "Benzadrina," explained the caretakers, for keeping you uuuppp alllll night," giving Mallory looks that needed no explanation.

"It's all yours," announced Z, "please take care of her because this is Loaf's little baby." And now the moment of truth. "You can be on your way any time or we can pay Hannibal a visit."

Mallory eyed his fellow travelers, the expectant look on their faces oblivious. He decided to toy with them a little. "Well, we definitely do have to get down to business," he watched their expressions drop... "Tomorrow." The ladies literally jumped for joy and the Rangers took on their all too familier 'dirty old man' expressions.

"Who is Hannibal anyway?"

"Oh that's the name of the paddle wheeler," answered Z, "the Hannibal Hamlin. History quiz. Which one of you lovelies knows who he is? Ah, er, was?" This brought on no response. "I'm not surprised. Hardly anyone does. It's pretty surprising considering he was vice-president to Abraham Lincoln."

"Very funny," remarked a skeptical Mallory. "Sorry, don't buy it. Everyone knows it's Andrew Johnson. No president Hamlin. I don't think so. Who was he really?" he asked.

"Ha! I've won so many bets on this one," laughed Z. "Seriously, he was VP during the first term. As the story goes he got fed up with the politics and war, slavery and all that. Add the incapability of the northern generals at the time and could anyone blame him? He wasn't that popular with the northern politicians anyway. Almost all of them except old Honest Abe himself. Get this, his last official act as Vice President was to bodily carry the new VP to his inauguration ceremony because he was too drunk to walk. That's some exit maneuver. I'd say that would be the last straw for Hannibal. He got up and walked out. Bravo! Some said he whistled Dixie as he was leaving. Probably to the horror of any within hearing distance. There was no love lost between Hannibal and the members of Yankee Congress. He's almost totally rubbed out of the history books. I've seen only one picture of him. He's at the inaugural ceremony and he's sitting next to Johnson. He's glowering in the picture and you can almost see the smoke coming out of his years. Anyway, needless to say he became a hero in the south, insomuch that he is the only person from the North to have a riverboat named after him. True story? It's all hearsay but a dubious distinction actually. And what's more we get to go out with Hannibal tonight!" Z was so pleased to have taken them all so completely by surprise. He would collect on the bet some time and was satisfied to be able to give a well deserved history lesson. "It's a general consensus in our clan that you can keep George Washington, Teddy Roosevelt, JFK or anyone else for that matter, Hannibal Hamlin: he's our man!"

"Wow, what a story," remarked Victoria. "You know, someone could actually write a book about that. Come to think of it, ever since we met, everything we've gone through could be a book, but who would believe it?"

"That's the beauty of it. It's all true even though it sounds like fiction," countered Mallory.

"If they make a movie out of it, Marlon Brando could play me," announced Townsend.

"I'll settle for Aahnuld," suggested Souza.

"More better Heckle and Jekyll," laughed Mallory.

"The men turned to Victoria and visually sized her up. They had to leave that one alone. "All right you perverts, I can read your filthy minds," with that they broke into some serious verbal hijinx until a powerful blast of a whistle interrupted the fun.

The crew of the Hannibal Hamlin were securing the lines by the time they arrived. The sternwheeler looked like it had come directly out of a time warp. It was painted gray and butternut yellow, the colors of the Confederate States of America and flew the 'Stars and Bars' on its flagpole. Built in 1862, she was originally named the Nathan Bedford Forrest who is credited for inventing Guerrilla Warfare. It was used mainly as a troop transport on the Mississippi during the Civil War until it got caught in the crossfire of Sherman's march to the sea. It had to be dry docked at the Savannah, Georgia shipyards and was mistakenly tagged beyond repair. There it sat until the 1880s destined for salvage when it was discovered upon closer inspection that the engines were not only intact, but in pristine condition. It then went through a major facelift, and then commissioned the Hannibal Hamlin. For the next forty years it was used for sightseeing and occasional private functions. Hannibal caught the attention of the Mob during prohibition and became a floating speakeasy. When prohibition lifted, the Mob sold it to the Mexican government and was brought to the Sea of Cortez to continue its nefarious activities. This continued until after WWII and then was brought dockside to be converted into a hotel. The company eventually went belly-up and it sat virtually unmolested until the early 70's then caught the attention of some California entre manures and Hawaii farmers. It was reconditioned once again, and riverboat gambling becomes popular, the rest is history"

"Entre manure?"

"A slip of the tongue."

"Right. As in bullshit artists."

"My God, it's absolutely beautiful," remarked a stunned Victoria, "and so big."

"It weighs eighty six tons and can house up to four hundred passengers at once. There's four deck levels including the engine room. It's 99.8 feet long, 27 feet wide, and has only a 4.5 foot draft. The steam engines still run perfectly but we installed a couple of one thousand horsepower Detroit Diesels as backup in case we get into a pinch," explained Z.

"We?" quizzed Mallory, "don't tell me, I've already figured it out. You're the Entremanures. Humph."

"Well well well, look what fell out of the sky. Nice landing Z, you're getting better." Down the gangway came a sight out of the 19th century. Dressed in the uniform of the Confederate States Navy complete with a feather plume in his hat came a tall gangly man with a full white beard and an eyepatch. As he approached, he lifted the patch to reveal two blue green eyes that contained the mirth of a half century. If he had been hired just for his looks, he would have been perfect for the job. Add the knowledge of how to run the century old boat and there wouldn't be a better candidate. "Good afternoon. My name is captain Tim Le Ballister, and who might you be?" Captain Le Ballister walked right by the men, totally ignoring them, went straight toward the ladies, bowing, then kissing their hand as he spoke. The move caught Mallory by surprise, but not Z nor the Rangers; they already had his number.

"Nice to see you too, Turtle," said Z sarcastically.

"Don't bother me. Can't you see I'm busy?" barked the captain. He was playing his role to the hilt. "This is important business. You clowns can wait."

Mallory caught the gist of the situation and let it slide. It was now obvious that they were all old friends and barbs would fly back and forth just as it had been going on all along so far.

Le Ballister broke into a huge grin and addressed everybody. "Hi. My name is Tim or Turtle if you like. Save introductions because Randall called me earlier to give me fair warning and filled me in. You are already totally set up. State rooms for all in VIP and your evening wear is on your beds. HT knows where to go and I have work to do. See you at the captain's table tonight. He imperiously marched off.

HT led the way to the top deck to the hallway right behind the wheelhouse. Mallory noticed that the entire crew were in Rebel Navy uniforms. They were about their business except for the occasional wolf whistle when the ladies passed by. When they reached the staterooms they were reserved for so and so on each door knob, as everything was pre planned, which it was. As each door was opened they found that the rooms were set up for double occupancy with a door on the inside that connected the rooms all the way down the hall. The doors were open to reveal the fact that all seven rooms were connected and everybody could eventually have their choice of where to sleep. Each also had the choice of having their own private sanctuary or being involved in one giant get-together. These people plan for everything thought Mallory. He had been disappointed with the setup until he saw the interconnecting doors. Then it became clear to him that the stateroom doors were just a front and the whole hallway was connected if need be. The rooms had been 'assigned' just to get the correct person to their evening wear.

The 'evening wear' turned out to be costumes from the Civil War era. When the ladies saw theirs, they immediately slammed the doors. From the shrieks and giggles it wasn't hard to tell they were going to be dressed to kill. Mallory found a suit similar to Jackson's, except it was white. When he noticed a 'suitcase' he figured no doubt he was a carpetbagger. At the moment nothing else really mattered until he noticed that the bed was a duplicate of an old feather mattress. He pushed the suitcase aside to test how soft it might be, and found himself melting into bliss. He managed to crawl out a few hours later.

The badge had teeth was the only thing Mallory could remember, as he awoke out of a long, deep, well deserved nap. Somewhere in the vicinity of his hearing came an unfamiliar voice saying "exquisite" amidst the giggles of his girl 'friends'.

He lay there in a few minutes gathering his wits, and tried to formulate his dream. He already could only remember small pieces, but the main character was an enraged agent Fife with a man-eating badge. Mallory was backed into a corner with Victoria behind him and apparently there was nowhere to go. The chomping badge is approaching. That's when he woke up. He shook his head to clear the cobwebs, got out of his man eating bed and took a shower. Once clean and freshly shaved he put on the costume and admired himself in the mirror. Not too shabby he thought and tilted the top hat just for effect. He then took his walking cane and tapped lightly on the door the giggles had come from. He opened the door to find the ladies, Captain Le Ballister and Jackson at the table playing poker. Yeah, that kind. At their side was an open bottle of champagne. They gave him sly grins but that wasn't what caught his attention. It was Scarlett O'Hara in the flesh. The dresses were clearly designed to push up and expose their breasts. Definitely some kind of sexposure. The cut went down to almost their nipples to reveal a pair of absolutely gorgeous melons. The waistband was extra tight so as to accentuate a womanly hourglass figure and the hemline of their skirts were cut up the front to reveal the black fishnet stockings they wore. It was a combination of dancehall girl and southern belle and they wore it well. Either the Captain or Jackson managed to find a hairdresser because each of the ladies had their hair coiffed in a fashion of the 19th century, mostly piled on top in the mastery of pins and curls. Exquisite was absolutely the right word.

"Oh hello Connor. Care to join us?" asked Victoria. "You're the last one up. It seems you 'men' all had the same idea. You all fell out all afternoon." She spoke with a southern accent to complete the part, "you all" turning into "y'all." It was clear the girls were having a ball, and Mallory didn't want to spoil the fun. Before he could answer she added, "the rest of the guys are at the bar taking in the sights. Apparently all the ladies are dressed like this and the dinner party starts in about an hour." If that wasn't a hint, nothing was. "Besides, we're in good hands with Turtle and 'Grabbo' here." This was true, except Tim and Jackson looked like circling vultures ready to attack their prey. Mallory contained his little bit of jealousy, politely declined, and decided to go take in the sights. As he closed the door there was another burst of laughter and he stomped away in a huff trying to figure out why he felt that way. That was until he reached the bottom of the staircase and ran into a black eyed beauty that looked at him from behind a fan in front of her face. She sized him up from toe to head in that order and her look was more than suggestive. All that had just happened before was forgotten.

The sun had set behind the coastal mountains of Baja California turning the Sea of Cortez into gold. The full moon was rising out of the east to light up the night. Mallory found his way to the bar and his knees almost buckled when he saw his friends. Z and HT were dressed similar to Mallory except in black, but the Rangers were a totally different matter. Townsend's wide girth was accentuated by a giant black belt with a silver buckle and a crimson sash as well. He had a red and white striped shirt and white pants that went to his knees. His head was covered with a red bandana tied at the side and a big gold earring in his ear. Tucked in his belt was an oversized 'Arkansas Toothpick' to complete the picture. Souza, well, looked like Morgan the Pirate. Blue hat and topcoat covered a silk shirt with ruffles on the collar and at the cuffs. Black pants with white knee socks and gold gilded black boots with gold buckles on them. The picture was complete with a phony red beard that was attached to his face somehow. Out of one sleeve was a hook instead of a hand. The only thing missing was a parrot on one of these clown's shoulders. In actuality they looked more at home in this attire than anything else. And to top it all off with that fact was they were surrounded by Southern Belles already.

"It never fails," said Z as Mallory joined him at the bar. "Every time they show up they steal the show. They have those duds reserved for them only. Hell, they even have a fan club." Z was on the verge of maybe looking a little disgruntled, when he broke into a huge grin and a gut laugh. "But we have our hands full already, so what the hell."

"I'm not so sure, Captain Le Ballister and Jackson are busy cornering the market downstairs. We might be freelance tonight," answered Mallory.

"Oh don't worry about them, they're just getting the gals primed, so to speak. Grabbo is married with two kids and captain Le Ballister, let's just say he's 'Cock of the Walk' around here. In fact there's Grabbo's wife.

Z discreetly pointed to the black eyed beauty Mallory had to run into before. She caught their glance, removed her fan and blew them a kiss. Mallory's momentary dream went right down the drain. "Although they do have an agreement that lets them 'fool around' at times," he added, "and tonight's primetime; it's their monthly full moon cruise. This event is looked forward to by people around the globe. We were lucky Captain Magic called ahead. Le Ballister had to bump a few Club Med people to get us on board. Reservations are taken a year in advance and it's strictly word of mouth advertising. It also helps that we own the boat." Their conversation was interrupted by the blast of Hannibal's whistle. "That's the signal for all on board that's going aboard. Get ready, this is going to turn into a real circus."

By the time the second whistle blew a half hour later, the boat was packed to capacity and then some. A steady stream of nineteenth century partygoers came from all directions. The town bars emptied at once. Limousines and taxis from Club Med and even zodiacs from the moored boats outside delivered people in various stages of inebriation all dressed for the festivities. From Hookers to Southern Belles to High Society Dames and from Bandidos to Cowboys to Riverboat Gamblers, all had gone out of their way to play the part. A chorus of boos erupted when a limo pulled up and out came a squad of soldiers in Union Blue. Boo's turned into cheers when they waved a white flag and pointed to the large white P on their back designating prisoners. Next to the two pirates probably the most outstanding garb was a Fire and Brimstone Preacher followed by a string of the most lovely Alcolites ever to wear almost nothing. Wild Bill Hickok and probably what was supposed to be the Earp Brothers and Doc Holliday made their entry and even emissaries from the Indian nations made an appearance and came aboard. A band of bandidos arrived shooting up the town 'with blanks of course' on mules, but when they came to dockside most of them fell off their steeds they were so drunk. They were almost 86ed until they produced those bottles of little pink hearts and agreed to take two apiece to sober up. Everyone had one thing in common: to tear it up.

The third whistle came in three booming blasts and the Hannibal Hamlin cast off its lines as the paddlewheels began to turn taking the boat out on to the Sea of Cortez. About ten minutes out, three speed boats came out of a secluded cove with 'pirates' swinging their cutlasses demanding to board. They offloaded and then tied their boats in a string line behind the paddle wheeler. In reality they weren't really party crashers, they just liked to board that way. Then the band started to play in the main salon after the boarding party, as if they knew what was going to happen; which was true. The instruments included two guitars, a banjo, fiddle, juice harp, harmonica, a washboard, and a washtub bass. There were even a number of spoon players to accompany the washboard rhythm section. Their numbers would ebb and flow like the tides throughout the night. The main salon/banquet hall had a roulette wheel, dice tables, slot machines and a poker tournament throughout the room. On one side of the room was a stage for the Burlesque and Can-Can shows. An almost connected horseshoe designed table filled the entire room to facilitate dining for those who chose to eat. On the other side was a giant long bar. The room took almost the entire first floor and was large enough to fit all (four hundred plus) passengers at once. Which was exactly what was to happen that night.

    The Captain's Table was at the center of the horseshoe. It was open only on one end so food and drink servers could facilitate more efficiently. Le Ballister made his entrance to a rousing applause from the guests on board. On each arm were Sunshine and Surfer Sue. Jackson was escorting Victoria alongside, and it was easy to see they were all in their cups. They weren't staggering but they were well lit. A close call either way. They made their way to the center of the horseshoe like a King and his retinue overseeing his court. The ladies were stylishly set in their chairs next to the Captain. There was a ship's bell conveniently set behind the Captain's Chair and before he sat down he rang it once to get everyone's attention. "Ladies and gentlemen welcome aboard the Hannibal Hamlin. Courtesy is the word for the evening, and the casualty area is always open for those who need a break in the action. Enjoy." Le Ballister spoke like a true politician. He then sat down at the center of the table and the band struck up a peppy rendition of The Rose of Alabama. This particular tune started slow and picked up pace as it progressed. By the time it was over there were whoops and hollers everywhere in the shindig and it was immediately in full swing. Iced buckets of champagne were brought tableside for those who had chosen to indulge. The Bars were full as well as the gambling tables, and the dance floor was a mixture of Indians dancing with acolytes and so forth. The 'casualty area' was a dozen bunk beds stashed in a far corner. So far, only one of the 'bandidos' that had fallen off his mule was out of action. The pink hearts hadn't kicked in yet, but that was only a matter of time…

    Mallory stayed at the bar taking in the scene and polished off a few Margaritas which was the drink of the evening. The bartender definitely knew his stuff as shot glasses were out of the question. A generous three finger pour of Cuervo Gold tequila was topped off by a mixture that obviously came from real limes. Only half the rim of the glass is salted so the consumer could have their choice. The only difference from a common Margarita was the floater of 151 proof rum. A couple of these and Mallory was well on his way. After a brief conversation with one of the Acolytes he found out that the 'Preacher' was in reality the town Sheriff and the Acolytes ran the town escort service; but there was no charge for escorting that night. Mallory politely declined for the moment but left his option open by asking for a dance in the future. After a curtsy and a bow they parted ways and Mallory made his way to the table where captain Le Ballister was holding court.

    "…is called a 'open steam cycle.' The water is taken directly from the ocean and after being purified it is fed into the boilers by a feed pump. It is then converted into what is known as 'saturated steam' which is one hundred eighty seven degrees centigrade that is collected in the steam drum. It is then fed into a super heater that raises the temperature to two hundred thirty degrees centigrade from the coal-fired Scotch Boilers. The smoke that flows from the smokebox to the funnels is fed into the cylinders and expands; hence power. Oh, good evening Mister Mallory," captain Le Ballister might have been a wolf in sheep's clothing, but he was an articulate one at that.

"Hello everyone. Great party Captain, I hope I'm not interrupting…." Mallory had approached cautiously, one reason being he didn't want to disturb the Captain's dissertation, the other being the effects of the margaritas he drank were coming on strong.

"By all means, no. I was just explaining the benefits of steam power. If all engines ran like this we would have a lot cleaner air to breathe. And these engines are as good as the day they came out of Savannah over a hundred years ago." Captain Le Ballister was clearly proud of his boat and had every right to be so. He went on. "After the Detroit Diesels were installed we fired them up once just to see what they could do; a test run so to speak. Old Hannibal almost turned into a hydrofoil. It went so fast it seemed like it was floating on a cushion of air, so we closed them down. It's still good to know they're in there though, just in case we get caught in a pinch. One never knows…." Le Ballister exchanged wry smiles with Z who had joined the table, an unspoken covenant between them. Mallory couldn't help but wonder just how far their 'under the table' empire stretched.

His thought was interrupted by an explosion of laughter at the far end of the table. The Rangers had placed themselves at each end of the horseshoe. Mallory had noticed at each table setting a card with each guest's name embossed on it so everyone had a preconceived place to sit. As if reading his mind, Le Ballister explained, "we put Souza and Townsend there so the people at the end don't feel left out. If it were possible we would have a round table King Arthuresque so we all would feel equal. But we do have to keep the food and drinks flowing, which reminds me…" Captain Le Ballister turned around and gave two short rings on the bell, which was the signal for the food to be served. If anyone had any doubts of eating, the smells of the food being rolled in on the hand carts took care of that. Giant platters of southern fried chicken, mounds of smashed potatoes, collard greens and black eyed peas were put in the center. Eventually everyone found their place to sit and Mallory noticed they were evenly distributed so there were no factions that had come together, were sitting with each other. This allowed people to mingle and make new acquaintances during the meal. Le Ballister again read Mallory's mind. "That's one of the funnest things about this party; choosing where people are to sit. It's definitely a science and it rarely backfires". Mallory saw the reasoning behind this and was equally delighted to be sitting between one of the acolytes and the black eyed beauty. Victoria was seated with the Captain and the Preacher and the Rangers were holding court at each end of the horseshoe table amidst a bevy of beauties, their jolly persona taking control of the situation. They were naturals.

After an appetizer of split pea and ham hock soup, the melt-in-your-mouth entree was served. The hall actually momentarily quieted down as the food was devoured. A giant cake was pulled in and out popped a beauty wearing nothing but frosting. This set the standard for the rest of the evening. The stage lit up and when the curtain opened it revealed a string of can-can goddesses from heaven. Each leg-lift brought a cheer from the crowd. After a comedy routine the curtains closed and the band struck up again and the dance floor quickly filled. Without even asking, the black eyed beauty grabbed Mallory's hand and led him to the dance floor. He soon found himself rubbing against her beautiful curves that were in all the right places. He also felt a hot breath on the nape of his neck. This lady certainly was not shy, thought Mallory. After each tune, Le Ballister rang the bell and announced, "switch partners" and everyone had no choice but to comply. Now Mallory was holding one of the delicious can-can girls who was equally as uninhibited. After a couple of tunes Mallory found his way back to the bar and ran into Jackson. "It seems my woman has taken a liking to you," he chuckled. Before Mallory could think of an apology, He went on, "just in case you're curious, we do have an open style of relationship, so shoot your best shot if you like." He winked at Mallory and moved on to socialize.

Mallory's mind went momentarily blank. It had reached his saturation point. The events leading up to this moment had been non-stop. It was as if the mental breaker switch in the fuse box of his brain had blown. Blissful void. A combination of the responsibility he had accidentally stumbled into and the subsequent events thereof; throw in mind altering substances and on top of it all, having a partner as sensual and desirable as Victoria, and now he was on an antique paddlewheeler that could possibly turn from a free-for-all into an outright orgy was just about enough that he could handle. His cupeth overfloweth.

"Connor, are you all right?" Victoria noticed her partner's blank stare and that was new to her. During their brief partnership they had come very close, but this look was a new addition. She had been sitting with the Captain listening to another one of his anecdotes when she noticed Mallory walk by in a trance-like state. This caught her attention so she watched him approach the bar, have a brief conversation with Jackson and then it just looked like his lights went out, oblivious to the reverie around him. "Knock knock, is anybody home?" she joked.

Mallory turned and stared and then smiled, "the badge had teeth," he sang. Captain Le Ballister had noticed the situation and followed a concerned Victoria to the bar. One look at Mallory and his suspicions were confirmed. "Uh Oh…. The cooks have been at it again," he observed.

"Pardon me?" quizzed Victoria.

"Our cooks. They're Indians from Huatla. A place far up in the mountains south of Mexico City where the strongest Psilocybin Mushrooms on Earth come from. They're used for the religious ceremony held yearly in Puebla. Our cooks like to 'spike' the punch so to speak," explained Le Ballister. It's relatively harmless unless you don't know what hit you, it's actually fun if you are prepared.

"He's going to be alright, right?"

"Oh yeah. It'll pass. It's the spores from the mushroom that contain the psilocybin. My cooks just fry them up for the brown gravy. Quite tasty, actually. And it adds a little, ah, color; literally."

Mallory came back into focus. "Wow! Vicky! You look so beautiful! Let's Dance!" His voice was a touch higher, but it wasn't broken so they didn't have to fix it. Without waiting for an answer, Mallory led her to the dance floor where his moves became so animated it was clear he was enjoying himself, again.

Townsend had noticed the goings-on and came up to the captain. "Gravy?"

"Yep."

"Oh boy! Seconds for me," and he was off.
And the Moon smiled...

The blood vessels in his temples were like clockwork even before Mallory opened his eyeballs. He cautiously opened one and it felt like heavy grit sandpaper. Although he still had his suit on, he had made it to bed. How, was a mystery, but that didn't matter at the moment. There was a shape under the covers beside him that he didn't know who it belonged to. He closed his eyes again and tried to reconstruct the pieces of last night's puzzle.

It was a blur of dancing with a variety of beautiful women and something about a lifeboat and the black eyed beauty, then Townsend's voice saying, "don't fight it, flow with it. It's the hongos." hongos? What the hell was hongos? Then it came back to him; Hongos were Mushrooms. He had unwittingly become a pawn in a psilocybin experiment, but so had everybody else. Intense colorful hallucinations and all noise seemed to have a reverberating echo to it. Was it another dream or had he, or had he not, participated in a group grope? The portents pointed to the affirmative. The shape beside him sighed and rolled over and he was thankful to see it was Victoria. Then on his arm he noticed an assortment of garters he must have collected throughout the night. Then it suddenly dawned on him that even if he did remember, should he admit it....

There was a tap on the door and Mallory slowly got out of bed. As he walked to the door it felt like he was walking on glue. As he opened the door the hinges squeaked so bad it was like spikes being driven into his skull.... There in the corridor on the opposite wall was Townsend leaning with his arms crossed, with a bemused smile on his face.

"Good morning. I hope you feel better than you look," observed Townsend.

"What happened? Wa-" was all Mallory could muster.

"What you don't know won't hurt you. Let's just say you were the life of the party."

"Unnhhhh..."

"Here! Doctor's orders." Townsend produced two yellow pills plus a pink heart. "Percs and Bennies. Take these and lay back down. Trust me, you'll know when to get up. And here's some for Vicki if she wants." At the mention of her name, Victoria opened her eyes and smiled. She was in much better shape than Mallory. Just then, two of the acolytes came up and grabbed Townsend by each arm and ushered him down the hall. He managed a "duty calls. See you later," before he was gone.

Mallory sat back down on the bed and stared at the pills in his hand. Victoria passed him a bedside water glass and he tossed them in his mouth with a water chaser. He gave Victoria a weak smile and fell back into prone position, hoping Townsend's 'prescription' would make haste.

Victoria wasn't one to rub it in, nor was she prone to treat him like a baby. So she chose the middle path. "Well you sure were a piece of work last night. You might have had the most fun of all. I take it you don't remember much."

"Unngghhh."

"Stop your whining. You were swilling those margaritas like water and it's no wonder your head feels like an anvil. You were... Do you really want to know?"

"Unnnggghhhh."

"You were everywhere. I don't think there's a square inch of this boat you missed. You are a happy-go-lucky type of fun drunk, and that's what matters. Your imitation of Barney Fife was deplorable. You kept saying 'my badge has teeth', or 'bite me'. Most everyone thought it was funny, although after a while you started getting on some people's nerves. When you went to arrest the Preacher and take his girls into custody is when I came to the rescue. He's the Sheriff hereabouts, you know. So don't expect any sympathy from me. You earned it."

Mallory decided to feign amnesia. Although it was all coming back in bits and pieces, he told Victoria about his dream in hopes that it would at least alleviate something. The lifeboat, the group grope and how he got the garters he thought best to keep to himself. "I don't remember" has been a universal scapegoat since the beginning of time. Soon his hangover began to evaporate as Townsend's prescription kicked in. If there was ever a time to put the past behind and look ahead, this was one of them. He mentioned something to that effect and Victoria agreed. The party was over and the party was just about to begin.

"Well, that's it. You're ready to rumble," observed Z, who also was a little rough around the edges, but it hadn't kept him from functioning. It had been a ragged lineup that left the Hannibal Hamlin. The attendees that had boarded the night before we're slowly filing off, more than a little worse for wear. "Now you can see why this is only a monthly affair, because it takes that long for some to recover," he remarked as they were saying their goodbyes. Mallory actually had seen some that looked worse than he felt. But they didn't have Townsend's remedy either. It took a little prodding from uncle Ray and Dad, but by noon the Winnebago was loaded and the quartet ready to go. "I've also had reports that every time a vehicle got near the Winnebago, their security alarms would go off. It has people wondering…."

That was their cue. Townsend jumped into the driver's seat and Mallory rode shotgun. Souza and Victoria took the back seats. Z, HT and the caretakers made a beeline to the Bluebird. "See you later Turtle," chorused the Rangers.

"Turtle?" asked Mallory, "what's up with that?"

The Rangers were having a big laugh over captain Le Ballister's reaction. Finally Souza calmed down enough to explain: "That was his nickname when we dove for Black Coral. Tim Turtle. He became so notorious he had to fake his death: lost at sea. There were only a few of us in on the situation so we had to fake a wake and everything, all of the time holding a straight face. We think he's full of shit because he still uses his real name. So when no one is around within earshot, we rub it in a little. Turtle will get even. He always does."

The stories of the pranks the Black Coral divers had traded throughout the years were the subject of the day on the road to Guadalajara. Most of them were too unbelievable to be true, but considering the source and and the subjects involved, it was a definite possibility/probability. The effects of the remedy had kicked in and the ride turned into another event on wheels. By the time they reached Guadalajara they had come down and were road weary. They parked on the outskirts and within minutes their mobile condominium was prepared for a rest richly deserved.

One thing Mallory knew for sure in his first waking moments is that he was going to a hotel. Even if he could call them waking moments, he had been on the receiving end of one of the most miserable nights of sleep in his entire life. This was because of two reasons. The first one being he was suffering from a delayed reaction from the events leading up to this night: Maui, the hurricane, Wood's, the flying experiment, and finally the Hannibal Hamlin had been non-stop, not to mention the object they now labeled 'The Missing Link.' When Townsend's 'hangover cure' kicked in, his 'come down' had been delayed yet another day. They made his headache evaporate and they put a 'zing' into the rest of the day. The road trip was punctuated by the bottle of mezcal in which he had gotten the worm. It seemed like a good idea at the time, but now…(?) The second reason was the two human buzzsaws in the next room. The walls had been shaking all night long and the Rangers were oblivious to it all. Mallory had tried nudging, yelling and even throwing water to no avail. They would briefly stop, roll over and proceed to go right back into the Chainsaw Massacre of his night's sleep. On top of this Victoria had managed to steal his pillow in the night and was using them for ear muffs. More power to her, he thought, at least someone had the right idea.

He less than gingerly got out of bed and opened the door to a fusillade of snores from 'Daddy and Uncle Ray.' He slammed the door against the wall of sound emanating from the front of the Winnebago and sat back down on the bed. He glanced at the angelic figure who lay on her side with one ear buried in a pillow and the other pillow firmly secured by her arm covering the other. Next to her were the hangover cures she declined to take. This left Mallory no option. He silently went to the bedside table and grabbed them and the water, quickly threw down one and pocketed the rest, giving no thought whatsoever to their addictive tendencies. Besides, he could rationalize his bad night's sleep into the scenario. He braved the door once again and made a beeline to the peace and tranquility that lay outside, grabbing a bottle of Cerveza Pacifico along the way.

He stepped outside and came face to face with the Virgin Mary, or at least a sculptured version of the same. She was the overseer of one of the most beautiful little roadside parks he had ever seen. A eucalyptus forest with trees at least a hundred feet high surrounded the park. Hedges of multi-colored bougainvillea dotted the perimeter along with patches of yellow, red, and white hibiscus all In bloom. In the center stood the Virgin Mary elevated in ancient but well taken care of fountain with plumes of water coming from each corner, with birds of every description taking advantage of the situation. This park has been here for a long time thought Mallory as he took in the sights. If this was any indication of how Guadalajara was going to be, he liked it already. He sat down on one of the many picnic tables, popped open his beer and waited for everyone to wake up, and his 'headache cure' to kick in. A half hour later Mallory was beginning to feel his oats when the door to the Winnebago opened and out stepped Victoria with a bottle of Cerveza Pacifico in each hand. After taking in the shock of the beauty of her surroundings she approached the table where Mallory sat.

"Good morning. After last night, you can probably use one of these. Do you happen to know where those 'cures' are?" It sounded like one continuous sentence. Victoria had obviously suffered from the barrage of sound from the Rangers also. Mallory guiltily produced the last two and handed them over. "I'm surprised you saved any. Their snoring was bad enough, but you're groaning made it even worse."

Mallory related his hotel idea and it took no convincing whatsoever. Victoria went as far as to suggest a two day stay to recuperate and plan for what lay ahead. It had been reasonably easy so far, but the next stop was not the US of A and all that didn't go with it. They agreed to call Dr. Bloomfield to get an update on their status within the bureaucracy. When the Rangers finally awoke they took a bewildered stance, each blaming the other on the snoring. Their not-too-innocent faces bespoke of an eternal ongoing battle on the subject. Once refreshed and a few Cerveza Pacificos later, they headed towards the center of town.

Guadalajara, the secod largest city in Mexico, was a monument to old Spain. Age old cathedrals, forts and parks were spread throughout the city; a testament to the historical value of Spanish influence. Upon reaching the main plaza in the center of the city, they checked into the Hotel Francis, one of the oldest buildings standing. The hotel, originally built in 1610, had withstood wars, rebellions, and revolutions and was a tribute to the decorum of the 17th century. It had been renovated in 1981 and was declared a National Monument. When the travelers first laid eyes on it, there was no doubt in their minds that this was where they wanted to stay. They took three rooms on the second floor. Mallory and Victoria paired up and the ongoing snoring feud made each Ranger take their own room. The speleologists requested one down the hall as not to suffer the horrors of the night before. They pitied whoever had the ill luck to be next to the Rangers but it wasn't their problem; been there, done that. Victoria was particularly delighted with the 'birdcage' elevators that moved from floor to floor. They were rebuilt antiques and moved slowly but efficiently. The rooms had no air conditioning but the extra large ceiling fans made up for that. To Mallory it could have been a cardboard box for all he cared as long as it had a bed far away enough from the Rangers. And as soon as they opened the door to their room, he dropped his suitcase on the floor and walked like a Zombie to the bed and fell face first and didn't move for hours. He awoke late in the afternoon to the sound of Victoria coming back through the door. She had done what any red blooded American woman would do; went shopping.

"It lives," she muttered as she threw a small bag on the bed. "For you," she added and went directly into the bathroom. A short time later Mallory heard the shower tap running, so he rolled over and fell back out. When he opened his eyes again he was looking at a goddess from heaven. She had shopped well. She was wearing a white linen embroidered blouse with matching skirt, and wrapped around her hips was a hand knitted red sash to accentuate her hourglass figure. Laid down on the bed next to him was a white linen collarless shirt and pants, and on the floor a new pair of Huarache sandals. "They should fit, it's a one-size-fits-all type of wear. Take a shower." Pinching her nose. "You need it. It's dinner time."

Mallory did as he was told and after the shower he felt much better. When he came out of the bathroom, the room was empty with a note on the bed saying 'at the bar with uncle Ray and your dad.' Next to the bag Victoria had thrown earlier was a set of earplugs with a note saying 'for the trip.'

"Bless her heart," he said to himself as he tossed down a headache cure into his mouth. The pink heart he let slide; it was time for some serious R & R. He left the room and went downstairs to what turned out to be a piano bar. The Rangers were in the crowd up close and personal singing:

La Cucaracha, La Cucaracha
ya no puede caminar
porque no tiene, porque no tiene
la marihuana que fumar

And having a good old time. Somehow the Rangers had absconded with a pair of senioritas and we're trading shots of tequila.

"Hey son, pull up a chair and lighten your load," said Townsend jovially. "This is Solange and Alba. Ladies, this is my son Dick. He enunciated 'Dick' heavily and broke out into a gut laugh." Everyone got the joke except for the ladies.

'Dick' muttered a sterile "pleezed ta meetcha," still not quite awake enough to be in on the festivities. Mallory declined a shooter but accepted a bottle of Corona and a lime. Victoria planted a small peck on the cheek and blew in his ear. They were all way ahead of him in the inebriation department, but he was just pleased to be relatively back to the land of the living.

Townsend then added, "hey Dick, do you know how that song translates? Here goes. The cockroach, the cockroach, crawled across the floor, because he didn't have, because he didn't have any marijuana to smoke." More laughter from the tipsy group. Even Mallory managed a small chuckle. A few more rounds were consumed and then it was time for dinner.

The senoritas, who had been swept up by the charm, and wallets, of the Rangers suggested 'El Restaurante Mirador' located on the rim of the 'Plaza de Internationale.' Its outside courtyard overlooked the entire main plaza of the city. It was a local favorite for two reasons: The first being the Mariachi Band complete with musicians dressed in silver studded Charro outfits and wide brim hats playing violin, guitars, bass, and vihuela, a five string guitar. The second reason was their famous dish, Chile Relleno Roulette. This was a platter of chile rellenos, with one special extra hot green chili thrown in with the rest. It was completely disguised so no one could tell who got it until the first bite. It was a joke among the local population to lead gringos like lambs to slaughter. The platter was delivered among the tortillas, beans and rice and everyone served themselves tentatively, ready for the first bite. This was a special favorite of the musicians who gathered around the table to serenade and watch the fun. Mallory was convinced he was doomed from the start, as each participant took their first bite all at the same time, supposedly. Victoria and the senoritas passed their test, then Townsend. It was Mallory's turn and he raised the fork to his mouth figuring, no guts, no glory. He bit into the relleno and was relieved to find it wasn't him. All eyes turned to Souza. Just like another day in the park, he bit, stopped chewing for a second. His face turned magenta as he attempted a few more chews, then let it drop out of his mouth. "Aiyeeee!" chanted the Mariachis, but much to their surprise, Souza forked another bite and proceeded to polish off the whole relleno. "Arriba! Arriba!" went the whole crowd as Souza dropped his fork and looked around the table. He had overcome the impossible, but was incapable of speech. His face was beet red and he almost had tendrils of smoke coming out of his ears. The unwritten law was if anybody could eat the whole thing, the restaurant picked up the tab. Souza was an instant hero. When he finally could speak he invited the musicians to try Hawaiian red chili peppers someday. The Mariachis struck up a tune as the festivities gathered momentum. The topic of conversation after dinner was how 'Mariachi' became their name. No one really knew but there were three theories. The first was that it derived from the French word for marriage but there weren't any French people around at the time. The second was that it was the indigenous word for Pilla or Cirimo tree, in which the guitar is made and the third and most popular was that it was named after a virgin saint, Maria H, mah-ree-ah-ah-chay. The argument was as old as the city but it was a never ending source of entertainment. Mallory's tolerance level was at a low ebb so left the pack to their own demise. He strolled back to the room and laid down to the lullaby of the mariachis in the distance. He was soon out like a light.

The next morning arrived like a blink of an eye and he woke to the familiar lump under the blankets beside him. He had heard nothing of her entrance and had no idea how long she had carried on, so he got up quietly and let her sleep in. He went down to the hotel's central courtyard for breakfast and was surprised to see the Rangers and senoritas up already. He wasn't particularly pleased about the situation but joined the table anyway. The only difference from the night before was that the senoritas we're hanging all over the Rangers like they had been lifelong friends.

"Good morning son," chirped Townsend, "have a good night sleep? You look a hell of a lot better." He winked at Mallory, looking like a dog with a bone which was an apt analogy. Before Mallory could answer he went on. "We have just been given a history lesson." I bet you have thought Mallory. "This town was founded by 'Bloody Guzman', Nuneo Beltran de Guzman, actually. He came to New Spain after the conquest as first president of their 'Advensia'; a court to investigate the charges against Hernando Cortez, and replace the government since the fall of the Aztec Empire," lectured Townsend.

Souza joined in on the lesson. "In 1529 he stole the treasury's money and with five hundred discontented Conquistadors and ten thousand Indians, went north. After two failed attempts at settlement, the third was a success. He earned his nickname by the wholesale slaughter of the tribes in the area. Charges were finally brought against him and in 1536 he was taken back to Spain in chains where he died in prison. The only thing he had done right was give the city its name. In 1541, there was a failed uprising and from then on the city grew its roots and the rest is history." The recount of historical facts brought on an applause from the senoritas. The Rangers were clearly basking in their own particular conquest. Mallory thanked them for the history lesson and left the table for some peace and quiet. It was time to think things out.

He picked a secluded table in the corner by the fountain, the running water having a calming effect on his frayed nerves. He was perplexed ever since they landed on the mainland. It had been one continual party. If they were on such a monumental mission, then why were they having so much fun? Should that worry me? Or is it the fact that I know it's not going to last, he wondered. Then there's Victoria. His feelings for her were starting to run far deeper than a partnership or casual fling. And, partnership in what? The seriousness of the situation was intangible simply because they didn't know what they were dealing with. Not that he minded it, but the people who had helped them so far weren't exactly pillars of society. Was he supposed to be having such fun, maybe falling in love with a singularly most heavy commitment lying ahead? And what would happen when it's over? Will it ever be over? What is that damn thing?

His reverie was interrupted by Victoria approaching his table. She was still dressed in angelic white, but the waistband had turned into a head scarf and she was wearing a pair of dark sunglasses. She appeared a little bit pekid and a mite unsteady. She pulled up a chair and managed a meek "good morning" and poured herself a cup of coffee from the silver pot on the table.

"Ohhh, I don't feel so good."

"You look like how I felt yesterday," observed Mallory. "Don't fret, it'll pass. Take just one 'headache cure' and you'll be alright in no time. How did it go last night?"

She took off her shades and gave him a withering stare. "As soon as you left me those mariachis were on me like flies on sh… Ah, spots on dice. They were charming and all, but everytime my glass was empty they replaced it with a full one. By the time I could get away there were three lined up in a row for me to drink. When I stood up to go, the world started spinning. Richard and Raymond had to carry me back. She reached into her bag and took out the bottle of pink hearts and tossed them down with coffee, defying him to say anything. "Don't you ever leave me like that again Connor Mallory!"

Wow, I didn't know I was her guardian thought Mallory. Is that a good or bad sign, he pondered. He hoped for the good but was prepared for the bad: relationships hadn't really been his forte. There really wasn't any time to ponder this anyhow. He had to tread lightly over Victoria's last statement as to not open another can of worms; they had a truckload already. Besides, she was in enough of a fragile state.

"Sorry, I wasn't thinking," was another universal scapegoat. "Listen, I've been thinking. We've got to get a hold of Dr. Bloomfield for an update. Then we should try to get a hold of your ex uncle; be prepared as they say. Not until you're feeling better of course, but that shouldn't take long. The fun and games have to be put on the back burner," said Mallory.

As if reading his mind, Souza came up to the table. "Morning. We're going to escort the ladies home and we'll be right back. It's time we got back down to business. Back in a few." It was perfect timing. They had successfully breezed over the relationship scenario and were back on track to the road that lay ahead.

A few cups of coffee later, Victoria was feeling better and the Rangers had returned. They agreed to pack and go meet in the speleologists room for the phone calls. The three hours time difference would make it lunch hour up on Haleakala.

Dr. Harold Bloomfield was sitting in his office having a local style plate lunch. Things had subsided since the circus left town, all except for special agent Fife. He was like a pitbull refusing to let go after his bite. Bloomfield had a grudging admiration for Fife's tenacity and dedication to the assignment. After everyone had disappeared, Fife would show up at the most inopportune times in hopes of catching someone off guard. But Bloomfield had done his homework: the burial chamber did not exist according to any formal inquiry. The only thing he had done in that department was to call OHA, the Organization of Hawaiian Affairs, to let them know something had been found but it was on Federal property and a lot of paperwork would be involved if word got out. OHA wasn't particularly happy with the feds either, after all the legal battles in the courtroom they had been through, so what the feds didn't know wouldn't upset things.

'The Missing Link' was another matter. That one unlikely phone call from Victoria to her uncle outlaw was a big mistake. 20/20 hindsight. The speleologists had made their escape with the help from the Old Coots, but the issue was far from over, thanks to agent Fife. His thoughts were interrupted by the buzz In his pants. He had chosen the vibration signal instead of the auditory beep so's not to arouse any attention. He took his cell phone to the parking lot where the mule traffic jam had occurred and dialed the number.

"Foxes in sheep's clothing, may I help you?" It was Souza.

"Cut the crap you old barnacle, how's things going?" returned the good doctor.

Souza gave him a brief account of the ocean crossing, Woods, Guaymas and Guadalajara and wound it up by saying, "other than a few hangovers were holding up well. Here, Dicky wants to talk to you."

Laughter erupted in the background as Mallory's voice came online. "Hey doc, we're holding up well except for keeping up with these so-called 'guardians' you saddled us with. We'll be in the US tomorrow, so we wanted to know what we're facing."

"Well, your faces aren't in the news anymore, but Fife keeps snooping around. You haven't been forgotten, so be careful." Bloomfield gave Mallory a recount of the squelch of the burial chamber news and agent Fife's comings and goings. The idea of Richard Junior and Raydene Souza made his eyes roll up, but other than that it was a good idea. Goodbyes were said and Bloomfield pocketed his cell phone and went back to the observatory. He was optimistic about the circumstances but what he didn't know about was the directional listening device that had just picked up his every word.

Agent Fife put down his earphones and smiled. His patience had finally paid off. After suffering the humiliation of the failed car chase, he wasn't about to let up on this one. He now knew they were still in contact and there was something that had been found on Federal property they wanted kept secret. He only wished he could have heard what was said on the other end. And Bloomfield had no idea they were on to him, so maybe later he would find out more.

The dilapidated billboard on the roadside read 'Keep America Clean, Get A Haircut,' it's peeling paint a befitting testimonial to hypocrisy. Below it was a new sign reading 'You are now leaving Louisiana, welcome to Florida. The trip thus far had gone without a hitch. Just before El Paso, the speleologists donned their costumes and uncle Ray and Dad plastered down Mallory's hair with lemon pomade and gave Victoria an old fashioned 'rat' job. They breezed right through the border without a second glance. Texas' dry desert terrain eventually gave way to the bayous of Louisiana. The only problem there was the overnight stay with the mosquitoes. Victoria's gift of earplugs turned out to be a godsend. Everyone swore the mosquitoes flew in squadron formation, dive bombing all night long. Everyone recovered along the way. Florida, however, could get a little dicey. They had reached the 'Sons of the Beach' resort by phone but only had gotten a message machine. Things being as they were, no message was left. The only thing they could do was leave the phone off the hook so the machine would only record silence. If Tyrone 'Bull' Exley was as crafty as they thought, he would figure out who called and what was happening.

"That damn billboard road sign is from the sixties. Too bad they didn't update it for the punk rockers or the grunge era," observed Townsend. It was his turn at the wheel and Mallory was riding shotgun. Uncle Ray and his 'niece' we're taking a siesta.

"Florida has a reputation for being strict. But considering what they have to deal with, can't say as I blame them," answered Mallory.

"Yeah. Remember the television show 'Miami Vice?' There's probably even a grain of truth to some, if not most of it. That and the Cuban refugee problem. Victoria's uncle is right in the thick of it too; being down in Key West and all. It's only ninety miles from Cuba. He probably has a few stories."

"I'd bet on it."

"At that moment, the door to the bedroom opened and out came 'Raydene' minus her wig. She was a real study in contrasts. "Where are we?" she asked in between yawns. This was the last nap that she had needed to be rested enough and be on an even keel.

"We've just crossed into Florida. The Sunshine State or the Orange State. Take your pick," answered Mallory.

"More better hurricane state," observed Souza, just waking up himself. "Pull over. I've got to water some trees," he added.

That took no coaxing. They had actually been waiting for 'the Souzas' to wake up so they could do just that. "Florida State Visitors Bureau. Roadside stop two miles," announced Townsend.

One could possibly call it a premonition because Victoria put on her flaming orange wig. They reached the roadside pit stop and filed into the restrooms. When they came back out there was a Florida Highway Patrol car parked behind the Winnebago, the officer eyeing the California license plates with his billy club in his hands. Without breaking stride, Mallory approached the officer. It was showtime.

"Well howdee, officer. What can I do fer ya." He has been practicing his Okie accent and it came out well.

"Good afternoon folks. I was just noticing you've come a long way. What are y'all doing outhyar?" The officer was polite, but snoopy.

Mallory's mind raced back to the decrepit billboard sign but he didn't even flinch. "These here are our relatives from Huhwhyuh. We're taking em on a touh," answered Richard Jr. Do y'all gots ideas?" He changed the subject like a pro.

The officer stared at them for a moment and then said, "I've never seen one of these here Winnebagas, mind if I take a look?" His intentions plain as day. Before they could answer, he was in the door scrutinizing the interior. Satisfied, he came back out. "Just be careful. We've had bad seed from Caleyforney before, so we weed them out pronto. IDs?" The Rangers and speleologists produced their identification and when it dawned on the officer that the Rangers were Federal Government, he lightened up. "Whal you two are fer from home arentcha? Enjoy your stay. Have a nahs day." He sauntered over to his vehicle and sped off looking for someone else to roust.

"Well that was a wake up call," said Victoria. "We better be on our toes from now on." She turned to Mallory, "that was quite a performance. Come here you." She planted a big old sloppy lipstick imprint on his cheek. "That's for you."

"Gee, thanks," the lack of appreciation apparent in his tone of voice.

"It's a good thing you had your getups on," Townsend told the speleologists. He probably doesn't miss an episode of 'America's Most Wanted.' Souza nodded in agreement.

"You're fine ones to talk" countered Mallory. You two look like a cross between Pee Wee Herman and Meatloaf. Throw in a little Mister Rogers too." It was true. The Rangers had joined in on the fun and they were playing their roles. They wore gaudy Aloha shirts tucked into plaid Bermuda shorts that rose above their ample waistlines. White knee socks and their recently purchased Huarache sandals complemented their wardrobe. Townsend's yellow tinted sunglasses and Souza's coke bottle glasses complemented their pomaded plaster hair job. They could have easily passed as descendants of Ma and Pa Kettle or the Beverly Hillbillies. The hard part was holding a straight face.

Victoria had gone to the Visitors Bureau during the bantering and returned with road maps and tourist brochures. "Okay kids, let's break it up," she ordered. The men tucked tail and boarded the Winnebago. They switched seats to spell each other; Souza as pilot, Townsend co-pilot, and Victoria as a navigator. Mallory was just Mallory and it was just fine with him. Souza produced some pink hearts, took one and announced, "ladies and gentlemen, welcome to the Souza 500, fasten your seatbelts."

They powered to the Atlantic coast and then headed south, taking minor thoroughfares when deemed necessary. They completely avoided

Miami and by the time they got to Fort Lauderdale, the 'Souza 500' had run its course. On the southern outskirts of town they found a beachside park and hauled in for the night.

    The next morning Souza found a pay phone and dialed 'The Sons of the Beach' resort. He left a message saying he was a lieutenant from the Yorktown and he was interested in time-sharing his place in Hawaii and that he would be in Key West that afternoon. He left Victoria's cell number for contact. Before he got back to the Winnebago the phone was ringing.

    Victoria answered and a gravelly voice said, "Vicky, this is probably you. Hog's Breath Saloon, Duval Street at three. Love you. Bye." And hung up. Victoria looked at her phone, shrugged her shoulders and smiled, then gave a thumbs up. Soon they were on their way.

    They crossed Alligator Alley without seeing any of its inhabitants and the seven mile bridge that led to Key Largo, the first of the Keys. Victoria explained from one of the brochures that a man named Henry Flager had built a connecting Railroad in 1912. It took seven years, five hundred workers and almost his entire fortune until Labor Day of 1935 when it was destroyed by a hurricane. So he sold it to the State of Florida and it became the foundation of the now existing overseas highway. Townsend remarked something to the effect that it should be one of the wonders of the world, and actually it wasn't a bad idea. A hundred and twelve miles later they were in Key West. They almost christened their arrival by coming close to and almost running over an old derelict pushing a market basket full of his belongings at the beginning of Duval Street. He looked vaguely familiar, but as they proceeded down the street, so did almost everybody else. There were dozens of 'Ernest Hemingways' walking the streets. They were puzzled only until they saw the banner announcing the 'Hemingway Lookalike Contest' draped across the street. They all got a laugh out of that and Mallory remarked, "I hope that old guy with the push cart wins, he looked like he could use the prize money." All agreed on that.

The Hog's Breath lived up to its name. It looked seedy from the outside, but upon closer inspection it was like Wood's; done that way on purpose and also made with fine materials. They found a parking lot that could handle the Winnebago, got out and went inside. There were even more 'Ernests' at the bar, all comparing beards and whatnot. They lucked into a corner table, but there was no sign of uncle Tyrone. Now their road disguises were totally out of place and they even received a few curious side glances and snide remarks. The joke was clearly on them. The Rangers were having a fine old time playing their roles so they laid it on thick. They ordered "margereeters" loudly just to compound the issue. The speleologists had this feeling that they were shrinking, but bore the brunt of it. Still no sign of the bull and it was after three.

"This reminds me of our watering hole back home", observed Townsend, "The Sly Mongoose. Same atmosphere, different people." It was true. The establishment appeared to be the local hangout. Even the old bum with the pushcart received a few back slaps when he sat at the bar. After an hour of waiting, Victoria called her uncle's resort to no avail. Somewhat miffed, she ordered another round. When the round came along with it was a note on the 'Sons of the Beach' stationery naming a campground on the edge of town and a time; Five PM. The bewildered party paid for their drinks and returned to the Winnebago. Along the way Souza asked for directions and they arrived shortly thereafter. The campground was set up with electrical outlets in each parking space. There were a few other campers, some set up for longer than overnight stays. One in particular had a porch in front of the door and an awning built over it, a sign on the window reading 'management.' Mallory knocked on its door but got no response. They decided to set up shop, so they picked a parking slot under some trees in the corner, fifty yards from the turquoise waters of the Gulf of Mexico. The Rangers wasted no time in taking advantage of the warm seawater. They were splashing like ten year olds when the old man with the pushcart rounded the corner and headed for the management trailer, his back bent and his shoulders stooped. Mallory was about to remark something to the effect of feeling sorry for him when the old derelict turned and waved and without a word went inside. They were pleasantly surprised to learn that at least he had a place to stay. They were even more surprised when he came back out later, dressed in clean pressed khaki shirt and shorts. And more than that he was walking ramrod straight, directly towards them. As he approached, Victoria's jaw dropped. He broke into a huge grin and said, "hi Vicky, long time no see," for a stunned millisecond she was immobile. When recognition set in she jumped into his arms and he spun her around like a doll. He set her down gently and planted a kiss on her forehead. It was the only thing he could do because he was at least a foot taller than her. He turned to everyone else and jovially said, "hi there, I'm Ty Exley."

"The stoop shouldered old 'pushcart' man had transformed into a tanned, shoulder length silver haired specimen between seventy and twenty. His eyes were clear and held a steady gaze and had a firm grip as he pumped Mallory's hand. He was well over six feet tall and there wasn't an ounce of cellulite on his entire frame. For a man his age, one couldn't be in better shape. He introduced himself to the approaching Rangers and mildly reprimanded Souza to "watch his driving," then asked, "can you spare an old man a beer?" It was easy to see that Woody's stories were the absolute truth. The man emanated boundless positive energy. Beers were brought and Exley explained, "sorry for the subterfuge, but after that phone call, things have been… different. The Feds are really obvious, bordering on stupidity and stick out like sore thumbs, but I had to make sure they weren't on to you. They have no idea I'm the bum with the pushcart. With that he broke into an infectious gut laugh that was shared by all. "It took me a while to make sure it was you. Those disguises are hilarious. Bravo." Tyrone 'Bull' Exley was instantaneously likeable and he fit in immediately. Even the Rangers were awed. Exley led them to his porch where there were chairs and a table. He offered them seats and then went inside and came out with a large Igloo cooler. When he opened it up and they saw it was full of beer on ice, they marveled on how he handled it so easily. 'Bull' Exley was the true version of a senior 'man's man'. "Now what's this all about?" Before anyone could speak he turned on his porch radio and tapped his ears and pointed to his head. The meaning was understood.

The speleologists went through the same routine as they had done at the 'pillbox' and Woods, Victoria doing the narrative. Exley listened wordlessly without interruption. His eyes lit up slightly at the sight of the gourds as if rekindling a memory, but the scenario involving The Missing Link seemed to come as no surprise to him. He loved the story of Woody's silver star plaque. He gave the Rangers an appreciative nod every time their participation was involved. They even blushed slightly, knowing they were in the presence of greatness. When her story was finished, he got up from the table and paced back and forth with his hands clasped behind his back. They could almost hear the gears grinding in his head. The Rangers and speleologists waited patiently while Exley drew his mental picture. They could only imagine the incalculable deviousness that was forming in his brain. He stopped pacing and faced Mallory. "May I see the object?" It was more an order than a request. Mallory went to the Winnebago and returned with the backpack and laid it on the table. Exley stared at the backpack as if mentally debating whether to open it or not. He looked up towards the sky, then slowly around the table, and cautiously undid the straps. There was a distinguishable intake of breath when he pulled it out. They didn't think it possible, but there was actually a paleing in Exley's demeanor when he first viewed the object. He obviously knew more than they did. The casual aspect of his features disappeared instantly and was replaced by something that resembled superstition/reverence. He had been clearly moved; how or why, nobody knew. Not even him. No one made a sound while they let Exley calculate, only the sound of the radio static filled the air. Its reception had blanked out upon The Missing Link's arrival. Finally Exley looked around the table and said, "this is either the answer to a half-century mystery or the key to Pandora's Box. Or maybe both."

As the weight of the situation set in, everyone was lost in their own thoughts. As to punctuate it all, Exley produced a box of hand rolled Cuban cigars and passed them around. Victoria was going to politely decline but her uncle gently but firmly shoved one in her mouth. Like a Cowboy of old, he struck a match with his thumb nail. If they were going to go up the creek without paddles, they at least might as well go up in style. After a few satisfying puffs Exley put the object back in the backpack. With his eyes and a flick of his head he signaled Mallory to take it away. Soon the music was back on the radio. The cigars replaced conversation while Mallory was fulfilling the request. Still nobody said a word after he had returned. They were waiting for Exley to take the floor.

Victoria broke the spell. "Uncle, please don't hate us for coming to you. We just didn't know which way to turn." She was acutely serious.

Exley's eyes softened and then he smiled. "On the contrary my dear, you made the only possible move you could, or should. I just don't know whether to thank you or not," trying to lighten the situation. "This is only just Highest Priority National Security and also possible criminal charges. The life or death kind, that's all. It's going to require some pretty fancy footwork; I thrive on this shit!"

Everyone nodded in agreement. They had definitely come to the right place. They could either become heroes or be on the long end of a short rope, or anywhere in between. Exley's smooth confidence was reassuring, but they also knew this was going to take real teamwork, but oh was this quite a team. "Any suggestions?" Mallory asked.

"Not right away, no," answered the Bull. "I've pulled off a lot of different kinds of shenanigans before, but this is going to be my crowning achievement. First off, I'm going to treat you to dinner and a fantastic bottle of wine, or three. Then I'm going to see if you can keep up with this old codger on the dance floor. After all, life ain't no rehearsal." Victoria almost swooned and fell into her uncle's arms. The Rangers stood up and cheered and Mallory felt a sense of relief of which he hadn't felt since stumbling into all this. If they're we're going to another party, again, so be it. "The Hemingway look-alike contest culminates tonight and I'm in the finals. You see, I have to defend my championship." Why doesn't that surprise me, thought Mallory.

Just for the hell of it and just in case Fife's cronies were nosing around, they all dressed like Ernest Hemingway. Including Victoria. There was a novelty shop in town where they sold Hemingway beards and wigs for the occasion. Usually the finest were the ones with real beards and hair, but every once in a while someone would have the correct silhouette to be in the running. Sure enough the Rangers fit that category. The winners were chosen not only for their looks; because each finalist had to quote from memory, a passage out of one of Hemingway's many books. This is where the fun began. Some took this part quite seriously while others could give a shit less. It was also where the transient visitors were at a disadvantage. The locals knew that absolutely nothing was to be taken seriously and that sometimes a deliberate butcher-job of their lines worked in their favor. All of these variables were contributing factors for the dethroning of defending champ Tyrone 'Bull' Exley that night.

The finalists consisted of three locals including Exley, two upstate New Yorkers, Townsend and oh yes: Victoria. Souza had edged himself out by speaking Hawaiian pidgin English that flew over everyone's heads. Victoria had her own personal fan club because a woman entrant was a first. Up to then there had been men only, but since that barrier was now down, she was really popular. Victoria playing Raydene playing Ernest Hemingway was a real showpiece. The only people not cheering for her were the two New Yorkers. They were the type that took the occasion too seriously and appeared to be strutting around with broomsticks stuck up their nether regions. In the finals, the passages to be quoted we're stuck in a hat. The contestants had five minutes to memorize, then recited. They were judged by audience participation so Victoria swept the finals hands down, Exley and his neighbors followed, then the uptight New Yorkers and Townsend, not known for his oratory skills came in dead last. This didn't bother him in the slightest, in fact he bounced around like he had just won the lottery. His joy was the last straw for the disgruntled New Yorkers, so they stomped off in disgust, which brought on even more cheers.

Pictures were taken for the local newspaper and statistics taken down. When Victoria and Townsend both mentioned Hawaii they didn't realize the mistake before it was too late. One of the less gregarious 'Hemingways' got out of his seat and went to a payphone in the back. Both the Bull and Mallory noticed this, and the Bull quietly whispered under his breath, "I'll handle this." Mallory watched as the Bull approached the man asking for a light. Before the man could respond there was a non-discernible movement of the Bull's arm and the man's head flew back and his knees buckled. Before he could fall, the Bull grabbed him around the shoulder as if talking to an old buddy and escorted him out. A minute later he came back in minus his 'buddy' and sat back down. He winked at Mallory and said, "military training" and continued celebrating as if nothing had happened.

When Victoria could pull herself away from her congratulators, she came back over to the table and apologized. Townsend did also, but the embarrassment on his face had already told the tale. The Bull looked at them straight faced and then smiled. "No big deal. I had him spotted already. I was just seeing if and when he would make his move. Ever since your phone call, there's been at least one of them snooping around my tail every day. They come in shifts. He won't be missed until tomorrow morning. There's a drunk tank in the back here that I locked him up into. I know the owner and he's not going to let him out until someone asks about him. Try to tighten it up though." It was a simple but effective reprimand. "This is going to move up our schedule. We've got until morning to vanish. We'll have to formulate plans along the way".

They stayed at the event until it was polite enough to leave. Victoria enjoyed the accolades of being the first woman 'Ernest Hemingway' and Townsend being a runner-up. Bull Exley accepted the condolences of being toppled from his throne. He had won three years in a row. Souza and Mallory scoured the crowd in search of a possible second agent. When they could leave, Exley explained he would go to the Sons of the Beach and get his gear together and be back with his car at sunrise.

Victoria asked, "what about the guy in the drunk tank?"

The Bull looked at her and smiled. "Don't worry about him. I went back in there and gave him a judo chop on the medulla oblongata that will keep him out for hours. I produced a roll of duct tape and wrapped him up mummy style. He won't be going anywhere for quite some time. The owner will go in at noon faking like he's cleaning up and 'discover' him and set him free. By then we'll be on the continental US free and clear." He then added with a chuckle, "they might, however, put out an APB for four male and one female Ernest Hemingways, could be considered armed and dangerous." Then seriously, all kidding aside, "we've got to vamoose. I'll be back at sunrise. You won't be able to miss me," with that he turned and headed home.

The Rangers and speleologists stood there and watched the retreating general. Then Mallory said, "wow! I'm sure glad he's with us." Murmurs of agreement went around the group while they walked back to the campground and were so happy to find total peace and quiet, a rare commodity these days. The Hemingway party could be faintly heard in the distance but was of no consequence. Once the quiet set in they found themselves extremely exhausted. With no fanfare they headed to their own personal sleeping zone and passed out. Not even the Rangers' snoring disturbed the speleologists. Or maybe the Rangers were just too tired to even snore. One thing was for sure: they would never know.

Exley's idea of sunrise was the first glimpse of light in the sky at night. It was still nighttime to anyone else. The sound of approaching footsteps in the gravel outside and then a rap on the door was their alarm clock. Without waiting for an answer Exley opened the door. "Chop-chop. Time's a wastin," he announced upon entering. Tucked under his arm was a large thermos. He proceeded to empty its contents into cups. "Here. Try this. It'll get you going in no time." Then he was out the door.

The group slithered out of their beds and were greeted by cups of an espresso ish type coffee laced with whiskey. Exley was right. It had the punch to bring back the dead. They moved as new recruits at boot camp which wasn't that far from the truth. By the time they were out the door Exley was removing a car cover from something parked behind his trailer. Once removed, it revealed a treasure not seen too often in this day and age. Underneath was a bright red 1957 Cadillac convertible complete with black tuck and roll upholstery looking like it had just come off the showroom floor. The white top matched the extra wide white wall tires of that era. And to top it off it had a Hula Girl on the dashboard. Exley popped the hood and hooked up the battery, hit the ignition and the engine came to life instantly, purring like a lion. He went back to his trailer and returned with a suitcase and the Igloo cooler. He threw the suitcase in the trunk and the cooler in the back seat. He looked towards the Rangers and said, "care to take a ride? He didn't need to ask twice. They needed no coaxing in that department, except for who got to ride shotgun. Exley looked up at the brightening sky, nodded affirmatively, and took the top down. The speleologists felt a tinge of jealousy not being able to go also, but their turn would eventually certainly come.

The road west, well, if you could call it a road, was a blistering trail of catch the Cadillac. When Exley sped out of the park, peeling donuts in the gravel causing a sizable dust cloud, he yelled over his shoulder, "Red Garter Saloon, Bourbon Street" then was gone. The speleologists could do nothing else but comply. By now, their disguises had become their alter egos. They had no trouble finding the famous French Quarter in 'Naahlans', New Orleans in English. The Red Garter Saloon was one of the more popular places in the area. After a night on the town they opted for a Holiday Inn. The next morning Mallory and Victoria rode with the Bull, the next stop on the endurance run being Dallas. There the Bull ordered everyone into the Cadillac and then they took the route of the Kennedy Assassination, where they marveled in the folly of the lone gunman theory. By being there it was easy to see that it was virtually impossible for it to have happened that way. Exley explained, "I wanted you to see this so you would know what kind of assholes we're dealing with." He had taken the Cadillac, top down, and drove as fast as Kennedy had, just to punctuate the idiocy of the findings of the Warren Commission. This had a sobering effect on the group but it didn't last long because when the Bull pulled up to the plush Plaza Hotel he treated everyone to rooms and a gourmet meal. During dinner Exley brightened everyone's spirits by suggesting the next stop to be the Carlsbad caverns. This would be more or less the Disneyland of speleology. They could tour the deepest caves on Earth. And also they could make plans for the last and most dangerous leg of their journey; entry into Nellis Air Force Base and Area 51, Roswell. So far Exley hadn't let on what he was planning to do, because every time the subject came up, he would smile and say "I'm working on it." And coming from him, that was enough. The next morning they were well rested and up bright and early. Exley paid the tab with a wad of bills explaining the fact that there would be "no tracing credit cards." More affirmation they were in the right hands. They stopped at the Winnebago where Mallory and Victoria reluctantly got out of the Cadillac and by the time they had the Winnebago started, the Cadillac was long gone, out of sight. The speleologists were giddy as kids at Christmas knowing they were going to the caverns. They also knew that this would probably be the last enjoyable thing they would do before entering the jaws of the trap. Once inside, they would be at the mercy of their hosts; who quite possibly might not be that hospitable because of the way they had left Haleakala. Although this was looming in the back of their minds, it wasn't going to spoil the tour of Carlsbad. But after that…

The trip had taken a total of three days, Exley being a fanatic behind the wheel of what he fondly called 'the shark'. His reasoning for the nickname, he explained, was that he had once read Hunter S Thompson's Fear and Loathing in Las Vegas and had gotten such a kick out of the heroes exploits in their Cadillac, also called the shark, he decided to do the same. It was also a less than subtle diversion. One glimpse of this flying down the road and anything else on the highway seemed insignificant. At the Texas/New Mexico border this was proved valid. For once the speleologists had actually gotten a head start in the Winnebago. Exley had wanted to refill the cooler. They were ahead by a full five minutes when they were suddenly overtaken and passed by a red blur on the straightaway of Highway 375. Less than a minute later two Highway Patrol cars with lights flashing and sirens wailing passed in pursuit, totally ignoring the Winnebago. Minutes later the speleologists saw the Shark go over a rise miles in the distance with the law still in hot pursuit. The next time this occurred the Cadillac had widened the gap between them and shortly thereafter the patrol cars were seen returning after giving up the pursuit. As the law passed they didn't even give the Winnebago a second glance.

"Your uncle sure knows how to make a lasting impression," commented Mallory. "He will definitely have to take an alternate route back."

"Oh he just loves that car," answered Victoria. "He once told me it had the biggest engine ever made. Four four seven cubic inches with a supercharger whatever that means."

"When he was hooking up the battery I took a peek. He's got a modified Weber carburetor with a nitrous oxide feed. It's the same kinda thing they have in drag racers. All he needs is wings," chuckled Mallory. "We're almost at Whites City. For some reason he wants us to meet at the park campgrounds in front of the entrance to the caves. He says it's essential to be there before sunset. It'll be close." With that, Mallory put pedal to the metal.... It was becoming increasingly clear there was always a method to the Bull's madness.

They arrived with very little time to spare. When they pulled up they found Townsend and Souza yukking it up with their fellow Rangers. They had already secured VIP treatment, plus could go on their own personal tour of the caverns, and since Mallory and Victoria were speleologists, they required no guide. "This place is ours," explained a beaming Townsend. After brief introductions they were shown where to park the Winnebago overnight. They signed the registration ledgers and were given keys to the kingdom. All this had happened so fast and was such a pleasant surprise they had temporarily forgotten about the Bull. When Victoria finally noticed her Uncle was missing she spoke up.

"By the way, where's my..." Her question was interrupted by an ear piercing scream and over a hill from the direction of the entrance to the Caverns came Exley at a full sprint. They were all completely taken by surprise by this maneuver and were stunned into immobility. The Bull's uncharacteristic behavior had the speleologists completely baffled. Their curiosity didn't last long, because behind him came a huge black cloud of what was one million Mexican Freetail Bats in hot pursuit. Exley ran up to the group supposedly terror stricken, yelled "run for yer lives!!!", then doubled up and almost fell over laughing. Uncle Ray, Daddy, and the Park Rangers had been in on the situation. Once reality set in and the speleologists realized what was happening, Victoria started swinging her purse. When Mallory realized the gist of the situation he started laughing also. The men artfully dodged Victoria's purse as the harmless bats went out onto the desert for their evening meal. After venting her fury, she too joined in on the laughter. Once things settled down all she could say was, "oh boy, do I owe you one!" This was generally agreed by all.

When the hilarity subsided Exley was the first one able to talk. "Okay. Fun's over. Personally, I'm opting for a hotel room. I need a headquarters and an operations space. You can go exploring without me. I need some time to implement a plan and set it into motion. There's phone calls I have to make; you see I haven't been there for many moons and I have to find out who's running the show and what to circumvent to get to where we have to go. If they're still in the loop, I have some mighty influential friends inside that can help. There's also the 'prick factor'. That's all I can tell you for now. I'll know a lot more and will be able to explain much better after I've done some homework. There's nothing you can do right now except to stay out of my way. So go have fun and let me get down to business." The intensity of his look behind his words left no room for argument. The Bull was in his element. "I'm not going to lie to you. If this thing is what I think it is then we are going to shake up some heavily entrenched foundations. And what becomes of that is still too early to tell." If Exley's words sounded ominous it's because that's exactly what they were. The party was almost over and the real party was just about to begin.

The Bull jumped into his Cadillac. The speleologists and Rangers could only stare in semi shock. As he was leaving he shouted over his shoulder, "Oh, by the way, come into town for dinner, on me. They have a house specialty, bat stew." He pressed on the accelerator just in time to dodge a 180° swing of Victoria's purse.

Carlsbad Caverns, located in the Chihuahuan desert in southwest New Mexico is the home of the Mount Everest of speleology. A total of three miles long and almost a thousand feet in depth, it houses eighty plus caves. It's creation began approximately two hundred and fifty million years ago with the emergence of a four hundred mile long reef in an inland sea. The reef eventually formed sponges, algae, calcite and seashells. Cracks developed as the sea evaporated due to weather change, and the reef was buried under deposits of salts and gypsum. Sound familiar? It was this same cataclysm that sank Atlantis and Lemuria and caused the weather change and these very same cracks to develop. The rainwater, made acidic from the soil, seeped down slowly, dissolving limestone, and the exposed reef to eventually become the Guadalupe mountains. About five hundred thousand years ago, as a wetter and cooler climate prevailed due to Ulric's blunder, stalactites and stalagmites formed as rainwater percolated down, drop by drop, absorbing carbon dioxide gas from the air and soil. A weak acid was formed as the drops dissolved the limestone, and when it hit the caves that were formed by the folly of Ulric, the gas escaped, and the drops deposited their tiny mineral loads as crystals of calcite. Billions upon billions of drops later, stalactites formed on the roof and stalagmites on the floor of the caves. The ones that formed together made the cavern columns into pillars and in time mother nature had created one of the most glorious wonders of the entire planet. Way to go, Ulric…

The speleologists and Rangers declined the Bull's invitation to bat stew and descended in the elevator nine hundred feet down to a cafeteria at the bottom. Their VIP status gave them free reign of the area. They originally had planned to tour the next day, but once they arrived at the entrance to the big room, it was as if the speleologists had plugged themselves into an electrical socket. They became so energized by their surroundings there was no stopping them now. The 'big room' got its name simply because that is what it is. Eighteen hundred feet long by eleven hundred ten wide by two hundred twenty five in height, it has a circular trail that encompasses the "Hall of Giants,' the "Temple of the Sun" and the "Rock of Ages'; all appropriately named. Adjoining the big room is 'The King's Palace' 'The Queen's Chamber' 'The Papoose Chamber' and 'The Green Lake Room.' The tour normally lasts three hours, but the cave dwellers found they could have stayed for days. More often than not the Rangers had to bodily drag them along because they were so absorbed by its entirety that they would have to inspect every little thing. By the end of their tour exhaustion had set in and they were all delighted to have the elevator take them back up. Everyone was thankful to have the Winnebago situated as close to the exit that it could get. They walked like zombies, asleep before their heads hit their pillows.

After one of their better nights of sleep they awoke to a crystal New Mexico morning. The cool fresh air seemed like it came directly out of an oxygen bottle. The cloudless blue sky accentuated the brown hues of the desert. There was even a smattering of the red and yellow desert flowers since it was that time of year to bloom. The panoramic vista spread for miles and it seemed like one could reach out and touch the mountains twenty miles away. They all woke up refreshed and the surroundings made it even more so. Everyone took full advantage of the peace and tranquility of the morning, each keeping talk to a minimum as not to disturb the serene effect. Except for a few short comments, the most noise they made was the deep inhaling of the pristine desert air and an audible "ahhhh" upon exhaling. No one was in any particular hurry, knowing what lay ahead. Eventually they ran out of small talk and chores, so they piled into the Winnebago and headed for Whites City.

They found at the Bull at a Motel 6, his shiny shark a direct contrast to the faded paint job of the old hotel. Somewhere he had procured a map of Nellis Air Force Base and tacked it onto the wall. The desk he was sitting at was piled with notes he had written to himself and a list of names with phone numbers that he had checked off once contacted. He was at the last number when they entered.

"Yes that's correct. The Flamingo after sunset. A top secret need to know. No leaks. Out." He hung up the phone and gave them a weary smile. It appeared that he quite possibly hadn't gotten a wink of sleep last night, judging from the stacks of papers that had accumulated and the look on his face. "Good morning. Your timing is perfect. I've just finished up and it's time to move into action. Sit yourselves down. It's time for me to commit treason."

The last statement had a startling effect on all and they did as they were told. The Bull produced an insulated coffee pot and styrofoam cups and everyone prepared themselves for what was to come. "Okay. Now I'm going to violate the National Secrets Act by giving you classified information. Any retelling of this and you are liable to be shot." He let this sink in before going on. He got a pencil from the desk and went over to the map. This is Nellis Air Force Base and this here…" He took the pencil and drew a rough rectangle in the middle of the map. "Is what we call Dreamland, or Area 51 if you will. It's officially known as the Groom Lake Bombing and Gunnery Range, but in actuality is where we develop and test our top secret flying machines." He gave his listeners a penetrating stare, then smiled, his eyes twinkling. "I was moved here at the outset, shall we say, for my nefarious talents. I believe their reasoning behind this was, if they wanted to keep a lid on things, why not get the craftiest innovator that knows all the tricks and have them covered before anyone else can think them up. They were correct. After I threw that party on the Yorktown I was decommissioned and immediately flown to Washington DC. I was expecting the worst. But instead of receiving a general court martial, I was brought in to see the man himself, Franklin D. Roosevelt. He actually congratulated me for my talents and went as far to say that I had brought morale to such an all-time high and that I was probably responsible for winning the Battle of Midway. He then got serious and he and Cordell Hull made me sign papers for top security clearance. I was then let in on the Manhattan Project where I was more of a morale officer than a working stiff. But that doesn't apply here so let's move on. In 1945 I was sent to Nellis. At the time there were only two landing strips used as training for flyers and advanced weaponry of that time. 1947 changed all that. But that comes later. By 1955, Groom Lake was the test site for the then U-2 spy plane, and President Eisenhower restricted airspace over the entire Air Base. In 1958 the Atomic Energy Commission restricted 60 square miles on top of this. In '62, they stretched restrictions to 22 x 20 nautical miles and is still known as the 'Groom Box' today. All eighty nine thousand acres are patrolled by helicopters and guards, all armed to the teeth. There are ground sensors everywhere and signs stating 'trespassers will be shot' around the perimeter. From the outset until my retirement we developed and tested the U-2, the Blackbird, and the Mach 3 Interceptor, the MIG-21 and the Have Blue stealth fighter, all of which have been spotted as UFOs. But what could we tell everyone? No sorry, folks, they're not UFOs, but only our nation's top secret weaponry. Anyway, all this is nothing compared to what happened in July 1947." Exley's oratory skills were shining. He had the group mesmerized. He would pace the floor as if lost in thought, then stop to accentuate a point and at the same time giving a stare to make sure each point was taken. It was truly worthy of a stage.

"Shit. I thought we had gone back to war or there was a surprise inspection by the inspector general or something. It was right after the fourth of July and I had thrown a little get-together for the Army Corp of Engineers and the flight training personnel. They had all been restricted to base during construction and under the Official Secrets Act, so needless to say there wasn't much fun to be had." He stopped in front of Victoria and gave her a hand caught in the cookie jar look. Excuse me, my dear, all candor aside, I have to tell it like it happened." This brought a noncommittal shrug from her as to continue. "Anyway, for the festivities I slipped down to Las Vegas and hired an entire escort service for the night. They agreed to be brought out in blackened out buses; it was the only way to get them through security. Hell, I thought it made it even more exciting. Now since there's a lady present, I'll leave out the details. Let's just say everyone was a little ragged when the alarms went off. We thought we were caught with our pants down." Exley realized the instant when the pun came out of his mouth. By that time it was too late and the lecture went to pieces for a few minutes, the seriousness of the situation out the window. When things settled down, the Bull continued, "if it had been an inspection I probably would have been keelhauled or hung with piano wire or something. I had requisitioned the main hangar for the event and thank God it hadn't spread too far from there. We were descended upon by what I thought was every MP in the armed forces and a security blanket was put around the entire perimeter of the 'Green Box.'

What surprised us is when they formed up, their backs were to the base, facing outward. They were all fully armed with machine guns on jeeps in each corner." Exley stopped pacing and made himself a cup of Joe. It was becoming clear that he hadn't slept a wink. For a man his age(less) he was holding up well. "Once the perimeter was secured, they did a spot check of the interior." The Bull's face brightened up at this point like he was reliving the event. "I'll never forget this part as long as I live." Chuckling, "we were extremely busy gathering clothing and making the bar and the cots disappear when a MP Corporal stuck his head in the door. The look on his face was priceless. He turned sheet white then crimson, did an about-face and without a word went to his superiors. A few minutes later a squad of them marched up with their head honcho. By that time at least the ladies were dressed and the booze was made invisible. The commander was a lieutenant and he left the squad outside and marched stiffly into the hangar. His jaw hit the floor when he came inside. He was about to go ballistic when he spotted me. The fickle hand of fate was on our side, that time anyway, as he recognized me immediately. As it turned out, he had been stationed at Pearl during the Yorktown incident and he took me over to the side out of earshot and shook my hand. He then quickly explained that the Yorktown event was the best experience he had during the entire war. He was off duty at the time and had joined in on the fun. Then with a wink of his eye he came to attention, saluted, about faced and marched out of the hangar. I followed him out and overheard him explain that it just was a morale meeting and ordered the squad to carry on. And that was that. We were virtually ignored and that allowed us to clean up our mess. By the time we had the area secured a convoy of trucks had shown up and in the middle was a flatbed with a large lump of something completely covered in canvas. Naturally they pulled up directly outside our hangar. The MP Lieutenant went up to the commander of the convoy and had a few brief words with him. He was a lite colonel and I outranked him so that was a plus. He came up to me somewhat embarrassed and requested we vacate the premises. He clearly was under extreme duress so we ushered the ladies and construction personnel to the base cafeteria for breakfast. The flight training personnel were ordered back to their barracks. Then when the hangar was vacated the flatbed pulled inside. Behind the flatbed was an ambulance that went inside also. By this time I was extremely curious as to what the hell was going on, and since I was the ranking officer I was allowed to stay and there was nobody around that could order me otherwise. The ambulance was unloaded first. Out came three body bags and one stretcher. I had to do a double-take because although the lad on the stretchers' face was covered in an oxygen mask, he was definitely out of proportion. At the time I thought his head was just swollen, but what really got my attention was the fact that he had six fingers on his hands, like an extra pinky or something. Anyway, the bodies were taken to the base hospital and that's the last I saw of them. The bulk on the flatbed was taken off with a forklift and left covered in the middle of the hangar. Everyone was booted out and an armed guard was posted around the hangar twenty four hours a day for months to come. Shit, I wasn't even allowed in there, being a brigadier general and all. What I did see was scientists coming and going for months. On July 7th and 8th the newspapers were full of unconfirmed reports that a UFO had crash-landed in Roswell, New Mexico. A quick cover story came out explaining that it was a Mogul Weather Balloon that had crashed but I knew it was bullshit because I saw them dismantling one to look like crashed pieces and taken out to the crash site the day after the bulk had showed up". Exley stopped for a minute to let what he had just said to sink in. There really wasn't much to say, so he continued. "The Mogul was really used to monitor Soviet nuclear tests, so by that time I was convinced that there was a major cover up involved. All of a sudden ten more companies of Corps of Engineers showed up and their construction area was covered up with a security blanket at that time not yet known to mankind. They kept blasting deeper and deeper into the ground and miles of rebar and mountains of cement were taken down into the hole they had made. This took two years of nonstop, around the clock participation. When it was finally done, a regulation hangar was built on top of it and it appeared to be just that. All during this time the UFO phenomenon was spreading like wildfire. By the fifties it was out of control. Even though the ladies from our party had to sign 'under the penalty of death' documents, word leaked out anyway and the focus switched to here. Luckily it was after construction was finished so we could deny everything. That's why the restriction area has spread so far; everyone is just so fucking nosey even though they had every right to be so. So it was probably that party that set me up for things to come." The Bull chuckled and shook his head in bewilderment, a 'why me?' type of amusement on his face. "If it wasn't for that party I wouldn't have been there and seen what had happened. Hmph. Oh well, as the saying goes, no good deed goes unpunished. That's me alright." The Bull pondered this for a moment then went on. "Anyway, word got out to the higher-ups that I was present, so I was again brought back to Washington, this time to see Harry S. Truman. What a difference. Franklin had an easygoing personality and Truman, well, he was a stiff little prick if you ask me. But hell, anybody who had to bear the weight of dropping the A-bomb probably had to be. So while I'm there is when they officially let me in on that it really was Alien that had crash-landed. I really just wanted to say "duh" but I held it back. I was given top security clearance from then on and had the keys to Dreamland." Exley paused for a moment and asked for questions. The Rangers and speleologists were in a trance from absorbing what they had heard so far. They wordlessly looked around at each other then back to the Bull. "Okay, fasten your seatbelts because this is where you come in". The Bull paused again for effect to give his audience time to brace themselves. "Whether it's a blessing or a curse, I don't know, yet, but we'll soon find out. The extra-terrestrial craft itself looks like one of our stealth fighters. It should be the other way around because that's where we got the design from. The difference is, there are no corners; it's rounded at every seam and doesn't appear to have any connecting parts, their technology unknown. The material is also a mystery. What I do know is that thing you found is made from the same stuff, and quite possibly answers questions that have plagued us ever since the damn thing crashed. You see, when Major Jesse Marcel, of the 509th bomber group, came on the crash site, three of its occupants were outside the craft, and already dead. It appeared that they were still alive and survived the crash, but died after successfully destroying an object that was found beside them. You're 'missing link', just might possibly be exactly that; the missing link. They appeared to have the same dimensions, although the one that crashed was really banged up. The three dead ones did a good job. The fourth occupant died a few days later for reasons unknown to us. They appeared to have close to the same physiology as us, so we tried life support but that didn't work. After an autopsy we found that the internal organs weren't much different from ours, but without any signs of deterioration. The only difference being the extra fingers, and their heads being larger. But we believe that it is because their brains are larger. Also, their systems were so clean there's no telling how long their lifespans might be. Much longer than ours most definitely. Their medical technology must be vastly superior. Anyway, I'm digressing here, so back to my point. The object they destroyed we had already determined to be either a flight recorder like our black box, or possibly their propulsion system. One or the other, maybe both. Whatever it was, plugged into the console in the front of what we believe is the pilot seat. When the major arrived at the crash site, the light in the object was still blinking, although very weakly- it faded out shortly thereafter. But now, thanks to you, we actually might have a working model." It was good everyone was sitting down because the last piece of information paralyzed them all. They were instantly slam-dunked into somewhere between a best and worst case scenario. Exley sat down with them to let this all sink in.

They sat in stunned silence. There was nothing to say. Mallory sat up straight with his mouth open and his eyes blinking. Victoria was looking at him with the same expression. Souza had his elbows on his knees and stared at the floor. Townsend gazed out the window. Exley sympathized with them, but there was no room for empathy, nor the time. After a few minutes he took the map off the wall and began gathering his papers.

"Well gang, there you have it," said the Bull. "I've been saving this knowing what your reaction would be. I've been holding this in ever since I laid eyes on it, so you can imagine what kind of stress I've been under. But now it's time to move. I have a lead-lined suitcase coming to Vegas tomorrow, so when we get to Nellis we won't blow the lid off the joint.

I still have friends on the inside working now to get us directly down to the science level and getting us by the bureaucratic bullshit on top. That part is not together yet but hopefully will be by the time we arrive. For now the next step is Las Vegas. Chop Chop." Exley clapped his hands on his last two words to break their trance. He put the speleologists in the shark because it appeared they were hit the hardest. Townsend recovered first, so he drove the Winnebago. The mention of Las Vegas inspired them also. Within an hour they were on a journey that was either the beginning of the end or the end of the beginning. No one knew. There was only one way to find out.

CHAPTER 6

THE SPACE PATROL SOMEWHERE IN THE GALAXY

"This one is ready for development. Now all we have to do is choose the sentient beings to populate it. This part is crucial. Picking the candidates from our ongoing projects successfully is truly a gamble. If they can coexist they have a good chance of surviving." Rawar was thinking out loud. They really didn't have to do it, non-verbal communication was automatic.

"I think we might have to put that on hold," countered Oxomoxo. "I've been checking the monitors we set up around Earth and our gift is moving. And it's heading towards the remainder of our crashed scout ship."

"Great. It's nice to know at least someone is using the brains they've developed." Rawar, usually skeptical, at least conceded this. "They're all so different from each other. I can't help but wonder what form of personalities have developed this time".

Oxomoxo was ecstatic over Rawar's curiosity. The last time they discussed this, the idea of taking a closer look had come up. "Our gift isn't there yet, but it looks like that could possibly be where they're headed. They've just passed by the last heavily populated area and their trajectory is pointing directly towards there."

"Then we still have time to work on this one". Rawar watched his partner's expression drop. "But it will be on our next stop, if that is alright right with you…" He enjoyed toying with his co-pilot. He already knew the answer, but it was so much fun playing the game of the bet, anyway.

"Of course it's all right, especially if they put things together. Their technology level is much higher than the last time. Things should probably progress one way or another, faster." Oxomoxo was on to Rawar's fake disinterest. But he also enjoyed playing his part. After all, they still had the bet ongoing. "So what shall we name this one?" changing the subject.

"Your turn. Remember I named the last one, or what's left of it. This one is all yours."

Oxomoxo's mind was already on Earth. His pet project was going to start moving in one direction or another, soon. "Let's drop it for now. We'll get some of their animals there and let them battle it out for a while, and then it will be time to put a higher species there. Maybe we ought to get them from Earth since it's possible that it might not last much longer…"

"That is not a bad idea since we're going there anyway. We can observe possible candidates."

"Hopefully at least some of them have changed. I know we're not supposed to interfere. That idiot Ulric proves my point. If our gift gets into the hands of another one like him, we might as well get ready for more clean up duty."

"Let's finish this project, then we can go see what's happening on Earth, if it's still there. If so, we can grab one of the inhabitants to see what they're made of: the kind of language they speak and what some of their customs may be. Then if we have to go down there, so be it." They both were attempting to appear nonchalant about this, but inside they were boiling with excitement. A first-hand look at their pet project was a dream come true. If their gift could be used properly, Earth would be a complete success and unique in the fact that it had bounced back after almost total complete annihilation. This would prove to be their greatest achievement, yet. But usually it would always come down to that last crucial step. If the gift had fallen into the hands of those with potential to take this last step, the results would be glorious. If it was another Ulric, they didn't even want to ponder this. The Earth's tenacity had brought them back to a level of technology worthy of acknowledgement. Keeping an eye on the gift and being able to interact this time could possibly tip the scales for success, but even the slightest interaction could change things drastically. This time they would be dealing with humans on a higher level of advancement. Would this work in their favor or be a detriment? For all their thousands of years worth of achievements, it still came down to chance. But that's what made it interesting.

YUMA, ARIZONA

It was a moonless starlit sight. Not a breath of air was moving. On the outskirts of the California side of the border town of Yuma, Arizona was the remnants of what was once a general store. Yuma had seen it's day and so had the store. It had once been a favorite stopping point for the Hell's Angels motorcycle club because they were friends of the proprietor. But when the sand dune buggy rage hit, the city folk with money used the place as its center and the Angels moved on. Eventually the dune buggy rage fizzled out. Not because of the magnificent sand dunes that went for miles around, but just the fact that a more modern top-of-the-line outfit opened up a business in town. The only business the store snagged was because of the sign that read 'last stop for cold beer' on the roadside. The lack of trade seemed to have no effect because the Raiders were kicking the shit out of the Cowboys and 'evil Sam McGregor' was hating every minute of it. An old Navy man, prospector, collection agent and bounty hunter, this now general store proprietor was his only semi-decent trait, plus his love of wicked pranks he played on people made him the least popular person in the area. In other words, his name 'evil' fit him well. Even though he was now well along in years, one could tell that he had once been a burly barrel-chested monster that you wouldn't want to say "no" to, or just be on his bad side. His barrel chest had conspicuously dropped down beyond his waist and now his bark was worse than his bite. It was well into the third quarter when his TV reception went totally fuzzy. Thinking that his antenna fell over again, he went outside to put it back up. This was when he noticed a peculiar cloud hovering over his unkept yard and which seemed to have a slight hum emanating from it. All of a sudden he was blasted by a bright white light and woke up on the ground sometime later thinking he had fainted. He noticed that his antenna was in place and could hear the television loud and clear again so he went back inside. The only difference was that the game was long over now and he didn't know the final score. Now how in the hell was he going to know if he had won the pool or not?

Oxomoxo stared at the screen in the scout ship laboratory totally dumbfounded. Rawar, equally bewildered, was getting a kick out of his co-pilot's astonishment. "Well, you sure picked a winner," Rawar chortled, not wanting to rub it in too much. "If 'that' is a genuine example of how this species has evolved, we're in deep trouble."

"At least the brain probe gives us a working example of their language," Oxomoxo replied. "I just don't think that 'Goddamn,' 'son of a bitch,' 'motherfuking,' and 'hellofa' has too much to do with the way they communicate." Being the optimist he was, he countered, "if and when we do intercede, at least we'll be able to blend in."

"I wouldn't worry about that too much. We can always pick another one if need be. Besides, we tapped his entire memory bank so we can learn the basics; systems of exchange, transportation, values and mannerisms. I agree this human is far from suitable, but I still believe we can obtain the information we need to get by." Rawar could sense the disenchantment in his partner's mood. "Look, all we can do for now is take what we have, analyze it and keep our eye on things. It's up to who has the gift and what they do with it. All we can do now is watch and hope for the best." Although he also had serious doubts, Rawar was trying to sound as convincing as he could. "You're right, let's take what we have and go. It's up to them for now anyway. But if that human is a true example of what we're dealing with, I'm surprised they've even gotten this far. We're going to have to keep a very close watch."

To anyone who might have noticed, it was just one of the many shooting stars that flew across the heavens on a starlit desert night.

LAS VEGAS

The myriad of colorful lights on the strip in Las Vegas brought the speleologists back to semi consciousness. During the non-stop run from Whites City, Exley attempted to strike up a conversation, hoping to divert their attention from the information they had received. The speleologists were less than cordial. They managed a few one-line monotone comments at best. Exley didn't push the situation, knowing they had probably just received the jolt of their life. Instead, he put pedal to the metal and sent the shark flying down the highway like a bat out of Hell.

The Rangers to the contrary took a more leisurely pace, knowing it was impossible to keep up with the shark. They stopped at a convenience store and loaded up the Winnebago's refrigerator with beer. Being the seasoned old Vets they were, they had taken the information more in stride. Although the portents were colossal to say the least, they realized they would have to be pillars of strength for the speleologists to lean on if need be, and by the looks of how they took Exley's revelations, that was entirely possible. They arrived at the Flamingo Hotel a little over an hour after their friends, and were pleasantly surprised to find they had a reserved VIP room on the top floor. Also at the desk was a note from the Bull requesting them to meet him at the bar at nine, which gave them an hour to spare.

"Ah, there you are," beamed the Bull. "I was about to send out a search party. Just kidding. Listen, I tried to lighten the load all the way here, but I've come to believe Connor and Victoria have to work it out on their own. I told them as much and it appeared to set well with them. Plus who in their right mind wants to be around old codgers like us 24/7?" Exley paused to look around the room, then flagged down a cigar lady and bought three, getting her phone number in the process. The Rangers weren't that surprised when she said, "thanks Tyrone, maybe we'll see you later." The Bull did a reasonable facsimile of a Groucho

Marx impersonation leaning against the bar pumping his eyebrows up and down a couple of times as he blew a blue cloud of a donut smoke from his cigar she had just lit. Exley went on: "My queries were confirmed. I haven't been forgotten around here". He gave them a conspiratorial look and asked "what'll it be gentlemen? First round's on me."

The Rangers, after hearing Woody's stories and also seeing the Bull in action, knew they were in store for a memorable occasion. They opted for a Martini and a Gibson, the only difference being the olive or onion. Townsend was the first to ask, "just how bad off are they?"

The road here wasn't pretty. But when I suggested that I Shanghai you two and let them be, they started to brighten up. A front row table over at the Sahara for Harry Connick Jr's show didn't hurt either. So that's it boys, we're on our own."

This was music to the Rangers ears. They glanced at each other and nodded affirmatively and Souza was about to speak up when the Bull put his hand up and said, "not to worry. It's already taken care of," and left it at that. "Let's have a few drinks and I'll bring you up to date." Exley led them to a corner table where another round appeared out of nowhere. "On the house Tyrone," the waitress said as she leaned over purposely to deliver the drinks and replace the spotless ashtray giving them all a bird's-eye view of her ample curves underneath her already scantily clad uniform. The Rangers were also mesmerized by her womanly retreat. "Okole Maluna" toasted the Bull, which by this point didn't surprise them one bit.

"Brigadier General Tyrone 'Bull' Exley Retired wasn't the type to beat around the bush. He got directly down to the matters at hand. "Tomorrow at noon is Zero Hour. We have a staff car that's flying my old pennants picking us up here. In it will be the lead lined suitcase I requested and we'll put the thingamajig inside it. From there it's a direct frontal assault. My car with me in uniform will be ominous enough to get us through the front gate. Don't ask how I procured the staff car because I won't tell you. The second checkpoint is the tough one. That's the entry into Dreamland itself. Your Federal Ranger Identification should suffice and Connor and Vicky's aren't bad forgeries at all. If we're met with any resistance I'm just going to tell the truth. We are from the LURE program on Haleakala and we have brought Eyes Only Top Secret sensitive material for the science level. Doctor Bloomfield is going to call precisely at two oclock to confirm this. Our timing has to be perfect. Me breathing down the guard on duty's neck backed up by a call from LURE should do the trick." Exley paused to take a drink and order more. The voluptuous waitress was there in an instant and Exley merely smiled. "Usually this checkpoint requires more paperwork, but my mere presence seems to have an alarming effect on those around me, especially when in uniform and reaming someone a new asshole. It will help if you two are wearing your uniforms and badges, the more official the better. This should get us into the hangar and to the elevators that lead down into the bowels of Dreamland. I've set up a meeting with Mike Stevenson, the top dog and whoever else he wants there. That's when we'll spring the trap and reveal Mallory and Vicki's find. If it is what I think it is, we will be the cocks of the walk. Sooner or later somebody's going to figure out I don't work there anymore, but after they've seen what we have brought, that shouldn't propose a problem. If it does get sticky, then I'll take the flak. I'm very used to dealing with suits like these. The only foreseeable problem will be getting back out; we could possibly be there for a while." The Bull's eyes lit up. "That's why we're going to live it up tonight."

At that moment, a goddess dressed in a white chauffeurs uniform approached their table. "Mister Exley?"

"That would be me," grinned the Bull.

"Your automobile is here as requested," stated the goddess.

"Gentlemen, shall we?" formally announced Brigadier General Tyrone 'Bull' Exley retired.

The Rangers were not ones to look a gift horse in the mouth. The three 'gentlemen' followed her to the stretch limousine that awaited them outside. The only markings on it were the license plates that read 'friendly1.' She opened the door for them and they climbed in. She got in the chauffeur's seat and remarked, "you are quite a legend at our establishment, mister Exley."

"Yes dear, and I believe we are going to create another one."

"Look out old Macky's back!" The resonating crescendo of the last A-major seventh note of 'Mack the Knife' competed with the applause of the audience throughout the ballroom. It was Harry Connick Junior's third curtain call and the audience responded in kind. To the speleologists it was like a salve on an open wound.

If it hadn't been an experience enough already, Exley's revelations confounded the situation ad-infinitum. Neither Mallory nor Victoria could remember much about the road to Las Vegas; they were on an information overload. At least their mental fuse-boxes were in order. Without Exley's guiding hand they could have wound up in wandering around aimlessly in a daze anywhere. But here they were, absorbing the talent of one of the world's finest jazz pianists. In all his wisdom, Exley's idea turned out to be the perfect remedy.

"I'm really going to have to thank your uncle. That was the finest piano work I've ever heard," said a beaming Mallory. "It was just out of this world." Victoria stopped short and paled, realizing her pun. She stared in shock at Mallory who had been caught off guard also. Suddenly they both burst out laughing, more at themselves than the pun.

"Hey! How do you like that? We're laughing," Mallory said in relief.

"Thank God for small favors," added Victoria.

That was the last straw. They were back to relatively normal. They held hands and sipped champagne. The ballroom was abuzz with chatter. After the fine performance they were just two more people enjoying themselves. If it were possible, they would have prolonged that moment as long as they could. But each knew that what was to come was inevitable.

"Oh Connor I just don't know what to say," blurted Victoria. "Or think, or do, for that matter." She sighed, trying to keep her smile. It didn't work. "It's that part about getting shot or not getting out… It's all so overwhelming."

"You're not alone. I feel the same way. But look, even if we did just give it up and walk away we'd be left wondering about all the what ifs, and it would haunt us for the rest of our lives. Besides, if this whole adventure leading up to this comes to an instant halt, I'm certain I'd need a straitjacket." Mallory's logic hit home and it felt as good stating it as it did to Victoria hearing it.

She held his gaze for a moment and then said with a completely straight face, "Connor Mallory, I do know one thing," she said confidently, "I'm going to turn you every way but loose tonight. That, you can bet the farm on." Mallory's feeble attempt to hold a straight face was betrayed by the light in his eyes. "Great minds think alike." He then planted a kiss on her lips that brought "oohs" and "aahs" from the tables around them. Tomorrow would come; as it had a habit of doing so, but if there was ever a time to 'live for today' this was it. So they did.

"Room service." Mallory's eyes fluttered open and glanced at the clock. Ten sharp. He slept-walked over to the door and let the waiter in. On the cart was a pot of coffee, rolls, and a fruit bowl for each. Included was a handwritten note stating, 'rise and shine, it's showtime!' This was not the time to ponder the situation, it was time to get with the program. After one good morning kiss it was on with the show. They ravaged through breakfast and were into their second cup when there was a loud knock on the door. Before they could move, the door was opened by an embarrassed maid, and in marched the Brigadier with his two 'Adjutants.' The speleologists' jaws dropped.

Gone was the shoulder length silver hair and stubble beard. In place was a G.I. crew cut complete with white sidewalls. The starched and pressed uniform was laden with medals and rows of multicolored bars that only servicemen could decipher. Around his neck was the silver star. He was Poster Material, from his inhumanly close shave down to his mirror polished patent leather shoes. The Rangers appeared to have gone through the same form of transformation. Their hair was also close cropped and the uniforms they wore were fresh-out-the-box brand new. Their new boots weren't as polished as their commander, but were shiny enough to call intimidating. Mallory and Victoria were used to their 'crusty old muleskinners' mode and were totally astonished by what they were seeing. Their erect posture complemented their appearance.

Victoria, not quite believing what she was seeing, went over to the Rangers and slid her hand across their cheeks. She looked down at her hand and then back at the 'Adjutants' and shook her head, incapable of comment.

"Wow!" was Mallory's only response. There was really not much more one could say.

"Well kids, get into those silly get-ups of yours and let's get moving. My transportation is waiting." The transformation was even evident in the Bull's speech. No more easy going friendly mannerisms, just short clipped enunciated words, 'General' style. The speleologists jumped to attention like they were at boot camp, which was partially true. While they were preparing themselves, Exley lectured them on the plan they had gone through the night before. A plan which now seemed to be much more feasible after seeing this complete transformation. At twelve noon sharp they walked out the front door of the Flamingo with purpose in each stride to the awaiting vehicle complete with pennants on each side, the picture complete. They received more than a few glances from the guests around them. The General's car arrived with an extra driver to handle the Winnebago. They transferred the luggage and the Bull went to the trunk of his car and produced the lead lined suitcase complete with handcuff and chain. The Missing Link fit inside perfectly and was given to Townsend. The aftershock of Exley's revelations had dissipated and was replaced with total confidence. The Brigadier got in the back seat and said to the driver imperiously, "you may proceed." Call it an omen or not, but as the car pulled out of the driveway, a good sized movement of bird shit fell out of the sky and landed on the windshield. The driver attempted to wipe it off with the windshield wipers but only managed to spread it across the entire front glass. The General ordered him to pull over and clean it off. He was gruff and abrupt. The good natured part of his demeanor had completely disappeared.

Not once during the entire trip did Exley utter a word. He sat ramrod straight with his eyes affixed ahead on the road. His congeniality was replaced by a clinical shell. They were waved through the perimeter checkpoint with a salute to the pennants. Only then did Exley look at the speleologists with a wink and a nod. From there on it was strictly business. At the second checkpoint, the guard asked for identification and papers. The Bull went into action. He got out of the car and read the guard the riot-act. He was in his element. He'd ask a question or demand and answer, but every time the guard attempted a reply, Exley would interrupt him with another. The poor guard couldn't get a word in edgewise or an edge in wordwise. The guard finally said something to the effect of checking Security for confirmation which made the Bull turn crimson. He got directly two inches from the guards face and in low tones spoke for about thirty seconds, spittile flying with every word. During this time the guard seemed to visibly shrink until he finally came to attention, saluted and gave them the sign to pass through. The General returned the salute crisply and started back to the car. He halted halfway and returned back to the poor guard and got back in his face. This time he spoke in even lower tones. Whatever was said it made the guard turn ghostly white. The guard went to the telephone and in hurried tones talked to whoever was on the other end of the line. He repeatedly looked from the fuming General to the papers at his desk and paled even more. By the time the conversation was over it looked as if the unfortunate guard might have lost a couple years at the end of his life. This time he seemed almost apologetic as he waved them through. If the General was serious or not, he didn't give anything away. He parade-marched back to the car, got in and looked straight ahead. "Proceed to the hanger driver, pronto." When they arrived at the hangar there was a Jeep loaded with armed MP's waiting for them. Before they got out, the Bull said out of the side of his mouth "don't flinch. Cameras everywhere. Move! Fast!" Everyone got the picture so they followed the General's cues.

The MPs formed up around Townsend with the suitcase. Exley led the way, followed by the speleologists, Townsend and the MPs and then Souza and the driver. At the hangar, more MPs came to attention as they passed through the doors. Exley proceeded rigidly forward to the elevators. Here was another MP station. They all came to attention and a formal 'Changing of the Guard' occurred. When the elevator doors opened, the original MPs and the driver about-faced and went back out of the hangar, but not before the General said "remember, not a word to anyone; this comes from the top." The interior squad of MPs formed up around the party as they entered the elevator. Exley still maintained his rigid posture so everyone followed suit. As the elevator descended, Exley said to the MP in command "Tell 'He's broke' I want to see him right away. That's an order." The MP gave the General a quizzical look then said, "yes Sir. He's waiting for you at the bottom Sir." There was a slight quiver in his voice. When the elevator door opened, a Full Bird Colonel of the Military Police was waiting for them. He came to attention, saluted the General then relieved the interior squad of MP's of their duties. They saluted then went back up. The Bird Colonel about-faced and led them the way to the command post of Security to Dreamland. They went through a door that said 'Colonel Robert Hasbrook', Commander. The Colonel had the door open for all to pass through. When the door was shut Exley turned to the Colonel, "cameras?"

"None."

"All right gang, you can relax. We made it through." The Bull sat down and breathed a sigh of relief. "Howdy Boss, how've you been?"

The Colonel looked straight-faced at the Bull for a second, then broke out into a wide grin. "Goddamn Bull, what are you trying to do, shake up my whole Security Force?" He came over and shook hands then went to his desk and pulled out a bottle of Courvoisier and some glasses. "What the hell are you doing here? I thought we've finally gotten rid of you!"(?)

"Folks, this here is Bob Hasbrook, better known as a little 'Bobby He's broke', or if you really want to piss him off, Meatball." Exley ducked the steno pad that was thrown at him. "See what I mean? He's one of my old partners in almost everything," announced the Bull, ignoring Hasbrook's protests.

"I deny everything and demand proof," Hasbrook returned automatically. It sounded like a conditioned response. It was.

Introductions were made. When Townsend was introduced, Colonel Hasbrook eyed the suitcase but said nothing. Exley went on "this here's that little snot nosed Lieutenant that broke up my party way back when. He's not so little now."

At the mention of the party, Hasbrook deduced they knew a lot more about him than he thought they did and that this was not just a social call. "Shit, I've gotten this character's ass out of so much hot water so many times that I've lost count." He returned, "are you going to answer my question?"

The Bull's eyes twinkled. "The best defense is a good offense. I thought I'd test your boys out. What a pushover. We brought a little something that might be of interest to Stevenson. I didn't want to go through correct channels unless it's the real deal."

"Since when did you ever go through the 'correct channels', you devious SOB! That'll be the day." Hasbrook poured everyone a shot and they toasted.

"Seriously Bob, we just might be onto something. Where is he?"

"Come on you old fart. I already know about your meeting. They're all in the conference room. Waiting with bated breath I might add... We all know that anything you're involved with has to be something out of the ordinary. As soon as Stevenson got the message he's been like a kid on Christmas Eve. I mean it, they are all here. Have another snort. Miss Barbie, would you do the honors?" Hasbrook was out of the same mold as Exley, two peas in a pod, just not as quite seasoned.

"Thank you, Colonel Hasbrook. I'm going to need my video equipment for a complete presentation."

"That's all being taken care of as we speak. Your Winnebago has been secreted into a hangar and we took the liberty of doing it for you. It was actually a request from your Uncle." Hasbrook turned to the Bull, "knowing you, I also blacked out the security cameras in the conference room. I can reverse that, if you like?"

"Perfect. No, let's see what happens first. The fewer that know about this the better. For now. We've come a long way and the last part of having to play a snotty assed General took it out of me. I haven't gotten too much sleep lately either." Exley looked at his 'Adjutants' who nodded in agreement.

"I probably know why you haven't gotten any sleep, you horny old dog. And judging by the looks of your two 'adjutants' they were in on it with you. I too remember that party, you know," their verbal standoff quickly changed into fits of laughter and exchanges of episodes from their past. The light talk was brief, serving as a pressure-relief valve before the meeting. As the clock approached the prescribed hour a pall of seriousness permeated the atmosphere in the room.

Exley turned deadly serious… "The people you are about to meet are, shall we say, different. They rarely leave the premises and when they do, they are under escort. This place down here is their life and most of them have no desire to visit the outside world. They live, breathe, sleep and eat their work. To them nothing else matters. I only tell you this so you will be prepared. To them you might seem a little, 'off'. Just keep this in mind during the meeting." Hasbrook's statement had a sobering effect on everyone. But now at least they had an idea of what they could experience. Colonel Hasbrook opened his desk and pulled out a stack of papers and passed them around. "This is your basic security oath. From now on everything you see you haven't seen. It doesn't exist. You should probably deny ever coming this far anyway or you'll be hounded by the press. And any information leaked could be considered a violation of the Official Secrets Act and considered Treason. Sorry, but it's a must that you sign these." The Bull interjected, "this is usually passed out on top before even getting anywhere close to here. Bob is just covering his ass, and yours. If there is any flack to come down over this, it's going to fall on me because I brought you here." Exley paused to let this sink in, then went on, "on the other hand, you'll be protected, should you ever need it; it's like signing up with Team USA." Mallory glanced at Victoria who was lost in thought. He was about to suggest to the Rangers that maybe they have come far enough. But when he looked over at them, they were already signing the paper given to them. They passed them back to Colonel Hasbrook, shrugged and smiled back. No words needed to be said. The speleologists signed the document and passed them back to Hasbrook. "Thank you." was all that he needed to be said. What else was there to say?

"Well, on that cheery note, shall we go meet the think tank?" Exley's overly optimistic nuances were a direct contrast to the situation. "Bob, if any shit comes down while we're in there, fend them off until I can get us out. Then I'll deal with it." The statement was comforting and unnerving at the same time. Call it timing, because the clock hit three sharp. "It's time to go to the party, shall we dance?"

Before they went, Hasbrook added, "you got a call from a Doctor Harold Bloomfield and he wants you to call him when this is over. He's with LURE, so it's okay."

That was comforting, thought Mallory. They now were like fish in a tank. It was still 'okay' to call a friend if he wanted to. If he ever had any serious doubts about finding this thing before, they came to the surface now. But 'now' is too late. They were now in one of the most secure places on the planet and were under the 'protection' of the US Government. "Shit and shove me in it," he whispered under his breath, for which he got an elbow in the ribs from Victoria and a "uh huh" from the Rangers walking behind them. Hasbrook led them to yet another elevator with an armed guard who came to attention at their approach. He thought they had reached the bottom already and started wondering just how deep it could possibly go. Did he really want to know, he pondered? He didn't think so. The MP pressed a button and then a code that opened the elevator for them. He took a deep breath and entered with everyone into the abyss, he thought, as the doors closed.

Once again they followed Exley's example. Ramrod straight, spit and polished, he marched straight ahead. By the looks of him it was easy to tell the gears were turning inside his head. As to what, it was impossible to tell; his face was deadpan and didn't give away in the slightest what he was thinking. When the doors opened, even the Bull took an intake of breath in surprise of what stood in front of him

Standing at the doors, the man standing in front of them looked like an apparition out of the sixties, his unkept hair went way down below his shoulders. He looked like he might have once been in an acid rock band from San Francisco. He wore an ancient paisley shirt and faded, ripped blue jeans, and to complete the picture was a button proclaiming 'Flower

Power' on the frock coat he wore over his getup. Other than that he was of average height and weight although pale enough to be borderline albino. But that wasn't the reason for Exley's surprise. Along with the 'hippie' was a man in a wheelchair that looked as if he should have been dead at least a few decades ago. He was ancient. He still had a few wisps of hair on his head that were almost as long as the hippie's. His body had lost all of its tone years ago and resembled more of a cadaver than a living human being. But the most startling effect was his large blue eyes. They were set deep in his emaciated skull and had a penetrating quality to them that also seemed to hold the wisdom of the Ages. They also appeared to be the only part of him in working order. The eyes bounced off Exley, then to the speleologists where he gave Victoria a once over that would have befitted an amorous hound dog sizing up a pedigree poodle in heat. His gaze went to the Rangers and when he saw the suitcase it was as if he already knew what was in it. Then and only then did one side of his mouth come up in a semi-smile.

"Oh goody, it's the president of the world! Have I told you yet that he should be just that?" The hippie was talking to Victoria referring to the Bull. "I vote for him every year and who might you be?"

"Cool it Mike," Exley interrupted. "Let's get through introductions first before you scare the hell out of them."

"Yes yes yes. Let's do that. Okay. Mr. Potts." The emaciated man shut his eyes and grabbed onto the arms of his wheelchair. It was just in time too. The 'hippie' swung him around and pushed him like he was a toy into what looked like a small auditorium.

Exley took advantage of the brief break to address his 'adjutants'. "You two stay with me while they're giving their presentation. I've got a plan." He led the way into the theater-like room. At the other end of the room was a table with Victoria's video equipment hooked onto a large screen. On each side were tables with empty chairs. The 'hippie' pushed the wheelchair up to the center and when they were in place, people seemed to manifest out of the darkness and take their places at the tables. It was an eerie moment to say the least. It was as if they had been in hiding and then came out of the woodwork. The Rangers and speleologists huddled together like they were at the Alamo. They all sat down in silence and stared at each other. A Fellini movie had nothing on this.

This was the 'Brain Trust' of the United States of America. Although some appeared fairly normal, others could have easily landed a job in a Freak Show at a circus. In their care were the secrets of the most powerful government on Earth. And by looking at them one wouldn't think that in their hands was the balance of power of the entire planet. It took the newcomers a moment to adjust to the eeriness of the situation. They were thrust into frontstage center instantly and felt like they were being studied more as science projects than as fellow human beings.

Exley broke the silence. "Ahem. Gentlemen, these are doctors Connor Mallory and Victoria Barbie. And these two are Raymond Souza and Richard Townsend, Federal Park Rangers over at LURE on top of Maui's dormant volcano Haleakala, House of the Sun." The Bull used as much formality as possible for levity. "They have, as you will see, something that might be of vital interest to you." He turned to the speleologists. "Doctors, we will dispense with introductions of these gentlemen and for the time being their names will be on a need to know basis. Let me just introduce Mike Stevenson, and I'm happy to see Mr. Lezlie Potts is still with us and has been since the outset of the program." The 'hippie' came over and vigorously pumped each of their hands. Potts just looked at them straight in the eyes, said nothing and nodded. "Doctors, the floor is yours." Exley went over to Townsend, produced a key and unlocked the chain attached to his wrist. He set the suitcase on the table next to the video equipment. With a flick of his head he motioned the Rangers to a corner out of earshot and let the speleologists proceed.

Mallory took the floor and gave them a rundown on their original intent of finding a mythical lava tube connecting Maui and the Big Island, Hawaii, and the subsequent finding of the burial chamber. He included the mysterious 'blur' on their satellite photos and the effect of The Missing Link on their electrical systems. This caught the panel of scientists' attention. Victoria ran the video and cut it before the Awa root experience. Now the panel was completely attentive and some were murmuring between each other. When they were told of the findings up at Science City there was almost an insurrection of formal meeting procedure. Stevenson had to step in and bring the meeting back to a semblance of order. Once they had calmed down and got back in their seats, Mallory continued. He omitted the details from the top of Haleakala to Dreamland figuring that it also was on 'need to know basis,' and also the minor detail that they were in flight from the FBI. Since they were where they were it probably didn't matter anyway. The jaws of the trap had shut and they were at the mercy of their hosts. Only Exley's expertise could free them from their situation which was the only comforting thought they had at the moment. When the meeting calmed down he went over to the suitcase and opened it up. That's when all Hell broke loose.

What had to have been every alarm in the whole facility went off at once…. WHOOMPOW! 'Whoop whoops,' 'clang clangs,' and even the water from the fire extinguishing system joined in on the cacophony. Mallory slammed the suitcase shut but he was way too late. Hasbrook and a squad of armed MPs, guns at ready, filed into the auditorium. Stevenson was fast to act. He ran to Hasbrook who in turn about faced and fled to his office and shut the systems down. At that point there was no telling how far the alarms had gone and the extent of the attention it had drawn. The damage was done. For starters, everyone was wet. Hasbrook came back into the auditorium and told the MPs to stand down. Mallory and Victoria stood in the middle of it all hands raised, dripping wet. They lowered their hands when the MPs stopped pointing their firearms at them. There was a moment of stunned silence, all except for the Bull who was in the corner laughing at the scene. His laughter seemed to have a calming effect on everyone. Then the phone started ringing. Hasbrook leapt into action as did Stevenson. Everyone else just stood there, dripping. Towels were brought and gratefully accepted, as were the ways and means to bring back a resemblance of order. While Mallory and Victoria were drying themselves off and attempting to bring back a little dignity to their presentation, Lezlie Potts rolled over to them and spoke to them for the first time. "Well done" was all he said. His voice was surprisingly resonant.

At that moment Stevenson and Hasbrook came back from the phones. Hasbrook went directly over to the Bull and Stevenson came over to the speleologists, "a most extraordinary thing has occurred. All lights and even the propulsion system came on momentarily on our 'project' we have here. I believe this coincides with the opening of your suitcase. May I have another look?"

Stevenson looked to Mallory who looked to Victoria who looked to the Bull who looked to Colonel Hasbrook who nodded affirmatively. Mallory stood back and replied, "be my guest."

Stevenson cautiously went over to the suitcase and cracked the lid an inch then let it drop. Next, he opened it a bit further, slowly, as not to cause another similar disturbance. Once he found the alarms didn't go off, he opened it completely. Once he saw what was inside, he screamed "Aiyeee!" and started jumping around. He ran up to Victoria and hugged and kissed her before she could respond. He vigorously pumped Mallory's hand, again, and said "bless you bless you" repeatedly, then ran towards the Bull and the Rangers who by that time were prepared for almost anything. Exley held up his arms signaling Stevenson to keep his distance. "You've done it, Mister President. I knew I was right." By this time there was no holding back the rest of the scientists. Each took their turn examining the suitcase's contents, and thanking the speleologists. When it was clear enough, Lezlie Potts rolled up to the suitcase in his wheelchair. He looked at it thoughtfully for a moment, and then did the unexpected. He stood up out of his wheelchair! The scientists stood back aghast. Potts gathered up his stooped, decrepit body and slowly ambled over to the speleologists. Then straightened up as much as his body would allow. He grabbed Victoria's hand in his own and looked at them both. He then gave them a rare smile and said, "well, it seems you two found the keys to our spaceship."

In most cases, VIP treatment from the United States Government would have been gratifying, but to the speleologists, the Rangers and especially Tyrone 'Bull' Exley it was like being in Jail. They had unlimited credit at the Nellis P.X., a free tab at the Officers Club, and top secret classified security clearance status within the perimeter of the base. But that was as far as it went, literally. They were confined within the perimeters of the base. Leaving was out of the question. They understood the reasoning, but the big question in their minds was, for how long? For the first few days it had been a novelty, but now the novelty had worn off. When they began questioning this, they were met with "we'll have to get back to you on this," and that was it. No time frame was given for allowing them to leave.

The phone call to Doctor Bloomfield had also been puzzling. Ever since their departure, Science City had been under the scrutiny of Fife & Company. They had even gone as far as to put a twenty four hour guard around the lava tube/burial chamber entrance. Then one day they simply disappeared. And it just happened to be the day the speleologists arrived at Dreamland, and it didn't take a genius to put that one together.

The only brite spot in all this was meeting some of the Bull's old friends and acquaintances, his ex 'partners in crime.' so to speak. They would come by and swap stories of past escapades that were both enlightening and entertaining, but even that had trickled off to next to nothing.

The Bull had become increasingly agitated of late. He had even gone as far as tackling the Top Brass, but was met by a stone wall. To him, confinement to base was the ultimate slap in the face, and he clearly wasn't used to it, ready for it, nor did he like it one bit. He was like a caged lion at best. Repeated demands for answers had gone to deaf ears and that was beginning to wear thin real fast. The damn dam was about ready to break, and real soon.

The Rangers, on the other hand, were taking things placidly. They were spending most of their time at the Officers Club enjoying the deep well of free reign. They had gone as far as striking up relationships with a pair of W.A.F.'s, Women's Air Force, and sometimes didn't make it back to home at night.

Their 'home' was a three bedroom house on Generals Row. In fact it had been the Bull's old home before retirement. It seemed that after he left, no one wanted to move into the Great General's place so as to not defile it as a shrine to his existence. It was now used for visiting dignitaries and that's what they were; confined visiting dignitaries.

On top of this all, they had received no word concerning their discovery. After the meeting and presentation, they were politely thanked and The Missing Link was taken deeper into the bowels of Dreamland. They had been given empty promises of updates but to no avail. The only information they had received was through Colonel Hasbrook and even that was sporadic. Plus they didn't even know that it had fit perfectly into the crashed ship, and that the ship came instantly to life; what was happening from then on remained a mystery. Colonel Hasbrook had been sincerely apologetic explaining his, "hands were tied," but also promised a presentation was coming soon. They were all wandering around in the pointless forest.

It was a beautiful twilight evening and the speleologists we're having a brandy and coffee on the porch of the General's old home. Talk was minimal and the chill of the autumn air made the coffee a welcome addition. Their serenity was interrupted by the roar of a Jeep engine coming up the road that came to a screeching halt in front of the premises. Out stepped the unlikely trio of Colonel Bob Hasbrook, the Bull and finally none other than Mike Stevenson out of the confines of his Laboratory. In one hand the Bull carried a bottle of Scotch, in the other was the collar of Mike Stevenson whose feet barely touched the ground as they approached. Hasbrook smugly followed. The Bull more than less carried Stevenson up the steps and brusquely set him in a chair and slammed the Scotch bottle on the table causing the speleologists coffee cups to rattle. Hasbrook leaned against the entrance way, his reasoning obvious. The Bull retreated inside and returned with two extra chairs, one he set next to Stevenson and the other Hasbrook sat barring the entrance.

"Hi there folks! We're going to have us a little friendly impromptu interrogation." The Bull's smile was more of a grimace, but friendly nonetheless.

The smug look on Hasbrook's face told he was enjoying every minute of it. Stevenson's countenance however was how General George Armstrong Custer might have looked just before he was about to bite the big one. The Bull brought three glasses and poured double shots in each. "Here you go Mike, let's have a drink." It was definitely an order, not an offer. Stevenson might have been out of his element, but he was still a trooper. All three toasted "cheers," and they threw down the double shot, which was immediately replaced with more.

"Thanks Mr. President," said Stevenson meekly.

"God damn it! Cut that shit out! You know I'm not the goddamn president," roared The General.

"But you should be."

"That's immaterial. Have another drink."

Hasbrook had to turn his face away to keep from laughing. When he turned back around, his face was bright pink and he was biting his lip.

Stevenson threw down another. He might have not been used to it, but he wasn't a stranger either. After a third double shot he had visibly relaxed as the whiskey took effect.

Stevenson meagerly attempted to steer the conversation around the subject. The Bull allowed him to exchange pleasantries with the speleologists which allowed him to relax even more. But after his fourth shot, when his tongue had loosened up sufficiently, Exley nailed him to the wall.

"Okay Mike, enough is enough. You might like being cooped up in here but we don't. It's been over a week since we brought this thing to you. An explanation is way overdue." The Bull leaned over the table and was inches from Stevenson's face. The statement and gesture was simple and persuasive. Stevenson looked around the table then back at Hasbrook. There was no escape. He sighed deeply and began to speak.

"First of all, Mr. Pres… ah, let me tell you that we have not purposely left you out, it's just that there's so much more than we possibly could have imagined. To put it bluntly, what you have brought us could solve the energy problems for all Mankind. But there's more. And here's where we have only scratched the surface. That's what is taking so long. Not only does it make our ship come to life, but it is also a miniature encyclopedia of some sort. We have the finest encryption and code breakers on it as we speak, and they're even keeping me out of their way. What I do know is there is a language translation about from whence it came, to a language that was from Earth before our recorded history. The closest we have come is that it is relative to the earliest forms of latin texts known to us. And if our guess is right, it comes from way before then. They're making headway, but it's far from complete. The technology we're dealing with is light years ahead of us and we don't know how or why you came upon it as you did. It's like we have a puzzle with all the pieces, but don't know how to put it together, yet."

The Bull, who had been standing, let his rear end fall into the chair opposite Stevenson. He looked around the table at the astonishment on everyone's faces. He had watched the scientist make his speech, searching for inconsistencies but there were none. Then he looked Stevenson straight in the eyes searching for the slightest inclination of evading the truth.

"Who knows?" he asked.

Stevenson didn't hesitate. "Just those within the compound, and you all of course. We played the alarm systems going off as a mistake, but I don't know how long that will last. The information we do have so far is far from complete, so until we have what we think is a complete package, no one will know." Stevenson gave them a sly smile. "After all, a Base that doesn't exist doesn't have to obey public laws."

The Bull smiled at Stevenson's last statement. "You are not so bad after all Mike. However, when this information does leak, the shit's gonna hit the fan…" Then the Bull slightly paled. It was as if a revelation just hit him, hard. "Or it wouldn't at all." He got out of his chair and started pacing. Stevenson reached for the bottle and poured himself another, then wordlessly looked around for any takers, but there were none. "Okay Mike, I don't think you're hiding anything, yet. I want you to get back there and put together a presentation ASAP. We're all sick of being out in the cold on this and would actually like to get on with our lives; if we can. You know what I mean don't you? Thanks."

"I'll do what I can, Mr. Prez… ah, General. It will still take a few days to put what we have together. Am I correct to assume you don't want to go public with this?"

The Bull looked at Stevenson. "Mike, even you haven't been locked up here long enough to know the answer to that. Even if we wanted to, would they let us? And once the bureaucratic element gets involved what's going to happen? This is serious shit everybody. It's time to start dancing on eggshells."

CHAPTER 7

THE WHITE HOUSE

A chilly Autumn wind blew in gusts, causing the fallen leaves to fly in formations that looked like soldiers scrambling for life across a World War I battlefield. It was a morbid analogy, but to the observer this day it was apropo. She wasn't in the best of moods this day, nor had she been the whole past week. The pressures of the Office were taking their toll.

"Scandal," she accidentally said aloud, as if talking to herself. This small outburst was involuntary, acting like a pressure release from the turmoil inside her inner being.

"Excuse me Ms. President?" Her secretary Ana Barton quizzed.

"Oh, nothing Ana, I was just thinking out loud. It's nothing. Thank you, you may go now," said Beverly Brandt, the first woman President of the United States of America. She was almost to the point of being angry with herself for letting that word slip out for anyone to hear. That was the last thing she needed. Especially now.

She came from her observation at the window of the leaves flying around in the Autumn winds. She sat down at her desk in the Oval Office, put her elbows on the desk and rubbed her temples. I'll have to be a lot more careful, she thought to herself. One slip like that in the wrong ears and she could wind up in a political morass like the previous President(s)? And she liked the way he played the saxophone. If anyone found out about… The buzzer on the intercom interrupted her train of thought and it was a welcome relief. She pressed the button. "Yes?" she asked.

"It's the chairman of the Joint Chiefs Ms. President. He's on line one from the Pentagon." Ana Barton's voice sounded far off and tinny, even though she was in the next room.

Thank you Ana, tell him I'll be with him in a moment." She had to gather her thoughts, General Steve Cleveland, Chairman, Joint Chiefs, medals in Vietnam, The Gulf and Kosovo, 3 stars, Air Force. Fairly congenial, but a no nonsense personality. She would have to deal with him accordingly. She picked up her phone and pressed line one. "Yes General Cleveland, what can I do for you?"

"Good morning Ms. President," Cleveland, in typical military preciseness. "We have just received the news from our science facility at Nellis Air Force Base of a discovery that could have major implications. They were supremely vague about it over the phone, but are planning to have a formal presentation sometime next week. You are invited by Lezlie Potts himself. It must be very important, madam." Cleveland never wasted words. To him, his time was invaluable.

"Thank you general, I'll try to have my secretary fit you in. If you will please give her the details, thanks again." She hung up the phone. 'Potts', that old lecher in the wheelchair. When he looked at you, you felt transparent. And he had no qualms about covering every square inch of your body, she thought. But on the other hand, for him to call for a meeting, something of supreme importance must be going on. She pressed the intercom, "Ana, see if you can fit me in on the meeting the General called about. Priority one." She got an affirmative response, then cut the communication. The 'science facility', she knew, was in reality Dreamland. For information to be put into a formal presentation was truly an oddity. And by Lezlie Potts himself, even more of a mystery. Oh well, she thought. At least it would be a break from the dogma of running the biggest superpower on Planet Earth. Never in her wildest dreams would she have realized how precarious the position of being the front piece of a nation would turn out to be. Adding the extra scrutiny for being the first woman on the job compounded the issue ad infinitum. A road trip to Dreamland would seem like a vacation.

Her thoughts drifted back to the matters at hand. As things were, she constantly walked a political highwire when dealing with the everyday issues that her position required. Any minor slip in either direction would cause her to fall into the safety net, if there even was one. The great Wallenda had nothing on her. But if anybody ever got wind of the 'scandal' that was on her mind, it would be a political firing squad. That, for some perverse reason at the moment, didn't actually sound that bad. She smiled to herself over that, but her thoughts were once again interrupted by the sound from the intercom. Duty was calling.

Twenty years ago, if anyone would have told Beverly Brandt that she would one day be President of the United States she would have laughed in their face and thought them crazy. Her unlikely trail into the political arena had been a series of unrelated occurrences, her gender being first and foremost. She was born and raised in Carmel, California. One of the most beautiful areas in the region. Her scholastic achievements weren't that spectacular, but they were above average. Her environment had brought her respect for the sanctity and preservation of Mother Earth and was always participating in quests for better treatment of the planet. She was good at what she did, drawing the attention of the financially well-to-do folks of the area. And she had also become one tough cookie. Then came the books.

The books were in a series of eight. If one were to categorize for library or bookshelf purposes they could fit under Mysticism/Religion. Neither could fit totally either way, they were in a new thought interpretation. In reality they were books on Truth. They slipped through the quagmire of religious sect interpretation and as for mysticism, they merely got to the core of down-to-earth inner truths without the flowery BS that usually went along with that train of thought. And what's more, none of the major organized religions seemed to be able to argue with the principles she set forth, nor did they want to. How could they? It was just the Truth. The popularity of the series took off like wildfire. She was instantly thrust into the spotlight. When anyone wanted her opinion on something or another she would give a short winded answer, non offensive and logical that made it tough to argue with. Her popularity skyrocketed starting with bumper stickers and graffiti aficionados stating 'Beverly for President,' then along came 'Truth and Politics.' Who could have imagined? The seed was planted. Eventually she wound up in the Presidential Debates, her opponent's replies were typically long-winded and ambiguous. Her replies were concise, logical and to the point. Instead of a political windbag boring everyone to tears, there was someone actually coming up with simplistic answers to complex questions; a novelty in this day and age.

At first she considered this as going along with a good joke. But as her popularity grew she started realizing the enormity of it and went public to diffuse the situation. She tried to explain she had no desire whatsoever for any kind of political office. This backfired completely. The political climate was in her favor and she won by a margin sufficient to her cause.

Her musings were interrupted by the intercom. "That was very strange Ms. President. I just received word from a Colonel Hasbrook at Nellis. He was extremely evasive. He is the head of security there and wouldn't give up any pertinent information. I asked for someone who could, explaining it was for you and he said that only a Mr. Lezlie Potts could speak about it and he was unavailable. We did secure a time frame though; they have a presentation set for next week, Friday. We can take Air Force One Thursday afternoon and you can get a good night's rest during the flight. In the meantime I'll try to dig up this Mister Potts for you."

"Thank you, that'll be just fine." (Fucked up, insecure, neurotic and emotional.) "I want to speak with Potts, now! You tell them to make him available immediately!" She used this tone only occasionally when she deemed it necessary. "I want to speak with him yesterday. Do you understand?" She cut her secretary off before any reply, for effect. If she sounded perturbed enough it would usually bring results, sooner than later. A few minutes later she called Ms. Barton once again. "Ana, also

I want you to find out who else is attending this presentation. I want a complete list. Thank you." She was more polite this time, even though her request was still a direct order.

For the next few hours she dealt with paperwork concerning the matters of state. Especially with how to relatively keep her campaign promises. As usual, they were way out of proportion to reality. 'You can please some of the people some of the time, but you can't please them all, all of the time,' W.C. Fields' classic statement constantly echoing in the back of her mind. A tap on the door brought her back to the here and now. Ana Barton entered, "here is the list for the Nellis Presentation." Then she was gone. President Brandt finished what she had been doing before picking up the list. She picked it up, curiosity more than background homework, being at the forefront of her mind. She scanned the names and wasn't surprised to see who she expected. Armed Forces, CIA, FBI, NSA, but when she got to the bottom of the list she froze in horror. Her eyes widened and her jaw fell open. It was her worst nightmare come true. Her eyes froze on one name. She couldn't remove her eyes from that name. Was this some kind of joke? Or has someone finally penetrated her secret of secrets? Scandal. Had the word she accidentally uttered a few hours ago been a premonition? But there it was, in black and white. She was going to be in the same room with the only person that could topple her from her temporary pedestal. In one instant her personal world crumbled around her.

The organ music in the background rose to a crescendo as the man in the blindingly immaculate white suit finished up his Sermon. "Praise the almighty! Hallelujah!" His arms were outstretched and his eyes rolled up into the back of his oversized head. His last statement was almost a shout as if he was conversing with the heavens themselves. Then he faced the camera with a huge, toothy white smile. "And remember, a generous contribution into the coffers of the Almighty will most surely land you a spot with the most high for all eternity. Ah lehuv yueh!" The canned applause filled the rest of the airspace designated for the weekly TV hour. The lights dimmed as the organ music played on until the director signaled they were off air. The Reverend Chuck T. Mansin ripped off his clip-on bow tie and shouted, "can't you get those Hellfire lights any hotter? I was sweating fucking bullets in front of the whole goddam nation." It was true. A bead of sweat trickled down his forehead, across his cheek and all the way to his jowley neck carving a wide path through his thick cake of makeup. He threw his bow tie at the light man and added a voluminous "Fuck!" as he stomped off to his dressing room. The light man flipped him off as he retreated.

 He slammed the door of his dressing room with such force it caused his name plate to fall off the door, again. Instead of pissing him off further, this brought a minor degree of satisfaction causing a slight uplifting of the corners of his mouth into what one might mistake for a smile. It wasn't. He went directly to his desk and opened the drawer that held a half full bottle of Southern Comfort and poured a generous portion into a well used water glass. He threw the room temperature liquid down his throat and poured another. This time he set the dingy glass on the desk and removed his white suit jacket, revealing a silk white shirt that was drenched with sweat from the armpits outward. It was almost totally soaked and the noxious fumes emanating from it rivaled that of the greasy fingerprinted glass that contained the Southern Comfort. These sticky odors caused his assistant, Bill Bugel to gag when he entered the room with the special delivery letter he had just received. Bugel beat a hasty retreat after laying the envelope on the table managing a quick, "for you Reverend," as he left. To add to the pungent environment, the Reverend Mansin pulled a hand-rolled Cuban cigar out of the inside pocket of his coat, lit it carefully and sat down at his desk and kicked off his Gucci shoes thus adding yet another body odor to the room. He put his odiferous feet on the desk, leaned back, cigar in one hand and dingy water glass in the other, content in knowing he had just 'fleeced his sheep' once again for probably another hundred thou. He was a true example of a living contradiction.

 The road to becoming one of the country's leading TV evangelists could quite possibly be construed as a comedy of errors. He had realized his oratory skills early in life as an agitator and protester of the then unpopular Vietnam War. He was a natural in finding negative things to say and dwell on them in front of an audience, thus working them up to a frenzy about what's wrong. That was the climate of the time and he was taking full advantage of it. He could go on and on for hours pointing out anything and everything that wasn't right or needed room for correction, offering no answers nor alternate plans to make whatever the topic was, improved. His talent lay in pointing out the problems, but not offering up any solutions. He was like a pig in shit; getting laid almost everyday and all the free drugs he could handle. Then came two major events that changed his life. The first was the Ohio State University riot where he met 'her' and the second was when that asshole with his name murdered all those people in California. Two negative occurrences which he used to his advantage. At the Ohio riot he had worked the audience like putty in his hands. Shit, they were all mostly too stoned to know any better. Their formulative minds were wide open for any information to absorb. When the shit hit the fan, he grabbed 'her' and went and hid in the University Church. When the smoke lifted and the police had contained the riots, four people lay dead in the streets. While in the church he had taken full advantage of the situation by having his way with 'her.' Only later did he find out she was freshly married and her new husband was caught in the melee outside. But the damage was already done. Who could have imagined at the time she would turn out to be who she would be. And spending that night in a church had sparked a new train of thought in his mind.

The murders by his namesake in California had also offhandedly given him a boost in fame. That, plus the riot had caused him to go in hiding and forced him to formulate some kind of new alternate plan. It didn't take long for him to figure: why not turn political agitation into religious fervor? And if he was the other Charles Mansin, why not be the all loving, all forgiving side of an already famous name? This idea, plus new scandals surfacing about the already popular evangelists, paved the way for the formation of the 'Non-denominational Church of the Almighty.' A name that didn't step on toes nor contradict any other churches in the religious arena. Now all he needed then was the bucks to back it up.

His connections as a political radical helped in this department. During this period he had made alliances with many major drug smugglers and whatnot, and they were always looking for ways to launder their cash into the system. They were more than happy to jump on the bandwagon. This was a precarious time for Chuck. He was finally forced to shorten his name from Charles to Chuck to alleviate negative publicity. Because it was time to either produce results or receive cement shoes. The acquaintances he had made in the forgery business produced enough paperwork to make him a bona fide clergyman and now it was time to gather his flock. His first move was to start with a media blitz, getting the idea from Goebbels' Nazi propaganda machine. He put advertisements in every radical newspaper and magazine in the country; sufficiently bending the words to substantiate each of their points of view. Flyers were handed out in every hotspot of political or racial unrest, denouncing everything he had previously supported. He even went on to do a brief stint in professional wrestling as an Evangelist proclaiming "I love you" which stuck in the minds of young and old alike. He shunned alliances or meetings with other evangelists for fear of being exposed as the sham he truly was. He miraculously showed up at every major catastrophe he could: damning the people responsible to the fiery pits of eternity. His bubble was almost burst when 'that tortured soul' who assassinated Lennon proclaimed he was a member of the 'Non-denominational Church of the Almighty." which Chuck had to vehemently deny. His underground connections within the prison system took care of that. No mention was ever made again. Then, just when he was about to go under, he got the biggest break of all.

The girl from the church in Ohio hit it big with her books. He used his media tactics to support and promote them to the fullest extent. He even coined some of her phrases to serve his purpose and fit into his media attack. It was time to pick the fruit while it's still ripe. Naturally, when she figured out who it was supporting her, she called a private meeting.

She happened to be in New York on a promotional book signing tour during the aftermath of Lennon horror. The 'Reverend' conveniently made his presence known there also. A phony chance encounter was set up for the next day. No cameras, no reporters and no affiliation whatsoever was agreed upon. The Reverend could sense her paranoia and decided to twist the knife, heavily, and go for the whole ball of wax.

If one was inclined to do so, they could go as far as to call it blackmail. He had done his homework well and figured that the birth of her daughter fit into the time span of that night in Ohio. Neither one of them wanted the negative publicity, but it was she who stood to lose the most, namely her marriage and the possible legitimacy of her daughter. And it was on this point that the Reverend hammered home.

So an agreement was made that an 'anonymous' donation would go to the coffers of the 'Non-denominational Church of the Almighty.' And through her popularity as an author, a 'request' would be made for an hour long broadcast on syndicated television for the Reverend to spread his message throughout the land, all of which became a reality. The Reverend flim-flammed his way to the top of the popularity polls and the author, well, she just happened to become the President of the United States. They both agreed to never see each other again.

The explosion from the anal cavity of the Reverend Chuck T. Mansin erupted just as Bill Bugel came into the room. It was staggering. The cigar was half gone and so was the bottle. The Reverend took delight in the expression of his assistant's face. "Come in, sit down and have a drink with me, Bill." His tone was almost cordial but they both knew it was directly the opposite.

"Thanks but no, Reverend. I just came to see if you saw who the letter was from." Bugel spoke through his mouth trying not to inhale. To do so might cause him to faint. "I'll come back after you have read it." In the blink of an eye he was back out the door.

The Reverend chuckled over his assistant's discomfort. Then he picked up the letter. "The State Department. I'll be damned," he said to himself. He reached into his pocket and pulled out his switchblade and opened the letter. He sat up straight in his chair causing yet another anal eruption and a simultaneous burp of Southern Comfort. As he read its contents his face became devoid of any expression. He finished, then read it again. Then yelled "Bugel, get your ass in here!" The assistant came in holding his breath. "Find one of my early tapes and arrange it for the next few week's shows. Then get the limo and pack our bags. Make reservations at the Sahara in Vegas. We're going on vacation courtesy of the United States Government." Bugel nodded affirmatively and exhaled as he left the room.

The air conditioning fans, although working at full capacity couldn't contain the smoke that was filling the room.

There was a gray cloud towards the ceiling emanating from the various combustibles each person in the room was consuming. The tensor lamps at each chair illuminated them from the shoulders down and offered them the option of anonymity. It was an eerie scene, as if each person sitting there were headless. For some, this was a requirement. For others only a convenience. But protocol had been established years before, and to break it would be possible elimination from life itself.

The position they held had been handed down through generations. It wasn't what you knew but from whom you were born. Each position was as carefully guarded as the billions of every currency each represented. Nothing personal, only financial responsibility.

Furthermore, entrance to this room had their own separate entry ways. No one saw from whence they came. It was another safeguard. Names were non-existent, they were "The Trust". They went way beyond politics, the only common denominator was the making and hoarding of money and what they represented was far from simple. This small group held a financial stranglehold on the entire world. They did so by owning the Banks, Natural Resources and the Power Industries of every major country on the planet. Absolutely nothing could transpire without their ultimate approval. They financed wars and revolutions, then supplied the resources necessary to carry them out. They received personal gain by playing both sides against each other, at the cost of millions of other people's lives. Their movements throughout history were guided by supply and demand. The crux of the situation was that they were both supply, and demand. This had been going on since the beginnings of the Industrial Revolution. Their biggest boost came at the outset with the purchase of the Federal Reserve Bank of the United States in 1913. This enabled them to buy into every Oil and Power industry in the world. Every major financial institution was a subsidiary. Every drop of oil and all electricity and water was controlled by them. They owned terrorist groups, the mafia and strategically held seats in every major government on Earth. Their goal was simple: financial global domination and control.

The positions were held through bloodlines. Politics were beneath them. The common denominator between them was personal gain and want, in that order. Each seat represented a monopoly from various areas on the planet. They owned it all and wanted more. All that was left was outer space and they had plans for that also. Their secret was guarded through puppet organizations and governments. The glue that held it together was greed, and they were at the top of the mountain. On paper they didn't exist. They were the marionettes behind the public eye that controlled all the basic necessities required for life on Earth. The buck started and stopped here.

No congenialities were exchanged as they filed into the room from their various entryways. The only noise came from the overworked air conditioner and the movement of chairs as they settled in. From the looks of their hands that shone under the lamps, it was easy to tell that over two thirds were old and withered. The others were young and un-wrinkled which belied the fact that their predecessors had recently passed on. More often than not this came from natural causes, but not always; The one thing in common was that each set of hands had a plethora of gaudy baubles on them. The hands that lifted the gavel to bring the meeting to order had a good size diamond on it that could have been in a museum. It probably had. The hands belonged to a woman.

Earphones were used to translate languages. These were not optional because they also contained voice distortion gimmickry to further guarantee anonymity. It was a miniature United Nations based on ruthless greed.

The gavel came down three times to gather everyone's attention. The voice that came out of the headset sounded more like a computer than a human. "Emergency meeting of 'The Trust' is now in order." The voice droned on... "We have information from contacts within the US Government that a discovery has been made that might affect our grip on the economy. It is currently being held at Nellis Air Force Base and a formal presentation is taking place next week. Our operative will be there and will relay relative information. Questions?

"Should I make arrangements to have it stolen? Do we need to eliminate anyone?" Even through the headphones, the thick Sicilian accent could still be detected.

"Not at this moment, but forewarned is forearmed. Set that contingency in place. We will use it if necessary. Any others?" The silence hung suspended in the room as each member was left to their own thoughts. "That is all. You will be notified through proper channels of our next meeting." No goodbyes nor small talk was needed.

Soon the chairs were empty and the room vacated. The tensor lamps were shut down and the air conditioner relieved of duty. The only thing left was the thick smoke that began to stick to the walls.

Each member had their own separate exits that would take them down to various unrelated areas in the building, thus to eliminate chance meetings at ground level. If anyone of them were to be seen together, speculation would spread like wildfire. That was the last thing anyone needed. In the public eye some of them were even considered as enemies. If word ever got out that they were actually holding meetings together, their positions would be jeopardised. That could be seriously detrimental to their health.

The hand that had held the gavel was known to the others as Violet. Her elevator went directly down to an underground parking lot where her stretch limo was waiting. She wasted no time leaving the area. To the American public she was Mom, America and Apple Pie rolled into one. During WWII Millions were made on both sides of the fence only at the cost of the lives of countless innocent civilians. Without her business acumen the V1 and the V2 rocket project would never have gotten off the ground and conversely many German cities wouldn't have to be reduced to rubble. But a buck was a buck. Her husband eventually died and their offspring had met an early demise. So it was she who had to take the position within the 'Trust.' It wasn't voluntary, it was mandatory. Chairmanship was established by seniority and she was the matriarch. Once inside the limousine she picked up her phone and punched in a number. After a few rings, the voice on the other end of the line responded with a simple "yes?"

"General, it's me. Is this line secure?"

"Hold on," replied the voice. A few seconds later it returned. "I'm not positive, I'll call you back." Then the line went dead.

The next few minutes passed in silence until her car phone rang again. "I'm sorry for the delay, but this is the Pentagon and you just never know," announced General Cleveland. "What can I do for you?" Now, he thought to himself, omitting the last word. Dealing with this Bitch always put him in a precarious position.

"Just exactly what's going on, General? Is what I want to know. What does that asshole Potts have up his sleeve now?" Her elderly shrill voice spewed saliva at the mouthpiece of her phone.

If Cleveland would have been in her presence he would have shrunk in stature from her outburst. This Old Lady had enough venom in her baby toe to stop a bull elephant. But he was safely tucked inside his private office inside the Pentagon and she was in her limo probably going to her estate on Long Island. This allowed him enough courage to sound confident, hollow as it was. "They're being vague and evasive." You cunt. "Ma'am," he replied. "But what I have gotten so far, it has something to do with the propulsion system of their spacecraft. A breakthrough. That's all they're giving us at the moment. I'll know more after their presentation Friday." His answer was actually honest, which was a novelty in itself.

The Old Lady, usually short on patience, was taken by surprise. This is surely a development worthy of scrutiny. She softened her tone, "well that is interesting, General Cleveland. Please let me know what you find out as soon as possible. It could be beneficial to the both of us," she purred. She could change her personality like a tampon. "I'll be anxiously awaiting your next report. Have a pleasant day." You fucking puppet. "Goodbye."

A breakthrough in the propulsion system of the spacecraft. The repercussions from something like that could be staggering. For someone that wasn't even supposed to know about the spacecraft's existence, she was very pleased. What if they actually solved the problem? Maybe buying up outer space wasn't that far off after all. The miles passed by as she pondered possible contingencies. They could be limitless. She picked up the phone and punched in a number. "This line is secure," stated the voice at the other end. It was the same guttural accent that had been at the meeting. Without introductions, "Mr. Brown, your suggestion at the meeting is now more plausible. Organize your finest retrieval team to be ready at a moment's notice. Spare no expense."

"Is this Trust business?" asked the voice, obviously delighted in creating a little mayhem.

"Yes and no. If we get a jump on this we could stand to gain more pull within the Trust. But we have to stay within its parameters, for now. Otherwise, it's too dangerous. Capice?" Although they were both power hungry megalomaniacs, they were still outnumbered. "For the time being it's between just us. We'll keep it in the family. But if we have to release it within the Trust we'll come up smelling like roses for doing our homework."

"I'll get one team from the city and another from the old country. That way, if need be they can phase each other out." The line went dead.

Violet leaned back and inhaled deeply. More income at others' expense. Perfect. She was fond of that little mobster called Mr. Brown. Obviously when he had chosen a name for himself he wasn't thinking of a toilet. Regardless, the joke was on him. They thought alike. Plus he was good under the sheets. At that thought she reached into her purse and pulled out a syringe and her pungent portable vibrator, its odor similar to rancid tuna. It was time for a little self-inflicted reward.

MISSING LINK

The rain had gathered momentum in the last few hours, causing puddles to turn into miniature lakes. The man approaching the front door to FBI headquarters had to take a zig-zag course to get there, secretly wishing it was a moat to prevent his way. He hesitantly opened the door prepared for another day of Hell on Earth. Being the laughingstock of the Bureau didn't help his disposition one bit.

Ever since Agents Bernard Fife and Persons had returned from Hawaii with the unsuccessful mission under their belt they had been the brunt of every cow joke known to man. He would arrive at work to a daily chorus of hee haws and/or moooos in the morning which would set the stage for the rest of the day. This poor fucker was down low, someone had gone as far as to go to a novelty shop and get some artificial poop. What was even worse was the fact that his partner Agent Persons had quit shortly thereafter, so the fiasco left Fife alone to be on the receiving end of the jokes and pranks.

Then came the beard. Somehow, someway, 'they' had successfully left Hawaii, gotten all the way across the US, and wound up in the Florida Keys undetected. They were spotted at a Hemingway lookalike contest and escaped. Hence the beard. Yesterday, he had gotten to work and on his desk was a costume beard and a copy of For Whom the Bell Tolls on it, the meaning obvious. He was a marked man.

This day, he'd had so much of enough he was considering following Persons, but as usual, it's always darkest before the dawn. He apprehensively approached his desk expecting the worst, when his assistant informed him his presence was requested in the Section Chief's office as soon as he got in. Wonderful.

Now what? He thought. It couldn't get any worse, could it? It had been bad enough of late, but throw in all the flak he had to take his whole career because of his name, the hard sheen of his personality was beginning to crack.

Bernard Xavier Fife from Paduka, Illinois had received the nickname 'Barney' during his childhood. Although he bore no resemblance whatsoever to the TV character, sometimes his actions did. If accident prone was a viable term, 'Barney' was an accident magnet. As a child he was considered an uncoordinated klutz in sports, but it went way beyond the playing field. He was just plain clumsy. Things just seemed to happen to him. It got so bad that a real life accident was called a 'Barney'. So he was inadvertently involved in every mishap that occurred in Paduka and beyond.

This caused two things. A general alienation from making friends while growing up and the formulation of a hard shell around his feelings, two traits that contributed positively towards his chosen vocation. He has even managed to curb his clumsiness. His cold callousness came in handy as an FBI Agent. He had no trouble whatsoever enforcing the laws and busting people for any infraction of them. He had chosen well.

But after his adventure in Hawaii and the results thereof, the prodding and name calling had resurfaced and Bernie could only take so much. It was as if he had struggled his whole life to escape from, had come back to haunt him and slap him in the face once again. It was precariously close to the last straw.

He left his foul weather gear at his desk which was miraculously free of any prank material and headed towards the Section Chief's office. He heard no animal calls which was a relief in itself, and finally noticed that everyone was avoiding his stare. Whether this was a good omen or not he couldn't tell. Nor did he care. All that mattered at this point was the welcome relief. Maybe the axe had fallen and was descending straight towards his neck on the chopping block. One way or another he was about to find out.

"Go right in, you are expected Agent Fife," said secretary Ginger Susner. Gone was the amusement behind her eyes. Something was definitely amiss.

He tapped on the door and entered. The Chief motioned him to a chair and kept on reading the brief in front of him, occasionally looking up at Fife and back to the papers. After what seemed like an eternity passed the Chief finally set the papers down, he gave Fife a penetrating stare. "It seems, Agent Fife, that you are going to be able to vindicate yourself from this latest embarrassment. The people you were sent to bring in wound up at Nellis Air Force Base with something apparently of major importance. That part is vague. What we do know is they are currently garrisoned at the Base itself and are under the protection of the Security Force there. A meeting is scheduled next week Friday and you, Agent FIfe, are going to be there. You will be our eyes and ears and report anything that affects National Security. Make the necessary arrangements. That is all." The chief passed him the Brief and picked up another. It was an obvious dismissal. Fife picked up the document, then headed towards the door. "Oh. And Fife, I don't need to tell you that this could make or break your career. Any replay of Hawaii and you might as well not even come back."

Fife left the office floating on air. A chance to vindicate this latest embarrassment was meat and potatoes. He didn't need to be told his career was on the line, he felt that way himself. He floated over to his desk, sat down and read the brief. Shit, they were almost in custody already. He would be their shadow. He could mop up the previous mess he had created in one fell swoop. Bernie would not be 'Barney' again. He felt so ecstatic he decided to call in Persons. Persons was in the private sector now and it wouldn't hurt to stay out of FBI boundaries if need be. He could turn disaster into advancement, and the key to it all was secure at a military base. He would not lose them again. Besides, what could go wrong? Yeah.

CHAPTER 8

Dr. Harold Bloomfield was perplexed. Somehow, without his knowledge, new satellites appeared around the globe. And what's more, not one scientific community on the planet was claiming responsibility for them. It was as if they had appeared out of nowhere. Further scrutiny provided no answers. In other words, their function was unknown. They fit into no category he knew of, and he was supposed to be aware of them all. Unless…

His bewilderment was interrupted by the phone, only it wasn't a normal channel, it was the Hotline reserved for High Security communications. He nodded satisfactorily to himself. Maybe he was finally going to get some straight answers as to where the satellites came from. He picked up the phone. "This is Harold Bloomfield, how may I help you?" He sat straight up and his eyes bulged, choking on the tepid coffee he had been sipping.

"Dr. Bloomfield, this is President Brandt speaking. I understand that you were at the outset of the discovery that is currently at Nellis Air Force Base. Her tone was noncommittal and matter of fact.

"Ah, yes, uhh Ms. President. However…"

"Save it, doctor. There will be no recriminations over the unorthodox route it took to get there. It made it safely and that's that. She was secretly tickled that the FBI had been given the runaround. If anyone deserved a little flak it was them. But she had discovered along the way that the best way to weather her Presidency was to make as little waves as possible. No victim, no foul.

Bloomfield responded affirmatively as the President went on. "Their official presentation is Friday, and we want as complete of a picture as possible. Your presence is required to make it so. Please gather any applicable information and find your way there. As of now you have complete Security Clearance. The country will appreciate your input. Goodbye doctor."

Now that is a no nonsense woman thought Bloomfield as he wiped up the coffee he had sprayed on the table. His participation in diverting the FBI had weighed heavily on his shoulders, so he was relieved of that. But on the other hand, being taken from his private little sanctuary atop Haleakala and thrown into the High Security world of Dreamland was another matter. He was overwhelmed by a combination of exhilaration and apprehension, not knowing which emotion overshadowed which. He would gather what little data they had accumulated and make a trip to the Burial Chamber for a gourd or two. He knew of a couple of salty old Park Rangers who would appreciate that. Little did he know at the time what a big difference this little decision would make.

"This is scary. I've never seen him like this before. Something is definitely going to give, just what, I don't know," remarked a concerned Victoria. She was referring to her uncle.

"Well, whatever it is, I hope it happens fast. This is starting to get real old." Mallory's comment could either be taken as a statement or a complaint. Both were applicable.

"When he was acting like a caged lion, that was normal, for him. But when he turned into the docile 'yes man,' it is something I've never seen before. It's as if he's just given up." Victoria was clearly baffled as to her uncle's actions.

"Somehow, Muhammad Ali's 'rope a dope' comes to mind. There's more to this than meets the eye." Connor Mallory considered himself a good judge of character, but Brigadier General Tyrone 'Bull' Exley was in another League. The General's actions, or rather in-actions was a new twist in his myriad of personalities. It all coincides with his meeting with Dr. Bloomfield, and the gourds. He seemed to change right after that."

The night held the beginnings of a winter chill to it. The cloudless starlit night was beautiful to look at, but to get out in, was a different matter. Winter was rapidly approaching.

"Look! There's another one! If I didn't know any better I'd say it's the same one." She was pointing to another shooting star that made its way across the sky. "On a clear night like this they're easy to spot."

"I know. They seem to come with some form of regularity around here. And some of them do look identical.

"Maybe it's the aliens." Her joke had a very hollow quality to it. It was a feeble attempt to make light of an otherwise dismal evening. Their patience level was wearing thin. They had been given no clue as to what was going to happen next. This, plus add in the Bull's mysterious behavior, made their being kept uninformed close to unbearable. The only ones who didn't seem to mind were the Rangers. But they could be counted on to be able to handle almost anything. Having new girlfriends on the post didn't hurt either.

Mallory got back to the matter at hand. "When he met Dr. Bloomfield and first laid eyes on the gourds, I noticed a brief glimmer in his eyes. Then he covered it up when his personality changed. He's got something up his sleeve and is not letting anyone in on it. I wouldn't be surprised if it had something to do with the gathering he intends to throw tomorrow night." Mallory was mostly thinking out loud than carrying on a conversation.

"If there's one thing constant about my Uncle, he's as devious as they can get. But still yet, the way he acted at the presentation was a new twist even for him. It was as close to ass-kissing I've ever seen him become. Whatever the reason, I hope we find out soon." Victoria's observation was just a statement of fact; or the lack thereof. Just then another shooting star flew across the sky. It had a remarkable resemblance to the previous one.

The reality of the contents of the Presentation was beginning to set in. Its all encompassing ramifications were at first stunning, as were the potential of their findings limitless. It was almost too much to digest in one sitting. The foundations of the status quo for life on Earth were instantly metamorphose; a complete transformation inevitable. What was once thought of as taken for granted was past tense. In one sitting, mankind's basic values were forever changed.

Prior to the Presentation, a perimeter security blanket had been set up around Nellis Air Force Base the likes of which had never been seen before. Upon observation, the General likened it to "worse than Fort Knox," only on a much grander scale. When those who were to attend began arriving, it was easy to understand why. Members of the World Science Community, heads of state of the free world, FBI, CIA, NSA, NASA, The President of the United States and even members of the various dominant religions were in attendance. These, plus the Armed Forces guards for each, made it a true microcosm of humanity; one that would have made any terrorist's life dream come true. Hence the Security.

The presentation itself came in four parts. The first of which was narrated by the Bull himself, in his best camouflage personality. Then a brief summary of the speleologist's original intent and the subsequent accidental finding was accentuated by an edited video version of the expedition that was shown by Mallory and Victoria. For obvious reasons, the self incriminating parts were omitted. They had no bearing here. Next, came the revelation of the existence of the scout ship and the object's relevance to it. This was explained by Dr. Mike Stevenson and his team of Scientists. The first big blow came with the announcement of a solution of Einstein's Unified Field Theory and a working formula for electromagnetic energy. This in itself almost turned the meeting into complete unadulterated chaos, but the big blow came when the ancient Lezlie Potts wheeled himself up to the podium and stood up to deliver his narrative. In the past week he had been rejuvenated with a new vitality and took sincere pleasure in explaining the fact that the object was also a historical encyclopedia.

He went on to explain in as simple terms as possible, the intricacies of turning their encryption into Ancient Latin and to the best of their ability, then into modern English. The real blow came with the translation. With a sardonic grin he revealed the fact that the object admitted through historical text of the once existing continents of Atlantis and Lemuria and that the object had once been a gift to them to evolve their technology and awareness. He firmly accentuated that the Text stopped there, and the rest was shrouded in mystery. There was a stunned silence within the auditorium. The term 'you could hear a pin drop' was an understatement. The final blow came when it was revealed where the gift came from. "Rawar and Oxomoxo, we believe are their names and we are not the only Planets they have populated and nurtured to help evolve. They refer to a 'last crucial step' to join some sort of consortium. We have mixed ideas about this and can't settle on one. We will keep working on this and hope to come up with better answers. For now you can fill in the rest yourselves." Potts' strategy was a complete success. His last remark gave him time to wheel off the podium and exit stage left before the audience realized 'the rest' was that in reality, these were gaping holes of evidence to back up his theories. After the initial shock of the revelations wore off, Stevenson and company were left to fend off the barrage of questions that followed. The first to realize Potts' ploy was the Reverend Chuck T. Mansin. Always ready to grandstand, he stood up and shouted "blasphemy!" and was immediately escorted from the meeting, much to the chagrin of the President who covered her reaction well. What began as a minor buzz throughout the room soon turned into an uproar. Stevenson rushed to the podium and announced that pertinent information would be handed out in booklet form to the proper recipients, and that certain information would be withheld and would be released in the future through proper channels. Instead of pacifying the audience, his statement was like the first crack in a dam in which a flood was sure to follow.

Even if only temporary, it took the Bull to calm things down and bring the Presentation back to order. In precise military fashion, he marched up to the podium and announced that the booklets would be handed out during their departure along with mandatory signings of Official Secrets Documents. For the grand finale the lights were dimmed and on the video screen appeared the spacecraft hovering on its own accord in its hangar. The Bull added that any questions that could be answered at the moment would be in the booklet and that the meeting was over. His way with words left no room for argument. As they were leaving, a few noticed a shooting star fly across the heavens.

Back at their bungalow, Mallory and Victoria's conversation was interrupted by the sound of approaching vehicles. Two Jeeps pulled simultaneously in front, followed by what looked like a sedan in the distance. The Jeeps were driven by what looked like Women's Air Force officers and riding shotgun in each were Rangers Raymond Souza and Richard Townsend, their new beaus. Each had brought a passenger. In one was Brigadier General Tyrone Exley and in the other was Dr. Harold Bloomfield. The sedan in the distance pulled over and shut off its lights. Only the Bull and the Doctor got out. Souza and Townsend just waved as they sped off. They had been entertaining tonight. As the Bull stepped out, he went to attention, saluted the sedan and shouted, "good night! See you tomorrow!" Then he proceeded to stick one arm perpendicular to the other in a fashion that suggested another type of salute. Yeah, that one, it's Universal. So the Bull comes up the walkway followed by Dr. Bloomfield. Mallory and Victoria look at each other, their previous conversation and premature concern dissolving before their eyes.

"Hi you two. A little chilly tonight. Irish coffee all around? I've brought an old friend of yours." Before they could answer, he was off to the kitchen.

Victoria got up and gave the good doctor a hug and planted a kiss on his cheek. Mallory waved him to a seat. Bloomfield was clearly winded from trying to keep up with the Bull. He let out a sigh of relief as soon as his backside hit the cushion. "Hiya Doc, enjoy your whirlwind tour?" Mallory could only empathize. After all, he was only involved in a cross-country road race. Bloomfield nodded affirmatively as he let his ticker slow down to normal. The Bull returned to the porch with a tray that held a coffee pot, cups and a bottle of Jack Black. He ceremoniously poured two-finger shots and filled the rest with 100% Kona Coffee. "Cheers!" He loosened his military tie as he threw down the cup's contents and poured another, uttering a "ahhh, nectar of the gods," before he left for his room.

Bloomfield watched his retreat then asked, "does he ever slow down?"

"Rarely. Usually just when his head hits the pillow," answered Victoria. It's good to see he's becoming his old self again."

"Connor, why don't you take a couple cups to those shitheads down the street? Even a shithead can get cold on a night like this," bellowed the Bull from the back. The sound of the shower came on from the bathroom.

Mallory shrugged his shoulders, picked up the tray and headed down the street. The fog from his breath could be seen in the lamplight. When he returned he was smiling. "They looked embarrassed but were happy to accept the General's offer. So really doc, how goes it?"

Great, actually. I just got the grand tour of Dreamland from a Colonel Hasbrook. It took some gentle nudging from the General to get past Stevenson and his team, but apparently he carries a lot of weight around here. That spacecraft is impressive. I had to sign my private life away to get to see it, but it was well worth it." The Bull's Irish coffee had worked its wonder. "What do you suppose happens next?"

"That's the question of the day," interrupted the Bull as he returned to the porch. He had shed his military uniform for a thick light blue terry cloth bathrobe with the word 'Yorktown' embroidered on it. He was himself again. "And it is the primary reason I brought you here. And to see your friends of course. I believe it's time to formulate a little game plan." The Bull's eyes lit up to match his mischievous grin. "By the way, who's in the car?"

"Well, it's not any MPs I recognize. However I do believe I saw them talking to that General Cleveland yesterday. They are standard military issues," said Mallory.

"Why doesn't that surprise me? That Cleveland is a shifty character who kisses ass his way up the ladder. He was a reasonably good general before he joined the Joint Chiefs. Now he's just a puppet for somebody else. Just who it is, is another good question. His boss is supposed to be the President, but... The phone rang before he could finish. He picked it up, "yes? Oh, hi Bob, is this line clear? Hmmmm, okay. Six tomorrow night. I believe I'll have a little surprise for them." He was looking at Bloomfield during his last remark. "You, me, Souza and Townsend for morning coffee. Out." The General looked around the table wearing his best poker face. It was impossible to tell what the gears in his head were grinding now. "Damn, even the goddamn head of security doesn't know if his lines were tapped!" His outburst was genuine. "Well well Dr. Bloomfield, how long are you planning to stay with us?" The Bull's tone instantly changed to yesterday's character as he rose to turn on the radio. It was just enough to foil eavesdroppers. He returned to the table with a pencil and a notepad. As they carried on their conversation, what really was transpiring was being written down.

To the two men down the street with the directional listening device, it just sounded like polite conversation. They reported as such to General Cleveland. What was really happening was an entirely different matter. Cleveland suspiciously accepted their report. He knew the Bull all too well to believe he was as innocent as that, but what could he do? Their surveillance could only go as far as it went. The rest he would have to read in between the lines. But the General was better than that. At this point he was just glad to be on the same side, for now. He would include as such in his report to the 'CBFH, Cunt Bitch From Hell,' whoever she was. To call herself the 'Violet' was corny but effective. But she would have to wait until there was something of merit to report. As little contact as possible was the desired effect at this point. If he blew his cover, his side income would be gone and quite possibly his life. If he only would have stayed away from his drug involvement in Vietnam, he wouldn't be in the mess he was in now. But it was too late for that. All he could hope for was that she would have a heart attack or something, then and only then would his puppet strings be severed. Until then he would have to live with the blackmail. Or maybe he could slip a little dum-dum juice on her vibrator…

Have you switched the contents of the gourds? The Bull wrote. Bloomfield read the question then opened his briefcase. Inside were a dozen thermos bottles with their lids taped shut. He gave a thumbs up. The Bull looked at the bottles and gave the okay sign. He picked up another piece of paper and wrote 'tactics' at the top and proceeded to write. Mallory's eyes bulged as he began to read. Victoria's jaw dropped with a sharp intake of breath. Bloomfield turned ghost white at the first two sentences. He didn't need to read anymore because he had already done his part. Everything else was on a need to know basis. Besides, the audacity of the first two sentences was enough already. All he had to do now was leave for Haleakala tomorrow and call Captain Magic by cell phone somewhere out of range from Nellis and notify him to sail up the Sea of Cortez to Guaymas and wait for their return. From then on it was out of his hands, or so he thought. But life is just chock-full of little surprises.

Bam-Bam-Badam-Bamdam-Babam dam-Bambam. The staccato sound of an out of sync snare drum awoke Mallory at dawn. At first he thought it was a machine gun misfiring on the roof. The lump of Victoria under the covers beside him rolled over to reveal she had in her ear plugs. Blissful ignorance he thought as he got out of bed to see what the noise was all about. When he got to the porch he was in for the first of many surprises of the day. On the porch in his 'Yorktown' bathrobe was the General Tyrone 'Bull' Exley retired, dancing the Jig looking out the screen door. Mallory's first thought was that the Bull had finally gone over the edge. Here was a man, in almost freezing cold weather, butt-assed naked except for the bathrobe, dancing to a totally out of beat rhythm shouting "perfect" to nobody in particular. That was until he looked out the screen also.

What looked like little round ice cubes falling out of the sky were in reality hailstones, lots of them. There were so many already they were piling on top of each other completely covering the ground leaving no discernible boundary lines. It was one giant rolling mass of ground cover four inches thick and building. The blackened dome of the sky left no trace of it letting up for a while either. Since Mallory had read the Bull's 'tactics' notes, he could understand his elation. The hail was going to turn his already dangerous plan into possible, if not probable, suicide. But judging from the Bull's reaction, he either hadn't taken that into consideration or perhaps he finally had gone over the edge. Oh well, thought Mallory. In for a penny in for a pound. The dice wouldn't stop rolling until tonight's function anyway. Then it will either be boxcars or snake eyes. Either way, there was a good chance they wouldn't even live to find out. Luckily, the phone started ringing and broke his train of thought.

The Bull stopped dancing and went over and had to shout "yes" into the mouthpiece because of the incessant clatter of the ice hitting the corrugated tin roof. "At the moment I don't particularly give a shit if this is bugged. Anyone out in this weather deserves a little information. Isn't this glorious? Right. Officers club for breakfast. See you there. Oh, and goodbye to anyone else who is listening." The Bull's mood was jubilant. It was either because of the fortuitous turn of the weather or he was finally going to make something happen. Probably most likely, both.

"Ah, good morning Connor. Isn't this weather just glorious? Go wake up the little woman and tell her I've arranged for her to go shopping in Vegas with the Rangers' new gals. They are also going to pick up the Red Shark. It's getting real close to show time, and if we are lucky we'll live to make a curtain call. We're having breakfast with them and we can iron out the few remaining kinks. Boy, is this going to be a day to remember!" The Bull left for the bathroom for his morning constitutional.

Mallory went to the bedroom to wake Victoria but she was already up and moving. The shower was on and steam was billowing out the doorway. She peeked her head out from behind the shower curtain and said "did somebody say shopping?" Women… The word 'shopping' was the great motivator. When timed at the right place there's no telling what one could accomplish. "Connor, would you scrub my back?" Victoria's tone left no doubt in his mind that wasn't all she wanted scrubbed. Besides, he needed a shower also and it was going to be a long day. He walked into the bathroom and closed the door behind him. It was a good thing that the hailstones were pummeling the roof.

At the Officers Club for breakfast were the remnants of the presentation that on two days prior decided to stay over. Judging from their multiplicity they probably had their own separate motives. At one table sat Doctor Bloomfield with his bags packed and FBI Agent Fife. Mallory instantly put it together that this had been the Agent who had been chasing him down the Dormant Volcano. For that reason he went over to say goodbye and introduce himself. He needed no introduction but the good doctor went through the formalities anyway. Mallory was met with frosty indifference but it was nice to know your adversaries. At another table sat the Reverend Mansin and his assistant Bill Bugel. How he still managed to be here after his outburst of "blasphemy" was a mystery beyond Mallory. He must have some real good connections. Mallory had noticed the President had tried to avoid him like a plague the whole time, but he also sensed a familiarity between them. It was a one-sided relationship at best. But perhaps the most curious duo was General Cleveland and a civilian in a dark suit who definitely looked like a foreigner. He had shown up during the last half of the Presentation and had not introduced himself to anyone. Every time he was in this stranger's vicinity, Mallory had the distinct impression he was being watched, but he would always avert his gaze when Mallory pressed him. The man also had an unsavory vibe, the kind that might enjoy strangling a puppy. It was almost to the point of being unnerving so Mallory kept his distance, but always kept him in check. At a round table in the corner sat the Rangers and their new girlfriends. Victoria had already joined them and struck up a conversation, their topic, probably shopping. The Bull came in the door glowering and gave everyone the once over. Everyone avoided his stare except the round table. That's the way he wanted it, intimidation was always a handy thing to have around when preparing for an offensive thrust. As he approached the table, the Bull stopped in mid-stride, a look of a brainstorm clearly etched in the lines on his face. He about-faced and strode directly over to Bloomfield's table. In a voice designed purposely to overhear he expressed his condolences to Bloomfield for not being able to stay over for the party. Then as an afterthought he invited Agent Fife to the festivities, as he did also to the Reverend, General Cleveland and their sidekicks. He didn't stay long enough at each of the tables for them to accept or decline. It was just long enough however for the Bull and the mystery man to lock eyes and they were like two Gladiators sizing each other up before entering the arena, an analogy so very close to the truth.

"From what I've been given to understand, your 'Get-Togethers' have an effect on History itself," observed Mallory. The Bull had joined their table and after pleasantries were exchanged, the topic on everyone's mind was brought into the conversation.

"Aw, Connor, I just like to give credit where credit is due; and tonight will be no exception." The mischievousness in Exley's eyes were only for the round table to see. His back was to the rest of the room so everyone else had to read in-between the lines. What was said had a much larger connotation than the words coming out of his mouth, "and the people here deserve no less." The words sounded cordial, but the scowl that accompanied them told a different story. Then a bit louder, "by the way, has anyone seen the newspapers?"

It was a question he really didn't need to ask. The Presentation had been on Friday and it was now Sunday morning. Still no word had been given to the media of the Earth shaking events that had just taken place. By all accounts there should have been headlines in Saturday's news, but so far there had been no mention at all.

Townsend, out of character, spoke up first. "Yeah, that Charlie Brown got suckered into trying to kick Lucy's football again." It was a roundabout analogy, but an apt one at that. "You would think he'd learn he was given the runaround after what he's been through." That analogy was better.

Polite incidentals were exchanged during breakfast. They were boring enough to make the men on the other end of the listening device lose interest. A bug had been planted under each of the tables at the Officers Club years ago and it was taken for granted that there were no secrets here. As a matter of fact it was an ongoing joke around the Base. It was Standard Operating Procedure to protect the secrets of Nellis and Dreamland.

"Please try to get back from shopping for the party, ladies. Victoria is an integral part of the festivities." While the Bull was speaking he held up a piece of paper which said 'seven sharp outside the gate.' His look that accompanied it bespoke of punctuality. The three ladies nodded in unison. There was no room for deviation.

By the time their breakfast was over, the eavesdroppers were bored stiff. Their report held nothing of consequence. When Colonel Hasbrook read it he laughed out loud. His old partner in crime had really lulled his adversaries into a passive state. But he knew better. His old friend definitely had something up his sleeve. The General couldn't tell him anything that would jeopardize his position. To do so would make him have to choose sides. He knew where his loyalties lay, but lately he had been given reasons to question them. He was grateful to the Bull for understanding his position. But what would he do if the shit hit the fan? At this point it was a toss up.

"Just shut up and observe," barked Brigadier General Tyrone 'Bull' Exley. "This is a Master Alchemist at work." He had just poured half of the contents of the punch bowl down the drain, and refilled it with an equal amount of what was in the thermos bottles. Colonel Hasbrook, who had 'been there before', knew his friend was into some form of skullduggery or another. Part of him knew it was his ass on the line and the other part was filled with curiosity about what was about to happen. "What you don't know won't hurt you," the Bull added. Thus fueling both fires on the dichotomy he was presently forced to endure. The Bull had a remarkable resemblance to Doctors Frankenstein and/or Jekyll or perhaps a combination of both. Either way, he was taking sincere pleasure in spiking the punch. "Don't worry Boss, it's harmless. It's just a cushion enabling us to do what we need to do." That did it. Colonel Hasbrook had known his friend all too long enough to figure out his game plan, but he couldn't let on that he was on to his scheme. To do so might endanger them both. "Just take little sips. You will be glad you did." Hasbook tried his best not to let on that his revelation was rapidly coming to fruition right before his eyes.

"Ty, old buddy, I have a feeling it's going to be a while before I see you again. I'll do what I can to cover your ass." His remark was almost involuntary. It came from way down deep inside. What one might call gut instinct. The Bull stopped pouring and looked into his old friend's eyes. Instead of getting sincere which for a long time to come he would regret, he lifted his eyebrows, Groucho Marx style, and began pouring again. No words needed to be said from such lifelong friends.

The first to appear at the Bull's function was the Reverend Chuck T. Mansin and his assistant Bill Bugel. For some reason it appeared he had the 'keys to the kingdom' and could go wherever he chose. For what possible reason the Bull could not fathom, unless it had something to do with Beverly Brandt. The Reverend entered, pious as usual, dressed in Evangelistic white; he had a penchant for grabbing front stage center wherever and whenever possible. The Bull was just putting the finishing touch on the Punch in the form of a bag of strawberry flavored Kool-Aid. The Reverend's eyes lit up thinking that the General had added a little 100 proof something or another into the mix. Before the Bull could stop him he had a cup in his hand.

"Hi there General. I thought we'd come early to see if we could be of any assistance." The Reverend took a sip and gave a minor grimace.

"Ho! That's sweet. If you are in the market for a benediction for the festivities, I would be glad to help: Free of charge!" He took a bigger sip. "Oh boy!"

The Bull wasn't one to usually be caught off guard, but this was one of those few instances. Ever-ready to adapt to any given situation, he saw his Guinea Pig. At the thought of it he couldn't help laughing out loud. Beautiful! He thought, this asshole is going to regret the day he met me. "Why yes, Reverend, that would be mighty kosher of you," agreed the Bull. With no reaction to 'Kosher', the Bull's mind went into gear. "We'll put you right up here next to the podium. I'll do my welcome speech, pass around some Punch, and you can do your thing. At the end however, please include a toast for everybody. That would be absolutely magnificent." Try as he may, he couldn't get the vision of a Guinea Pig dressed in a white suit with the silver wig snorting away at the microphone. He turned Crimson and had to say "excuse me Reverend, I'll be right back." Barely able to contain himself, he rapidly walked to the men's room to splash water on his face.

The Reverend looked around the auditorium. It was empty except for Bill Bugel. He tossed down the contents of his cup and quickly dipped it into the bowl for another. One scowl towards Bugel and his assistant looked the other way. By the time the Bull returned he was well into his second cup. "Say that's quite a Punch General, a Punch with a punch as it were."

"Go easy on it, Reverend. It's got a secret ingredient in it, from Hawaii actually. It's a ceremonial"--- That was as far as he got. Mansin's legs gave out and all of a sudden he was sitting on the floor, the rest of the cup spread all over his immaculate white suit. Exley and Bugel helped him up and escorted him over to a chair.

"That's some potent shit, man, Fuckin A." The Reverend's inhibitions were rapidly deteriorating. His rambling incoherencies before he passed out were "fuck the President" or "I fucked the President." Something that made no sense at the time. Exley called for a stretcher feigning heat prostration which made no sense at all since it was winter outside. Nevertheless the Reverend was carried out just as the Scientists began to arrive. One last look towards Bugel, the Bull put his forefinger to his lips. Bugel smiled and returned a slight nod, once to let him know that he understood.

Once everyone was in attendance, the General began with a welcome speech. Once they had all filled their cups, the Bull called for a toast of congratulations then carried on with his filibuster as they refilled their cups. All accepted except for the stranger in the dark suit. When Townsend began to pour, darksuit put his hand over his cup and gave the Ranger a menacing stare. Finally the Bull ran out of words and ended by calling for another toast. He called Mallory up to explain the finer points of speleology. "Say anything. Just keep talking until they drop. I'll be right back."

One by one their heads began to fall, all except for the strangers'. When the Bull returned he was carrying the suitcase. Mallory's eyes almost popped out of his skull when he saw what he was carrying. The Bull stopped to deliver a judo chop to the stranger as he was evidently trying to get up. "Let's move!" He said as he led the way to the adjacent hangar that held the Winnebago. The two guards who also had accepted a cup were out cold. Mallory, the Bull and the Rangers piled into the Winnebago, the Bull in the driver's seat. "Hang on. I'm going to give you a little lesson in 'Destruction Derby'." With that he floored the Winnebago. With screeching tires they headed towards the entrance to the hangar. "Damn" uttered the General, when he noticed the doors were closed. He stepped on the accelerator to gather momentum. The doors flew open on impact. Miraculously, the alarms didn't go off. But as they left the hanger, they found they were being tailed by a Military Jeep. No time for hesitation now. They flew through the first checkpoint with the Jeep hot on their trail. The Jeep momentarily stopped at the checkpoint then continued pursuit. "Get ready, here we go," the Bull yelled, and as they approached the Guard house at the entrance to Nellis, the Bull swung the wheel a hard left and stomped on the brakes, just enough to bring the rear end around. The Winnebago went into a sideslip, helped by the melting hailstones on the tarmac. Instead of slowing down, the icy road permitted them to maintain speed and gather momentum. The Jeep was rapidly approaching. The Guards couldn't help but notice the sliding bulk of metal heading their way. They vacated the Guardhouse just as the Winnebago slammed full force sideways. The sound of breaking glass and crunching metal filled the air. Still no alarms. "Out!" the bull roared. Visibly shaken, Mallory and the Rangers found their legs. They filed out the trap door in the destroyed Travelall and found themselves facing two shotgun barrels held by the Guards.

"Stand down. That's an order!" The voice was that of Colonel Bob 'Boss Tuff, Meatball,' Hasbrook who had been in pursuit in the Jeep. He had come up in a skidding halt just in time to save them from being shot on the spot. The Guards lowered their rifles and came to attention when they saw from whom the order had come. Hasbrook marched up and surveyed the disaster. He smiled to himself. Tyrone 'Bull' Exley had managed to plant the Winnebago directly in the way of the outgoing and incoming vehicles. The lanes were blocked solid. He looked at the Fugitives and then at the Guardhouse and back again. "God damn, Bull you've really done it this time." The Red Shark was rapidly approaching out of the gloom. Hasbrook instantly put it together. "Go! It'll be my ass for this, but get the fuck outta here! Go!" The Shark came up to a screeching halt in front of the disaster. Victoria turned pale as she surveyed the scene. The Bull grabbed the keys and threw the suitcase in the trunk. He ran back to the driver's seat, but before he jumped in, he came to attention and saluted his old friend. Hasbrook came to attention and as his arm came up, the back of his head exploded and the front of his face blew off. He crumpled over faceless first, into a puddle of melted hailstones and blood and brain matter spreading in a large pool around what was left of his head. The Bull looked up to see the Dark Suit in the distance, revolver with a silencer in his hand. Darksuit mock-saluted with the smoking barrel, then took aim once again. The Bull flew into action, diving behind the door of the Red Shark. A 'thud' sounded in the door. The Bull crouched and put the Red Shark in drive to the sound of a bullet ricocheting off the pavement. He floored the Cadillac and the nitrous oxide tanks responded immediately. With smoke billowing off the tires it leapt into action like a racehorse out of the gate. The Cadillac flew down the highway away from Nellis Air Force Base, the only sound being the muttered curses of the driver as he vowed revenge. Directly overhead, what had appeared to be a star left its stationary position and shot off in the direction of Yuma, Arizona.

SPACE PATROL

"Oxomoxo, it's on the move again. Judging by what just happened down there, we must decide whether we are going to take an active part in this, or not." Rawar had been keeping a close watch via satellite tampering, their interest and curiosity mounting. Ever since their sensors had shown that the inhabitants had successfully figured out their Gifts' function, they now had to keep a closer watch.

Oxomoxo had been observing also. The downed scout ship had been 'powered on' for days and it also appeared they might have figured out a translation of its contents into their language. "One of them just took another's life and that is not good at all. Since some of them are still at that level, it could be a disaster. I'm for going down there." That statement didn't need to be said. They had been at this for eons together and knew each other's minds. Still yet, Oxomoxo had to cast his vote.

"The problem is, just exactly what are we going to do? It appears some of them have transcended the taking of life, but not nearly enough have reached that level and it's mandatory that they do. It depends entirely on what type of Humans have our gift and what they plan to do with it." Rawar's observation was astute. Without realizing it, he had cast his vote.

"You are absolutely correct. We should go and see just what level of humans now possess it. If they are of the more evolved species, we can discourage those that are not: Until when they can find a way to put it to beneficial use." Oxomoxo was delighted at the chance to get a closer look. The fate of this project might hang in the balance.

"They are headed in the direction of where we inspected that strange human. Any more of them like that and it's hopeless. We should go back there and observe, then we might not have to interfere." The idea of having to deal with that human again made his skin crawl, but Rawar was committed.

"Are you sure you don't want to cancel our bet? We both want this project to evolve…" Oxomoxo's enthusiasm was infectious. The chance for a closer look was agreed upon.

"Absolutely not. This project is just starting to get interesting. The inhabitants are so diverse, anything could happen. Our bet just makes it more fun." Rawar was finding he was becoming as interested as his co-pilot--. They were actually going to get a closer look at the 'Fruits of their Labor'. They both hoped they wouldn't be disappointed.

YUMA, ARIZONA

'Evil' Sam McGregor never knew what hit him. He was passed out in front of his TV with a beer in his hand. The can was warm and had tipped over into his crotch that he never felt. Typical. The next thing he knew he was awoken by a strange hum emanating from his backyard followed by something crashing into his barn. When he went to inspect, his last coherent thought was a feeling similar to hitting his funny bone, except it was felt all over his entire body. Oxomoxo and Rawar had put him in a state of suspended animation. A whole week would pass by before he could remember a thing. They picked him up, which wasn't an easy thing to do, him weighing close to three hundred pounds and laid him on his bed. When he came to, the only thing that had happened were his bodily functions, and he was not wearing them well. They inspected the dwelling and they weren't very impressed. They went through his wardrobe to find some appropriate clothing. It was all way too large but it would have to do for now. Then they proceeded to his kitchen and found the refrigerator. They were appalled by the sight of the flesh of animals, raw and disgusting. But, even though the beverage he drank tasted terrible, the feeling that went along with it was actually quite pleasing. They needed transportation, so they found their way to Evil Sam's garage. And in it was an old but reliable Chevrolet truck. After a brief study and a few grasshopper jumps, they figured out how to drive a stick shift. Luckily, they had assumed correctly what an American Express card was, so they loaded up their tracking device and found boxes of the peculiar beverage they had just experienced. No trouble deciding there. With the truck loaded with their tracking gear and a few boxes of 'Budlite,' Oxomoxo and Rawar were off and down the road in pursuit of their Gift.

CHAPTER 9

SOUTHWEST USA

"Well, isn't this just wonderful, Mallory groaned. "First we mugged tourists, then we are the head of a robbery ring and now we are probably Public Enemy number one. I am not going to ask what's next!"

"Relax, it's obvious they weren't going to go public with this," returned the Bull. "You have no idea of what they're capable of when it comes to National Security. We would have either wound up in some type of witness protection plan like puppets on a string, or maybe just totally eliminated to protect the discovery. I started smelling a rat when there was no news anywhere the next day. Those people don't fool around. Just look what happened to Colonel Hasbrook." The Bull's last statement made him clench his jaw. Justice would be served to Darksuit, whoever and wherever he was.

"But what are we going to do now? I'm surprised there's no roadblocks already." Mallory's innocent spelunking project was rapidly deteriorating into one giant clusterfuck and their last maneuver had made them fugitives from every conceivable law enforcement agency in the US of A.

"I don't know… Yet. Since the alarms didn't go off I think Colonel Hasbrook in his last glorious hour gave us some breathing room." As an afterthought the Bull added "something else happened when I grabbed our find. As I was putting it in the lead suitcase, Lezlie Potts rolled up out of the shadows. He had been watching me the whole time. He reached into his pocket and gave me a disk and said, "it's all there. Take it. We have a copy, and just turned around and rolled away. Shit, I thought he might have pulled out a gun or something."

The Red Shark's speedometer went up to 120. Thanks to the nitrous oxide tanks it had been past that number for the last hour. They had totally bypassed Las Vegas and were heading south, a red rocket flying down the straightaway, destination Nogales, Arizona/Mexico. If the Bull's prediction about Colonel Hasbrook was correct, they would be out of the country before they were found. If he was wrong…

The Rangers had been unusually quiet since their escape. The excitement of the moment made nobody notice at first. When it finally dawned on the Bull, he glanced back to see if they might have caught a stray bullet. But there they were, sleeping like babies, oblivious to the chaos around them. Victoria was out also, probably the victim of a vicious shopping spree. At first it puzzled him, but it didn't take long to put it together. Rangers, plus free Ava Root Punch, equals sleep. It was Townsend who first came out of his blissful unconsciousness. It took a few minutes to dust the cobwebs from his mind before his idea hit him. "Hey guys, I just remembered a way to get into Mexico. In between Tucson and Nogales is an army base called Fort Huachuca. There is a town outside called Sierra Vista, named after the mountain range there. I got stationed there after I was drafted in '65. Anyway, up in the mountains there's a place called Parker Lake. We'd go there to goof-off and swim while off duty. That's where we stumbled onto this old fire road that snakes through the mountains, all the way through to the Mexican side. We used it to smuggle pot across the border and were quite successful I might add, but that's another story." Townsend's brainstorm was deliverance.

The Bull lovingly padded the dashboard of the Red Shark. "Can this handle the roads and are they patrolled is the question." It was a statement.

"It's Department of Forestry Land on the US side, and only once did I see anyone inspecting the roads, and they were Forestry Rangers just like us, so we'd fit right in. The state of the roads are anybody's guess. They were marginal then, but that was almost forty years ago. It's a gamble, but shit, compared to what?" Townsend's confidence was questionable.

"A firing squad at the Mexican Border." Mallory's cheery disposition wasn't necessarily at a high. One could go so far as to say he was downright grumpy. But no one was there to crucify him for his indiscretion, they just had a higher tolerance level at the moment. All knew, however, that complaining would do absolutely no good whatsoever.

"Connor is right of course, although a bit blunt. But our choices are a touch limited: a possible roadblock at the border vs getting stuck in the mountains, oh goodie."

"And sleeping with the rattlesnakes," added Mallory.

"Oh stop your whining you big baby," Victoria was awake now. "Shut up or you're not going to get any…"

"Any what?" Mallory barked. But his statement quickly fizzled out when he realized what 'any' was. Oh, the power of women held over a man, thought Mallory. You fall for them, get hooked, then you're doomed. A no-win situation.

"A ring in his nose and a ring on her hand," Souza sang a line out of an old Savoy Brown tune. It broke the ice that had been rapidly forming. Townsend, then Victoria, then the Bull joined in and they let Mallory steep in his own misery. It didn't last long…

LONG ISLAND

"They what?" shrieked Violet. "I don't care what you have to do or how you do it, but get that whatever it is back! Eliminate them, torture them, whatever. But get it back!" Her rage had caused spittle to fly in all directions, soaking the mouthpiece of her phone. She looked at it, and began to throw it against the wall, but then thought the better of it. "Convene an emergency meeting. We must retrieve it before word gets out. If it does, we'll be ruined." Her last words had such a high pitch to it, it could have broken glass. She was furious and was throwing a child's temper tantrum. "Spare no expense. We must find that object! Out."

Then she threw the phone against the wall. It didn't do her any good at all. The Old Lady wasn't used to not being in control. After all, she was a pillar of society; literally. She continued her tantrum in the office of her Long Island home until there was nothing left to break. She picked up what was left of her phone and when she realized it was broken, she started continuously pounding it on her desk like a child in their 'terrible twos', screeching and pounding. It wasn't a pretty sight. And on top of it all her connection hadn't shown up and she was going through cold turkey. If anyone would have been in her vicinity they would have run the other way. Luckily, this wasn't the case. She continued pounding until her hands were bloody and the phone in pieces. A spoiled brat that didn't get her way. Finally whimpering, she sat down in her chair, but failed to notice its legs she had broken. The chair gave away and she wound up on the floor pounding and kicking again.

The emergency meeting convened and it was the same scenario, except for the hands of the chairperson that were heavily bandaged. This made them clumsy to handle the gavel that brought the meeting to order. Only Brown had a vague idea of what might have occured. Their relationship wasn't entirely business. They all took time to read the contents of the pamphlet that had been placed in front of them. It was a synopsis of what happened at Dreamland, and ending with the escape of the object. Sharp intakes of breath and gasps of astonishment were the only sounds in the room. It held the possible demise of the stranglehold they had on the entire world's economies. If word got out about the amazing leap in energy technology they would be ruined, their companies ruined and worthless. The population of the planet wouldn't depend on them. It was a worst-case scenario come true and they had to stop it at all costs; or face ruination. Brown took the floor. "I was there and saw the whole thing for myself. It was incredible. Free energy and limitless. We must find a way to seize and control it. Otherwise we are obsolete. At least I nailed the fucking colonel who allowed them to escape."

"You can leave your gutter language outside Mr. Brown," reprimanded Violet. "What we want to know is what's being done about it. This is your area of expertise, sir." The 'sir' had a derogatory tone to it. Her voice sounded hoarse for some reason.

"First we have to find them. Then I'm going to cut their fucking nuts off! Oops, sorry." Brown wasn't used to answering to anybody. His family had been in the business of crime from day one. To the others he was loathsome, but necessary.

"We must leak word of a healthy reward for their whereabouts and capture, dead or alive. It doesn't matter as long as we recover the thing and bury it. How about General Cleveland?" she asked.

"They have no clue. The colonel I snuffed was the head of security and he disconnected the alarm system. They were gone before anyone knew it," answered Brown. "Cleveland however did get authorization from the President to use their satellite tracking systems, so it's only a matter of time. This object emanates some sort of pulse so it's impossible to hide unless it's kept in the lead suitcase. And once it's open, we'll have them."

"Those liberal bastards in Washington can ruin us too. We must have it or we're finished." Violets' statement was tainted with hypocrisy. "Mr. Brown, use your family connections. They will be heavily compensated."

The meeting ended with the gavel falling on the floor. The chairwoman was having trouble holding it. All their asses were on the line and they knew it. Unless they got the object back in their possession.

"Bluebird travel. Your pleasure is our business." Captain Magic's attempt to sound official was feeble at best. The last two weeks had taken its toll.

"Randy, this is Harold Bloomfield. I'm afraid our friends are in serious trouble." Bloomfield proceeded to give Captain Magic a synopsis of what had happened which sobered him up immediately. "They are attempting to flee to Guaymas and from the little I know about this General Exley, they probably will make it."

"If they do, we'll be waiting for them. What about you?"

"I'm headed back to Haleakala. Word is out about the Burial Chamber and it goes all the way to the Presidency. I'm going to have my hands full." Bloomfield also knew that it was linked to the fugitives and he would have to watch his step. "There's a chance I'm being followed, so I'll keep communication to a minimum."

"Okay doc. It's going to take a couple of hours to gather the crew. They're spread out all over creation. But we should be there by tomorrow morning." Captain Magic always was fully committed to his friends in need and this was a prime example. It was showtime. "Where are you by the way?"

"I'm at the Janet terminal in Las Vegas airport. I just came from Nellis. One hop to LA, then home. Bar unforeseen circumstances." At this rate he realized that anything was possible. It was.

"Well then, hopefully we will see you soon. Aloha and thanks. Out."

"Bloomfield was satisfied at a task accomplished. Now all he could hope for is that Exley would live up to his reputation. Judging from what little contact they'd had, he was confident that The General would find a way. What he didn't know was that Agent Fife's civilian counterpart, retired Agent Persons, had just picked up his side of the conversation via a sound scanner and was relaying the information back to Fife.

Fife in turn was not going to be the laughing stock of the Agency again. Yet the fugitives had managed to escape once more. Thanks to the idea of bringing his old partner into it, he now knew their destination. It was time to gamble his career and contact General Cleveland, then go it alone with his civilian partner. Then and only then would he be exonerated from his past mistakes.

General Steve Cleveland knew which side of his bread the butter was on. He graciously thanked Fife for his discretion and immediately contacted Violet. She in turn alerted Brown and company and he assured her there would be a welcoming committee awaiting them in Guaymas. The chase was on. Their only mistake was their underestimation of the resourcefulness of General Tyrone 'Bull' Exley 'retired', the crew of the Flying Cloud and Bluebird Travel. But nobody ever said that learning the hard way would ever be easy.

It took the Reverend Chuck T. Mansin a full 24 hours to come out of his stupor, and another six to gather his wits. By then the Fugitives were well on their way and the mess at Nellis Guardhouse cleaned up. Any questions had been met with tight lips. His only consolation at the moment was the knowledge that Mother Earth was being propagated by Aliens. But goddamn, what would that information do to his ministry? He would go broke, that's what. His only course of action would be to apply a little pressure on his old squeeze to keep abreast of the situation and if need be, change the format of his ministry. He would milk his flock while he could, but also be ready to disavow the Christian Doctrine and invent a new one if and when the information were released. For all his shortcomings, he was not adverse to taking advantage of any given situation. If he played his cards right, either way he could come out smelling like a rose.

Beverly Brandt, on the other hand, had a Country to run. She was confident that the Joint Chiefs and her Cabinet could handle the situation at Nellis. Meanwhile she was a busy gal. She agreed to keep that con man Mansin informed through indirect channels. Although looming in her background was the detrimental information he held over her head, but she could hold him at bay by agreeing to keep him informed. One curious occurrence however, was the invitation to tea from the grand Old Lady from Long Island.

She had always been firm about the privacy factor and that the meeting should be as soon as possible. President Brandt couldn't help but wonder if the development at Nellis and the invitation were somehow connected. Most probably she figured. Rumors circulated that the Old Lady's web of power was far reaching. Nothing could ever be proved of course, yet the rumors were there. In the brief span of a few days, the future was drastically altered, the benefits of the discovery incalculable. General Cleveland had convinced her to keep a lid on it until a viable course of action could be found. This was fine with her because she knew it would shake the very foundations of the balance of power in the Oil and Power Industries and they were surely not going to take that lightly without some form of compensation. A path beneficial to all would have to be created and that would take time. For now she would deal with the problems at hand, then take a break and go to tea with her husband Jack. It would be like a mini-vacation, or so she thought.

"Oh yeah, now this is living!" shouted the Bull to the mountain tops. There was a light coating of snow on the ground and he had jumped into Parker Lake and swam out to the float offshore in the middle of the lake just like a member of the Polar Bear Club. He mounted the float, did something that resembled a Tarzan yell, then dove back in and swam back to the shore. His audience stared at him in aghast from the warmth of their sleeping bags. The sun peeked out of the overcast sky lending a pastel quality to the mountain range spread out before them. Beige and mint green with intermittent white from the snowfall dominated their surroundings. The steel blue grey water of Lake Parker was about as inviting as a melting ice tray, except for one with a constitution such as 'Bull' Exley. Besides the fact that his lips were blue and fog escaped with his every word, it appeared that he was actually enjoying himself. "What a way to wake up! The water is absolutely invigorating! You should try it!"

"Uncle, you are either batshit crazy or a bona fide member of the Polar Bear Club. A little of both I'm afraid." Victoria's 'uncle outlaw' never ceased to amaze her. Her remark brought a smile to his face. The other men were speechless. Of all the things they had heard and seen about him, this one was the capper.

"Don't knock it until you've tried it. It's a once in a lifetime opportunity, for me at least. I don't even like the cold." This statement baffled them even further. "Come on kids, time's a wasting. We've got some road to cover. I'll boil some water on the Coleman stove." The Bull was jogging in place, clouds or fog escaping his mouth. He added movement to his jog as the rest reluctantly got out of their sleeping bags. Soon the robust aroma of 'cowboy coffee' filled the air as they finished rolling up their bags.

"These were certainly a good call," remarked Mallory to the Rangers. He was referring to the sleeping bags they had found at an army surplus store back up the road aways.

"It was either these or huddle together for body warmth." The Rangers eyed Victoria hungrily. They found toying with her most enjoyable. All knew it was harmless.

"Don't force me to get my purse, you horny old dogs. You already know what I can do with it." Her tone was mock-vicious and she used it well.

Everyone was trying their best to be jovial, but in actuality the murder of Colonel Bob Hasbrook weighed heavily on all of them. So far they could almost call their adventure fun, that is until the moment Hasbrook's brain matter adorned the pavement at Nellis Air Force Base. It had happened so fast and they left so soon that the reality of the situation crept up slowly, only to hang over their minds like the clouds presently over the Sierra Vista Mountains. It was here during coffee that it came to the surface.

"Uncle, did your friend have any family?" Victoria's spoke diplomatically. She wanted to circumvent the harsh reality as lightly as possible.

"Yes and no dear," answered the Bull. This naturally got everyone's attention. "Not officially anyway. He's got three daughters all from different mothers, none of them married. In his younger days he was a regular Casanova, but his wild ways cost him his relationships. Judging from what you saw of him, you probably would have never guessed in his earlier years he was a comedian/magician/musician. All of which he could apply at any given moment. One time, he dressed up in a tux and complete with top hat he put on a magic show for my grandmother. He had her totally mesmerized." The Bull had to stop momentarily, to remove some of the moisture from his eyes. "Hell, I could go on and on about this guy's adventures. Sufficient it to say he lived a full and happy number of lifetimes and we'll leave it at that." The Bull fondly reminisced until he visibly turned stone cold. "That S.O.B. that shot him is going to get his just rewards." The Bull had to get up and busy himself to control his emotions. He loaded the sleeping gear and Coleman stove into the trunk of the Red Shark while the rest finished their coffee. The mood turned a little lighter when Mallory reached the bottom of his cup and gagged on a mouthful of coffee grounds.

Souza explained, "cowboy coffee: the grounds go straight into the boiling water."

"Thanks for the warning," spluttered Mallory as he attempted to brush the adhering grounds off his person. Although his move was entirely unintentional, it did act as a salve and lighten the situation on the open wound of Hasbrook's murder.

"Let's go! The sooner we get across the border the safer we'll be. Vicki, I want you in the front and the heavyweights in the back for traction. We might just need it. So far the roads have been passable, but you never know." Call it a premonition or not, the Bull's statement had a basis in common sense. As they left, no one noticed the old blue truck that pulled up in the distance.

Their misplaced expectations for the human race came like a slap in the face to Rawar and Oxomoxo. What little hope they had left was rapidly dissolving before their horrified eyes. Totally acclimated to the pure air of their mothership, it didn't take long to detect the sickly aroma of burnt fossil fuels. A hole in the exhaust pipe of McGregor's truck didn't help either. As they bounced down the road in pursuit of their rapidly fleeing Missing Link, the carbon dioxide poisoning gave them both the first headaches they'd had for a long while. The only solace came in the form of that peculiar beverage they had absconded with from 'Evil Sams'. When they came upon their first densely populated area, they almost turned around to go back to their scout ship, grab the Missing Link, then leave Earth to its own demise. The only thing that kept them on route was a combination of curiosity and awe and downright disbelief. Their advanced evolution allows them to read the energy field or 'aura' around each living thing. It came in the form of various shades of the color spectrum. Each color represents a personality trait, while the shade represents its intensity. Almost every human they'd observed lit up like a pulsating Christmas tree. While plants and animals more or less had a steady pulse of their own particular shade of color. And what they'd seen so far didn't look that promising. But they also knew this was their own personal creation, and it's destiny lay further on down the road.

"Oxomoxo, hand me another one of these 'Budlites'. They seem to help my throbbing head a little bit." "It's these fumes" returned Oxomoxo. Rawar had picked up the knack of driving quickly and found a radio station to his liking. He marveled at the different types of music but found what was called 'rock and roll' the most palatable. Then also had found that their tracking gear eliminated most of the static and this particular station came from a place called Tucson. Oxomoxo passed him a Budlite and he got a particularly large belch out of his first swig. "They can't be all that bad if they invented this."

"From what we've seen so far, I'm surprised this planet is still in one piece." Oxomoxo's demeanor was somewhat less effervescent. Of the auras they've encountered so far, few were capable of even coming close to the last crucial step. Unfortunately there was no way to help them figure that out. That, they had to do themselves. "You were smart to keep the bet going."

"One way or another we are going to find out soon. There they are at that body of water." Rawar pulled the truck to a stop. They had just come over the last rise that descended into the plateau that held Lake Parker. The Red Shark was just pulling out. "Let's keep a safe distance until we can figure out what type of humans they are." They both climbed out of McGregor's truck to take in the fresh mountain air. By the time the Red Shark went over the last rise, their headaches had dissipated.

"Isn't it ironic that the fate of their planet could possibly depend on just them? Hopefully, they are like Andar of Lemuria. But if they resemble that imbecile Ulric, we might as well procure a pair and leave before they destroy themselves. Oxomoxo was thinking out loud again. They really didn't need to discuss it at the moment. They thought the Earth's chances were rapidly dwindling, but they had seen so little and there was so much more. Besides, there was still 'rock and roll' and Budlite.

"They all can't be that bad" interjected Rawar, as he popped another Budlite. He smiled at his co-pilot and had empathy for his misgivings.

"One thing is for sure, they have come a long way, again. Just where they're going is probably left up to those humans up ahead."

Oxomoxo's headache had disappeared and it helped his mood a lot. "Well, let's just follow and find out. We've learned from the past that chance is a mighty big factor and since their personalities are so diverse, we just might get lucky."

"That's the spirit! Have another Budlite." They both got a chuckle out of this and got into the truck. They knew that Earth's destiny was in the hands of those up ahead. What they didn't know was what type of people they were, although the auras they carried looked promising.

CHAPTER 10

NORTHEAST USA

The sleet was almost horizontal as the small motorcade pulled up to the gates of the Long Island Estate. Somewhere, a hidden camera announced their presence and the heavily fortified gate opened as they approached. Even though it was just for a little while, Jack and Beverly Brandt were happy to leave the confines of her present position. The harsh weather was actually an enhancement. It reminded them of Carmel, California and a past that seemed so very, very long ago… Thunder boomed in the distance as Jack opened the door for his wife. A gust of wind almost tore the umbrella out of his hands and in a matter of seconds he felt more like Jack Frost than Jack Brandt. "Grab my arm dear, so you don't blow away. Your Country needs you." He was always looking for ways to lighten the burden off his wife's shoulders. He had the gift of making light of almost any given situation. "It's just like home, only with a different coastline."

Beverly Brandt looked at her husband and laughed. He was instantly coated in white against the backdrop of the gray-black clouds hanging over the Atlantic Ocean. She was about to remark on this when the thick oak front door opened. A butler in a heavily starched, crease free uniform motioned them inside. His nil-personality face and plastered down hair job had a distinct resemblance to Adolf Hitler, which caused both of their smiles to freeze on their faces. They looked at each other out of the corners of their eyes and then back at the butler, their superficial smiles stuck as they proceeded to enter the domain of the Old Lady of Long Island.

"Good afternoon Ms President, so good of you to come." Violet had a face for every occasion. "And you too, Mr. Brandt," as an afterthought. She looked at him as though he might have been a leper. Her holier-than-thou tone of voice completed the facade. Jack Brandt, the eternal optimist, disliked her immediately. He nodded politely and didn't say a word. Adolf relieved them of their overcoats and umbrella.

"Thank you, madam. Any break from my duties are infrequent and most welcome." Her politician's personality was instantly called for, as was her inherent womanly instinct that told her she was in the presence of a deadly enemy.

"My dear, you will soon find out that this is certainly not a social call. We have some urgent matters to discuss, and I believe you will find, shouldn't be made public." Her cold eyes matched that of her cryptic statement. "We will have tea out in the gazebo. Unless you would prefer something stronger of course."

"Tea is just fine," (fucked up, insecure, neurotic and emotional.) "Thank you."

Violet led them to a promontory on the peninsula. The trail was encased in a sheltered hallway that led to the octagon shaped gazebo perched on the cliff. Although the vibrations were suffocating, the view was magnificent. "My late husband built this to be alone with his thoughts. History has been altered in this very room." The giant surf from the storm that pounded the coastline could be felt within the gazebo. It was awe-inspiring to be right next to it and yet not be in it. "And it is quite possible that it will be altered today." She winced as she poured the tea. Her hands were still recovering. A wave crashed against the cliff causing the cups to rattle.

The President opted for a spoonful honey. This brought her time to gather her thoughts. Jack sat beside her stone-faced, his usual perpetual smile nonexistent. "Madam, I wasn't aware that you were involved in Matters of State." She was doing her best to feel her out and be affable at the same time. The Old Lady didn't make it easy.

"Young lady, I still do that and more." This old bitch had raised her voice to the President of the United States and what little protocol existed, disintegrated. "You really have no idea just how much power I wield because your term is only four years. My family has been involved since 1913 and I own you. So you should better pay attention."

Jack Brandt stood up to protest. "Listen…"

"Sit down and shut up! Now!" The Old Lady reached into the briefcase that had been placed there earlier and produced a folder. "Let's get down to the point. I am a member of an organization that when pooled together control the financial stability and natural resources of this country. And all the other countries considered to be super powers for that matter. In generalized terms, our organization is the backbone of the world. We are also aware of what has taken place at Nellis Air Force Base and believe it poses a threat to us. We have always operated in secrecy, but due to these recent developments we are forced to take an active role in the disposition of the facts recently encountered." Violet slapped the folder on the table. It was titled 'Nellis Presentation.' She reached into her briefcase and produced another folder. "You can take my word for it or read it for yourselves. By me just knowing about it should satisfy you."

President Brandt sat immobilized. She was incapable of comment. Rumors about a supposed 'elite' that was operating behind the public eye was exposing its monstrous face right before their very eyes.

"We need your full cooperation in the seizure and containment of this information until a way can be found to control its disbursement. Until then it must be kept from the public. Just like this…" Then she placed the other folder on the table. It was entitled 'Church of the Almighty/Reverend Chuck Mansin.'

Beverly Brandt's composure completely disintegrated. She stared frozen at the folder, all color drained from her face. The folder's contents were obvious. She tore her eyes from the folder and gaped at the Old Bitch. Behind the old crones eyes was a malignant glow that defied all human decency.

"I'm sure you see the need for the utmost discretion in these matters." She glanced at the top folder and back again. "Your candor and diplomacy can produce the required results needed to keep this secret, for now. We are also aware that the discovery's whereabouts is currently unknown." Which was a lie. "We must work together to bring it back into our custody at all costs before the information is leaked.

Any objection the President might have had died in her throat upon the appearance of the second folder. Any pretext of this meeting being anything other than it was, no longer existed: Blackmail. One encounter with this old woman convinced her she was capable of the most evil acts of degradation. Beverly Brandt caved in. "What do you suggest?" Her voice was barely audible.

"Confiscate any pertinent information and file it under the Official Secrets Act. That is until we can find a way to capitalize on it." The Old Lady wasn't about to beat around the bush. Besides, she felt the need for another fix coming on. "You may have these folders to look over. Naturally they are copies." She pushed the folders across the table. "And I warn you. Don't try anything funny, we have eyes and ears everywhere." As to punctuate the situation another wave slammed into the cliffside.

The constant discharge of the fury of the ocean was the only sound as the two most powerful ladies on the face of the planet sized each other up. It could have been a face-off on the dirt streets of Dodge City or Tombstone, Arizona. The air in the room was charged with electricity. Like the inevitability of an upcoming gunfight, but with no guns, only purses, and there's some that would say it was quite a lot worse. Anyone who has ever seen a cat fight could testify to that.

Beverly Brandt wordlessly stared at her nemesis. The President was not born yesterday. Her formative years had been during the drug crazed sixties and she had been around the block enough times to know an addict when she saw one. And this one across the table was rapidly coming in need of some help. If there was a chink in the old lady's armor, this undoubtedly was it. She seized the opportunity and decided to test the waters. "This is wonderful tea, may I have another cup?" She picked up her teacup and accidentally-on-purpose dropped it on the floor.

Neither her husband nor the Old Lady expected this response, there was a slight intake of breath and the widening of her eyes. Jack exchanged glances with his wife. He had known her long enough to understand that she was onto something, and her return look convinced him of that. She had given him that all-too-familiar non committal placid smile before, the one she used when dealing with the various personalities that her job required. It was time to sit back and watch the show.

Somewhat flustered, Violet rang to Adolf for more tea and another cup. In the minutes it took to arrive, the old bitch had visibly taken a turn for the worse. Her fidgeting was noticeable and a telltale sheen of sweat had formed on her forehead. "Now if you'll excuse me I have to…"

"Madam, I don't believe that I should have this under the Official Secrets Act. That could draw too much attention." The President's tone was light. The one she used to placate Ambassadors of unfriendly countries. It was an art form.

"That is up to you. Now if you will excuse me I really do have to…"

"How will we stay in communication? We obviously have to keep this just between us."

"You will be notified!"

And on it went. A barrage of various related and unrelated questions and rebuttal were thrown at the old addict who was by now approaching the first stages of acute withdrawal. Her answers became curt and dismissive. But Beverly hung in there, buying time. Soon Jack picked up on the scenario and he asked her for another cup also. That was the last straw.

"You have to go immediately! Right now! I have other business to attend to that require my undivided attention." Her shrill voice had risen and octave and she was clearly hurting. She forced the folders into the President's hands, then Adolf could rapidly escort them to the door and off the property. When Adolf returned with their overcoats and umbrella, Jack straightened to attention, slapped his arm out and shouted "sieg heil", about-faced then 'goose-stepped to their ride.

On the way back to Washington, Beverly confessed all and much to her surprise she found out Jack had known about most of it for quite some time. She even made light of the fact that's why their own daughter had gone wrong, but both knew it was years of pressure finally released. By the time they got back to the White House they were ready to practice making another child; so that's exactly what they did.

"That has to be the strangest pair of people I have ever seen in my entire life," remarked Connor Mallory, as he watched the old blue truck recede in the distance. He was the first to make a remark after the surreal encounter. They were all standing around the rescued Red Shark. Souza, Mallory and Townsend were completely mud splattered from attempting to push from behind. The road appeared passable on the surface, but that was just a dry coating from the sun. They had wrestled with it for about an hour; jumping up and down on the rear bumper as Victoria put pedal to the metal with the tires proceeding to sink deeper into the mud. The spinning tires completely coated the men, giving each of them a distinct resemblance to Swamp Thing. Victoria was remarking as such when she noticed the truck that must have just pulled up. The strange pair didn't say anything, but just pulled up to the rear of the shark and helped them out of the quagmire. And without a word, proceeded on their way. As they passed by however, they gave the fugitives a once-over, then looked at each other and smiled at what seemed to be like some sort of personal joke between them and proceeded onward, leaving them standing there perplexed and free of their predicament. No one mentioned the fact that the look they gave them made each of them feel transparent. None of them knew that they each had experienced the same sensation.

"Don't count on it," advised the Bull. He looked like he had seen a ghost. The three swamp things looked in his direction and he gave them all a look that was new to them.

"Huh?"

"Don't count on it," repeated the Bull.

"I don't get it," returned Mallory.

"You don't have to," he countered. The gears in his head were turning and everyone knew him well enough to leave it well enough alone. "I believe eventually it will explain itself." This confused them even further but they chose to let it go. For now.

Victoria tossed the 'swamp things' towels so they could repair the damage as best they could, eyeing her uncle as she did so. He was staring at the last rise the truck had disappeared over and she could see he was lost in thought. She jumped into the shotgun seat and kept a steady gaze on him, until he finally came out of his reverie and looked back, a queer look on his face.

"Penny for your thoughts," she whispered.

The Bull smiled at his niece-outlaw. "Not now. I think I'll let the dominoes fall as they may." He had an all-knowing twinkle in his eye. "This could get really interesting." Which left her even more completely in the fog, but she knew him well enough to know there was a method to his madness. So she let it go. When the 'swamp things' returned to human form they piled in the back.

"Maybe we should keep up with the truck in case we get stuck again," suggested Mallory. Everyone was of the same mind but it was he that put it into words.

"That's what I plan to do, but at a safe distance," the Bull answered. He was trying his best to negotiate the ruts but at the same time keeping an eye on the road far ahead.

"Why? You don't think those weirdos are dangerous, do you?" Victoria was incredulous.

"Far from it. It's just that if they wanted to stick around and chat, they would have. There's only one road so they're not going anywhere else. Unless we get stuck again of course. Besides," the Bull laughed out loud. "They had a few cases of beer in the back." He got a real good laugh out of this which made no sense at all to the others. It was as if he had his own personal source of entertainment that he wasn't sharing. The Red Shark, not exactly what one would call an off-road vehicle, slowly picked its way down the windy road, destination Mexico. It was slow traveling. The winter storm had done its fair share of damage to the road. They had to make a stop once more overnight. At sunset they found a grove of stunted Birch and Fir trees on a plateau overlooking the hills they had just traversed. Mother Nature gave them yet another spectacular show. The sky lit up a brilliant Orange, Pink then a Raw Sienna fading into Magenta and then a very Deep Purple. The Rangers put their forestry talents into action by building quick lean-to while Mallory, Victoria, and the Bull gathered deadwood from the grove and built the fire. After eating, the rains came off and on and the lean-tos' proved themselves functional as they all lined up underneath. After a plethora of snide remarks concerning her gender, Victoria opted for the Red Shark leaving the chauvinists on their own. With no one to razz, the boys quickly fell out for an excellent night of dreamless sleep. Besides the intermittent Chinese water tortures, no one was even bothered by each other's snoring. The rain helped alleviate that. The rest of the trip held no sign of the rescuers with the blue truck. Only the Bull was confident that they were somewhere in the vicinity. There was a certain item in the trunk of the Red Shark that made sure of that. Although it had been years since the episode in the Dreamland hangar, the Bull instantly recognized the resemblance between the two in the truck and the unfortunate form that had been on the stretcher. Mallory's remark really was true to form except for the "people" part, plus it was always nice to have a new ace up his sleeve; it was as good as gold and it was only going to get better, or so he hoped.

Everyone awoke the next morning fully refreshed. There was definitely something to be said about sleeping out in the wilderness. One could go as far as to say it's medicinal. Only Mallory found himself somewhat less rejuvenated. He had been plagued with the recurring dream of the badge with teeth. He made no statements referring to it because of the lingering memory regarding the mushroom gravy episode aboard the Hannibal Hamlin. It was a 'live and learn' scenario and once was enough. One cup apiece of Souza's 'cowboy coffee' and they were ready to be on their way. Destiny awaited. Little did they know at the time what a severe understatement that would turn out to be. Oh, but would they eventually find out.

"The female one in the group has offspring," announced Oxomoxo jubilantly. "I could read it in her aura." He hadn't been this exuberant in a very long long time. It was a welcome sensation to have something to be enthusiastic about for a change.

"Does she know yet?" asked Rawar, equally as happy about the change.

"No, probably not. Unless she recognizes what humans call intuition. It's too early to tell." Ever since their chance encounter that just occurred, they were rejuvenated with a new vigor for the project. They had noticed each of the groups auras were on the far side of the spectrum that represented potential for higher consciousness. The ones possessing their Gift were what they were hoping for and it filled the Space Patrol with a new vision for the human race. The grim reality of the state of affairs they had seen so far wasn't that comforting, but now, since their Gift was in the possession of such as these, the chances of advancement took a turn in their favor. Things were looking up. "What a relief," exhaled Oxomoxo, a sigh that came from deep within.

"Our bet is just getting better and better. We got really lucky this time." Although Rawar shared his co-pilot's enthusiasm, he was the more pragmatic of the two. "They're all so much different from each other which makes things harder to predict. They have come so very far, yet they're capable of so much more. It pains me to think of what possibly could happen if they put our gift to use." They rode on in silence for a while contemplating the possibilities. "Those capable of the next crucial step are outnumbered. We should probably stay close by for a while to see if it stays in their possession. That is what we are doing here, isn't it?"

That was an excellent question. But neither of them really knew the answer entirely. Now that they knew their gift was in proper hands, just what in this world were they supposed to do about it? Interaction was against the Rules and they already had stretched those to the limit. If they made a habit of doing this, how could they ignore their other ongoing projects? Even though this one had come back from the brink of extinction, there were no others following a similar path. Oxomoxo was pondering this when he came to a conclusion. "You know Rawar, what it really comes down to is the temperaments of the first pair we put on any given project. Their genes carry on through each generation so we should be very selective when we do this." He realized he had just solved a problem that had plagued them for Millennia. And it was so simple.

Neither of them said anything further although they were both thinking the same thing. After all, up-close-and-personal was their desired effect.

SEA OF CORTEZ

Bernard Fife and Gregory Persons weren't exactly what one would call 'blending in'. It wasn't necessarily their tourist get-ups and pale skin in the temperate zone that gave them away, it was their less than gregarious personalities that did it. Actually, they stuck out like sore thumbs. They were oblivious to the merriment around them. They were also used to being able to push their weight around behind their badges. After a while they were being avoided like the plague. The partying youngsters around them sensed their 'out of place' demeanor and some suspected that maybe their parents might have sent them down to bust them and send them home. This caused most of them not to notice the other new contingent of dark suits to arrive and check into a beachside hotel. The darksuits looked more like a business convention arriving for a formal meeting. No one took the time to notice the weighted down suitcases they brought with them, nor the bulges in their jackets where a firearm would be. Fife and Persons almost missed them also, but still paid them no mind, because of a certain Red Cadillac that had just pulled up to the harbor. They also neglected to put two and two together when a blast from the whistle from the paddle wheeler coincided with their arrival. Private investigators they were not.

"Care for some more coffee senor?" The waitress interrupted their 'stake out' and the timing was in their favor. She had come up to the table and blocked the view from the fugitives; all they saw was her backside standing in front of a pair of gringos dressed in tourist attire. By the time the coffee was declined, the fugitives failed to notice them. Fife quickly paid the tab and they weren't noticed. As they rounded the corner of the Cantina they looked back to make sure they weren't being followed. Before they could look back to where they were going, they ran head-on into one of the bigger 'conventioneers' and Fife found his backside hitting the ground. It was like walking directly into a wall, except this wall was made of muscle.

"Hey, why don't you watch where… oh, uh, excuse me." Fife's surprise turned into shock as he looked up at the man in the dark suit towering above him. The man with an exceedingly raspy voice said "I think you should go back to wherever you came from." The voice was more of a resonant whisper; that of an over the hill Blues singer or that of a Prizefighter that had been hit in the throat too many times. He was not the type to be ignored.

Fife was used to having an official Badge to back him up, but here now, there was only Persons. In his present situation he thought it only mandatory to show off for his ex-partner. "Now see here mister, I'm a Federal Agent currently work---" That was the last thing he knew for hours. By the time he and Persons woke up, they were in an alleyway, stripped of their Identification and valuables. The Red Shark was nowhere to be seen along with the Paddle Wheeler and the old schooner that had been tied alongside it, the only signs of anything happening was the two Federale cars at the harbor entrance and an ambulance just pulling away. Their work lights were out so there appeared to be no emergency. Tourists and young partygoers we're talking to the Officers in animated gestures. He couldn't hear what they were saying but one tourist enunciated a loud "boom" during his recital. It was then that Fife noticed a throbbing in his skull. One look at his ex-partner and then in a mirror and he started putting the pieces back together. They had missed everything; all except for a solid thumping by a man in a dark suit, and there was no sign of him nor his associates either. He did notice however, notice all of the extra flotsam in the water that had not been there before. Something of major consequence had happened while he and Persons had been laid out in the alley. And he had no idea what it was. His only course of action was to relieve himself of the beef burrito he'd eaten earlier. This move made him ever popular with the inhabitants of the alley. Mangy stray cats came from all around to lap up what he had just regurgitated. Persons joined in on the fun by tossing his cookies also. It was truly a sorry sight. Especially to the pair of strange onlookers in a blue truck who had just happened to be passing by at the time.

The Bull took a liking to the Old Coots and the Raiders immediately. Upon arrival, a launch from the Hannibal Hamlin and a zodiac from the Flying Cloud were dispatched to shore with a welcoming committee. To punctuate the scene, the Bluebird circled the harbor then went into one of Z's patented Kamikaze 'dive-bombs' only to come to a landing inches above the Sea of Cortez, just offshore from the newcomers. Z would claim later that it was the best landing of his short career as a pilot. The first to arrive at dockside was Turtle and Jackson dressed in their finest regalia from the previous century. Next came Captain Magic, Slo Mo, The Colonel and Cue Ball. The rest of the crew under the dictatorship of Funk Dog were readying the Flying Cloud for immediate departure if need be. Introductions were swapped and the Bull was genuinely impressed with the contingent of characters that made up 'their side.' Exley recognized Captain Magic as his father's son immediately. He explained that the 'shit eating grin' is what gave him away. Z, HT and the caretakers were the last to arrive and the Bull wasted no time laying on the charm. By the time they reached the Cantina Agents Fife and Persons had vacated, the Bull had Sunshine and Surfer Sue on each arm. As they sat at a table to celebrate their safe passage, Souza and Townsend brought them up to speed explaining the first leg of their journey to the Florida Keys. Then Victoria and Mallory took over, finishing up at the Carlsbad Caverns. The audience took particular delight in the fact that Victoria was crowned the first woman Ernest Hemingway. Merriment filled the table as the exploits of their trip (so far) were explained. The table turned somber when the Bull reiterated the findings and the catastrophe at Nellis. Exley kept the blue truck's inhabitants' identity to himself. There was enough on their plates already.

While the stories were being swapped, no one noticed when Mr. Brown grabbed a stool at the bar just within listening distance. He had traded in his suit for some appropriate wear conducive to the area and added a baseball cap and sunglasses to complete his disguise. It was actually a fairly good job because nobody paid him any mind. He listened for the length of a mug of beer and surmised there was nothing of consequence to be gained from eavesdropping. Just as he was about ready to leave, the towering giant Fife and Persons ran into, joined him at the bar. His size and stature not only drew the party's attention, but everybody else's also. The Bull sensed familiarity because of his dark suit, but that was as far as it got; the caretakers' presence took care of that. Brown situated himself so his back was turned towards the table, so they failed to make the connection. In low tones the giant explained the encounter with the FBI and finished it off by showing Brown Fife and Persons badges. Brown turned crimson. He was furious over not being given the complete picture from Violet. He gave rapid-fire orders to his assistant then slammed some Pesos down for the beer and stomped out of the bar. Patience was not one of his virtues. He went directly to the boatyard to pay for the two speedboats he had reserved. Soon the team of Darksuits were loading into what looked like their luggage into the boat. This drew little attention because people from all walks of life at one time or another descended on this little town of Guaymas. The most curious however were two peculiar little fellows standing by an old blue truck. They had attempted to blend in by feigning being fishermen at dockside. It worked well because they were able to observe every move around the harbor. After the Darksuits finished loading, they boarded the speedboats and each took off in separate directions. The giant darksuit remained on shore. After the boats were out of sight, he reached into his inside jacket pocket and pulled out a cellphone. A few texts of send and receive later, satisfied, he returned it to his pocket. He sauntered over to a Mercado and bought a newspaper, came back and sat down to mock read. No one took notice that it was in Spanish.

"What happens next?" It was a simple but monumental question. "Or better yet, what can we do to help?" Captain Magic's usual good nature had a more intense quality to it now that the Missing Links' capabilities were known. At this point in time it was truly auspicious indeed. The fun and games were over. But little did he know at the time how true this was.

All eyes turned to the Bull. He hadn't asked for it, but now it seemed like he was the head honcho. It was more than less automatic since he had the wherewithal to deal with things at this level. But this was even a new level to him. And he took it in stride: so what if the future of mankind and the world as a whole rested on his shoulders? It was just another one of Life's challenges. He looked at each of their expectant faces and knew then that just when he least expected it, he would be facing the most challenging episode of his life's career (so far). And this to him was the elixir of life. After a deep sigh he answered, "well, it seems that the powers that be are trying to keep this secret. Probably because they want to figure out a way to take control and then capitalize on it. In a way, they were sorta correct. But what's the motive? That's the moot point. And more to the point, what was the motive of those that gave this to us? Who are they? Where are they and more to the point, what in the world does it have to do with us? I don't get it and that's the trouble. I don't believe these motives coincide." The Bull was thinking of the two in the truck. He instinctively knew they were somewhere close by; like an itch you couldn't scratch, or a question you couldn't answer. But why? He could only surmise they were there, only to observe, for now. "So this is what I think we should do; and that is, take it back to where it came from." Exley was well known for throwing curveballs when you least expected it, but this was beyond comprehension. He went on: "as you know, Lezlie Potts gave me a disk with all the information pertaining to the 'Missing Link', or so I hope. We have the Missing Link itself, but what good does that do? Now it's the Disc that matters. At the time, it really hadn't sunk in, but that crafty old bastard Potts was way ahead of us. Besides, he told me they have a copy. Now that I think of it, I wouldn't be surprised if he's keeping that to himself." A smile of genuine respect appeared on

Exley's face. "We don't know with whom we are dealing with, so we have to do what they would least expect, and that is take it back to the LURE Observatory. Once there we can view the information and hopefully utilize it; make a working model to give to the world, so no one faction can dominate another. But do not be misled… There are those that will want to stop us; Colonel Hasbrook's death testifies to that. Ladies and Gentlemen, we are at war, and we don't know who with. But I have a feeling that that is going to change. The table was silent for a minute, then nods of agreement were unanimous.

Captain Magic was the first to break the spell. "General, do you like sailing?" Nothing else needed to be said.

"Young man, your boat's a little smaller than what I'm used to, but shit, any port in a storm. On the sail over we can figure out ways to make the information available to the public. I'm for it." The Bull became instantly like a racehorse at the gate.

"The Flying Cloud is probably ready by now," announced Captain Magic. The excitement of the moment was condensed and palpable. "We can get our provisions at Cabo San Lucas and be home within a week, winds permitting of course."

The ever-crafty Tyrone Exley suggested "let's board the Hannibal Hamlin, then slip over the back side unnoticed, just in case…" It wasn't necessary to finish the rest.

Captain LeBallister spoke up. "It'd be probably a good idea to switch clothing while onboard, just in case…" Turtle had a devious twinkle in his eye that testified to the fact that he had been there and done that before. "Jacksons wife can put on Victoria's wig. That should do the trick. As for looking like the Rangers, a few pillows in the right places should suffice. Hats and uniforms for the rest and then anyone who might be interested, won't be able to tell who's who."

"Great, we'll go and do the switch and slip out after dark." The Bull was genuinely pleased. With a little coaching he could be their mentor, and they, his proteges. It was a satisfying moment. Too bad it wasn't going to last for long.

These unlikely heroes filed out of the Cantina and headed for dockside. On the way, the Bull remembered to apologize for the Winnebago. HT answered something to the effect of a "sacrifice for a worthy cause" and went on to explain the Cloud of Title it had and could never be traced to them, then passed it off to the 'hazards of duty'. During the conversation Exley noticed the pair of 'fishermen' by the blue truck. The group had briefly stopped at the Red Shark to gather some of their belongings. When the Bull fished out the lead lined suitcase from the trunk, he gave them a slight, but perceptible nod and lifted it for a brief instance for them to see. Satisfied they understood, he joined the others who had missed the whole scenario.

The 'fishermen' stared back in surprise but made no move that might have given it away, plus, the maneuver had been covered by the Red Shark's trunk lid, so it stayed between only them. Call it instinct, but the Bull figured that they were probably allies, and they were truly in short supply of those at the moment. The Darksuits' face remained buried in the newspaper and missed the whole exchange.

Their belongings returned, the group boarded the paddle wheeler's launch and the Flying Cloud's zodiac and headed offshore. Darksuit reached for his cellphone and alerted his cohorts of their movements which caught the eye of the 'fishermen'. The speedboats simultaneously rounded the headland only just in time to see the fugitives board the sternwheeler. The driver of the Zodiac appeared furious about being too late. Their plans thwarted, temporarily he ordered the boats to stay closer, now they had to wait to make their move until after nightfall.

Once his fury was spent, Mr. Brown sized up the situation. He had intended to catch them halfway between the old boat and the shoreline, relieve them of the Item at gunpoint, then be on their way. Any opposition would be met with force. But once he had calmed down he decided the Hannibal Hamlin would be much easier pickings. Plus, a clandestine boarding by night would be less conspicuous and make their getaway much easier. He relayed the plan to the darksuits' other boat that they should stand down and feign enjoying the sunset. Then at dark the deed would be carried out and in their possession would be the most valuable artifact on the face of the Earth, and oh, did he have plans for that. Those snobs at the 'Trust' had been looking down their noses for years and now the shoe would be on the other foot. It would be time for them to renegotiate. That horrid old bitch had held the gavel for much too long. She would finally be reduced to the slimy old drug addict in heat that she was. He would no longer require to 'service' her and put up with that god-awful stench her body fluids emanated. And as for those other assholes, they would just have to follow suit; with the Trust in possession of that thing they would be able to dictate Global Policy in their favor. His thoughts were interrupted by the vibration of his cellphone, "Boss, they're on the move again." It was the giant Darksuit at dockside, reporting in. Mr. Brown quickly surveyed the situation then gave the orders; "We'll take them just after they leave and rendezvous out of town. Meat, go get the van and retrieve us there. Out." The huge Darksuit known as 'Meat' moved immediately towards their twelve-passenger van they had come south in. There was a spot north of town where the speed boats could be beached and they could make their way back to the Border. Meat, not known for his mental prowess, never took into consideration that he might be being followed. Although he didn't know it at the time, his presence and movements had aroused the curiosity of the 'fishermen,' one of which was hot on his tail.

General Tyrone 'Bull' Exley, dressed appropriately in a Confederate General's uniform, stepped into the wheelhouse of the Hannibal Hamlin. He walked proudly over to where Captain Le Ballister was observing out the window, as if perhaps in a previous lifetime he had actually worn the uniform for real. 'Turtle' turned and appraised him with an affirmative nod, then returned to his observations. "It seems that your suspicions were correct, General. Those two boatloads don't belong here. Here, take a look." Le Ballister passed the Bull an old-fashioned spyglass. The Bull scanned both boats that had situated themselves on either side of the sternwheeler. As he centered in on the driver of the second boat, recognition set in. His normal, amiable countenance instantly dissolved, replaced by stone cold determination bent on retaliation.

"Captain Le Ballister, do you have any firearms on board? The Bull's question was more of a growl than a statement. His face was set with grim determination. The resemblance to Robert E. Lee was uncanny.

A startled Le Ballister opened a cabinet and produced a sawed-off shotgun. "Just this and a few Colt 44's we use for decoration. They do work though." Then as an afterthought he added, "then of course there's our five pounders at the bow and aft by the wheels. They're basically for show, nothing more."

The Bull's eyes lit up. "Just man them and load 'em with anything you've got. It seems that this old tub is going to see some more action. And be sure to fire up your boilers to the max. We just might need 'em."

"I've got something better than that, we installed..."

"Captain, whatever tricks you have up your sleeve, be prepared to use them. We are going to need all the help we can get." The Bull charged out the door and made his way to the Gambling Room where everyone had gathered to joke with each other about their new looks. The gaiety of the moment evaporated upon his hasty approach. "We've got company" was all he needed to say. Two Pirates, a Dancehall Girl and a couple of Riverboat Gamblers listened attentively as the Confederate General explained the situation. "Z, HT and the Caretakers are going to create a diversion. Our stand-ins are readying themselves to go ashore as we speak. They even have a suitcase full of rocks, to throw in the water just in case. I don't need to tell you that this could get a bit dicey." The General's tone was militarily a matter of fact, the seriousness of the situation made it so. "With a little luck everything should go smooth..." He didn't get to finish because all hell broke loose.

Dusk arrived upon the Sea of Cortez. The Sun had set over the mountains of Baja California and a northeasterly breeze caused the water to shimmer from the light from a waning moon. The Bluebird had recently taken off and was making it's habitual fly-by, flapping its wings in its usual farewell. This time however, it was a signal for the mock-fugitives to disembark. The only distinguishing characteristics were Victoria's obnoxious red-orange wig that was being worn by Jackson's black eyed beauty and the suitcase full of rocks. The visibility at dusk failed to reveal to those on the boats that there was anything different happening.

The Bull's speech was interrupted by the sounds of automatic weapons and the report of a shotgun blast. A brief second of instantaneous indecision was interrupted by the Bull bellowing the order to "move out." The Rangers/Pirates quickly escorted Victoria over to the Flying Cloud tied up alongside the paddlewheeler, undoing the bow and stern lines as they did so. The Bull, bent on vengeance headed in the other direction towards the sounds of battle.

After the mock-fugitives had disembarked, an impatient Mr. Brown gave the order to seize them. They came from both directions at once with automatic weapons firing directly in their path intending to block their way. An errant bullet hit the air filled zodiac causing it to sink immediately. Mr. Brown got his first surprise when he observed the red-orange wig floating in the water when they were making their first pass. The second surprise came shortly thereafter in the form of a shotgun blast disintegrating their windshield and grazing his cheek, momentarily causing him to disengage the throttle. The launch piloted by Jackson, upon seeing his wife blown into the water, made a quick U-turn to come to the rescue. This caused Mr. Brown's boat to become directly in the line of fire of the other speedboat. Not known for his superior intelligence, the other speedboat's pilot followed in pursuit, guns blazing. Stray bullets hit Brown's engine, killing it instantly. The crew of Darksuits jumped over the side, leaving Mr. Brown to meet his fate alone. He pulled out his pistol he had used on Colonel Hasbrook, and scanned the water for anyone to shoot at, friend or foe. The wake of the other passing speedboat caused him to lose his footing and he found himself on his backside, butt first in a rapidly rising water line. His third and final surprise came when he stood back up and was facing directly down the barrel of the five pound cannon mounted on the bow of the Hannibal Hamlin. Standing next to it was none other than Brigadier General Tyrone 'Bull' Exley (retired?) Himself, torch in hand. Exley saluted Brown just like he had done after murdering Colonel Bob Hasbrook and lit the fuse. A thundering 'whoompow' filled the air as Brown dove for his life overboard. The split-second delay of the fuse to cannon is what saved his life. Before he hit the water, the speedboat disintegrated into tiny pieces of flotsam and the force of the explosion threw him like a rag doll across the water. The next thing he remembered was being fished out of the sea by his cohorts in the other boat, and now descending on them was a nightmare out of Hell.

Bull Exley has had a lot of satisfying moments in his lifetime, but this one was somewhere close to the very top. He only wished he had more time to gloat over this, but his thoughts were interrupted by a strange rumbling sensation coming from below deck through his feet. As the survivors from the first skirmish were being saved from the Sea of Cortez, the rumbling came to a crescendo. The other speedboat had given up pursuit and returned to fish the limp Mr. Brown out of the water. Jackson added insult to injury by tossing the rock-filled suitcase overboard.

Brown's first coherent moment caught Jackson's maneuver, but that wasn't what caused him to stare momentarily in horror. Heading in their direction was a colossus seemingly floating on air. Several tons of iron, aged old wood, steam, howling whistles and two brand-spanking-new Detroit Diesel engines were on collision course with their little fiberglass speed boat. Add a chorus of Rebel yells, a couple of Pirates and a dead eye sure shot manning the cannon on the bow, one could probably call it a legitimate version of Hell on Earth for them.

But that wasn't all. The Bluebird had decided to join in on the fun by taking potshots with a signal flare gun from above. All delusions of grandeur evaporated before Brown's eyes. Now it was merely a matter of survival.

The giant Darksuit known as 'Meat' had missed the whole exchange. Not necessarily known for a high IQ, he had first failed to discern the fact that there was now only one boat left. The sight he beheld upon pulling up to their pre-arranged rendezvous could have easily come directly out of a Hollywood movie script. Make that a B-movie. Heading in his direction was a zig-zagging speed boat being pursued by a paddle wheeler turned hydrofoil, and a seaplane turned Kamikaze dive-bombing with what appeared to be skyrockets. And what was even more surreal was the fact that the old boat was gaining on them. As Meat watched in astonishment, he failed to notice the old blue truck pull up a few yards away. The thought popped into Meat's head is that he would have liked to have had some popcorn and a soda pop to enjoy the show, but that thought quickly vanished when the flare hit the target and the speed boat lit up like a Roman Candle. All he could see before the boat disintegrated were black silhouettes, some on fire, jumping off the boat and into the water. To add to this outlandish scene the paddlewheeler full of hollering crewmembers set its course directly over the flaming remains of the speedboat, sending whatever that was left to the bottom. Then to top it all off, the strangely clad person manning the cannon took aim on him. The potshot was relatively harmless as it fell way short, as if it was done purely for spite. The weirdo on the boat removed his hat and bowed as they passed by, amidst cheers and jeers from the rest of the crew. Two in particular appearing to be pirates were waving their cutlasses and giving the 'universal gesture' with the other hand. It was then when he noticed a figure struggling to get out of the water. At first he was hard to spot because he was blackened from head to toe. But as he got closer, an astonished Meat discovered that the lone survivor was face (or what was left of it) to face with the boss himself. The fact was confirmed when the apparition rasped "you fucking idiot, help me up!"

Brown was completely charred. His once full Italian mane of hair was singed to his skull and the only part of him not blackened were his eye sockets. What was left of his clothes were in tatters and Meat could see that his entire body was covered with blisters, and he smelled like a combination of diesel oil and Bar-B-Q'd flesh. This poor fucker was fucked.

After the initial shock of his appearance, Meat attempted to help him to the van, which was immediately met with screams of protest. Mr Brown was one giant heat blister and there wasn't one spot on his body not afflicted. Meat could only stand there and watch his boss hobble to the van. If there is truly such a thing as karma, Mr. Brown had gotten more than his fair share of just rewards. Whether it was an act of mercy or not, they would never be able to tell: but for the rest of his life, Meat would swear they were attacked by little green men with ray guns. As for Mr. Brown, he never knew what hit him.

As they were attempting to flee the scene, Rawar came up from behind and gave them a dose of his Sound-Vibration Ray, knocking them into the next morning. When they were picked up by the Federales and blamed for the destruction from the night before, they were taken to jail, then transported to prison in Mexico City. For all intents and purposes they just ceased to exist. This would turn out only to be temporary because as Brown recovered, promises of compensation were kept and they eventually bribed their way out. By then Mr. Brown was just an embarrassment and he had lost all credibility within the 'Trust'. Any mention of the 'Trust' and he would be dead meat: not a pun, just a fact. His megalomania died out like a sputtering candle. His only driving force at this point in his life was retribution on General Tyrone 'Bull' Exley (retired) and company. And for that alone he would live for vengeance.

CHAPTER 11

BAJA CALIFORNIA

The turquoise mountain of water turned cylindrical as it ended its march across the Pacific Ocean, finally releasing its energy on the reef of the pristine coastline of Cabo San Lucas. Its rider had caught it when it first feathered; riding into the trough at the bottom, then carving his surfboard up onto the face as the moving mountain of water threw tons of gallons of ocean onto the reef. He floated like a gliding bird momentarily, then returned to the bottom again and repeated the maneuver, carving an 'S' on the face of this majestic monster; painting a temporary masterpiece on nature's bounty that would soon become only a memory to those who had witnessed it and he who lived it. To add to the spectators' delight, the surf rider stuck his hand in the face of the wave, causing him to slow down and disappear behind the curtain of the water being thrown over him as the wave met the shoreline, only to reappear at its end by being spit out by the force of the breaking wave, sending his surfboard spinning out over the back. It was truly a poetic dance with mother nature that could be repeated over and over again with different results. This particular type of artwork didn't pay the bills, but certainly appeared to be soul-satisfying, which it was.

"Now, that is the life!" said an admiring Bull Exley. "If I were years younger, that is definitely what I would be doing!" The rider had retrieved his surfboard, waved, then paddled out for more.

"His name is 'Piggy Boy'. He is Mouse's brother. You'll probably meet him later at the Mousetrap", returned Captain Magic. They were slowly motoring towards their mooring outside of town. The peninsula that separated the Pacific Ocean from the Sea of Cortez was a surfer's paradise, and also temporarily a well kept secret. "They both used to live on Maui. Mouse runs a sportfisher and owns a bar; The Mousetrap. And Piggie boy, he surfs: I'll have to leave it at that. Captain Magic's meaning was ambiguous, which is what it was meant to be. The area was certainly conducive for dropping out, which is exactly what many of the residents intended, the Libby brothers included.

After the fireworks in Guaymas had ceased, Le Ballister shut down his Detroit Diesels and scoured the water for survivors. There weren't any. Only the Bull had seen the black apparition reach the shoreline where Meat was waiting. What followed he kept to himself. On their return pass he had seen the inhabitants of the blue truck approach the van, and for a millisecond he thought he had felt a minor vibration other than the engines under him. It was hard to tell, but it didn't betray the fact that Meat slumped over at the same time. Then Rawar had looked directly at him, and for a second he thought he was being given an examination, which unbeknownst to him, he was. The Bull waved at Rawar and he waved back. And that was that. There was no doubt or question in the Bull's mind that he would be seeing them again. The Hannibal Hamlin caught up with the Flying Cloud and the Bull and the Rangers/Pirates went aboard. There was no time for goodbyes because the Federales were finally pulling up at dockside, a consistent habit of theirs was to wait until the action was over, then pick up the pieces and look for someone to extort dinero from. Le Ballister managed a "see you in the further" as they drifted away. The Bull came to attention and saluted them as they left. No words were necessary. The Flying Cloud cut the shimmering moonlit water like a hot knife through butter. By the next morning they were at the headlands that separated the Sea and Ocean and all was calm, for the time being.

"Eet most bea gud fer ya ta be een soch eh loivley day." Mallory's Irish brogue was impressive whenever he decided to use it, but sometimes it accidentally slipped out occasionally; on purpose or not. They were the only ones' topside. The others were taking a well deserved siesta. Captain Magic and the Bull had taken the Flying Cloud down the Sea of Cortez and Mallory was the first to appear on deck. His sleep was interrupted again by the recurring dream of the badge with teeth, and this time he was glad it happened because he was able to catch the show that Piggy Boy was putting on.

With no Zodiac to speak of, the crew had to wait at its mooring for a savior from shore. This time it came in the form of a rowboat being powered by a little man with a giant smile. The smile contained two oversized front teeth that left no introductions necessary for 'Mouse' Libby, proprietor of The Mousetrap. By the time everyone was rowed to shore they had all gotten their morning exercise, taking turns at the oars. Everyone was treated to a breakfast of tortillas, eggs scrambled and salza. The salsa was optional, reserved only for those with masochistic tendencies. Mallory, as usual, found out the hard way.

Shortly thereafter the sound of the approaching Bluebird filled the air. After only one pass and no kamikaze dive bombs, it came to a gentle landing alongside the Flying Cloud. Curiosity of this strange behavior was satisfied when their Zodiac was filled to the brim with the rest of the Raiders, and out of the pilot seat came old Woody himself, plaque in hand. Z was no fool; if he hadn't gotten the rest of the ensemble he would've never heard the end of it. After all, the chance of meeting a living legend sometimes came only once in a lifetime, and only if one was lucky. And for Woody it was a special reunion, and a chance to reminisce one more time, the part of their lives that changed History, with the man himself.

Woody was the first one out of the Zodiac. He marched directly up to the General and saluted, "First Lieutenant Woodward reporting for duty, Sir!" The "sir" enunciated louder for effect. The Bull returned the salute and the two old warhorses sized each other up. When the Bull eyed the plaque, he smiled.

"Well well, Lieutenant, I see you earned your 'stripes' at our little repartee." Naturally he was referring to the ladies undergarments that surrounded the medal. The Bull then looked at Z, "Excellent Marksmanship son," referring to the hit on the speedboat. Z responded by swelling up like a peacock. T-Boy, Loaf and HT were introduced and apologies were again given for the Winnebago and was met with the same response.

Victoria broke in by saying, "We'll leave you 'gentlemen', and I use the term loosely, to your own destruction. We have some shop… eh, preparations to attend to for the voyage home. She hadn't been talking much lately, due to a peculiar nauseating sensation she was having, and they usually were coming in the morning. Uh oh! But an excuse to go 'preparing' brought on temporary relief. Mallory was just beginning to notice her change on the trip from Guaymas, but there had been no break in the action to mention anything about it. Captain Magic produced a list he had made during the night. With that, the girls were gone, but not before Piggy Boy showed up to escort them around. It was obvious they had made acquaintances before. Mouse just shrugged and smiled.

In the interim, more stories of the Bull's legendary exploits were exposed, winding up with the latest escapade aboard the Hannibal Hamlin. It was then that he revealed the fact that the leader of the attack force was Hasbrook's murderer and that he had survived, barely. It wasn't the most preferable subject to end the discussion with, but it was necessary. "I don't think he will be bothering us for quite a while, thanks to Z and his flare gun. The fact that he even survived was a miracle in itself, even though he turned into a human torch." This statement brought a semblance of satisfaction, but they all knew that it was a hollow victory at best, and there was still more to come. By the end of the afternoon provisions were secured and the Flying Cloud was ready to sail. An invitation to stay overnight was politely declined, but a request for a rain check eagerly agreed upon. When the Bull found that the only place left to sleep was in the caretaker's berth, he reluctantly agreed to be given such a fate while the twinkle in his eyes and the various shades of pink on his face said otherwise. Amidst raucous laughter and fond farewells the crew boarded the schooner and headed towards the sunset with a fair wind and a following sea. After its traditional wing wave, the Bluebird headed north. To all who had participated so far it was a sad parting. Little did they know at the time how intertwined their lives would bring them to be in the future.

WASHINGTON, D.C.

Beverly Brandt wondered just who in their right mind would ever want this job. She concluded that it must have something to do with ego fulfillment, and that just wasn't her. If she wasn't the first woman President, she might have considered resigning her position, but she knew deep down inside that it just wouldn't do. She opened the top drawer of her desk in the Oval Office and produced the two folders. After staring at them for some time, lost in thought, she opened the first, entitled 'Nellis Presentation'. Not surprised, she found it contained all the information regarded as Top Secret about the item now known as the 'Missing Link'. She had a grudging admiration for the Old Lady whose sources seemingly penetrated the structure of the Government. Just who this was, she absolutely had to find out: a little disinformation sent their way could tip the scales back into their favor, or at least even them up. She found this maneuver disgusting, but necessary; hence her conclusion: "This job sucks" she said to herself as she closed the folder and reached for the other one. Apprehensively, she opened it.

It would have been far worse if she hadn't come clean to her husband, and finding out he had known all along was an incalculable weight off her shoulders. She smiled at the memory of what had occurred after the meeting with the old woman of Long Island. It was the best sex they've had shared in a very long time; inhibitions were nonexistent. And there in front of her, in black and white were all the gory details of her involvement with the Reverend Mansin. And that old Bitch still thought that she could hold this over her head. But in reality, the only one she cared about already knew, and as for the political ramifications, well, they could take this job and shove it.

Her thoughts were interrupted once again by the buzzing of the intercom. Ana Barton's voice announced, "Ms. President, it's General Cleveland of the Joint Chiefs. He insists that it's urgent." Something clicked in the back of her mind but it didn't register: it was just there. She was pleased with Cleveland's timing, because it went along with her current train of thought. She gave the affirmative order to put him through.

"Good morning Ms. President." Clevelands backside-licking tone was ever present. "We have received information from Agent Fife who has been undercover in Guaymas, Mexico, that General Exley and company showed up there. He let the good news sink in before delivering the rest. "Unfortunately they collided with an unknown aggressive contingent also in the area and lost the trail once again. Details are forthcoming…" Clevelands performance was convincing, although paper thin.

"Thank you General" (?) "I would like to see Agent Fife upon his arrival. Please keep me abreast of any new developments. Goodbye." Beverly Brandt hung up the phone perplexed. Just what in the hell is going on? Why is the FBI and the Joint Chiefs in bed together on this? And just who sent them down there? And an 'unknown contingent'? It certainly didn't take a rocket scientist to figure that one out. The old Bitch had lied to her from the get-go. All of a sudden her gut instincts were pulling for the Fugitives on the run. There she was, the figurehead of a nation, siding with those supposedly detrimental to their sovereignty, and something deep within her was convincing her it was the correct choice. She leaned back, smiled to herself and exhaled deeply. Her duality of purpose was put right in front of her and she couldn't help but admire the so-called 'bad guys', and be forced to appear to be against them. But that was the only route she could travel at this point, and that was to keep up appearances all the while trying to root out the rot within and without the Government and expose it for what it was. She would have to keep her inner thoughts to herself and her husband Jack, and secretly hope that Exley could evade this situation until she could expose the rot. It was then that she realized that the future fate of the entire globe could possibly rest on her actions from then on and she could actually do something to help. Maybe this job didn't suck so much after all....

This realization was fuel for thought. Although the variables were spinning seemingly unconnected, there had to be a thread somewhere and Exley was buying her time to find it. It was the dichotomy of the situation that led her to her brainstorm. She laughed out loud at the thought of it. She had guided her entire life in pursuit of the truth and there it was, staring back right in front of her. After taking a few minutes to wallow in self-satisfaction, she pressed the intercom button. "Ana, this is Priority One. Top Secret. This is what I want you to do…"

The Reverend Chuck T. Mansin was working on a new angle. Although he was vaguely curious as to why there had been no news about Nellis, he wasn't about to upset the status-quo. His weekly television program was lining his pockets substantially and he wasn't about to upset that, yet. But somehow the Almighty had put him in a position to be first off the block if and when the information were released, and goddam if he wasn't going to be ready for that. He had debated whether to drop subtle hints during his weekly oratory, or just come out with it and drop the bomb on the whole Christian Doctrine. The key lay in knowing when the information should be released. So he opted to drop very light hints like "Beware of wolves in sheep's clothing," or "With the end comes a new beginning" and such. He timed these statements superbly so they were left out to hang and catch the listener's attention, that he liked to call his "dangling participle." Oh, and also there was that fucking Official Secrets Act release that they had made him sign. For all his character flaws our Chucky Boy was certainly no dummy. They had him by the balls and he knew it. His ace in the hole was the information he held over Beverly Brandt's head and he would milk it for what it was worth. In the meantime he would prepare for 'The Church of The Universal Brotherhood', and be ready to turn to it at any given moment. Holy shit, if he was to be the first one out of the gate with this, all those other religious crackpots could lick his…

"Ah, excuse me Reverend, but this just came for you." Bill Bugel's interruptions were tolerated but not appreciated. Mansin was about to remark on this until he saw the Presidential Seal on the envelope. He curtly dismissed his assistant and poured himself another double shot. After throwing it down he poured another and opened the envelope. A sadistic smile rose on his face as he read the invitation. "Well well, crime does pay after all, Bev," he said no one in particular. His self esteem just climbed up another level. An invitation to a White House briefing was as good as gold. Just to be identified with these people his popularity, and pocketbook would go off the charts. Time was approaching when he would be the richest fucking preacher on the planet, or so he thought.

After a few more belts and an excessive amount of mouthwash, Reverend Chuck T. Mansin donned his blinding white suit and approached the TV podium. There was a spring in his step as the alcohol in his system made him think he was invincible. He delivered his sermon with only the slightest amount of slurring and announced he was having an important meeting with the President of the United States and promised that his next sermon would be a revelation to all. After suggesting that contributions would bring them salvation and his patented "Ah luv yueh", the lights faded and he strutted like a fighting-cock back to his dressing room, but not before giving orders to Bugel to make preparations for Washington D.C. It was time to work out the kinks in his new program. By this time next week he would be cock of the walk. But for now he would unwind a little bit with someone from a certain escort service to take off the edge. His weekly sojourn into debauchery was one of his favorite pastimes. The escort service provided all the toys: from the white powder to the handcuffs and everything else in-between. And he took advantage of it all at the expense of his flock's religious fervor. He really wasn't concerned because soon he would be king of the heap. Just what, he didn't know at the time, and just what the fuck was a heap anyhow? Well, maybe somebody's got me confused with someone who gives a shit.

Agent Bernrd Fife was both elated and apprehensive at the same time. Upon returning to the home office he was uncertain as to what the future would be. He was convinced he had probably blown another assignment and was returning for his walking papers, but there was the VIP treatment on the way back, and then the Presidential Invitation upon his arrival. There had been no harassment from the usual assholes at the Section Office and even his station chief treated him respectfully. What surprised him even more was that reinstated Agent Persons had received an invitation also. The whole section had given them no clue as to the purpose of the visit, but Fife correctly surmised it most likely had to be something to do with the Guaymas situation.

So, after pocketing the invitation, Bernie went on a shopping spree: a new suit and bow tie, starched shirt, shoe shine and haircut, even though he didn't need one. The next morning he was polished up like a brand new penny.

At the White House gate he and Agent Persons were politely directed to a side entrance where they were informed they would be meeting with the President in a room reserved only for private ceremonies. A few minutes later after they were seated, the President came in accompanied by General Cleveland, a look of genuine bewilderment on his face. "Good morning, gentlemen, please remain seated. This will not take very long and I'll be brief." In uncharacteristically informal tones, what followed was more than less an interrogation as to the whys and hows of the Agents' appearance in Guaymas, Mexico. Fife's explanation included taking the initiative to include then ex-agent Persons on the Nellis Detail and the subsequent overhearing of Dr. Harold Bloomfield's conversation. He then indicated to General Cleveland as to who he reported to, deducing that he was the top ranking officer to be entrusted with such delicate information. This brought a raised eyebrow from the President's otherwise poker face. At the culmination of the interview, the Agents were given commendations for 'extraordinary measures for extraordinary times', then were invited to the forthcoming press conference that was to follow. General Cleveland, looking a bit uneasy, escorted them out to the White House lawn.

Fife was dancing on air. What could have been the final axe to fall turned out to be a reciprocal of Certificates of Merit. And on top of that they were given a one month off paid vacation. There wasn't even a choice in the matter. He would return to Hawaii for a well deserved break and to lick his wounds from the beating he had taken from that mob-type gorilla in Mexico. From there he could also visit his new acquaintance Harold Bloomfield atop Haleakala Volcano, this time as a tourist instead of a Federal Agent. After a cavalcade of "Barneys" things were finally taking a turn for the better.

When they reached the White House lawn elation turned into astonishment. There, seated behind the Presidential podium was that strange scientist Mike Stevenson and that decrepit old man in the wheelchair Professor Potts from Nellis. Next to them was that freak of a Preacher dressed typically in white with his cast-iron silver hairdo. The scientist looked like a petrified bird or a fish out of water; either was apropos. The old man looked as if he had taken a drink from the fountain of youth as he sat there looking like a 'cat-with-a-feather-in-his-mouth' type of grin. The Reverend was all puffed up like a game cock except for his red nose that pointed to the fact that he was under the influence of something or another. Besides the General and the two Agents, the only others in attendance were photographers and news correspondents. The President, escorted by her husband Jack approached the podium, an acutely smug look on her face. It was then that she dropped the bombshell...

The concentrated ingredients of Heroin and Cocaine, commonly known as a 'speedball', were currently coursing their way through the old woman's veins. As the rush subsided she let her pungent vibrator slip through her hand and drop to the floor of the gazebo. The butler known as Adolf knew better than to disturb her in these 'moments', so he quietly laid the silver platter of coffee, croissants and morning newspaper on the table and slipped out unnoticed. As he walked back up the corridor to the mansion overlooking Long Island Sound, he was stopped in his tracks by the ear-piercing shriek that came from the gazebo. He turned and at a jog-trot changed directions to find the source of the old woman's discomfort. Upon his return he found her out cold; either from fainting or possibly the final overdose that would eventually have to come. On top of her was the scattered remains of the morning paper. He bent over her to check to see if there was still a pulse. There was. He quickly surmised she must have fainted from something she had seen in the paper. He picked up the phone and dialed 911 for an ambulance, gathered the newspaper and headed for the front door to await for its arrival. As he scanned the front page his eyes widened in surprise.

Washington Post: December 7th, 2001. Headlines: The Good The Bad and The Ugly: President reveals affair with Preacher! In an unprecedented move, President Beverly Brandt requested possible Impeachment Hearings due to an extramarital affair with the controversial Reverend Chuck T. Mansin. She had decided to "clean out the dirty laundry and face the consequences." The announcement was made with the Reverend in attendance who clearly was taken by surprise and consequently had to be physically subdued and taken away. He is not available for comment. Prior to the announcement, President Brandt had given FBI agents Bernard Fife and Gregory Persons Good Conduct Citations in a private ceremony. What then followed was the formal blockbuster announcement of "recent developments" in technology and the admittance of the existence of a UFO. Details at this point are not available due to the existence of what she terms as "unsavory elements." In a race to gain control of what is now known as the "Missing Link."

She then introduced and appointed recluse genius Lezlie Potts and his assistant Mike Stevenson, head scientist at Nellis Air Force Base to head up a new committee that would handle the Information here-to-fore. Details will be available forthwith. "We cannot release any information at this point until the cancer within our Government is removed," she said. In attendance with the FBI agents was Joint Chiefs General Steve Cleveland who clearly appeared to be perplexed by it all. He left before answering any questions.

After closing the Press Conference President Brandt left arm in arm with husband Jack.

As did her bid to drop out of the Presidential race, the announcement brought out reverse results. Instead of Impeachment Hearings, the move solidified her position and she was termed by the Press as "gutsy and honest" and that she was "human, just like us." The lies and deceit of previous Presidents reinforced the public reaction and the fact that her adulterous behavior occurred before her term, not during, actually increased her popularity; not because it happened, but by her honest admittance that it once existed. It actually drew more headlines than the spaceship. In its thirst for gossip, the public was more interested in extramarital affairs than extraterrestrial technology. As it turned out, the President took more of the heat than the Missing Link, which makes one wonder if that is what she intended in the first place. The first Woman President of the United States had unequivocally proved that she was certainly no dummy.

The Reverend Chuck T. Mansin was committed to a sanatorium. Inconceivable statements concerning "Aliens among us" had sealed his fate. Rumors of blackmail had surfaced and his weekly TV show was taken off the air.

General Cleveland though, was on the hot seat. His precarious position had been reinforced by Fife's revelation of his involvement in Guaymas. In an effort to stay any further investigation, he quickly formed a Task Force to find the Missing Link, reporting only to the President, his resolve in the matter allayed any suspicion that might have otherwise come his way. Even if only temporary, this, plus the fact that the old Bitch had finally gone over the edge gave him some breathing room. If he could find the Missing Link quickly, it would absolve him of any previous chicanery. His career was on the line and he knew it.

His 'task force' included the CIA, NSA and this time formally the FBI and Special Ops teams from each of the Armed Forces, ready to move at a moment's notice. Acquisition of the Missing Link could bring

Clevelands' salvation and quite possibly another feather in his cap in the form of another star on his uniform of an otherwise sordid career. He had successfully covered up his involvement in drug smuggling out of Vietnam, but it wasn't entirely impossible that it could re-surface if it was brought under the scrutiny of further investigation. He also had to consider the possibility of the old Bitch losing her mind and revealing all. A contingency plan for eliminating that threat had to be considered. All in all, General Cleveland had his hands full juggling all these past infractions, and it didn't appear that it would get any better until this missing whatever it was, was retrieved. Until then, he would be like a bloodhound in hot pursuit.

None of this was known to any of those aboard the Flying Cloud. In blissful ignorance they crossed the Pacific Ocean with prevailing winds helping them along the way. In a little over a week they reached the Ala Wai Harbor in Honolulu where they were met by Captain Pickle and First Mate Moonpie aboard the White Wings and transported them back to Maui. The Caretakers had to reluctantly part with the Bull. During the voyage he had cornered the market and was the object of their affections, much to the delight of all. The Rangers flew back to Maui to prepare the way for Dr. Bloomfield to study the disk, and the disposition of the Missing Link. By the time they were safely back at the Pill Box they were made aware of the recent developments. They were now the world's most wanted and their whereabouts were still unknown.

The Bull's eyes lit up when he spotted the cache of Harley-Davidsons. He immediately claimed the necessity of surveying the terrain, and after a talented makeover by Captain Magic of a long hair wig, an assortment of temporary tattoos and a costume beard, The Bull, Captain Magic and Slo Mo took off on a 'circle the island' tour. They were gone overnight and returned severely worse for wear. The Bull and Captain Magic, clearly suffering the effects from the night before, almost had to be carried in by Slo Mo. When asked about their whereabouts Slo Mo rolled his eyes and shrugged his shoulders and left it at that. After sleeping it off, their claims of "being waylaid in Lahaina" was met with indifference by the rest of the 'Old Coots', only Victoria's blossoming maternal instincts showed any disapproval of their behavior. "Why don't you boys just grow up!" she barked, then stomped off to let them ponder their predicament. After cringing solely for her benefit, their crafty all-knowing smiles betrayed the fact that they'd had a wonderful night living it up in Lahaina. A big meal and a good night's sleep, punctuated by a little of the Old Coots 'fruits of labor' and they were ready to get back down to business. The next morning they joined the caravan of sunrise watchers atop the slopes of Haleakala at the rim and the LURE Observatory. Their passing went totally unnoticed, arriving safely into the hands of Dr. Harold Bloomfield at the Science Facility. The Old Coots went back down the mountain minus the Bull, Victoria, and Mallory. Their passage was a complete success. To the rest of the world they had simply ceased to exist, for the time being.

"After the announcement of the discovery of the burial chamber, it was a circus," explained Bloomfield. "The OHA, the Organization of Hawaiian Affairs claimed sovereignty. But since it exists in a Federal National Park on Federal Land, naturally there's a lot of red tape. Since then it's been relatively quiet. OHA has sealed it off and the Government has refused them access. So for now it's a standoff." Bloomfield added with a grin, "Rangers Townsend and Souza have taken it upon themselves to protect it. How's that for irony?"

"It's like entrusting the Crown Jewels to Morgan the Pirate," observed Mallory with a chuckle. "I hope this OHA took an inventory, especially the gourds."

"Actually, that is why the OHA is tolerant. The Rangers presented them with a few, sort of like pacifiers as it were. Whatever, so far it seems to be working." Although Bloomfield was surprised by their bold move, he was happy to see them safely back in one piece. The temptation of being 'hands on' in the development of the information gathered from the Missing Link was impossible to resist. It was a chance of a lifetime. "Well, folks, shall we see what's on the disk?"

SPACE PATROL

"How can they treat each other so?" asked Oxomoxo, more to himself than his co-pilot. "If I didn't see it for myself, I would find it too hard to believe!" he grumbled. Their hopes turned to disappointment, then changed back again with every new development. This particular project was an emotional roller coaster. The diversity of the human race was at times interesting, then could change to appalling with each new turn of events. After observing the wholesale slaughter on the Sea of Cortez they were truly mystified. The humans now in possession of their gift they judged possibly capable of the crucial next step in evolution. Unfortunately they had been forced to take lives, an abhorrence to the Consortium. Although they realized that it was solely for self-defense, it still was further proof of the precarious state this Planet was in.

"Pass me another one of those 'Budlites', would you?" They definitely were not a cure, but it certainly seemed to help. That was another example. It was true that these 'Budlites' did bring temporary relief from Earth's polluted air, but once those effects wore off, it was replaced by an even bigger headache. They also found that a few the next morning would bring relief from that, and now they were beginning to wonder if that was even a good thing.

Rawar passed Oxomoxo another and opened one for himself. He took a huge gulp and took particular delight in the belch that followed. And now they had started having contests on whose were the loudest. Now that was a good thing. It was folly, but also fun. But having to drink another one the next day to cure the effects from the day before was questionable. "None of these creatures are anywhere close to perfect, some are just more evolved than others, that's all, and further proof that we will have to be more selective on future projects." 'Meat' and Mr. Brown came to mind. "Those two I had to knock out were particularly lower consciousness. Imagine if our gift were to have fallen into their hands; we might as well just take a pair, leave and kiss this planet goodbye. But still..." He left the rest unsaid, he didn't need to finish because they both had a very good idea of whom to take.

After the events in Guaymas and the Missing Link's safe departure, they had decided to return to their Scout Ship. This time they took the easier route on paved roads and as they approached the Nogales border they were sickened by the filth and squalor of the Mexican side only to be as equally surprised when they crossed into the US. It was beyond them how people of the same town could live so unequally without sharing with each other. Sharing was an integral part of the last crucial step and the humans here were either not aware of it or simply just didn't care. It was right there in front of them but they did nothing about it. They were speechless as they passed through the separate standards of living. On the way south they had taken notice of it, but here at the US/Mexican border, the blatant disregard for each others' mutual welfare was most obvious; and disheartening.

"They seem to be more attached to their possessions than they are to each other," observed Oxomoxo again. "If everything were distributed more evenly there would be less lack of want for all, maybe even total. Why can't they realize this?" He was deeply moved by the selfishness of the Human Race. They were so close to being beyond help it filled Oxomoxo with a new determination. At least their gift lay in the hands of someone capable of getting it right this time, or was it? What little ray of hope that existed was with whom they hoped were the right people. It was like Rawar had been reading his thoughts.

"I believe the older one knows who we are. First he showed us he had it in what they call a suitcase and then on another occasion he acknowledged us. So then I took a closer look at his energy field and he is proof that their potential still exists. The others are also close to the same category, albeit different levels. And that's the beauty of it." Rawar and Oxomoxo were of the same mind, although neither of them would admit it, after all, they had their bet to consider. The hope for this project, slim as it was, still existed. To speak of any other outcome was premature. Besides, at this point the Human Race needed all the help it could get, plus their tenacity intrigued them. So no mention of any alternate plan was made in case the planet self-destructed again. All involvement from this point on would be towards preserving their pet project, and to do that they had to locate the fugitives before any harm came to them. "Let's take some of these 'Budlites' with us. Besides the pregnant female, they're the best thing we've come across." Out of all the curiosities they've encountered so far, this peculiar beverage had the most potential. But when factoring in its addictive properties, he couldn't decide if it was a good idea or not. Rawar broke in on their train of thought. "It will be good to get back to the Mothership, I've seen enough. For now."

YUMA, ARIZONA

'Evil' Sam McGregor's usual morning hangover was nonexistent. In fact he couldn't remember how long it had been since he felt so rested. He felt so good that the hole in the roof of his barn wasn't a source of aggravation. Just what in the hell caused it remained a mystery. Most likely it was the same assholes that took his beer and truck. Goddammotherfuckers anyway. But in his rejuvenated state it just didn't matter to him. What did matter however is when he figured out what day it was. A nine day sleep was fucking impossible, plus, that dream he had felt so real. The pricks in it weren't monsters, nor were they humans. These fucks had bigger heads and six fingers, beady little fuckin eyes and almost no ears. And how in the hell did his truck get so muddy? First it's gone and then it's not. To mention anything about it would just cause more bullshit and that's the last thing he needed any more of. Those who knew him thought he was a goddamn crackpot anyhow. Fuck them anyway; he felt good, so whatever. He only wished he could get that dream off his mind. Shit!

"We've exhausted all our resources Ms. President and it simply doesn't work. The composition of these materials is of 'Unknown Origin'. Our technology level doesn't permit us to duplicate it." Potts' conclusions were delivered with a grim finality.

The conference room in the White House was shrouded in apparent disappointment. President Brandt stood at the window watching the snowfall while Potts, his assistant Mike Stevenson and General Steve

Cleveland sat at the conference table each in their own particular world of thought. On the surface they all appeared to be of the same mind, but beneath was an entirely different scenario. They were secretly elated for different reasons, all except for Stevenson; his new toy was broken. The President just realized that her gut-instinct was pulling for the fugitives; they were buying the time to ferret out the old Bitch's spies. General Cleveland would be empowered with more resources at his disposal to catch them and at the same time covering her not-so-lily-white backside. And Potts had the biggest secret of all. The Disk. And along with that came the responsibility of the information useful for the betterment of all mankind. And for that reason he wasn't about to part with it; until he found out who stood where. So he was going to hold his cards close to his chest and not flinch, that is until he found out where the stench came from, in the form of just who killed Hasbrook and why. Each person held their poker face well.

"General Cleveland, do we have any idea yet as to where it's gone?" asked the President. And please tell me no, she thought to herself.

"We lost the trail in Guaymas, but the incidents that were reported there point to the fact that they probably left by boat." And gave me some breathing room to cover my ass. "That Exley is a devious SOB. They could be anywhere."

"The object itself does them no good whatsoever, nor us for that matter." But the disk does. Potts knew his statement was unnecessary but he said it for appearance's sake.

"Just why would he take the key to our spaceship?" interjected a distraught Stevenson, the wind was clearly out of his sails.

"That is the key question Mr. Stevenson." When she realized what she'd said she added, "No pun intended," red faced. "The Brigadier General doesn't strike me as the criminal type, yet his actions are beginning to leave a trail of dead bodies and whatnot". The 'whatnot' being as ambiguous as it could get.

"It is also becoming harder to keep this quiet thanks to him." Cleveland, in his best effort to pass the buck, had to use any means necessary to keep the spotlight off himself. "Charges could be brought…"

"It is possible that is why he took it in the first place." Potts' interruption was timely. "Just what right do we have to keep this from the public, General?" The more time he spent with Cleveland, convinced him that he had made the correct decision; giving Exley a copy of the Disk was one thing, but he wondered if letting him abscond with the Missing Link itself had been the correct move. That is until he had to work in conjunction with this asshole; Lezlie Potts began to wonder if Exley was way ahead of him. It was a mutual admiration.

"Now gentlemen, we're not here to argue..." Beverly Brandt was enjoying this but she certainly couldn't let on. "We need to find a way to get some answers, and quickly." She felt like a referee in a Pro Wrestling match; where cheating was mandatory and the ref was purposely made to look like an idiot. "And find a way to locate the Missing Link without causing harm to anyone." The President's direct approach brought the meeting back to order. "Suggestions?"

"With all due respect to Mr. Potts here, we still have to keep its status a secret. It's value is limitless, but if word was to get out that it is out there, somewhere..." Cleveland pointed out the window. "The race to possess it could turn into chaos." He gave Potts a superficial smile. Where is Brown when I need him? He thought.

"Somehow we need to get word to General Exley that we can go no further without analyzing its composition." And let him keep the disk. Potts gave Cleveland a blank stare. "Without letting on to the public that it's out of our possession."

"If, and when General Exley opens the lead lined suitcase our satellites will pick it up and we'll have him. Until then our hands are tied." Where are you Brown?

"Then we can attempt to make contact. If we try to physically subdue them, Exley will probably find a way to elude us, again." As he was speaking, it came to Potts just where they might have gone. "If we were to take a violent approach, we might never see them, or it, again."

"The Brigadier is a slippery one at that, thank God." The President smiled inwardly. "General Cleveland, put our spy satellites on full alert, Priority One. We must establish a line of communication ASAP. So far, Exley has shown no signs of using the Missing Link for personal gain, although any justification for his actions are way beyond me." The President looked at Cleveland as she addressed him.

The meeting adjourned and the President went back to the business of running a Superpower. Potts and Stevenson watched the General walk off. They looked at each other and back again at the retreating General. No words needed to be said; they had his number. His own code of ethics were like blunders. He couldn't see beyond them. Potts looked at his distraught assistant. He felt genuinely sorry for him. The elation of having a working spaceship only to have the rug pulled out from under him had taken its toll. But there was no time for whining now. Alot rested on his next decision; quite possibly the future of the entire planet. With a sly grin on his age-old wizened face he asked, "Mike, have you ever been to Hawaii?

CHAPTER 12

"It's quite simple, really. When you close the distance between the magnets situated at opposite poles, you create more energy. If you lock them together encased in a Vacuum Chamber, it will then create a surrounding force field. When it is enclosed in this chamber the energy can be harnessed. It can then feed the generator while the generator is feeding it, sustaining each other simultaneously. The size and number of magnets are the variables. With enough of them working continuously against and with each other, you can defy Gravity itself. Our only problem is the materials themselves. They are not of this Earth. Is anybody familiar with the Fibonacci sequence? No wait, I'm getting ahead of myself. Let's just say it has to do with directing the magnetic energy/power. We'll save that for later." Dr. Bloomfield's explanation of the Disks' contents was in layman's terms, but it was unanimously effective.

The LURE observatory was the birthplace of new-age technology, or rather the rebirth of an age-old one. Deep in the bowels of the science facility they gathered to witness the first working model and there it was; a miniature mock-up of the Nellis spacecraft hovering in a large vacuum chamber with no support, no noise and no energy spent. The onlookers stared in respectful awe, lost in their own thoughts and incapable of speech. "There is much more to it than that, of course, but here it is, a legitimate working model of Einstein's Unified Field Theory," Bloomfield added proudly. "His Theory of Relativity was done at an early age. Until now, no scientist on Earth has been able to explain this one."

The Bull was the first one to speak. "Makes you wonder what happened to Atlantis and Lemuria" He didn't have to fill in the rest. Mallory did.

"Obviously it must have fallen into the wrong hands and they abused its power." Nods of agreement here and there. The significance of this auspicious moment was sinking in. It was in their hands now and just what was to be done with it? In an effort to lighten the portents of their impending future Mallory asked, "what happens if it is out of a Gravitational Field? Does it still work?"

"Good question. Don't know. It could be that's why the item is made of different compounds that are unknown to us. It's possible that it can create anti-gravity in space. There would be only one way to find that out, and that is to go there."

The Bull smiled to himself, he knew of a certain pair that had that answer. "Those weirdos we met were smart cookies. Their Kind gave the Atlanteans and Lemurians only half of the keys; the power for it only to work in gravity. Just enough rope to hang themselves, which is apparently what happened; also not to endanger wherever they had come from. Damn smart of them I'd say." He hoped that soon he would have the opportunity to find out. If the chance presented itself, a confrontation would be imminent.

Victoria spoke for the first time. "The question is, now what are we going to do with it? Our track record speaks for itself. Plus the fact that we aren't that popular right now doesn't help much at all."

"No one faction or government can control it. It's all or none. Since it is potential free energy, the existing power monopolies are going to want to keep it quiet or get control of it for themselves. We've gotten a taste for that already and it's only just begun." The Bull stated the obvious and just to emphasize the fact he added, "As of now we are in a really deep shit."

Why don't we just send it back to Potts and let them worry about it?" Mallory moaned. He knew it was futile, but if he could just go back to his spelunking project, preferably with Victoria, that would be just fine with him. But being in that place at that time made it too late for that now.

His wishful thinking backfired. "Connor Mallory, that's the most selfish thing I've heard you say yet!" Victoria barked. "You ought to be ashamed of yourself! She stomped off to the ladies room leaving the cringing men to themselves.

"Watch your step son, she's been getting very emotional lately." The Bull tried to sound comforting.

"Yeah, I've noticed."

When she came back it was clear she had left to cry, which puzzled the men even further. Only she knew she was late for her monthly ordeal. "Have any of you 'gentlemen' taken into consideration what impact this is going to have on almost everything? Take religion. To what lengths will they go to keep this new revelation quiet?"

The Bull laughed out loud. It was his only course of action. "If that 'reverend' and I use the term loosely, Mansin' is any indication, we are sinking deeper into the shitpile as we speak."

"That does it!" bellowed Dr. Harold Bloomfield. "Here we are, involved in what is probably the most important discovery ever! And all you're doing about it is whine! What is wrong with all of you?" He might as well have told them to go stand in a corner. The results would have been the same. "All of you go out and get some fresh air. And do not come back until you have something constructive to say." He winked at the Bull as he yelled and they all scurried towards the door just as the Rangers burst into check on the commotion. They had been guarding the perimeters outside. One look at the situation and they about-faced and fled with the others. Once outside they looked at each other and started laughing. Bloomfield's ploy was a complete success. After a few minutes Bloomfield also came outside and sternly announced, "Now children, are you ready to play nice again?"

"Yes Professor," they chorused like school kids as they followed him back in.

"Why me? Why now? Why, period?" A certain amount of credibility can be attached to Murphy's laws, especially when it's applied to Federal Bureau of Investigation agent Bernard 'Barney' Fife. Out of all the places on the whole entire planet why did he have to, at this point in time, pull up to the parking lot of the LURE Observatory, now? Couldn't it have been thirty seconds later or five minutes before? No! It just had to be when the last people on Earth he wanted to see were filing into the Science Facility. Damn it! He was on vacation! He slumped over and let his head hit the top of the steering wheel of his rental car, an involuntary mournful groan coming from deep within. Then misery turned incredulity changed into opportunity in the blink of an eye. After all, he was a Company Man, and a decorated one at that!

Deluded visions befuddled his mind. Bernard Fife, superhero of the world and savior of the Yeunahtad States Uf Ayemerika to the rescue for truth, liberty and justice blah blah blah. It must have been the altitude; mental pictures swimming in his head. Magazine covers, syndicated news interviews, centerfold of Playgirl(?) Well no, not that far… Get a grip Bernie, one can stretch reality only so far; back to opportunity.

Fife sat there for a while weighing his chances. This was being handed to him on a goddamn platter and he wasn't about going to blow it, again. First, a little reconnaissance was in order, if Doctor Bloomfield was going to hide the fact that the fugitives were there, he would act accordingly. He had been a week into his vacation and it was possible that something had transpired without his knowledge. If he went in there guns blazing and their presence was a known fact, God knows what kind of shitpile he would find on his desk back at the office. He had already suffered enough for a lifetime and then some. It would be better if Bernie were to investigate first and then make a move later. Oh and he knew who to contact. That General Cleveland had already gotten him to the White House, what would they award him next? If only he would have thought of the old cliche 'watch out for what you wish for, it might come true.'

Agent Fife decided to call first. His cell phone was now a permanent fixture. That would soften the element of surprise and get Bloomfield to lay his cards on the table, so to speak. Then he could feign ignorance and set the appropriate measures in motion. Exley and his band of fugitives were in the bag and they didn't know it. He could nail them all in one fell swoop; even the accomplices on the motorcycles that had led him on that merry chase down this frigging volcano the last time. Oh, paybacks would be double. In the meantime he was a one-man team and that was okay with him because he would take all the credit, and/or blame, for this one.

He punched in the number. "Hello Dr. Bloomfield? This is Bernard Fife. I'm on vacation and I thought I'd pay you a visit." There was a pause on the other end of the line. Did he detect a slight intake of breath? "Well, actually I'm right outside in the parking lot. If it's any trouble I'll come back another time. Really? Fine. I'll come right in." Bernie looked in his mirror and patted down his bothersome cowlick, then licked his thumb and ran it across his eyebrows. If he was going to save face he might as well do it looking good. Bernard Fife, alias Barney, alias Maxwell Smart was ready for action.

Unbeknownst to Fife, Murphy and his Law were already hard at work in the form of Rangers Townsend and Souza. They had observed the whole routine. A quick call via their standard issue two-way radio and everyone inside was on full alert. Fife didn't know that they knew he knew they were there. And that's all it took for Agent Fife's delusions of grandeur to completely fall to pieces.

He was met by a cordial Bloomfield and given the grand tour of the Science Facility, all except where Exley and company were gathering pertinent material for their planned retreat. The Rangers, pranksters at heart, flattened one of Fife's tires and stole the spare. It wasn't really necessary but it was fun. Fife should have smelled a Rat,(in this case two) but he was so caught up in himself he failed to make the connection. The Rangers, good Samaritans that they were, even helped Fife out of his temporary predicament. They just happened to have a can of Fix-A-Flat which they purposely filled only halfway. In the interim, Fife made a call to alert General Cleveland who in turn called out the Reserve Maui National Guard, not exactly the sharpest pencils in the pack and also the

Regular Coast Guard that had a small station at the Ma'alaea boat harbor. Fife was told to stay put until backup arrived, and in the meantime he was to observe; all he saw were the Rangers loading equipment into the back of their four wheel drive Jeep Cherokee Chief for a trip down the mountain. Bloomfield came out once again to invite Fife to lunch. This distraction, plus the flat tire ordeal had allowed enough time for Victoria, Mallory, and the Bull to sneak into the back of the Jeep, away from prying eyes, namely those of agent Bernard 'Barney' Fife. All was ready for the shit to hit the fan which it did.

If it hadn't been for the Rangers catching him in the act, Fife might not have underestimated his adversaries as much. Be that as it may, it didn't dawn on him until it was too late and they too had made their escape with Exley; that is until he finally put it together as they were pulling away. They smiled and waved as they passed by and all of the sudden the reality of his realization came in like a slap in the face. His eyes bulged and he screamed like he was about to give birth. Then he started his car and limped out of the parking lot, only to come to a halt as the half full fix-a-flat leaked out of the unplugged tire. But as fate would have it, the convoy of the National Guard was just pulling up as he was rolling to a standstill. They would have been there earlier if they hadn't been held up by a certain motorcycle gang on the cruise. Fife looked like he was going to shit a concrete block. After flashing his badge he ordered pursuit, a grim vision of deja vu formulating in his mind.

"Load your weapons! Full ammo pack! These people must be stopped!" His shrill voice must have jumped an octave. The National Guard sergeant in charge gave him an exceedingly strange look, then did as he was told and relayed the orders. Shit Howdy, he was a good ole boy from Arkansas and wouldn't mind a little target practice anyhow. "After them, they must be stopped at all costs!" With whoops of joy, the convoy barreled down the mountain. Too bad they didn't know the roads.

"Fasten your seatbelts kids, we're going for a joyride!" yelled Townsend at the wheel. It was his turn to give a driving clinic. At the sight of the pursuing convoy, he didn't waste any time. He jammed the Cherokee into four-wheel drive and left the curving roads, heading straight down the mountain. With each slice of the highway they became airborne, only to land in the soft earth of the dormant volcano. "Oh yeah, I've always wanted to do this!" The others looked as if they didn't particularly share his enthusiasm. Down the mountain they went, gathering momentum and approaching breakneck speed. The speleologists thought they had an experience the first time, but this one was lunatic fringe. As they got further down, the turns became wider, which gave them more room on the straightaways. They passed a herd of cattle being led to water by a pair of Paniolos, (Hawaiian Cowboys). With horns honking the Cherokee burst around the edge of the herd, Souza waving and pointing up the hill. The Paniolos were old friends and one glance up the hill told the story: they could be of assistance. They steered the steers directly in the path of the oncoming Jeeps who in turn unsuccessfully tried to swerve out of the way. After this maneuver, out of the eight vehicles that had begun pursuit, three were left. The five that didn't make it were left in assorted various stages of destruction strewn over the mountainside. The first one attempted going left around the herd and hit a slick combination of mud and cow shit, which caused it to roll a number of times before coming to a halt in the middle of a pasture. It was hard to tell whether they looked or smelled worse. The Jeep and its passengers were completely covered in the stuff. The next two Jeeps, not wanting to duplicate the mistake, attempted going right, the way around but after negotiating a small rise, found themselves in the reservoir in which the cattle were heading. They were soaking wet, but at least they were clean. The fourth vehicle plowed straight ahead and ran directly into one of the bigger cows also covering them with shitmud plus an added coating of blood and entrails. The Paniolos didn't even seem to mind; they would eat plenty of steak for a while. It was the fifth and final accident that was hard to tell exactly what happened. Somehow it had miraculously made it through the cows unschathed, but the journey cost them control of the vehicle and they twisted and turned, bumped and jumped into one of the many eucalyptus forests that grew in patches on the side of the mountain. As they entered, the passengers bailed out and the sound of tearing metal and crashing trees was the only telltale sign of destruction until it finally came to a halt fifty yards deep. There was only a momentary sound of hissing steam until the forest was rocked by an explosion and a subsequent fireball. It was truly a miracle that nobody was seriously injured, except for some minor cuts and bruises, one broken arm and one dead cow. The Paniolos enjoyed the show so much that they invited the survivors to a barbecue that night; steaks of course.

The remaining Jeeps weren't having much better luck. A standard military issue Jeep has much less weight than a fully loaded Cherokee Chief and they were being bounced around like a ping pong ball. It was amazing in itself that they were even able to remain in the vehicle. The only thing that saved them was their ability to follow the tire tracks of the Cherokee. But the Cherokee has a wider track so they could only follow one groove. The other side was like driving on a washboard. Fife made a futile attempt to fire a rifle but the shots weren't even close. One ricocheted off a rock and the sound of the shots were the only evidence left of the chase. This only caused Townsend to drive faster and widen the gap between them. Souza was double-seat-belted and Mallory and the Bull each had a firm grip on Victoria in the back seat. If it wasn't for the seat belts their heads would have probably popped out through the roof. As they gained distance they finally had time to slow down and take stock of the situation. Four hulks of misshapen metal and one cloud of smoke coming from inside the eucalyptus trees was all they could see, until the remaining three came over a rise, bouncing in the distance, way too far to catch up. They could see Fife standing on the passenger side of the Jeep attempting to take aim. Every time they hit a bump he would have to grab on with both hands to keep from flying out. The next two bumps were particularly accentuated. The first one Fife appeared to be holding his mouth and on the next he completely disappeared, all except for two legs that were sticking out upside down in the passenger seat. It looked ridiculous. Townsend decided to toy with them even further by letting them close the gap then speed up again, just enough for them to maintain pursuit. By the time they reached the open road at the bottom none of the remaining jeeps, nor their drivers, were in any condition to catch up with them. Just before they left them in the dust, Townsend decided to add insult to injury. When they got back on the pavement he stopped the Cherokee and got out, proceeded to the side of the road, dropped his pants and gave them a view of his generous backside, slapping it for effect. He pulled his trousers back up, blew them a kiss and slowly but deliberately meandered back to the drivers seat. All they could hear was a gut-wrenching scream in the distance. It didn't take a rocket scientist to know who that came from. An hour later they met the Old Coots back at the pill box.

After slowing up the convoy, the gang had taken refuge in one of the eucalyptus forests to remain: in order to see if they might be of any further assistance. They saw the whole show and concluded it was worth the price of admission and then some. They had gone innocently up to the Paniolos to offer any help and received a large chunk of freshly butchered strip loin for their efforts. The feast was going to be extra special tonight. They all agreed that agent Fife at least deserved a toast, which they did a number of times. Oh, and one for Murphy of course.

LONG ISLAND

The Reverend Chuck T. Mansin couldn't believe his luck nor the turn of events that had brought him from a completely crashed empire to the lap of luxury out on this Long Island Estate. They had actually manhandled him, the Evangelist of evangelists off the White House property and in guarded condition committed to their hoity-toity clinic to be under 'observation' as they called it. Shit, it was like being in a goddamn jail, the only difference being that the guards wore white and called themselves fucking doctors. He had a doctor outside his room day and night and everyone avoided him like the plague. That is except for the old lady that had been admitted the day after him, apparently from an overdose of drugs. Once she had detoxed, she was let in on the co-ed meals and recreation sessions. Word gets around even in places like this, and once she found out who he was, she was like his shadow, and the only one who seemed to take an interest in what everyone else thought was nuts. He couldn't blame them, but why her? She was some high falutin old hag, and he, a washed up preacher, enveloped in a cloud of rumors that he had been blackmailing the President during her term. Did she have some kind of disjointed fantasy towards the criminal element or was it some other ulterior motive? Either/ or, he didn't particularly give a fuck, nor was he about to look a gift horse in the mouth. She had some kind of extracurricular pull and had gotten them both released together and he was invited out to her Long Island Estate to recover. Here he was, persona non grata to the rest of the world, sitting out in a gazebo with the finest whiskey and cigars at his disposal, overlooking one of the most magnificent vistas the Atlantic Coast had to offer and her Nazi butler would come by occasionally with a tray of uppers, downers and mood enhancers in pill form that he could help himself to. He was a pig in shit, but all the while echoing in the back of his mind was what in the hell she wanted from him. She was polite and cordial on the surface, but behind her eyes lurked something totally sinister he couldn't put his finger on. Then came the mob type visitor she had a private conference with. He definitely was not a pillar of society, the bulge inside his coat testified to that. Even out in the Gazebo he could hear her yelling and the only word discernible was 'Brown' because she yelled that word louder a number of times. Whatever the reason, it wasn't his business; or so he thought.

The out of control conversation went on for about a half hour. The end accented by a slammed door and screeching tires. Then all was back to serene once again. The serenity was interrupted by the sound of footfalls coming down the corridor towards the gazebo. Upon the old woman's entrance it didn't take a brain surgeon to notice that she was on something. The Reverend had been around the block too many times not to have noticed that. In her hand was a folder which she dropped on the table next to Mansin. He eyed the folder and then her. Behind her dilated eyeballs was a more abhorrent malignancy that was beyond even him. The folder had one word on it. Brandt.

She sat at the table opposite him and glanced at the folder then delivered a penetrating stare. "Reverend, I believe it's time we have a business discussion." Her tone was most obvious.

The Reverend picked up the folder and without a word thumbed through it. The only sound was the crashing of the surf on the cliffs and rain from the storm pushing off the Atlantic. Mansin was surprised by the thoroughness of its contents; substantiated proof of all the allegations against him. Here across the table was someone in his own league. With a look that matched hers he answered "Yes, I believe we do. What can we do for each other?"

Agent Bernard Fife was beside himself. Not only had he managed to allow his query to evade him once again, but he chipped the entire front row of the upper bridge of teeth in the process. In an attempt to fire the rifle during the chase down the mountain and hang on at the same time, the bumps had wreaked havoc on his mouth. He immediately had to visit what he would later call an old Japanese "hatchet dentist" for some temporary repairs, only to find after a healthy dose of sodium pentathol, a completely irregular set of discolored caps in the place of what was once was his 'Bureau Smile', a trophy as it were. And to add even more insult to injury before he could return to give his unsuccessful report, the office had gotten wind of his accident and upon his arrival, a set of wind-up false teeth were going clackity-clack across his desk. Perfect timing on the pranksters part. It was just too much for those in the office to contain themselves. Bernie came in, mouth closed of course, and when he saw the teeth marching noisily across his desk, his eyes bulged and the entire room fell to pieces. It was a worst-case scenario in the flesh. To him it was the living end of a wholehearted career he simply wasn't suited for, or so he thought at this moment in time. I feel sorry for this poor fucker even writing about him. Right-o.

When born into this life, love has no inhibitions, grudges or prejudices; or any other emotion for that matter. Well, this was Bernie; a blank slate. After the initial shock of the moment, his cup was empty. When his brain started to re-function, he reached into his pocket for his badge to throw it on the desk when: "Agent Fife, you are summoned immediately to the Pentagon for a meeting with General Cleveland of the Joint Chiefs." His supervisor, not usually known for a sympathetic bone in his body, took it upon himself to alleviate the situation, and his timing couldn't have been better. The overbearing tonal quality of his voice brought things back into perspective. Fife was still an integral part of the ongoing project within the Bureau, not to mention the world, was involved in.

Agent Fife refocused and took his hand out of his pocket. He quickly thought to himself that it couldn't be any worse than it is at the moment, about-faced and headed out the door. With the clackity clack of the teeth winding down into silence.

General Cleveland had his scapegoat, his sacrificial lamb, and it was in the form of Agent Bernard Fife. The Agent was also coming in handy for keeping the spotlight off himself. His antics, embarrassing as they were, had kept Cleveland away from being the focus of attention. And that in itself made Bernie indispensable in the eyes of the General. Ever since that horrid old Bitch had gone over the edge he had been walking on eggshells. If any connection was to be made to her, his career and quite possibly his freedom would be instant history. If the incriminating folder she had on him was ever to be made public knowledge, he could kiss his precious prestigious backside goodbye. Not to mention all the dollars he was racking in on the sly. So even though he found it personally degrading to be polite to this idiot with a badge, it was also a must-needs situation.

What could Violet be up to? He wondered. Especially with that freak of a preacher whatshisname. Oh yeah, Chuck Mansin. His name itself brought horrifying connotations. Surely she must have something on him also. He had successfully burned his own bridges by just the fact of being involved with the then would be President. The hypocritical nature of his position and his actions was surely enough to make him worthless. But the underhanded capabilities of that wicked old lady went far beyond his imagination, so he always found it necessary to take that into consideration, just for the mere fact of self-preservation.

His thoughts were interrupted by the entrance of Agent Fife. "Ah, good morning agent Fi... Good God man! What happened to your mouth?"

Fife was instantly self-conscious. But on the other hand it happened in the line of duty, so he played it to the hilt. "Good morning General. It happened during pursuit of those criminals down the mountain on Maui. It's a dormant volcano and they took a most suicidal route. I had no choice but to follow, and my driver was a Reserve National Guard..."

"That's alright Agent, I'll read it in your report." Any mention of Cleveland's involvement with this boob he cut short. Besides, he already had read the report and it had played down the incident involving Fife's injury as if they were trying to sweep it under the carpet. But seeing it first-hand shed new light on the situation. Cleveland quickly concluded that the old dentist previously must have been on the losing side during World War II and it was his own small way at gaining some retribution.

"Held up somewhere."

"Ah, er, what was that again?"

"I said we have the Island completely blanketed so they must be held up somewhere."

"Oh, yes. Excellent. And the material you confiscated at the observatory. Did you bring it with you?"

"What little there was. Mostly just some notes. Either they all have brilliant memories, or they received some sort of help we don't know about." Fife handed him a small briefcase. "They're all in here."

Cleveland opened the briefcase and scanned the notes, he was baffled by the thoroughness of them. Surely they couldn't have gotten all this at the Nellis Presentation. There had to be some kind of activity on the inside. A leak. It was most likely that it was that Colonel that got shot. If not, they still had plenty of work cut out to do. "Yes, I see what you mean. What about this Dr. Bloomfield?"

"He managed to slip through our fingers during the chase. So far, there's no trail of him." Fife was clearly agitated and the General could see this. He would have to handle the Agent with kid gloves, for now.

"I'm sure you've done your best." Yeah, right. "And you being caught right in the middle of your well-deserved vacation." A vision of the Don Knotts' television character came to mind and he still had to stifle a laugh. If this idiot was any example of the FBI's capabilities, we are in serious trouble, he concluded. "Agent Fife, you always seem to be in the right spot at the right time. I commend you for that." How lucky can we get? "Finish your vacation and try and see if you can get your mouth repaired. Please."

"If it's all the same to you General, I'd like to return and be hands on; I feel partly to blame that they escaped again."

Partly? You've got to be kidding. "As you wish, Agent." Go see how much more you can screw up. "Use all means at your disposal and report directly to me." I'm going to need all the ammo I can get to keep them off my trail, he thought. For all his failings, this Agent Fife was a perfect fall guy. "That is all." And keep smiling.

Fife lapsed and smiled which made the General involuntarily cringe. Both of them were embarrassed. Cleveland added again, "and do try to get those teeth fixed."

"Burp. Damn good steak," Exley remarked. "There's something to be said about freshly butchered meat." His belch was intentional. In the Orient this was considered as a compliment. He had picked this habit up during his tour of duty in Hawaii and beyond during World War II. Not only was belching satisfying but also complementary to the host. It would also offend those without this culinary realization which made it doubly fun. That, however, wasn't the case here in the pill box.

"It's probably the good grass they eat or the contented environment they live in." A foregone conclusion by Dr. Harold Bloomfield. "And the price is right too."

Townsend added, "the Paniolos are a couple of Raymond's cousins. They're all over the Islands. If it hadn't been for them we probably wouldn't be sitting here." Nods of agreement went throughout the pill boxes' sitting room.

Soon a pungent after-dinner cloud of Maui's finest filled the room. If they had to be interned, they might as well go stressless. Days had passed since the Townsend 'driving clinic' and their faces were plastered all over Network TV and local newspapers. Once again they were now proclaimed as "thieves of Federal and State secrets, guilty of acts of Treason, and they were America's Most Wanted. They wore it well.

Captain Magic had immediately flown the caretakers over from the Flying Cloud to ferry in supplies to the pill box. Victoria was given a makeover. A little sun tan in a bottle, plus a black wig, add in a pillow and she blended in with many of the other local ladies on the Islands: all except for her pale eyes. But in this day and age, cross breeding had made even that not too much of an oddity. She was then allowed to go on the shopping runs to alleviate her recently-acquired discomfort. It was like a tonic; send a woman shopping and all else is forgotten; kinda-sorta. This of course also brought relief to Mallory who was finding her behavior curious of late. A number of times he caught her staring at him and he couldn't put a finger on the reasoning. Sometimes one is oblivious to the obvious and this was the case now. Only her Uncle was beginning to suspect that something was amiss with his niece. Victoria had considered breaking the news, but things were complicated enough already, so it was still her own personal secret. Hers, Oxomoxo and Rawar's.

Captain Magic strode in holding his cell phone. "Pack it up folks, we're taking a quick helicopter ride tonight in the early a.m. It's all set. We'll be dropped outside the harbor with life rafts and will row to our boat. If all goes smoothly, nobody will notice a thing." The announcement brought sighs of relief from the 'internees', even a good thing can get old after a while sometimes. The Bull was especially ready. He had been like a caged lion ready to pounce during the last 24 hours. There was simply just too much to accomplish and they couldn't do anything sitting there. The fact that he was the only one not to partake in the herb was also a factor. He claimed that it smelled wonderful, but he had enough habits already. Everyone else enjoyed the break, but the Bull's was a mind in motion. Being the unproclaimed leader with the weight of the world on his shoulders contributed also. Other than his concern for Victoria, he was always mentally calculating the tasks that lay ahead. Oh and did he have a doozy of a plan; one that would certainly mess with the minds of those after them.

"Penny for your thoughts." Mallory had the uncanny knack of almost reading his mind. Although the Bull wanted to share his ideas, they hadn't been totally worked out yet. All depended on them getting safely back to the West Coast undetected. And it is also contingent on the unscrupulous capabilities of that of the Raiders in which he had total faith. Their track record was unblemished, as were the Old Coots, the Rangers, Doc Bloomfield, and even those two new 'lovebirds'; the Speleologists. All in all, it was quite a crew indeed.

"Ah, just thinking ahead. We're supposed to be the bad guys and we're not. Plus being a good guy sucks. The one thing I have decided is getting the Missing Link back to Potts. It does us no good whatsoever and he did give us the Disc. I believe it's safe with him and only him. Now I'm working on the 'how' of it." Exley wanted that info to sink in for a while and then he would call for a vote. What he couldn't reveal was his knowledge of Oxomoxo and Rawar. He simply didn't know where their interests lay. He didn't know if they did either. His gut instinct told him that they were putting them to some sort of test. When he had locked eyes with Rawar he had felt like he was being scrutinized, as though he was transparent. And since they were all basically good people that posed no threat, he felt at the moment they could be watching out for us, just to what extent he couldn't know. Shit! They were Aliens!

Mallory observed the Bull. He could tell his mind was working overtime and would keep them informed whenever possible. But along with that he could detect something the Bull knew and he didn't. Oh well, ignorance can be bliss he thought. "Well, just let me know if there's anything I can help you with, we are all in this together, you know."

The Bull smiled at the speleologist. Victoria snagged a good one, he thought. He knew they were in love but wasn't sure if they knew it yet. Oh boy, would time definitely tell. "I'll do just that son. Meanwhile you just take good care of our Girl."

Just before liftoff, the Bull, cagey old veteran that he was, opened the lead lined suitcase just for a second. This caused the alarms of both the heliport and airport to go off, simultaneously. Amidst the confusion they lifted into the night sky unnoticed. While those on the ground were looking for the source of the confusion, the helicopter made its escape. The suitcase had also set off the satellite tracking systems and soon the airport and heliport were smothered with National Guard and Law Enforcement individuals, all searching for a non-existent prey. In one brilliant maneuver, The bloodhounds were put completely off the scent. Cleveland was being made an ass of, and he was finding it harder to steer the blame elsewhere. Fife arrived the next morning only to find he had missed the boat. On his flight there was a peculiar man completely covered in bandages; as if once he had been severely burned. Only the malevolence in his eyes told that he was on some sort of mission of pure hatred. During the flight he had been mostly avoided because of his appearance, and demeanor. He emanated negativity. Mr. Brown was back.

CHAPTER 13

BLACK SITE

The headless people in the smoke filled room were somewhat apprehensive. A stranger in their midst was out of the ordinary. To the best of their knowledge it had never happened before. And most likely would never happen again. But here he was, in the middle of the surrounding tables that were occupied by the members of the Trust, a stranger in their midst, albeit a blindfolded one at that. Violet had called it mandatory that he wear one. Any attempt on his part to keep track of where they were going would be met with severe recrimination; as in not living to see the light of another day. As if he could have kept track anyway. Adolf had blindfolded him on Long Island, complete with a black hood over his already covered eyes; the type used for hanging people, and that alone was satisfactory intimidation enough. He was then ushered into the old crone's limousine for an hour plus ride into what he guessed was the City. It smelled like it anyway. Then he was taken on an extremely long elevator ride and set down in the middle of the darkened room. Once his blindfold was removed, he found what little light there was only revealed his captors' torsos, their heads lost in the darkness. Add the fact that there was an extra light shining directly on him, it was next to impossible to detect anything, let alone identities, as if he wanted to anyway. No thanks.

The Reverend Chuck T. Mansin couldn't help but admire their thoroughness and it was on this that he remarked when he first spoke, only to be immediately reprimanded for uttering a sound. If intimidation was part of their design, they were most successful.

'Violent' laid her cards on the table. She and her constituents were buying into Religion, and he possibly was going to be their front man, and scapegoat if necessary. During their first confrontation she made it clear that the information in the folder would go to the appropriate authorities if he refused to cooperate. This would surely draw him a prison term, considering who it was that he had been blackmailing. They really thought their conditions were unnecessary, considering his position; there was nowhere to go but up. And these weirdos were going to back him? Their zeal for anonymity he found a bit excessive, but then again he didn't know with whom he was dealing with anyway. That was fine with him, the woman was plenty of enough already.

"Your knowledge of what transpired at Nellis Air Force Base we find most appealing." Even distorted and through headphones, Violet's voice was discernible. "However, your unscrupulous behavior is not." Mansin knew her last statement was bullshit, otherwise he wouldn't even be there. "We must be prepared for all contingencies, especially if that information is to be released. You were the Preacher of Record there, and that in itself gives us a jump-start. We want to capitalize on this and feel you can give us the correct leverage."

Mansin was starting to get the picture. These people, whoever they were, wanted in on his 'Church of the Universal Brotherhood.' He related his ideas to them and received no negative response, which in itself was positive. He was beginning to wonder just how gullible were they? As the meeting progressed, it dawned on him that they were not only thinking of Earth itself, but churches elsewhere! What? Shit, were they planning to buy the fucking Universe? Little did he know, then.

The meeting ended with a vote. It was almost unanimous; one abstainee. Mansin would start putting together sermons that included the new technology denouncing the old doctrines and replacing them with alien intervention and consequent new revelations. At this rate he would have to create a whole new fuckin bible. What the hell? If it sells, why not?

He was then once again blindfolded and led back to the limousine. For the moment, nothing else needed to be said. The only noise on the way back was the peculiar muffled vibration accompanied by moaning, which was then replaced by a god-awful stench. When Mansin finally realized what had just occurred and the source of the really bad odor that by that time permeated the whole cab, he couldn't help himself.

"UHHUGGRRAAAAGRGHHHCHUGGGRAHYHHH!" He vomited profusely.

SPACE PATROL

Rawar and Oxomoxo were in a quandary. Although they were of the same mind, neither would admit it. Their project Earth and its inhabitants had come to this stage of evolution once again. This time they had intervened more than they had ever done before. Their involvement kept everything in a very precarious position. Without it, the Missing Link would probably be in the wrong hands and their pet project doomed. But the durability of Earth was without question. The last time it came too close to total annihilation and they knew it. Hence, help. At this stage of development its fate could go either way. The Space Patrol had put in too much time and energy to give in now. And part of their job was to transfer two (or more) of the species to their recently finished new orb. They wanted to do it, but they couldn't and they couldn't even if they wanted to: Quandary. It was that close. Plus, their recent visit hadn't reinforced their decision either way. That 'Evil' Sam McGregor, plus Exley, add the pregnant female and the collaborators from each camp really confused the issue to say the least. If anything, it made any choice in the matter more difficult. They had started this whole business, so they had to see it through to the end. Or to a new beginning. Quandary.

"Three, two, one and disengage." The magnetic hum could almost be heard instead of felt as Rawar complied with Oxomoxo's request. They were on top of their game when it came to approaching gravitational pull of any given sphere. It hadn't always been that way. A millisecond either way could make the difference of thousands of miles of any approach. Once, they misjudged and switched off too late, causing their ship to burn in the atmosphere. By the time they reached the surface their machine was a worthless pile of waste product beyond salvage. But that was eons ago and they had learned from that mistake. "Gravitational orbit achieved Rawar. Absolutely perfect." Oxomoxo was proud of their teamwork.

Time and distance measurement in space is no longer applicable nor appropriate. Nevertheless, in the span of a half a dozen 'awareness rest periods.' The Space Patrol traversed from Earth to what was yet to be named another finished product. The pinpoint precision of their approach had taken them from the approximate speed of the light, directly into orbit velocity; just inside the gravitational pull of 'no name' the timing was as close to perfect as it could get.

They were grateful for the duration, for their adventure on Earth proved to be psychologically and physiologically taxing. The combination of the impurities in the air, the lingering effects of the Budlite and the subconscious level of Earth's inhabitants had made haste for their departure. Their recovery had taken more 'awareness breaks' than they cared to admit. Be that as it may, they were happy to leave, but at the same time they were looking forward to returning, a curious sensation they had not yet experienced. This confused them even further in deciding whether interacting with the project's species was a good idea or not. Either/or, it was too late anyway. They had a lot to digest.

"'No name' is our best work yet," exalted Oxomoxo. "It is groundwork for a possible utopian society." As they made their first orbit, they marveled at their handiwork. 'No name' was about two thirds Earth's size, but close to a duplicate. The major differences were that the land masses and oceans were more evenly distributed; like Earth had been before Ulric's blunder and subsequent cataclysm. And more importantly, what oceans existed were situated more towards the poles and the land masses closer to the equatorial regions; thus creating abundant tropical environments capable of creating large amounts of photosynthesis and oxygen. The future inhabitants would have much friendlier weather. The only possible detriment would be if the water at the poles froze too much and got too heavy. This, combined with the centrifugal force from the spin could quite possibly cause a ninety degree axis tilt making the poles the equator and vice versa. It had happened before and there was nothing that could be done about it. It depended on the inner turmoil of the inhabitants and of course what they did with magnetic energy once they were given it. Oxomoxo and Rawar had been contemplating the problem already and the last thing they needed was to compound the issue.

"It's ready to populate." Rawar looked at his co-pilot and was convinced he was thinking the same thing. With who, went unsaid. They still had unfinished business elsewhere. Oxomoxo didn't exactly answer, but said "This one will require some real careful planning. It has the potential for our crowning achievement." His excitement was diminished only by his concern of the happenings back on Earth. During their absence the problems might have fixed themselves, or they could possibly have a mess to clean up. For them one civilization at a time was the basic principal, so they set their mothership in orbit and took a scout down to the surface.

The quality of the pure rich air and unadulterated atmosphere created potential for abundant life in many forms. The vegetation completely adapted to a point where no dead foliage was detected. The greenish sky testified to the purity of the air as did the deep dark blue of the syrupy water. A red orange sun smiled over all as well as the two yellow ochre moons perfectly situated one hundred twenty degrees apart. A few deep breaths of this, and any leftover edge from Earth completely dissipated. 'No name' had a life of its own; it was oozing with a healthy environment. When they set foot on the surface they detected a slight vibration under their feet. Oxomoxo commented: "The insides are still settling. It's too soon to populate. 'No name' is too young." As if on cue, it rumbled. And instead of lava, numerous geysers of steam blew out from the core causing the sky to turn into one giant rainbow, a more beautiful sight had never been seen. They planted their token apple tree and were shocked to see it minutely tremble and in a matter of minutes the tree happily took solid root and absorbed a deeper richer tone that matched the environment. The Space Patrol looked at each other with the knowledge of a job well done. One low orbit with the scout ship, numerous seeds from various projects were scattered; confident in the fact that they would root and grow.

"Well, it's time." Oxomoxo was obvious. "Let's go see what happened. In a way I hope it has gone either way, but not before…"

"Save it Oxomoxo. I have a good idea what you were going to say. It's too early. We are committed to see it through. They still have a chance, slim as it may be." Rawar was forced to bring things back into perspective. And then he had to add, "If it's still in one piece that is."

"You are right of course," agreed Oxomoxo and with a twinkle in his large blue eyes he added, "If they still exist, let's go see if we can get a recipe for that Budlite." This brought an agreeable chuckle from Rawar. Soon the magnetic hum engaged and in a flash of light they were gone.

WASHINGTON, D.C.

The tension in the situation room was understandable, had those in attendance known the agendas that lay under the surface. Their faces spoke of sincerity, but for each it was a mandatory facade to fulfill their role. If any of them knew where each others' true sentiments lay, the whole purpose of the meeting would be for naught.

"If Bull Exley doesn't want to be found, it's just not going to happen. I've known that cagey SOB too long to underestimate him." General Cleveland's frustration was detectable in his speech. One might have thought it was because of his inability to subdue the fugitives but that was insignificant compared to his unknown tie to the Trust. If that were to be found out it could be labeled as Treason and the veil was wearing thin. Besides, for the situation at hand he had his fall guy, in the form of Agent Bernard Fife. "I'm convinced that the fiasco of a wild goose chase at the airport was purposely set up by him to cover their trail." And it worked. In this case his sincerity was real. They set up a security blanket for three days at Kahului airport upsetting the schedules for all inter island and mainland bound flights, suffering the wrath of all the commuters in the process, adding embarrassment to inefficiency.

The President's poker face didn't let on that she was loving every minute of it. This ass kisser was getting his just rewards. "Be that as it may, General, I'm getting pressure from those that attended the Nellis Presentation to issue a statement. And frankly, I don't know what to, or not, to tell them." President Brandt had to play her part, but by now secretly she was pulling for the fugitives. At any given moment she could hold a press conference and let the public know what really was happening. But that would serve no purpose at the moment. Firstly it would take General Cleveland off the hot seat, and in her opinion his backside hadn't been cooked enough. Secondly she had unconfirmed suspicions about him. And third, it would bring more undue heat down on the fugitives, which reminded her... "Besides, have we received any ransom notes or any notes at all? Just what is the method of Exley's madness?" If she could postpone any announcement, she might be able to expose Cleveland as the leak she thought he was.

"Ms. President if I may interject, from what interaction I've had with this General Exley, he doesn't strike me as the self serving type." Professor Lezlie Potts spoke the words running through the President's head. "If he was doing any of this for personal gain we would already know about it." Little did they know that it was he who was responsible for helping them with the escape, and with the Missing Link. Lezlie Potts had played his part. And that was understandable since he and General Tyrone 'Bull' Exley Retired had all the pertinent information in disc form. It was their secret and it had to stay that way until somebody showed their cards. The information it held was just too important to let fall into the wrong hands. So he decided to drop a bombshell: "This is what I believe. I wouldn't be surprised if he was making an effort to find a way to give it to all, instead of just some, which to me is what should be done anyway." The air just got sucked out of the room.

"Preposterous!" Cleveland came straight to attention like his backside had just been shocked. "We are the Superpower of the planet! It has to be us that controls its usage!" And the Trust, thought the General. His outburst brought a look of sheer disgust from Lezlie Potts and curious bewilderment from the First Lady.

"General, Mr.Potts quite possibly may be right. As of yet we have received no letters of demand from Exley or anyone else for that matter. And who are we to monopolize control of such a universal gift? Her tone was condescending and Cleveland realized he better tread lightly. The President turned to Potts, "What course of action do you suggest? Has anything come to mind yet? Professor, surely we must do something to placate the masses."

Potts looked thoughtful for a moment, then replied. "Nothing can be made public yet of course, and that is where our problem lies." He eyed the General then went on, "I believe that is why Exley took it in the first place; he was afraid we might want to keep it just for ourselves, and judging from our track record, I can't say as I blame him one bit." Cleveland was put in his place and the President beamed. "We can delay those who were at the Presentation by announcing we are working on a finished product, but that will last only for so long. In the meantime we must try to completely defuse Exley and company as being wanted criminals, it's only making it harder on them to show their true intentions. This element…" Potts gestured toward the ever-shrinking General, "is exactly the reason they are in hiding." And to twist the knife even further he added, "If I were younger I'd have probably done the same thing."

General Cleveland cooly addressed the Professor "Well Professor, your 'goody-two-shoes' assessment is all fine and dandy. But what if you are wrong? What if Exley is intending to sell it to our enemies? Where does that leave us? In a way the General could not be argued with. His viewpoint, although narrow minded, had to be taken into consideration. The balance of power was totally lopsided in the United States' favor and General Cleveland wanted to keep it that way. He drove his point further, "No! I am not going to sit by and watch the United States go down the drain. In fact, I'm going to do the opposite! I am going to step up the manhunt to bring them to justice." His tempo resembled a Chuck Mansin sermon. He might as well have been standing on a soapbox. Even though his scope was limited he was fervently behind it. Rah Rah.

Potts could only sit there and take it. If only this numbskull knew what I had in my possession, he thought. But then again, this was further support for keeping his secret for the time being. "My apologies General. Of course you are right." This guy needs a muzzle; the thought of it brought a wry smile to his face. He was thankful they couldn't read his mind.

As was the Presidents', but for a different reason. "Gentlemen, both of these points of view are valid. Mainly because we simply do not know what General Exley is planning." She had to stifle a chuckle. "It is plausible, however improbable, that it may be that he is up to anything considered subversive. But we must protect the sovereignty of our Country. May I suggest more of a low profile approach in apprehending them? At this point in time it does neither of us any good whatsoever bringing heat down upon them." She felt like a Referee again. "Take them off the news and give them some breathing room. It may be that's just what we all need. General, it is your move and I expect some results. Soon." This loose cannon is going to get a surveillance team, she thought. And who better than this Agent Fife? "I believe they are thick as thieves anyway." Better not to let one hand know what the other is doing. "That is all for the time being, good day."

The meeting ended with no justifiable conclusions, but it did bring them one step closer to a final result. Cleveland was given more clout so he could bury himself and the President's suspicions were confirmed enough to warrant him followed. Potts had become more convinced that his course of action had been the right thing to do and his Ace in the hole stayed undisclosed, for the time being. He also decided that if and when he were to reveal the Disks' existence, it would be for the President's eyes and ears alone. The President could only sit back and let circumstances run their course. She thought she made an unconfirmed alliance with professor Potts whose thoughts ran along the same line. Agent Bernard Fife would be contacted and the players would be set in motion and the repercussions fall as they may. Although nothing of substance was concluded, each player was comfortable and steadfast in their own position. The rest would depend on Brigadier General Tyrone 'Bull' Exley Retired and the web he would weave with his friends' help.

CHAPTER 14

WEST COAST USA

When the Flying Cloud slid into Newport Harbor and the zodiacs docked at Wood's, the Bull was delighted to see the Red Shark parked out in front. It looked like it belonged there. Upon entering, they found Jackson and his black eyed beauty seated at the bar with the Raiders considerably in their cups. It was soon discovered that he too had once been a Raider before retiring into anonymity in the Sea of Cortez aboard the Hannibal Hamlin. When queried about this, his answer was "I deny everything and demand proof," and it sounded like an automatic response. It was. He humorously added "I get around." The Bull didn't believe it for one second but pumped his hand rigorously anyway and thanked him for returning his Baby. Exley assessed the situation and quickly concluded that nothing of consequence would be gained that day. With a "If you can't beat 'em join 'em" attitude, they attempted to play catch-up with limited results. Woody was so taken with the General being in his establishment that the 'closed' sign joined the door, and he declared "Open bar," and a non-stop lavish buffet of seafoods were consumed throughout the afternoon into the evening. It was such a royal banquet that no one could take it upon themselves to leave. The booths were once again turned into beds and those with the wherewithal to make it back to the schooner did so. Everyone had to turn in early. It was a fitting homecoming for those who remembered any of it.

The voyage across the Pacific was nothing like the one before. With mostly inclement weather, they faced nonstop mid winter rain squalls that cloaked their entire voyage. This however didn't inhibit the spirits of the crew at all. Any excuse to be up close and personal with Mother Nature's bounty was met with exuberance. The Old Coots were in their element everywhere, actually, and they were loving every minute of it. With limited help from their guests, the methodical crewsmanship was like clockwork. The caretakers kept the Bull and the Rangers busy while Mallory and Victoria formed their own special cocoon inside their cabin. Even Dr. Bloomfield was paid a visit, much to the delight of all. His reddened face the next morning was met with catcalls in which he didn't seem to mind at all. Why would he? With steady strong Tradewinds out of the northeast they made record time completely rejuvenated; that is until the banquet Woody threw upon their arrival.

The Bull was typically the first topside to enjoy the serenity of early morning Newport Harbor. The sky dome was gray overcast and not a breath of wind was stirring. It was moments like these that made older age worthwhile, he thought. The air off the surrounding San Bernardino mountains was crisp and cool at a dead still, making the oily water glass as yet untouched by the many boats that would soon be passing through the area. Newport Beach, a hub of the Los Angeles metropolitan Zoo was often referred to as the unofficial borderline of northern and southern California. Usually busy, moments like these came few and far between and cherished. He was also glad for this time because his undeclared leadership was going to require some fancy footwork in the days ahead. Ah, he had a plan all right, but etched in the back of his mind was that one unknown factor; that of the curious pair that was not of this Earth.

His reverie was interrupted by the appearance of a pekid-looking Connor Mallory, a little worse for wear. Mallory surveyed the situation correctly and with a brief "Mornin," sat down next to the Bull in silence. The unique calm of the moment was to be enjoyed while it could, for it was quite possibly going to be their last for quite a while. In that assumption they were completely correct.

A bit later, Mallory, unable to contain himself any longer, was the first to speak. "General, I received some disturbing news last night."

"You mean she finally told you? Congratulations."

"You knew already? For how long? Why didn't you te…"

"Son, when you get as seasoned as me, you learn things. I've suspected for a couple of weeks. But the female mind is a delicate piece of work. You try to upset the balance as little as possible and sometimes that makes it worse. Who knows? Not me! And when it concerns matters such as these? Yeah, I knew enough to leave it alone; but I think it's great! The timing could have been a little more favorable, but then again you never know."

"Who else…"

"Relax. I'm her Uncle. She doesn't even know I've figured it out already. Connor, I've known Vicky ever since she was a babe in arms. Her mother is my sister in-law, and a mighty pretty one at that. She had the same look when she was pregnant. Those far away stares, the erratic behavior, the skin, it starts to glow. You are a very lucky man, Connor Mallory. Actually, I've been wondering where I could pick up a shotgun; just kidding." The Bull got a big kick out of Mallory's bewildered expression.

Naturally, the commotion brought out Captain Magic and the rest of the Old Coots topside, curious about what was afoot. Most of the morning involved lots of back slapping and shrieks of glee from the womenfolk. Victoria naturally was treated like a Queen. It was like everybody was a 'calabash' auntie or uncle, which for the most part, couldn't have been anymore true. The matters at hand were temporarily forgotten as the day turned into another celebratory function. The word "shotgun" came up more often than not, but only in jest. In actuality everyone was elated and knew these matters would take their own course. Little did they know at the time how auspicious this situation really was.

Later that afternoon the 'brain trust' was huddled together in the back booth. The Raiders, the Bull, Captain Magic and the Rangers planned into the evening. Every once in a while a, "aha ha haha haha" would explode, like elementary school kids planning some kind of prank on their teacher. Their demeanor spoke of tomfoolery but their expressions were deadly serious. Once, Mallory attempted to crash the meeting but was quickly ushered away. When it was over, the Bull came back to the bar and dropped himself down in one of the easy chairs. After a deep sigh he broke into a huge grin and announced, "Damn! I like these guys!" By this time, curiosity was running rampant with the rest of the Crew. When quizzed about the results, the Bull stopped them in mid-sentence with a "Later. First, let's eat." Which they did. The exquisite buffet furnished by Woody was fit for a king. Or in this case, a Queen. Victoria became the center of attraction as every type of Oyster dish known to man was first put in front of her to sample. The reason being that everyone wanted 'their baby' to eat healthy and grow strong.

Victoria was beaming. With a smile for all she said, "I could get used to this." Then a tear would roll down her cheek and she'd do a complete reversal and start sobbing. "Oh, you are all just so wonderful." Then tears of happiness gushed like a flash flood. Mallory could only sit on the sideline like a spectator. The Bull only reinforced his feelings by stating "Relax Connor, it's only the beginning," that brought looks of bemusement from some and empathy from the others. When things settled down and Victoria's mood swing came around again, the Bull called for everyone's attention.

"Well friends, I'm sure you've noticed that we have come up with a tentative game plan." He might as well have been a cat with a feather in his mouth. "Since there are so many unknown variables, naturally we'll have to play it as it goes, but basically it's going to go like this…" The Bull glanced over to T-boy who passed him a map. He unfolded it and revealed a map of the United States with a route highlighted in yellow magic marker from the west to the east coasts; destination, New Orleans, Louisiana. He gave everyone time to digest this, then went on: "OK. We all know the seriousness of this situation, but hey, why not make it enjoyable? We can, so we will. First and foremost we must always attempt to do the unexpected. Last time we went south, so now we go north, then east. Raymond and Richard will act as our cover as Official Rangers.

They more than less have keys to every National Park across the entire continent. They are our guides and we are something resembling a 'Sierra Club', which is innocent and plausible enough to possibly get us through the whole way, undetected. That part we don't know, nor will we." The Bull paused to let this sink in. Nods of approval went throughout the room so he continued, looking directly at his niece. "Now Vicky, your new 'condition' makes me rather hope you will not come, but I know you'll have no part of that. So instead, we are going to expand into a caravan. I can't fathom why, but the Raiders are going to furnish us with even more transportation. They seem to have a very deep bag of tricks, so here it is; the ladies, for Victoria's sake, Doc Bloomfield and myself, the Rangers, Raiders, and we're borrowing Slo Mo for muscle, and Jackson. They have the wherewithal to improvise, and are Sierra Club members visiting National Parks across the USA. Tourist garb, cameras, the whole scenario. We start at Yosemite and head East. It's not complicated unless we choose to make it so, but we can make it work for us. Now..." He paused for effect. "Just in case we are found, we'll be able to scatter in all directions, making it extremely harder on those trying to stop us. That's fourteen in all in our new Sierra Club guise. That..." Another pause, this time stone faced. "Should make for a very interesting trek." The Bull raised his eyebrows twice ala Groucho Marx style then threw down a couple of Oyster Shooters.

The ladies had been sitting at a table of their own, mostly for the support of Victoria. When they learned they all got to go, they were ecstatic. To them the meeting was over, they had plans to make, and of course it involved shopping. But this was not to be the case. The Bull strode over to their table and glanced appreciatively: "Observe. Four magnificently beautiful women in a red Cadillac convertible. If that's not an 'attention grabber' I don't know what is. With them at the front of our caravan I doubt seriously that anyone will be paying much attention to the rest of us. Throw in Slo Mo for muscle and we have our sidetrack complete.

Victoria perked up with a mischievous grin, suggesting "He can be our business representative, or pimp as you men like to say." Naturally this would require some more shopping.

"Not a bad idea, since the Missing Link will be with you." Before anyone could object, the Bull continued, "Face it. We're expendable. The ladies are not, especially with Victoria's new condition. If we're discovered, we can lead them on a merry chase while you go about your 'business'. Besides, your safety is paramount to all of us as is this scheme we've gotten ourselves into." Murmurs of agreement reinforced the Bulls' statement.

Mallory wasn't too keen on the idea of being away from the mother of his child, but had to agree it was for the best. "What happens in New Orleans?" he asked.

"Plenty, son, plenty." The Bull's eyes momentarily twinkled. "When we get close, I will have Doc Bloomfield contact Lezlie Potts. We'll set up a rendezvous to return the link. It's obvious he has similar viewpoints as us, and it will also get the Doctor off the hook, just in case there's any recriminations over all this. Hell, if Cleveland has any say in this, they'd probably lock me up and throw away the key."

"That's where we come in," interjected Captain Magic. He looked at his Crew and it was plain to see they were beginning to feel left out. "Well boys, do you feel like a little sailing excursion to New Orleans?" Captain Magic's question brought a unanimous cheer from the Old Coots. "Good. Because we're heading for Panama at first light." The cheers turned into reluctant groans, then cheers again in a matter of seconds. Something like, "ohyahoooooyay."

The Raiders and Rangers were standing on the side and were getting to be hardly able to contain themselves. It was clear that they knew something else the others didn't. Exley glanced over at them and nodded affirmatively. The twinkle came back and that's when he dropped the bombshell. "Oh, yeah. I almost forgot. This time of year they throw a little party over there. It's calle the Mardi Gras."

HAWAII

Brown had no business whatsoever being out under the Hawaiian sun, and his tender skin was having serious objections about it. True, he had worn the bandages during the flight solely for the purpose of keeping his identity unknown and in that he was a success. But the bandages themselves drew attention and the stewardesses acted like some kind of 'sisters of mercy', taking pity on him when all he wanted was to be left the hell alone. When he arrived in Hawaii he removed them and achieved better results. Instead of pity the general reaction from people around him was shock. And rightfully so; he looked like an Albino that once had a serious acne problem, that is until he went out into the relentless Hawaiian sun.

His skin had recovered steadily in the dungeons of the Mexican jail. Then, after the bribes succeeded, he actually received the medical attention that country had to offer, which wasn't really that much. But nevertheless he slowly began to recover, and with each day his hate for Tyrone 'Bull' Exley became his only reason for living. Sometimes so much as to blot out the pain of his recovery process. Tons of dollars later, when he was eventually released, the downfall of his social status was secondary compared to the retribution he planned to inflict on his nemesis and anyone that happened to get caught in the crossfire. With the information he had at his disposal he could blackmail his way back up the social ladder, but that was inconsequential compared to the matters at hand. And that involved following this bumbling FBI Agent until he caught a break.

It hadn't been that hard locating Fife once released from Mexico. Not only had he been on the news, but he turned out to be the laughing stock of the Agency, and they were more than happy to cooperate. One call is all it took posing as a magazine reporter wanting to do a story on the newly decorated agent responsible for the 'heroes' in Mexico. Mexico. If it wasn't for Fife's necessity, Brown would have snuffed him out himself; maybe later he would. In the meantime he had to follow this idiot to probably one of the last places on Earth his skin would tolerate: Hawaii.

Mr. Brown was livid. Internally and externally. Even before his mishap, sunbathing went totally against his grain and now it was completely out of the question. Even the slightest amount of ultraviolet rays on the tenderized surface of his skin brought on sun blisters in some places and magenta colored sunburn on the rest. And to make it even worse, the accident had caused his skin to fail to be able to assimilate the sun's rays and turn it into a tan, thus compounding his discomfort daily. And why on God's green earth had this asshole flown two thousand miles across the Pacific Ocean to have dental work done?

After almost two weeks of abject misery, Brown was finally given his reprieve. Fife had received an important phone call and was being summoned back to Washington, DC. A bribe at the front desk had given him all the appropriate information he needed, and he had already made reservations according to Fife's schedule for the same flight back. This FBI asshole had been so involved with his mouth he had never taken notice of the gross monstrosity following him. Now it was time to call in a few markers he'd gathered throughout his nefarious career, namely in the form of Violet. He had learned through undisclosed resources that she was now shacking up with that hypocrite preacher and that was just more ammo for him. Even though he was persona-non-grata in the Trust, he was still a force to be reckoned with. He would like to survive and bring on the downfall of Exley and anyone else in his path to achieving that end. If he was to die in the process, so be it; he would take any and all of those ingrates with him, it just didn't matter any more.

All this had been running through his mind as he prepared for the flight back. He reapplied the bandages over his face, busting open sun blisters in the process. Now the pus oozing from them had congealed to form splotches all over his bandaged face, making his appearance even more disgusting than before. So much the better; now maybe those fucking stewardesses would stay the hell away. So what if the removal of the bandages was going to hurt like hell; it would only fuel the fire of vengeance. He smiled at the prospect of it. Somebody, if not everybody including Exley most of all, was going to pay the price along with him. And he didn't care who.

Fife was beside himself. What on earth had he done to rate this, he wondered. He had been summoned back to what he thought would be the Agency by his section chief, and that was normal procedure. But upon his arrival he was quickly ushered into an awaiting limousine with American Flags in the front, complete with motorcycle escort as if it was a motorcade. At first he thought it couldn't be possible, but sure enough, they were heading directly towards the White House. One thing that was for sure is he didn't know what to think about any of it. He was torn between elation and apprehension or a combination of both. And on top of it all, there was no sign of General Cleveland, unless he was there already, wherever 'there' was. Agent Bernard Fife was going to meet somebody, perhaps even the President herself, at the White House. Thank God he'd had his mouth repaired.

The flight back from Hawaii had been inconsequential, all except for the general murmur of the stewardesses concerning someone in coach class whose head was completely bandaged. Apparently he was extremely disagreeable to the point where they were discussing his uncooperative behavior during the whole flight. Fife's curiosity got the best of him and he had to steal a glance at the cause of their discomfort. Much to his surprise the man was vaguely familiar but he couldn't figure how. Had he seen him before in passing? Or, was it just a mere coincidence? He pondered this off and on during the flight, but it was quickly forgotten when he was met by the special envoy at the airport. He was waved through the White House checkpoints and escorted to the same room where he'd received his letter of commendation prior to the President's blockbuster announcement. For the briefest of moments he wondered what had happened to that freak of a preacher, but this was cut short upon the entrance of the President and much to his surprise, no one else except for her husband Jack.

"Good morning Agent Fife. Thank you for coming on such short notice." The President's stature was much less formal than before. Add her husband and negate that stuffy general and Fife could go as far as to describe it as downright casual. "I'm sorry to have had to cut your well deserved vacation short, but we have necessary immediate business concerning your relationship with General Cleveland to discuss." The look that accompanied such a devastating statement by her almost knocked him out of his chair. So much for casual he concluded. Was this finally the end then?

"Ah, uh, I'm at your disposal, maam, uh, Madam." He stuttered. Garbage disposal he thought.

"Relax, Agent. The fact is, we need your help. And it's not of the official variety." Her tone backed up her statement and Fife's fading career reappeared.

"I'm not quite sure what you're getting at, Madam President." This time his comment came out smoothly. What he had quickly deduced as the 'hot seat' turned into an easy chair of opportunity. And with the luck he had been having lately, he would take it anyway it came.

The President proceeded to tell Fife what she could about the leak in her inner circle and her suspicions about General Cleveland. Although he had been out cold in an alley during the Guaymas fiasco courtesy of some behemoth in a dark suit, the pieces of the puzzle started to fit together better with the existence of an outside element. It also took considerable heat off his vulnerable position. Fife believed in his heart that he had already received his fair share of bad breaks, and then some. And it was a revelation indeed that Cleveland might have been responsible for some, if not most of them. Fife also knew he was not out of harm's way, yet. If he had gone through correct channels instead of attempting a shortcut in the Guaymas affair, this all might have been over and done with already. At the time he had thought it a clever move, but if Cleveland was using this information for his own personal ends and also creating Fife as the fall guy in the process, then it was time to turn the tables.

A tentative plan to deliver some disinformation at the soonest opportune time in the future was decided upon. Until then, Fife would keep the President abreast of his interactions with the General in the hopes of cementing the link with that god-awful woman from Long Island. Fife left the meeting with high hopes and as the President watched him leave, she couldn't get the vision of Maxwell Smart out of her head. It was amusing, but if any further incident was to blow up in their face, General Cleveland would surely go down and Fife would only be embarrassed, again. Now it was time to let Professor Potts in on the situation and hope and pray for some contact with General Exley retired. If Cleveland and heaven forbid the old Bitch were to get to Exley first, there would be hell to pay. That was the worst-case scenario. The best-case was to get to Exley before her and of course expose Violets' whole conglomerate and put them in their place; which was away for a very long time. Until the Brigadier and company declared themselves, they would just have to wait. Just where in the hell were they?

For all his inequities, Cleveland was certainly no fool. He was well aware of Fife's meeting with the President and the thin ice he was treading on. But he was also stuck in the clutches of Violet. He had no choice but to cooperate. By now, his only avenue of pursuit was to keep Fife at bay, and he also decided to fight fire with fire. Violet and that preacher were definitely up to something underhanded; just what, wasn't important, at least to him. What did matter now was the fact of their relationship. Since she held his dealings in Vietnam over his head, why not get some dirt on her and this preacher? Negate blackmails as it were. It was his only avenue of possible escape. He had once held a chance meeting with Mr. Brown of the Trust. But he had disappeared after the Guaymas disaster. If he could find some way to form an alliance with him, he could quite possibly get out of this mess unscathed. Little did he know at the time how soon their paths were about to cross.

The atmosphere in the bedroom out on the Long Island Estate was contradictory in nature. The double sliding door windows opened out to a lofty panoramic view reserved only for the filthy rich. The Atlantic Coast was having one of its few pristine mild weather mornings of winter. They came few and far between; usually at the end or the beginning of a winter storm. This calm in particular was right between two storms of the more ferocious variety. The first of which included Gale Force winds with horizontal sheets of rain. The kind that would keep anyone in their right mind indoors. And according to the weather stations, it was going to be followed up by ones with equal ferocity. The ocean was sheet glass and the sky had patches of deep winter blue, lending a pastel quality to the surroundings of the Long Island Estate. A calm before the storm scenario. The rays of the Sun that shone in the windows were enveloped in blue clouds of cigar smoke and that pungent odor was rivaled only by the stench of something abhorrent. "Must you smoke those things after sex? Every time? They're absolutely horrible!" complained 'Violent': His nickname for her was appropo.

Reverend Chuck T. Mansin eyed his sex partner underneath the sheets. She was putting away her hypodermic kit she kept at bedside. Her pallor bespoke of the rush one gets after shooting what was called a 'speedball' (a combination of heroin and cocaine) and the blood vessels on her face were working overtime and she was as pink as one gets as if she had been out under the sun instead of under the sheets behind the windows. "To each his own," he answered. He held back the comment regarding the aroma of her vibrator. In truth he could do without the cigar, but it was the only thing that he could do to combat the shtank of her well used machine. Besides, he was a pig in shit; or off tuna as it were.

Mansin jumped out of bed and slid open the door. The fresh air off the Atlantic was a cool and welcome relief. A military helicopter was receding in the distance. It was curious, but he paid it no mind. At first he thought it was just her vibrator working overtime that had been abnormally loud. But the appearance of the helicopter confirmed that it wasn't just the buzz of her sex toy. He smiled to himself and said nothing. 'Violent' was oblivious to it all anyway. Her before and after doses of hard drugs confirmed that. If someone was taking an interest in her sexual deviations it was no skin off his back, his reputation was shot anyway. He took a deep breath of fresh air, thankful to get away from the aroma emanating from the room. To punctuate the moment a voluminous flatulant explosion erupted from his anal cavity. It was a blessing that he was by the open sliding door; the room was noxious enough already.

He looked over to excuse himself but she was beyond coherency so he let another one go.

Cleveland unscrewed the telescopic lens off the camera. He had hit the jackpot. The brief break in the weather permitted him to do some advanced reconnaissance, or so he thought. But there they were, caught in the act only a deviant could love. And although he would have preferred more, the three rolls of the film be brought would probably suffice. The automatic motor-driven shutter had caught them in one glorious act after another; from pre-sex illicit drug use, through sex toy warm ups and then to the grand finale of anal penetration locked up in chains. Ugh. All in all it was a thoroughly disgusting performance. But in Cleveland's mind, it was a complete success. He disliked having to stoop to this level, but when in Rome… Now it was just a matter of developing and formulating a little package for presentation. General Steve Cleveland of the Joint Chiefs had his dirt.

Unbeknownst to Cleveland though, was another shutter in action, and that particular camera was in the hands of Mr. Brown. He and the General had been on the same wavelength in the blackmail department, but his photos had caught Cleveland in the act of catching them in the act, which made his, all the more valuable. He didn't even bother photographing the deviant addicts, because his film, combined with Cleveland's, would make a tidy little package indeed. Besides, he had once been in the Reverend's shoes and just the memory of it was repulsive enough. Satisfied, he climbed back down the ancient weathered Oak tree he had been hiding in and slipped back out the way he came.

NEWPORT HARBOR

"Loaf, it's coming all too clear how and why you got your name." remarked the Bull admiringly as eyed the two RVs that had taken up most of the limited space of Wood's parking lot. The pair of colossal homes on wheels were the biggest and the most luxurious that money could buy. They were both well past the point of what one would call decadent.

"Well, if you're planning to travel, you might as well go in style." Loaf's slow and even drawl matched that of his nickname. His tall and once lanky frame had become slightly pudgy and he was a perfect match to the vehicles before them. He could blend in naturally with the thousands that had chosen this mode of travel, and by the looks of him he had done so a number of times. "These are our Babies. The one you 'borrowed' in Mexico was expendable." The hint was obvious and rightfully so. These were in a complete other league as far as luxury went. And just to clarify matters he added, "But if you do find you have to sacrifice them for the cause, do not hesitate. After all, it's only metal."

The 'metal' before them was built by two different companies. The larger of the two was a Rexhall C-34 'American Clipper Vision' that comfortably housed six. It was powered by a Chevy 454 cubic inch engine, the biggest in the industry and could easily break the speed limit at will. The second one, although a couple of feet smaller was more functional. The 'Friendship' built by Gulfstream was complete with a slide-out stove in the rear for tailgate parties and such, or that's what it appeared to be. In actuality, the Raiders had modified this area solely for the purpose of discouraging pursuit. The stove was just a shell that housed two ten gallon cans of heavy-duty motor oil and an assorted variety of tire flatteners that could be dropped at any opportune moment, thus eliminating any of those that might want to hinder their roll, or harass them. It wasn't a modern tactic, but it certainly was effective. Loaf explained that he got the idea from an old Keystone Kops comedy in which they had been chasing moonshiners; it had been tested only once because that was all they needed. The only other modifications were the trap doors on the floors in each of them. The RVs had every conceivable optional equipment available, even including awnings for outdoor activities, and disc satellites for television and other 'communications.'

"The only thing that's missing is a Jacuzzi." With Loaf's easy-going manner one couldn't tell whether he was serious or not. And judging from these characters, anything was a possibility.

Exley was about to remark on this, but the words didn't have a chance because around the corner came a sight that temporarily immobilized him. Loaf had a whimsical gleam in his eyes that told they had saved the best for last. All four ladies, with Slo Mo in the driver's seat, pulled up in the Red Shark, with what looked as if it should be in a classic antique car show, in tow. Built by Rolls Royce at least a half century earlier, was an old rounded trailer home so shiny, it seemed encased in chrome. It looked like it just came off the showroom floor yesterday. The Bull was uncommonly speechless and could only stand there and gawk. If the gals in the Caddy weren't stunning enough, this brought it beyond the realm of comprehension.

"And this little gem we reserve for special occasions," announced Loaf proudly. "The interior is just as plush as the exterior. You made mention of the fact that you wanted a distraction to keep the attention away from yourselves? Well this oughta do the trick".

Rarely was Tyrone Exley at a loss for words. This was one of those few occasions. He had seen photographs, but never one up close and personal. The exterior was almost blinding. Add four absolutely stunning females in a red convertible Cadillac and it was a picture complete. He glanced at Loaf approvingly and without a word walked around the trailer. He had to touch it lightly once to see if it was real. When he opened the door they all heard him gasp. The inside was purple velvet; everything: furniture, walls, the bed, the pillows, "Wow," he uttered under his breath, then walked back towards those enjoying his reaction. When he finally found words he said, "just when I think I've heard and seen it all," the meaning obvious.

"We run a High Class Business," said Victoria jokingly. If that was even close to the truth, it would be the hottest ticket on the planet. Just the thought of it brought a shiver to the Bull. "This should definitely take the heat of you 'gentlemen', although I still have doubts about carrying the Missing Link with us," she added.

"Oh no. So much the better. Who would ever suspect you were doing something other than what it appears. It couldn't be better," replied the Bull, once again capable of speech.

The Bull attempted sleeping and travel arrangements but to no avail. Everyone had learned from past experience what it was like to be anywhere near the Rangers while they were attempting to sleep. They all knew about the Rangers' snoring capabilities. Eventually it was decided upon that they would get the Rolls-Royce and could snore to their hearts' content, without bothering anyone. The two couples would sleep in the Friendship and the bachelors would share the American Clipper. The caretakers made the point be known that they would be circulating, which brought no objections whatsoever from anyone at all. Once this was all agreed upon, the ladies were released to go shopping; to Fashion Isle, one of the most plush Malls anywhere. They jumped into the Red Shark and peeled out of the parking lot as if the men didn't exist. Alba, the black eyed bombshell was at the wheel and it quickly became increasingly clear that she had gotten her driver's license in Mexico City. Nevertheless they eventually made it back safely with the trunk and back seat completely stocked with amenities that challenged the imagination; their mission a total success. The Rangers, after a considerable amount of mock consternation, walked off to inspect their 'sleeping arrangements'; elbowing each other in the ribs all the way, as if they had just played some sort of master prank on everyone. Woody insisted on forcing condiments and selections from his private stock of Gourmet Delicacies. It wasn't met with much aversion. HT and Z announced they were going to back out on the trip to act as a rearguard as it were, and also as a backup in case their flying expertise was required again. Little did they know at the time what a monumental decision that would turn out to be.

The Flying Cloud was loaded for the trip south as were the RVs and the Red Shark. By late afternoon the preparations were finished and everything was ready to roll.

The Bull in a sudden brainstorm announced the fact that he, HT and Z were going to fly a little detour below the Mexican Border that afternoon. Along with them was going the lead lined suitcase to be opened down South to set those in pursuit off the track. It was a superb idea, but in the best laid plans of mice and men, Murphy and his law was going to eventually step in. During the wild ride down the

Haleakala crater, the bouncing and jostling of the suitcase had taken its toll. Standard Military Components weren't made like they used to be. The boys took the Bluebird all the way down to the southern tip of Baja California. It was here that they opened the suitcase and let out the pulse for those who might want to be tracking them. When the Bull closed the suitcase, unbeknownst to him one of the latches had come loose, just enough for a very faint signal to be dispersed. It would take some time before Cleveland and company would figure this slight signal was one and the same, and then all Hell would break loose. Until then the ploy was a complete success.

Not so with Oxomoxo and Rawar. Their advanced technology allowed them to pinpoint the Missing Link from then on. None of any of those involved would know how this would eventually come into play. Ignorant of the fact of the signal, the caravan turned north in the morning. The Flying Cloud sailed south for the Panama Canal and an eventual rendezvous in seven to ten days in New Orleans, depending on the winds. A Military blanket descended on Cabo San Lucas, only to find they had been outwitted by the Bull again. By this time the caravan had gotten out of the LA Basin, their first stop to be Yosemite National Park, and from there a hopefully enjoyable trip down to New Orleans. But this was not to be.

CHAPTER 15

THE WHITE HOUSE

In most cases, with old age comes senility. Not so with Professor Lezlie Potts. His mind worked like a fine-tuned Swiss watch and was as strong as a steel trap. And with the advent of the new developments brought on by that rascal General, it was like a rebirth in direction for him. In his time he had seen so many Presidential Terms come and go, he had developed an inherent distrust of the Government in general. It was obvious that they were merely puppets; the true power lay behind the public eye that dictated policy down to those holding Public Office. Just who they were remained a mystery, but what they represented was obvious; Money, Power, the Military Industrial Complex, etcetera. Although his basic instinct told him otherwise, he was fond of the lady presently holding the office of the Presidency. The previous terms had been shrouded in controversy. But this one had actually held a press conference admitting her inequities. After all, she was only human. What did people expect? Some kind of lily white saint that had never made a mistake? Hogwash. She had also gained more respect after their last meeting, and now he was on his way to another confrontation.

He held in his possession the secret of secrets, but even that was limited. Without the knowledge of the properties of the components of the Missing Link, the Magnetic Energy was limited to only Earth's sphere of gravity. The Missing Link's components were labeled as 'Unknown Origin'. They were much sturdier than that of Earth's Basic Metals. Even so, for that alone to fall into the wrong hands and be used improperly would surely bring on mass destruction. That was precisely why he let that Rascal General abscond with it. At least he had a level head. But that move he knew was only temporary. Eventually the Missing Link would be found unless there was some sort of divine intervention, hopefully in the form of those who brought it here in the first place, namely in the form of Oxomoxo and Rawar. But for the present situation, all he could have done is buy time, and in that he was successful. For now he could only hold back and watch things unfold. Besides, he was getting a real kick out of Exley giving them the run-around.

Potts was delighted to see the President enter the conference room without General Cleveland. Their previous meeting had cemented his decision to keep his secret to himself. Cleveland, he concluded, was a borderline megalomaniac and the last person on Earth he would let the information he held go to. It was a welcome relief not to have to deal with this level of consciousness. The President smiled and sat down.

"Good day Professor, thank you for coming." She passed Potts a folder she had been carrying. "These are the notes we procured from Haleakala. I'm sorry but they're only copies, but General Cleveland insisted on keeping the originals claiming Military Priority. The President's tone and word inflection gave away the fact she thought the same as he.

Potts thumbed through the papers and could tell they had studied the Disk. Thank God the information here was incomplete. He looked at the President. "It seems that they have been doing their homework." It was all he could give away until she showed her true colors.

"Yes. Well that isn't the reason I asked you here." She proceeded to inform Potts of her suspicions about General Cleveland and his possible link to an outside enterprise, including at the end her meeting with Agent Fife. All of Potts' suspicions were confirmed right then and there. He also believed that she was on the right track, so he decided to give away a little. Bend the truth as it were.

"Madam President, I believe I might have the 'dis-information' you seek." His wizened old eyes brightened at the prospect of it. "We can lead General Cleveland to believe we have the necessary information at Nellis. And even he can't overstep a Presidential Order. This should take at least a part of his concentration off of Exley and hopefully they will make contact before they get caught." He couldn't let on that he actually did have the information, but it just might cause Cleveland to reveal his outside connection. It was a step in the right direction.

"And in so doing we might expose Cleveland's connections." The President took the thought right out of Potts' head.

"Yes and thank you. I am awfully glad to see where you're coming from. You are probably pulling for Exley also, aren't you?" That was as much as he could give away. For now.

President Brandt gave Potts a mock surprised look, then smiled. "Well let's just put it this way: I would never admit to it in public."

They both got a laugh and felt comfortable with their newfound alliance. But still yet, the rest was left up to Exley and company. And for them, things were going to get very thick.

Plots and counterplots were set in motion. Blackmail was spreading like wildfire. The infallible General Exley had made a mistake. The United States Government, the Trust and the Mob were all forming small armies to apprehend the fugitives. A wizened old professor held the secret of secrets. The FBI was being used as a pawn. Impatient Governments were expecting more information, and the Missing Link was bouncing around in the trunk of a red pimp-mobile driven by what appeared to be call girls. A more unlikely scenario couldn't be conceived. So beautiful!?!

If any of this were to be known by the Space Patrol, they might have intervened or, possibly taken their Gift for the human 'race' and left, sealing the Earth's fate. But they were half a Galaxy away heading in this direction, ignorant of the state of affairs transpiring on their pet project. All they knew was their gift was on the move again, heading for a possible crash-course that could ultimately affect the history of mankind on Earth for all time to come. Murphy's law was running rampant and it was not just limited to our tiny little Planet floating around in the vast infinite regions of outer space. For at that moment…

"Oxomoxo, a meteor has hit one of our babies. It looks like we have a mess to clean up." Rawar interrupted his concentration on the flight of the Missing Link. Oxomoxo was puzzled as to why the pulse was so faint.

"That is really too bad. Our Gift is being transported somewhere, plus the signal is weak." Oxomoxo couldn't decide whether the mishap was a relief or not. He already knew he was overly involved with the goings on at their pet project, but it was also so close to a 'make or break' situation, he couldn't help himself. And they did have a new planet to inhabit. "I suppose we better go and clean it up before the debris fouls something else up. Where is it located?"

"In the opposite direction, naturally. I have a good idea what you're thinking, but they have to overcome their own evolutionary process. We have interfered too much already." Rawar empathized with his co-pilot, but Rules were Rules, and they had been stretching those limits quite a bit lately. Then to lighten the situation he added, "You will just have to wait a bit longer for your Budlite."

The remark caught him off guard, but nevertheless it was a success. "Very funny. But you are right. Let's go." Although their detour didn't account for too much Earth time, it was definitely enough for the cow patties to hit the windmill.

The Long Island Estate had been a hive of activity lately. After Mr. Brown resurfaced via telephone call to her private number, a separate meeting was agreed upon. Brown appeared with his set of photographs and at first Violet was infuriated, but soon it was replaced by a cool, calculated, Icy calm. Now she would have to play all sides. She would have to be polite and appear to be working with General Cleveland, and be ready to turn on him at any given moment; Brown had produced the photographs to prove that. As for Brown, a little side gambit wouldn't hurt in case the other plans didn't work out. And above all, the Trust had to have the Missing Link first at all costs, otherwise, no Trust. What she didn't know was that Brown was doing the same thing.

Prior to calling her, he had reintroduced himself to General Cleveland and showed him the same prints that had caught him in the act; so, she didn't know that he knew that she knew Cleveland was probably going to threaten blackmail. Both Cleveland and Brown had their stacks of photographs for what they thought was their protection, but what they didn't know was that in reality Violet couldn't care less about it. She was just too old to really give a shit. And Brown had his own separate agenda to get the Missing Link before the both of them; using them for what he could, and Cleveland had his own personal Ace in the hole, namely his position, on thin ice as it was. Both men had a forced truce because the photographs wouldn't do either of them any good, and their relationship would have to remain private. Sound confusing? It is.

And it was under this scenario that their necessary secret meeting took place. The frosty air outside the gazebo matched that of the atmosphere inside. Although they were doing their damnedest to conceal the fact. Brown arrived first and was conversing with the Preacher about nothing in general when Cleveland strode in, led by Adolf. They would have to act as if they hadn't met since Nellis:

"Good afternoon General Cleveland." You fucking asshole. "I trust you weren't followed?" And get us all busted. Her congeniality was drug-induced, but effective. "May I introduce Mr. Brown? You might remember him from Nellis Air Force Base." The two men exchanged falsified cordialities. "And this is the Reverend Mansin; he is my house guest." And my sex toy as you well know, you fuckers.

Cleveland was still finding it hard to get used to Brown's butchered face, but he disguised it well. Besides, Brown had the photographs that could bury him by either the US government or Violet. The ice he was treading on couldn't have been thinner, but he did not falter. "Yes. Well, now that we're all together," and at each other's throats, "I've brought some interesting news for us all." That will hopefully get you out of my face forever. "I believe we have located General Exley." Eat that, you shitheads.

Violet had been pouring some Tea to calm her nerves. The statement froze her in place. "Oh really?" Spill it before I have your balls nailed to the wall, you prick. "How delightful." I need a fix.

"Yes. Our satellite tracking system has picked up a slight signal. We're not positive, but we believe it is our Fugitives. We're organizing a task force as we speak." And will hopefully get to them before you scumbags.

"And just where do you think they are, General?" Brown was trying his best to conceal his impatience. He had to contact the Family, and quickly.

Cleveland was enjoying his brief upper hand, temporarily as it was. Grovel you fuckers. "Well, as you know, this last incident in Mexico was just a ploy. Actually they are headed..." He stalled on purpose, just to tease the shit out of them. "North, and if the satellites are correct, for some reason they have stopped at Yosemite National Park." I wish I could show the old cunt my photos.

"That's great news. Thank you." You piss ant. "We will make expedient use of this information." And nail them before you, asshole.

"You are most welcome." Right. "Now I must be on my way." And hopefully never see you again, you withered old Bitch. "We should be up there by midday at the latest. So do what you can in the meantime." And hopefully get yourselves fucked over in the process. Cleveland was so sick of being polite to this loathsome pair and the feeling was mutual. But he had done what was required of him to cover his ass. At least he had his dirt on her, and if he was to go down, so would she.

"Good afternoon," cunt.

"Goodbye," piss ant.

"See you later," asshole.

The devious pair watched him go. Violet was starting to feel the need. "Mr. Brown, you can go now." God you're ugly. "I have to call an emergency meeting. We must get to them before he does." And I need a fix.

Brown eyed the old crone. He knew what was happening. He then glanced at the Preacher who had stayed out of the way the whole time. The Preacher's slight grimace told him that he understood also. "At your convenience," you strung out bitch. "Let me know what you might need." And I'll be one step ahead of you.

The meeting adjourned and they went their separate ways. Cleveland had been so lost in the confusion of his own thoughts that he neglected to notice Agent Fife had been following him to and from the meeting. Brown left shortly thereafter and headed towards Upstate New York where the Family awaited, armed to the teeth. After a quick fix, Violet alerted the already waiting hit squad from the Trust. Everyone was assembling to pounce on the unsuspecting prey.

At the moment, the only thing working in the Fugitives' favor was the mutual distrust and the ever increasing hatred that was festering in each group opposing them. They all wanted each others' failure just as much as their success. And this factor would prove to weigh heavily in the eventual results. Newton, Einstein and Murphy; all laws would come into play.

CHAPTER 16

YOSEMITE NATIONAL PARK

One of the few good things to come as a direct result from Ulric's blunder was the creation of Yosemite Valley. As the Earth's mantles crashed together and resituated themselves during the axis tilt, a seven mile long and one mile wide cut in the Earth was created on the western slopes of the Sierra Nevada mountains. Where the Merced River flows beneath towering cliffs, peaks as high as 13,000 feet formed the eastern boundary punctuated by the majestic 3000 foot vertical walls of El Capitan, one of the most breathtaking spots on the entire planet.

And on this particular day one's breath could be seen emanating as small clouds; due to the mid-winter chill of this early February day, which would also prove to be a major factor in the turn of events that were soon to follow.

The three hundred twenty mile trip from LA went without a hitch; that is except for all the near fender benders that almost occurred due to all the attention being paid to the gorgeous creatures in the red Cadillac. The only real calamity happened when a dude on a motorcycle craned his neck a little too long and slammed head on into a public mailbox in Sonoma County, and that mistake caused a bigger dent in the rider's pride than on the front fender of his bike. Other than that the caravan made it to the Tioga Pass entrance to Yosemite in little over a half a day.

Rangers Townsend and Souza played their parts expertly when obtaining Permits for camping. They even managed to check out a pair of standard issue Department of Forestry sidearms, mainly used for discouraging the bear population of the area; two Colt 45s complete with holsters and badges. And it was a good thing that they did. On a drive through Tuolumne Meadows, more than a few bear families were observed getting increasingly friendly with the tourists driving by. In one instance, a bear was actually standing with its front paws on the hood of a car, much to the mortification of the tourists encased within. Without hesitation Townsend pulled out his pistol and shot in its general vicinity and the bear slowly turned, glowered, then skulked off as if it was some kind of minor irritation. This wasn't, however, what the pistols were to come in handy for.

The caravan opted to set up camp at Wawona, situated next to Mariposa Grove, home of the largest living things on Earth. Sequoias as large as twenty nine feet in diameter and two hundred ninety feet tall populate this area and are estimated to be approximately in the range of 3000 years old. To experience the immensity and the majesty of these giants lets one know how short and minuscule our lives really are. After the long trek and a gourmet BBQ, the plummeting temperature sent everyone to go down for an early night's rest, but not before checking the area for their neighbors, those friendly bears.

The Bull was typically the first to rise and immediately set out on a perimeter check for bear prints while water was heating for Cowboy Coffee. To his relief, there were none. The waxing crescent moon hung ochre in the sky amidst the yellows and pinks of sunrise clouds. Soon the aroma of good strong French Roast sporadically drew out the others like moths to a light bulb. What they found was the Bull doing his best impersonation of a penguin flapping his arms and jumping around to keep warm with white clouds expiring with each exhale. It was an entertaining way to start the morning, but soon each found themselves imitating the imitator. Temperatures ranged from a crisp fifty five degrees to a less than comfortable twenty six average during this time of year, and it was going to be a while before the sun found its way above the towering trees surrounding them. Until then temperatures would remain at a low ebb and the coffee with optional brandy shots would have to do to alleviate the discomfort. The surroundings helped also.

The women took it upon themselves for chef duty. Victoria offered to help but they would have no part of it, accrediting her condition for the reason. After a hearty breakfast of cast iron pan fried bacon, home fries and scramblers, plans were made for each to go in their own separate directions, to take advantage of the one day off, although all agreed that just one day would barely scratch the surface of exploring one of the most beautiful spots on Earth. Townsend wanted to expand his knowledge of his Indian Heritage and opted to explore the White Wolf Lodge and Porcupine Flat; The Raiders and Souza would accompany him. The ladies of course wanted to accost Yosemite Valley and the village therein, due the wide range of shops in the area. Slo Mo, Jackson and Mallory were dragged along with them to the sound of dragging heels. It was a full load for the Red Shark but they happily made do. Bloomfield and the Bull weren't going anywhere. They were quite happy to give their old bones a richly deserved break and soak up the majesty of the Sequoias.

Exley was beginning to feel apprehensive for no apparent reason. Things were just going too smoothly and for some reason he couldn't put his finger on, something inherent in him knew it wouldn't last. He requisitioned one of the Rangers' sidearms claiming it was the bears, but he felt within that it was something else, and he didn't get this far in life for not following his gut instinct. With a grandmaster's poker face he told the explorers to keep their cell phones handy, just in case. Then he sent them on their merry way. Only Mallory and Townsend picked up on it; the tension behind his eyes; and it was a good thing that they did. For at the moment Mr. Brown and his mercenaries were entering the Arch Rock entrance from the West that led directly into the valley and General Cleveland was preparing to land their fully loaded nine passenger Bell-Boeing tilt-rotor aircraft atop Glacier Point that overlooked the entire Valley. The Bull felt rather than saw their approach, for the hairs on the back of his neck stood at attention. Call it a sixth sense, but he knew that some form of a nemesis was in the vicinity.

For an hour he mentally debated with his instincts. There was nothing viable he could see or touch, but yet again there was this feeling within he couldn't ignore. The deciding factor came with the approach of the top of the line aircraft that was flying too low to be passing by. It just didn't fit into the picture. He went for a set of binoculars and observed its approach. When it stopped in mid-air, tilted its rotors and dropped as a helicopter would above Glacier Point, it was then that he decided that an inspection was due.

But not before he contacted his cohorts via Globestar Satellite Telephone. He mentally gave thanks to Captain Magic for their parting gift, vowing to hopefully be able to thank him personally in the near future.

Raymond Souza answered the call. "Ray, it looks like we may have some trouble on our hands. Go to the Valley and gather the others. I think it's time to beat feet on the street." His tone conveyed urgency and Souza picked up on it immediately.

"Done."

Fate led Mr. Brown directly to the Red Shark parked at Yosemite Village. It was an automobile hard to forget. He remembered it from Guaymas. Had he arrived fifteen minutes sooner, he would have seen from whence it had come. But this was not the case. Like a hound dog on the scent the excitement stirred within him: knowing the one that disfigured his face was somewhere close by. Retribution was at hand. His heart pounded and his breathing increased, which would prove to be his undoing. Although he didn't know it, all he would have had to do is crack the trunk, grab the Missing Link and be on his merry way. But he was so bent on inflicting harm that it clouded his judgment; for this was his time to do away with those who had caused all his problems.

Unbeknownst to him, he was caught in the crosshairs of the telescopic sight mounted on the rifle held by General Cleveland, where he sat atop El Capitan overlooking the whole scenario. He quickly alerted everyone to pick a target, for they weren't that hard to spot. For all his failings, General Cleveland was not a cold-blooded murderer and he certainly was not going to let Brown and his mercenaries decimate the fugitives, not if he could help it.

Mr. Brown's hit squads' method of travel had been two gunmetal grey Econoline Vans with tinted windows, real unobtrusive vehicles. Right. And it was in one of these he situated himself to stalk his prey. The other Van he directed to the other side of the parking lot so as to catch the fugitives in a crossfire. It was a simple but effective plan.

The wait didn't last long. The first one Brown spotted was that little prick that had upset his boat ride. Then came the two speleologists that had found that accursed thing from space, followed by two pretty things hanging on each arm of someone that looked like he might have belonged in a professional wrestling ring. But there was no General Tyrone 'Bull' Exley Retired. This caused indecision on Brown's part. Torn between gathering the prize and vengeance caused him to pause in his initiative. The unknowing party slipped out of what looked like an art gallery, and entered a museum; totally ignorant of the gun barrels pointing at them. Brown's breathing quickened. This time he would not fool around, he decided to bring down the big guy and the little prick. The speleologists he would let live, that is until he wrung the whereabouts of Exley out of them. The ladies he would let go unless they got in the way, for even he was a connoisseur of fine female flesh.

The Raiders and Rangers were making record time down Tioga Pass road. They twisted and turned at breakneck speed down the curvy road, almost rolling the Rexhall C-34 around the last curve leading into the Valley. They had run more than a few disgruntled tourists off the road in the process. It was Souza's turn to show off his driving expertise while Townsend rode shotgun, pistol in hand. Loaf had managed to materialize a sawed-off shotgun seemingly out of nowhere, conjuring up a "for emergencies" excuse that was taken for granted. As they entered the parking area their friends were just emerging from the museum.

T-Boy was the first to spot Brown. His breathing had caused clouds of fog to come out of his mouth. But it wasn't the fog his eagle eyes were concerned with; it was the pistol in his hand that was pointing towards their friends. "There!" he shouted and pointed to the van. Souza floored the Travelall.

Brown was about to pull the trigger when the RV slammed into the rear end of the van. The errant shot caught Slo Mo in the arm as Brown was catapulted through the front windshield, his already disfigured face becoming a reasonable facsimile of raw blood sausage from the flying glass. In the chaos that ensued bullets ricocheted off the stone walls of the museum coming from all directions at once. The roar from Loaf's shotgun eliminated one of the directions, the boom of the Colt 45 another. Caught totally by surprise, the mercenaries were quickly decimated. What the Raiders and the Rangers couldn't figure out is how and why they went down so quickly. The answer lay with General Steve Cleveland.

Atop El Capitan, Cleveland had ordered cover fire. His elite fighting force was equipped with telescopic sights and silencers and the mercenaries were like sitting ducks. A few shots were directed at the rock walls of the museum so's to discourage the fugitives from entering the fray. In that it was a complete success. Cleveland was gloating over this when out of nowhere came the cold steel of a gun barrel against his ear.

"Well hello there, 'dead than red', long time no see."

"Bull! How? Where…"

"Your men are like smoke stacks out here in the cold air old buddy. I thought I'd stop by to see what you're up to." Exley's tone was as congenial as if they were at a tea party. But that quickly changed when he spotted the carnage below. "You sonofabitch! I ought to…"

"Slow down asshole. We just saved their lives. Cleveland hastily explained the situation and the fire left the Bull's eyes.

After quickly ascertaining the situation at hand, the Bull called out to Cleveland's fighting force. "Thank you very much gentlemen. Now I must ask you to discard your weapons." The team members were clearly perplexed. Here in front of them was their not so popular boss, held at gunpoint by the man they had been sent to find and to some, considered as Royalty. One by one they reluctantly set down their weapons and raised their hands. "You're not prisoners. It's just that your boss here is trying to discourage a date I have to keep." Then to lighten the atmosphere he added, "he's the jealous type." The Bull then pulled out his phone and contacted his friends. "Is everyone all right?" was his first question.

This time it was Townsend who answered. "Minimal damage," he answered groggily. "Slo Mo took a hit in the arm but it hit just the muscle, and he's got plenty of that to spare. Jackson was strafed by rock fragments from the building; there were shots from elsewhere. We're a little banged up from Souza's version of Demolition Derby, otherwise the only casualty is another one of the Raiders' vehicles.

"I can see that. What about the enemy?"

"There's a few down with non life-threatening injuries. One took a shotgun blast courtesy of Loaf. But he was hidden in a bush and just looked like hamburger. I'm afraid my aim is a little too good so there's one dead." Townsend paused, "Bull, the one who went through the windshield was the snake that killed Colonel Hasbrook, and he managed to slither away with rest. They had another Van."

At the mention of this, Exley's blood turned cold. His instincts were correct. After a minute of mental anguish he suggested "take everybody to the medical clinic. It's there somewhere. You look pretty beat up."

"Where are you?"

"Look up."

"What?"

"Look on top of El Capitan. Cleveland is up here with his own welcoming committee." Townsend complied and sure enough they were easy to spot; all standing with clouds of fog emanating from their breath. Townsend and Exley exchanged waves and signed off. The sounds of approaching sirens pierced the air and soon enough, the Local Authorities had control of the situation. All those in need of medical attention were ushered to the clinic. The rest were involved in backslapping for a job well done; except for Loaf who was staring at his now demolished Land Cruiser. The Bull then turned his attention back to Cleveland and company. "Hey, there's a few things I need to know."

"Such as? You get nothing out of me you traitor!" Although his conviction sounded hollow he considered himself to be a good soldier.

"Traitor (?) Right! What about Vietnam old buddy?" At the mention of this, Cleveland turned ghost white, all the wind out of his sails. "Relax. After all, people in glass houses, you know. Besides, that's all in the past."

"You knew?"

The Bull turned serious. "To even be in that stupid war required being on something, and I see no fault in cushioning the soldiers' misery. I've done that myself from time to time, although I never made any money on it..."

Cleveland stared at the ground and knew he was beaten. "I still won't talk Bull." It was meager defiance at best.

Exley studied the surroundings and then his eyes lit up. "We'll see about that." He turned to the others. "Boys, I'm awfully sorry about this. Maybe someday you'll find it in your hearts to forgive me." If the last conversation wasn't enough, this comment mixed up their loyalties even further. The Bull read their minds. "Pick up your weapons barrel first and stack them in the aircraft. Which one of you is the Pilot?"

"Ah am suh." This came from a dark haired lieutenant on the left, he looked no more than mid-twenty. His accent deep south.

The Bulls eyes lit up even further. He made a split second decision. "Consider yourself drafted into our rebel army."

The word "rebel" seemed to strike a chord from deep within the lad's ancestry. He came to attention and saluted. "That'll suit me just fahne, suh."

"All right gentlemen let's move out," the Bull stated imperiously. But instead of leading them back to the aircraft, he indicated that they walk single file towards the ski lift that went up Badger Pass. "General Cleveland, are you sure you won't tell me what I need to know? How did you find us?"

Silence.

"Too bad. It's your bed and now you get to sleep in it. Boys, strip down to your thermal underwear. Lieutenant, gather their uniforms." The elite fighting force glowered at their commander and complied. "Okay. Pile on guys. Nice legs, Cleve." The Bull pointed to the ski lift. Although they were quickly becoming cold, they were still getting a kick out of the Bull's treatment of Cleveland. They formed up and marched towards the ski lift, Cleveland following. And just to add more insult to injury the Bull asked the lieutenant, "Son, have you ever been to the Mardi Gras?"

"Plenty of tahms, suh. It's the best damn pahty in the Confederate States of Yuhmerica." His allegiance was only obvious.

The Bull laughed heartily. "Mister, I like you already." The 'elite fighting force' loaded onto their respective chairs and Cleveland was the last. "Well old buddy, I know you won't believe this, but we're going to give the thing back. Give a message to President Brandt that the exchange will happen in Nahlans and it will go directly into the hands of Professor Potts. No one else. Have a nice ride." He turned to the ski lift operator, "stop this thing halfway up for a few minutes so they can really enjoy their predicament. We're actually old friends and this is just a practical joke." Although the operator didn't believe it for one second, he nodded affirmatively. He was caught up in the moment. "Now Lieutenant, let's see what our new toy can do. Bye, Cleve."

Traitor! I'll see you get Leavenworth for this!" Cleveland's teeth were chattering already.

The Bull pondered for a second, "Yes, you just might." Then they were on their way. Just to twist the knife a little further, he added, "Look for me in the French Quarter. I'll be in a gorilla suit."

As the 'elite' fighting force receded in the distance, the Bull turned to the pilot.

"Son, can that aircraft of yours land in Yosemite Valley?"

"Lahk a buttahfly on a flowah petal, suh" answered the pilot confidently.

"Great. We've got business there. And by the way, I'm not a 'sir' anymore. People call me Bull."

"That's right fahne with me. Ahm J-Boy."

J-Boy's flying expertise matched that of his personality. Cool under pressure and congenial on the surface. The capabilities of the tilt-rotor aircraft impressed the Bull and J-Boy, true to his butterfly analogy, dropped effortlessly into the parking lot next to the Red Shark. The commotion caught the attention of the Local Sheriff but it was alleviated by the explanation from the Rangers. Slo Mo, arm in a sling and Jackson with a face covered in bandages were loaded into the aircraft under the ministrations of the ladies turned nurses. The Bull strode over to the wreckage and the Raiders who were busy unloading and loading their personal belongings into the Cadillac. Loaf was taking it like a champ again although the pain in his eyes was evident. At the Bull's approach Loaf turned and before Exley could utter an apology he smiled and mentioned "Insurance." All goods were transferred by the time the tow arrived. It was then that the Bull noticed the speleologists were missing. "Where's Connor and my Niece?"

Under a grimace of pain Slo Mo answered, "they're still in the clinic getting an ultrasound." Which explained it all.

When Mallory and Victoria finally approached, they were beaming. Arms wrapped around each other's waist, they proudly announced "it's a Girl." This broke the spell of the last episode as congratulations flew back and forth. As usual, Mallory the mind reader, read the Bull's thoughts. An announcement of a marriage proposal and acceptance was met with cheers, New Orleans being where the ceremony would take place.

When Brown regained consciousness he immediately flew into a monumental tantrum. By the time his energy was spent, his hands resembled his face; the constant pounding on the walls of the Van had turned them into mincemeat. To anyone passing by, the Van might have resembled a microwave popcorn bag on wheels in the process of popping and expanding. His tirade could have filled a dictionary of curse words all except for two: Exley and Bull. Those he kept repeating again and again, inserting them over and over. The mercenaries that survived could only stand back and observe until it was over. By then the inside of the van was a blood-spattered mess and outward dents were everywhere. Then came the removal of the glass splinters from Brown's face which started the whole show all over again. This time morphine had to be administered.

When he 'came to' the second time, the Van was stationary. There wasn't a square inch on his body that didn't hurt. This did nothing to help his mood one bit. But the exertion plus his injuries slowed him down considerably. He looked through the slit in his all too familiar bandages and asked "where are we?"

"Mariposa Grove" came back in barely discernible English. The accent was guttural Sicilian.

"What happened?" He asked through a fog. The explanation brought on another volley of cursing, this time less vehement; the morphine had taken care of that. He attempted to get out of the van but his world started spinning and he fainted, not before noticing a peculiarly shaped silver antique trailer parked across the campground. He was far too gone to make the connection. The giant Darksuit called 'Meat' administered another ampule of morphine to keep Brown down and out. His devout Catholic ears had heard enough blasphemy and the boss needed time to recuperate anyway. It seemed like a good idea at the time, but he would pay for it later. The surviving mercenaries decided to kill some time by exploring the Sequoia Grove. They were just out of sight when the Red Shark came rolling into the campgrounds.

The momentary lapse in the action came back into focus upon sight of the mercenaries' other van. Warily, everyone got out of the Red Shark and prepared for another ambush. There was none. For that matter there was no one in sight. They took advantage of the situation by hitching up the Rolls-Royce trailer. Still no one in sight. By the time the Friendship Gulfstream RV was recovered they were ready to go. It had been agreed upon to meet the next morning at the Grand Canyon where the Bull and J-Boy took off to gather "a little surprise." Everyone knew the Bull long enough not to bother asking any further questions, so it was left at that. Swiftly and silently as possible they left the campground; but this required a pass alongside the Van. As they passed by, they marveled at the dents on the exterior. It was as if there had been some sort of explosion in the interior. What's more, there was a muffled cacophony of cursing coming from the inside behind what was left of the tinted windows. They wasted no time investigating, there had been enough interaction already. In a momentary brainstorm, Townsend pulled out the 45 and shot out the tires, which brought on what seemed like some sort of howl from the inside. Whatever it was, it wasn't happy. They left as the Van was settling onto the ground.

Mr Brown's prey was a hands reach away but he was too fucked up to move. He was incapable of another tantrum, he hurt too much. He could not apprehend the fugitives, the morphine took care of that. He couldn't cry, period. His only option was to howl like a wounded animal and that, he did well. The gunshots alerted the survivors and they came running. But upon arrival, concern turned into apprehension due to the noise emanating from inside the Van. Meat opened the door and jumped back. The site he beheld was too much even for him. Brown's eyes were glazed from a combination of drugs and fury. He had ripped his bandages off and was scratching and reopening his fresh flesh wounds on his already disfigured face. If that wasn't horrible enough, he was rubbing the squirting blood all over his body. He resembled a half-chewed hot dog smothered in ketchup. Brown was over the edge. Gone. Meat then noticed the firearm beside him and became instantly convinced Brown was going to commit suicide. Too bad he was wrong. He glanced at the pistol, then back at Brown and began to say "Boss, I…" That was as far as he got. Brown picked up the pistol and instead of putting it to his head, shot the Sicilian right between the eyes. The other survivors stepped back and prepared for the worst. But amazingly the murder seemed to have a calming effect on Brown. He refocused and took a deep breath and sighed; as one might do if they had just completed something satisfying. It was truly a surreal moment in the making.

After the echo of the gunshot faded away there was dead silence. The only sounds were the wind in the branches of the trees and the birds that lived in them. The surviving mercenaries stood shock still incapable to figure out what to do about what was going to happen next. Considering the circumstances, anything was possible. Surprisingly, Brown regained his composure and came back to his senses, what little he had left of them. The first order of business was to get rid of Meat and then fix the tires. Meat wound up in a wheelchair in the men's room of the museum. They had only one spare tire and needed another. Townsend had taken out only one side of the vehicle. They tried a can of Fix-A-Flat but unfortunately no amount of that gunk would plug a bullet hole. With each passing moment, the fugitives were putting miles between them. This did nothing to improve Brown's mood. So the chore was completed in record time. In less than two hours they were on Highway 41, the only road the fugitives could have possibly taken, on the trail of their prey.

By the time they were able to escape the confines of the Badger Pass ski lift, Cleveland and his elite fighting force were close to collapse from exposure. The only thing that kept the General going was acute embarrassment and a new level of dedication for bringing down Brigadier General Tyrone 'Bull' Exley Retired. When they finally reached the top of the ski lift Cleveland immediately confiscated a phone claiming "National Emergency," and by the time they made it back down, a reception committee of Park Rangers were there to meet them. They were quite a sight: teeth chattering, blue in the face with purple lips dressed only in thermal underwear, they were given hot coffee and National Forestry Service uniforms. Cleveland and his gang had been the brunt of numerous wisecracks and the Rangers tried their best to hide the smirks on their faces. It took quite some time for the 'elite' force to thaw out and during this process Cleveland arranged for two Forestry Service Vehicles to keep them in the hunt. He then made two telephone calls. The first was to Violet in which he suffered a bombardment of comments regarding his ineptness, and the second to the President regarding the loss of one of the Government's latest developmental aircraft. His story was met with a cool reception which did not help much. Cleveland's desire for retribution filled him with a new level of dedication to the task at hand. His not so spotless career was in dire jeopardy and he knew it. The only thing working in his favor was the knowledge of the fugitives' destination and that was only if Bull Exley was telling the truth and not sending them on another wild goose chase. Considering the source, anything was possible. The only thing he really knew was that sitting around pondering the situation wouldn't get them anywhere. His dignity somewhat restored, he ordered his troops into the waiting vehicles. With some luck and perseverance they could possibly catch them on the way to New Orleans. The chase was on; Cleveland following Brown in pursuit of the fugitives on the only highway leading in that direction. Easy pickings. What could possibly go wrong?

Agents Fife and Persons arrived after it was all over. Without the luxury of knowing Clevelands' original destination it had taken time and considerable Badge flashing to get some answers. Without their Presidential order they would have gotten nowhere, fast. Eventually, Yosemite was determined as their destination and direct travel arrangements had taken some time. Although they didn't know it, they had passed the Van and the Ranger vehicles going the other way as they were entering the Park itself. When they arrived a massive cleanup was happening in the parking lot and they didn't make the connection until some questions were answered. By that time, the fugitives and their pursuers were well on their way; at least a couple of hours ahead of them.

By then, Fife had already made the connection between General Cleveland and the 'Grand Old Lady' on Long Island, but that alone wouldn't vindicate him from his past mistakes. And Agent Bernard Fife must absolutely see this through to the end!? After all, he was on special orders from the President. Then after consulting a map, he determined there was only one route to New Orleans the fugitives would take. What he didn't know was who else was on it. Without hesitation, he reversed direction and began pursuit, delusions of grandeur once again formulating in his mind.

CHAPTER 17

THE U.S. ALL OVER THE PLACE

Both the President and Violet had one thing in common; the distrust of their men in the Field. General Cleveland's allegiance was certainly in question, and Mr. Brown was definitely looking out for himself. And this was the time not to have any doubts in the matter. Almost simultaneously they took matters into their own hands. After a brief discussion with Agent Fife by phone, the President delegated a force of FBI Agents to New Orleans. Violet called an emergency meeting of the Trust to create another Task Force for the same purpose; to pursue the pursuers to get the prize: in this case, the Missing Link, which was still bouncing around in the trunk of the Red Shark and still emitting the faint pulse for those to follow. Of course it had to be the Mardi Gras, but everyone would be in costumes, and that could work in their favor.

Or not.

Despite the fact that they were being followed, the fugitives took it slow and easy. A ricochet bullet had hit the oil pan of the Red Shark and although it was a very small puncture, oil began to leak slowly. Cadillacs are notorious for their durability. But when Mallory set the nitrous oxide fuel injection into overdrive the oil was forced out faster due to the higher RPM's. So by the time they noticed the problem, they were out in the middle of nowhere, hundreds of miles away from their destination, the

Grand Canyon. If it hadn't been for Loaf's ingenuity, they would have been stranded. The stove in the back of the Friendship Gulfstream was loaded with the stuff. It was used and overweight, but it would just have to do. So it was stop and go traveling, but only when it was absolutely necessary. At first they would wait for the red oil light on the dashboard to signal the pressure was down. But after a while the light stayed on permanently, which required some more TLC and a sharper watch; on the engine and the horizon behind them.

"This old Warhorse is giving up the Ghost" muttered Townsend during one of the last peaceful stops they would be allowed to make. "It's amazing it's made it this far."

"They built them to last back then is why," returned Slo Mo through clenched teeth. Although he had been milking sympathy to the maximum degree from the women, the gunshot wound was still no lightweight injury. "If we had time to patch the hole, this Beast would probably last another few decades."

"Fat chance around here" observed T-Boy as he scanned the horizons. As if on cue, a set of headlights came over the rise a few miles behind them. "We should probably get a move on."

Luckily for them it was a BMW appearing to be in time trials for a road race. It came from behind, and without hesitation passed both vehicles going a lot of miles per hour faster. The black eyed beauty delivered a harangue of curse words in Spanish to the driver that never heard a word, nevertheless it sounded good and she received a round of applause from the others. It lightened the moment and brought a brief respite from the tension. Slowly, they plodded down the highway giving the grand old car the breaks it so richly deserved. The distance between those in pursuit was quickly decreasing. But the fickle hand of fate, in the form of Murphy and his law, was soon to come into play.

Or was it Sir Isaac Newton; because what goes up certainly does come down and for every action there is a reaction. Or perhaps Albert Einstein was closer to the point, because energy does equal mass times the velocity of light; except in this case it was the velocity of a car. Whatever reasoning comes into play it was probably a combination of all of the above. I'd bet on Murphy.

If the driver of the Beamer hadn't been momentarily sidetracked by the sight of the goddesses in the bright red Cadillac, or if the jackrabbit wouldn't have been in the road when he returned his eyes from the rearview mirror back to the road, and there wasn't a small rise and a slight curve on the straightaway at that very moment, it probably never would have happened.

Obviously, for a split-second the driver's mind was in the Cadillac with the ladies instead of his own car. The straightaway had been ongoing with an occasional rise for miles. The curve was unexpected. The Jackrabbit was transfixed by the oncoming headlights, causing it to stay stationary as if hypnotized. When the driver's mind came back to the matters at hand, a slight tap on the brakes and readjustment to the curve in the road at this speed caused it to first roll sideways and then end over end for at least a quarter mile of sparks flying and metal crunching, eventually to come to a halt upside down in the middle of the road billowing steam in a puddle of gas. This was the opening of a multi-act play that would stretch all the way across the United States and wind up in some far-off corner of the Universe.

Miraculously, the driver was thrown from the car at the beginning of the onslaught, only to wind up spread-eagled in the middle of the road, face up looking at the sky. The last thing he saw before losing consciousness was a shooting star flying across the sky and it seemed to him that it stopped, which later would be accredited as a hallucination before entering shock.

The fugitives' momentary glee was immediately cut short upon viewing the accident. Before they reached the remains of the car they spotted the body. Even though this was the first time their paths have crossed was less than desirable, this was still a human being. The fugitives approached, and much to their astonishment the driver was still breathing and relatively unscathed. After a quick once-over it was discerned that he could be moved and it was unceremoniously done due to the appearance of another set of headlights looming in the distance.

Brown and his entourage were behind a rise when the accident occurred and didn't see a thing. The BMW had passed them also and the last thing they expected was for it to be between them and their prey. So bent on vengeance was he that it clouded his logic. He wanted them dead, all dead. He spotted them earlier just before sunset and the furthest thing from his mind was that it could be anyone else but his target. The BMW was simply out of the question. So, during the approach he gave orders to open fire which is literally what happened. The stray bullets caught the gas puddle and the hulk of twisted metal erupted into a fireball igniting into the sky. Not only did this alert the fugitives, but it also blocked the road for quite some time. Brown even failed to notice it wasn't his prey until the flames died away. When he did finally figure it out, he flew into a rage that would have made the Devil himself blush. Meanwhile, the fugitives were continuously putting more distance between them. As if it were an omen, a shooting star flew across the sky.

The fugitives had caught the whole show and were convinced it was their nemesis hot on their trail. 'Hot' was an understatement; the whole road seemed to be on fire. By this time they had their oil problem down to a science. Even though it was slower going, without the nitrous oxide overdrive they would only have to stop every ten miles or so to refill the crankcase. They functioned like a professional road race pit crew; clockwork. And the Red Shark was showing its appreciation. The red light on the dashboard even went off. Although it was only temporary, the old classic was keeping them out of harm's way, for the time being.

Cleveland saw the fireball as a glow in the night sky. But even that was enough to put two and two together. He ordered the Company to drive with only parking lights. That, plus Brown's attention to the road ahead allowed them to catch up unobserved. He toyed with the idea of confronting them but decided against it. He might as well let them do the dirty work as his reasoning. And why not? After all was said and done he could just slip in and grab the prize claiming National Security, and also gain plenty of leverage for dealing with that old Bitch from Long Island. This whole shitpile could actually work! And in his favor if he played his cards right; There, ahead on the road was Violet's fall guy, who also had one of his own: Agent Bernard Fife. Just where was he, anyway?

"Ms. President, they are both directly ahead of me on the road to the Grand Canyon. They are within sight. No, they don't know I'm here and it's going to stay that way. What's curious is that they don't seem to be working together. Cleveland is following the mercenaries who are following Bull Exley and I'm following them. Odd, but true, Madam President. If something changes I'll let you know. Until then we're going to stay out of sight. Yes and thank you. Out." Fife was puffed up like a fighting cock. His surveillance was working like a charm. No more practical jokes on his desk for him, he thought to himself. "Bernie cool" he said out loud accidentally.

"Huh?" Persons looked at him quizzically.

"Oh it's… uh, never mind." Fife was too caught up in himself to qualify an answer. To do so was beneath him. His partner wouldn't understand anyway.

SPACE PATROL

"The inhabitants here are just too violent. There's no hope for them," observed a disgruntled Rawar. They had been tracking the faint pulse and viewed with horror the events at Yosemite and on the road to the Grand Canyon. "We should just take our gift back and leave them to their own demise," he added. Considering what they had seen so far, he had a good point.

"You mean you are calling off the bet?" asked Oxomoxo, appealing to his convivial nature. "I'm surprised at you." Rawar stole a glance at his co-pilot and couldn't help but notice a smirk on his face and gleam in his eyes. This bet had been going up and down for ages and he knew there was no way out. He turned his attention back to the screen, curiosity getting the better of him.

"No, not really, it's just that they're evolving so slowly when they are so close to the crucial step." Rawar gave away his true feelings. Deep down he was pulling for this project just as much as Oxomoxo. But when they observed this type of behavior… This just happened to be one of those times when they didn't feel that confident. This Planet Earth was by far the most complicated, and interesting.

Oxomoxo read his mind. "Besides, those with our gift are basically good natured and they haven't committed their true intentions. There's still hope for them yet." Oxomoxo was right, of course, but he usually had the tendency of giving them the benefit of the doubt. "There's also our new Project to consider."

"I suppose," Rawar's thoughts went immediately to the episode when he locked eyes with Bull Exley. "There's still a faint glimmer of hope." The older one's energy field had only the slightest traces of negativity and that was way above their norm. But after all, nothing is perfect. "No, I'm not backing out. The bet stands."

"I don't understand why they are not exploiting their newfound knowledge. Surely after connecting it with the scout ship they must know what they have. Oxomoxo spoke of what was running through Rawar's mind. Neither of them had an answer.

"That's probably what all the violence is about. It's times like these when I'd like to intervene, but that would only cheat the evolutionary process. They have to do it on their own terms, for better or worse." Rawar's tone was cynical but he was absolutely correct.

Both of their thoughts drifted to the new project and its population issue. The answer was simple and right in front of them, but so much time and energy had been put into planet Earth, that abandonment was out of the question; they must see it through to the End. If those currently in possession of their gift were the type of humans that could handle its use, the project still had a chance to evolve.

Their energy fields' showed their potential. If the gift were to fall into the hands of the type of people chasing them, the project's days would certainly be numbered, its fate sealed and the project decided. In that context the idea was appealing, although it meant another mess to clean up; and only if the Space Patrol had the time to gather some life forms to populate their new project. And even though Rawar and

Oxomoxo hadn't discussed it openly, both were of the shame notion: that the fugitives themselves were the front running candidates for the population of their latest project. To whisk them away now would severely limit the chances of Earths' survival; to wait too long would destroy the chances entirely. They had no choice but to keep watch on the fugitives and do what they could without direct intervention. The enthusiasm they derived from the quandary they were in was an elixir; they lived for moments such as these, their purpose defined. One could go as far as to say that they were fate itself, and to the people of Planet Earth, they couldn't be any closer to the truth. And the 'fates' were going to step in and do some juggling.

"He's coming around" came a female voice out of the velvet fog that was his mind. The driver of the Beamer's eyes fluttered open and he immediately tried to sit up only to be brought down again by the pounding in his head. He also found himself being gently held down by four sets of soft female hands. He involuntarily squeezed his eyes shut to blot out the pain, but when he reopened them and came into focus, he found that the hands belonged to four gorgeous creatures that must belong to Heaven. Except Heaven isn't supposed to have pain. Then he remembered the Cadillac, the jackrabbit and that strange shooting star.

His car. The joyride. What the fuck happened? He lay there still, and let his eyes do the roaming. Sure enough, the ladies were real. Weren't they in the Cadillac? Then grim reality came flooding back to him. "Wwwhere am I?"

"You are in the back of our recreational vehicle," answered one of the beauties. "And lucky to be alive."

"When I saw you ladies I'd thought I'd died and went to Heaven." He attempted to turn on the charm but it wasn't working.

"You are a road hazard sir," came from the black eyed beauty that was holding his head in her lap. Her eyes weren't that friendly. "You almost killed everyone here."

He held up one finger. "I was distracted by your beauty." Two fingers, "there was a jackrabbit on the… Did you see that shooting star?" This time he figured his charm would be fruitless. So he became pragmatic.

"Find out if he knows who he is. If he's got a concussion." The male voice was less than cordial. It came from the driver's seat.

For the first time the stranger considered his predicament. He was in an RV possibly being held hostage by people he had almost hit with his car? Where is the car? He decided to come clean. "My name is…" It immediately came to mind whether he should give his real name or not. "Geno Morelli. I am a Gynecologist from San Francisco. I am, or was, on vacation heading for the Mardi Gras in New Orleans." This brought on a cacophony of laughter from those in the vehicle. He relaxed a bit.

"Well, his brain works. Ha! You putting us on? A gynecologist, right." The voice was also male. But all of a sudden the voice had a face; and was looming over him. He looked like a pro wrestler and his arm was already in a sling. "Any bones broke?"

Doctor Morelli took a personal survey and nothing seemed to be broken, although he felt like he had been on a medieval torture rack. "No. Everything seems to be in one piece. What about you? That looks like a gunshot wound. I'm a doctor. Can I help?" It was hard for them to contain themselves. The laughter would stop, then one snicker and they were off again. After even more laughter regarding his Profession, he decided he wasn't in deep shit. Even if he was, there wasn't much he could do about it anyway.

After some brief introductions he was permitted to take a look at Slo Mo's arm. He went to work and cleansed the wound, asking no questions. When he learned of the fate of his car and noticed their tight-lipped attitude, he laid back down and went to sleep.

For what seemed like days but was in reality only hours, the Doctor came around again. This time he kept his eyes shut and ears open as to ascertain his position with these strangers. In less than an hour he deduced that they were on the run and partially responsible for the destruction of his vehicle. The biggest piece of information however was that they too were heading to Mardi Gras. He considered the few alternatives he had and decided to try and snag a ride. This decision would haunt him for the rest of his days. When he came back around he hadn't realized he had slipped away again. This time his hands were tied.

"Whatsthemeaningofthis!" He roared his indignation and when he was done he found himself staring down the twin barrels of a sawed-off shotgun, the black eyed beauty on the other end.

"You talk in your sleep señor." A smile that was not really a smile was on her face.

"Now, do you want to tell us now just who you really are?" The male voice again. The big guy. "Who's Bam Bam?"

"Oh oh."

The confession rolled off his tongue and as it turned out, he hadn't strayed that far from the truth. He had just omitted a few things, like losing his license and becoming a Con Man. At the shotgun's urging he told most of his whole story. During this time Loaf had come up to scrutinize his face. When Morelli was done, Loaf asked "Are you by any chance Dr. C?"

At this, Dr.Morelli turned ghost white, expecting the recoil from the shotgun at any given moment. This gave him a brief amount of time to contemplate: does one even hear anything after the trigger is pulled? No recoil, or anything for that matter came from the gun. Loaf then added, "Relax Doc, you are among friends. We are in the same business." All the color started coming back into Morelli's face and he actually could smile, just a bit. Loaf spoke again, "Ladies and gentleman you are amongst Royalty. This here is Doctor C., Professor of Clitology, or 'Clitologist' as it were."

This took a moment for it to sink in, due to the stunned disbelief. Then his ropes were cut. Morelli was truly famous. He had actually convinced the female gender of most of the whole Planet that he could produce 'hard-ons' in the female anatomy which was undeniably ludacris. At first it started out as a joke, but eventually he made millions on it, only to disappear because of its dysfunction. He was a hero to chauvinist pigs around the world. For the ladies, it was a different story. Everyone in the vehicle knew of Doctor C; except for the black eyed beauty and she held the shotgun. So they purposely neglected to enlighten her. Victoria and the caretakers were free thinkers enough not to give a shit. By the time the black eyed beauty figured it out, she had been relieved of the shotgun. And it was a good thing too because it still looked like she wanted to scratch his eyes out. At the next pit stop, Geno Morelli was transferred to the Red Shark with the Rangers. They were delighted by such distinguished company.

By the time they reached Lee's Ferry at the beginning of the Grand Canyon, Wyoming's Green River was close to overflowing which raised up the many rapids in the Canyon's two hundred twenty seven mile course.

At some places the Canyon is as much as eighteen miles wide. Here the river flows easy. But in the narrows at these times it's close to impossible to navigate. This however, wasn't the fugitives' number one problem. The Red Shark was taking a beating and their pursuers were surely to be closing the gap. At any given moment all Hell could break loose and the Red Shark couldn't take another high speed chase. Tension was building; especially between the black eyed beauty and Dr.C. Due to her strict Spanish Catholic upbringing, the Doctor's con was abhorrent to her and her hot Latino blood didn't help things much either.

The Red Shark rolled to a halt enveloped in billowing clouds, ranging from an oily blackish gray to steam white; depending on which parts of the engine it was coming from. The noise was horrendous. The pistons sounded like they were pounding their way through the engine block, the clattering valves sounded like they wanted to self-destruct and the shriek of what was left of the water in the radiator sounded like a whistle from a freight train. It hurt to even look at, let alone listen to. Even the onlookers expressed their sympathy for such a grand old classic to meet such a fate as this; truly a shame.

When the Rangers got out of the car it was easy to tell that driving it in this condition had been an emotional drain. Even their soot blackened faces highlighted their frown wrinkles. They got out, shambled over to the curb and plopped down with their elbows on their knees and palms on their cheeks and stared at the ground for a long time. "This is like losing a Relative, maybe worse" Souza said glumly.

"At least the Bull doesn't have to see her like this" returned Townsend.

The Globestar Satellite Telephone rang. Not wanting to be the bearer of bad tidings, Townsend reluctantly answered the call. He wasted no time describing the past episode and the present situation, wanting it to be as quick and painless as possible. The Bull's lack of attachment to materialistic possessions was apparent in his reaction. It came in two words: "Too bad". And that was that. Townsend looked at the phone as if it was the Bull himself. He should have been incredulous. But nothing pertaining to Tyrone 'Bull' Exley surprised them anymore.

"We're leaving John Wayne Airport in Orange County now. I had to pick up a few 'necessities'. We should catch up to you by this afternoon. Get out of there ASAP. You could get boxed in too easily. If you have to leave the Red Shark, so be it. But she's a tough old gal, and I think you can get a few more miles out of her by doing this…" Townsend marveled at the simplicity of the Bull's plan. He wondered who 'we' was and how he got back so quick? He didn't bother to ask. Sooner or later it'll all come out in the wash if and when it's supposed to. The Bull finished by adding, "Head for Pikes Peak and an old gold rush town called Cripple Creek. We should catch up to you by then. Give my best to everyone. Out."

'Everyone' would have preferred an explanation but Townsend was already moving. The Bull's point about "getting boxed in" hit home. And if they were going to take the time reviving the Red Shark it was now. Townsend slipped under the Cadillac for a peek and came up with a satisfactory grunt. He directed Souza to the Lee's Ferry General Store for the heaviest weight motor oil and a can of oil treatment goop, if they had it. He looked at the others and raised his eyebrows a couple of times and without a word, went to work.

Townsend drained what little oil remained from the Red Shark and returned it to the 'stove.' "You never know when this might come in handy," he explained. Next, he removed a bullet from his pistol, and while he was at it, reloaded. He then found a good sized rock that would substitute for a hammer and pounded the leading edges of the casing inward. He looked over to each of the others who by this time were mystified. He stopped at Doctor Morelli, "Give me your jacket," and he complied. Townsend took off the jacket and ripped the lapel pocket off. "Thanks." He threw the jacket back and before Doctor C could register a complaint Townsend headed back under the Red Shark. Never one to shirk center stage, he laid it on thick. He held the casing between his thumb and forefinger and showed it to everyone like a Magician would at an audience. He did the same with Morelli's jacket pocket. He then proceeded to wrap the casing in the cloth as if he was going to make it disappear. He did the thumb and forefinger bit once more for theatrics. He grabbed the rock and slid under the car. After some pounding he returned minus his 'stage props', curtsied and showed his empty hands. "Viola." He turned to his assistant, "Mister Souza, you may proceed." Souza got the corny picture and emptied oil into the engine block saying, "forty weight," as he did so, joining in on the fun. Townsend inspected the oil pan once again and gave it a few more taps with the rock. Then started the engine. Since it had time to cool down and also receive a transfusion, it purred like a kitten. Next came the radiator. It had suffered from overheating and the radiator itself had been well used. Townsend produced a can of coarse ground pepper and showed it to the audience then poured it in with water. When the pepper grinds were swollen they managed to slow down the leak to a manageable dribble. Townsend and Souza took a bow as if soaking up the adulation of their audience. "Thank you, thank you, thank you very much," mimicking Elvis.

"If you weren't so successful, I'd throw tomatoes," razzed Mallory. "Where did you learn that trick?"

Townsend came to himself again. "It's an old army trick. The Bull utilized it during World War II. If it's a bullet hole, plug it up with a bullet. He said the life of a patch will vary, depending on what you put the engine through." Townsend left the statement hanging, the meaning obvious. No one needed any more incentive than that. They hastened towards the vehicles without discussing seating arrangements, whoever was closest to each vehicle taking precedence. It was more like natural selection. The Rolls-Royce trailer had been doubling as a sickbay so Slo

Mo, Sunshine, Jackson, and his black eyed beauty headed there. Victoria opted to be with her man and joined him in the Red Shark along with Townsend who had by this time adopted the Cadillac along with Doctors Bloomfield and C. Souza and the Raiders followed up in the Friendship Gulfstream with Surfer Sue who had been shadowing T-Boy of late.

If they had cut it any closer, the Canyon could have turned into a bloodbath. No sooner than they had departed was when Brown and his mercenaries showed up, bent on destruction. By this time Brown's patience was hanging by a thread, making the lives of the mercenaries miserable. On more than one occasion they had considered just throwing him out and being done with it. But they hadn't been paid yet so they were forced to endure and suffer the insults and complaints that went on nonstop during the ride. It took only a few minutes to discern that the fugitives had left already. So they filled their gas tank at the General Store and continued on their way, looking for blood.

Cleveland showed up shortly thereafter. They had been pacing the mercenaries so's not to be seen. He could have just as easily notified proper authorities and blanketed the area. But his cause had become more personal, and besides, he didn't want to share the credit for recovering the Missing Link; he needed all the clout he could get, to save face of what was left of his rapidly dissolving career. His grudge towards Bull Exley was clouding his logic and he neglected to call in for help. It wasn't the first mistake he had made.

As for the Agents Persons and Fife, they had what they thought was the world by the tail. All they had to do is observe and report in and with any luck maybe those ahead of him might fight it out and knock each other off. Then they would simply sift through the wreckage and abscond with the Missing Link, and receive even more accolades for a job well done. This was probably the biggest dream of all. They had no idea of the depths of Brown's hatred for the transparency of Cleveland's position. They had to retrieve the Missing Link or die in the process; no other option was plausible. Only the successful completion of their mission could possibly redeem them and bring back their previous status.

Failure was inconceivable. Had they known this, they might have taken a different approach.

The die was cast. All were like racehorses heading down the track a few lengths apart for the home stretch, with the dark horse in the form of "Bull" Exley bringing up the rear and closing the gap. The finish line for now was Pikes Peak. The fugitives' horse could be named Ingenuity, Brown's horse, Hatred, and Cleveland's, Desperation. Agents Fife and Persons' horse; just plain old Dumb Luck. Exley's would definitely have to be Pegasus, because it had wings. It was an apt analogy, except for the fact that in a race like this, there were no rules. The race was on and the future of the planet hung in the balance.

CHAPTER 18

EAST COAST USA

"There must be such a thing as karma after all" muttered a thoroughly disgruntled Reverend Chuck T. Mansin to himself. Oops! He caught himself thinking out loud again. That could be dangerous, he thought, this time to himself. Warily, he glanced around to see if he had been overheard, but she was oblivious to it all, her Habit saw to that. For the first time in his life he was a kept man and not in control of his own destiny. At first, the luxury and amenities of the Long Island Estate had placated his instincts but the novelty had long since worn off and he was left being a house guest; as 'Violents' personal sex toy. And even that wasn't working anymore. But that, he rationalized, was due to the repetitive acts his one eyed lizard was suffering to endure. And even his lizard couldn't turn a blind one eye to how repulsive that was. What's worse is she didn't seem to care. "With these," she explained one morning, hugging her syringe and vibrator, "I can take care of myself." Thank God for that. He did wonder however, if this might affect his stability in the household. So far it hadn't, but his male ego found it hard to accept the fact that he was there for something other than his physical prowess. He was a stud all right, but wasn't he also a pawn in this? Maybe I should get some Rogaine, he thought. Or was it Viagra? And that he laughed out loud and took another slug from his bottle of Southern Comfort. "That's all I need; is to give my dick a haircut."

"What's that?"

Oh shit. He was thinking out loud again and she was coming out of her drug induced euphoria. He was about to say it was nothing but then decided to explain. After all, even someone as unholy as this still had to have some form of a sense of humor. Or did she? He also didn't want to feed her paranoid delusions by elevating her suspicions of him. After explaining the difference between Rogaine and Viagra and the mental picture he derived from it, she actually got a good laugh. But it wasn't that she was laughing about.

"My dear Reverend," she paused to glare at him. "You don't think your purpose for being here is to plug my hole, do you?" He was amazed how she could change personalities like turning on a light switch. "You're just a convenience, or were…" Her voice became shrill with that all too familiar malevolent gleam in her eye. "But I would like to see you give your dick a haircut." Switch. There she went again, back to her school girl laughter.

Mansin was relieved again. He had dodged another bullet. But how long could he go on? This strung out schizophrenic lunatic megalomaniac beside him was one of the most, if not the most powerful women on the planet and he was becoming increasingly weary of being involved in it. He took another long pull off the bottle as she did herself up again. With luck, she'd OD. And that would be the beginning to a new end or vice-a-versa. He had even considered slipping her a 'Mickey', but he could never tell where that fucking Adolf was lurking. He was convinced that the walls of the old mansion had secret passageways and rightfully so, for even at that moment he was being scrutinized; it was Adolf's secret personal maze and he loved playing in them. And when this wasn't the case there were always the hidden cameras. They all had been installed when her husband was alive, for his nefarious activities went far beyond that of 'Violents'. He began to feel like a fly caught in a spider's web and in actuality, it couldn't have been nearer to the truth.

Maybe he should lift a few of her diamonds, flee somewhere like India and open up an ashram. Fuck, anything is better than this. He'd had enough, especially since the phone call she received yesterday. After she flew into her typical rage at the caller, she had been tight lipped and even somewhat smug. He tried to lightly inquire but she wouldn't give anything up; he was out of the loop. He considered taking the information he had and going over to President Brandt. That would probably keep him out of jail, but not much more than that. He would wind up with zilch. He was mulling these possibilities over in his mind when his train of thought was interrupted.

'Violent' momentarily came out of her stupor long enough to say "Oh, I forgot to tell you. Pack your bags. We're going to the Mardi Gras." Then slipped back into wherever she goes in that condition.

"The Mardi Gras, what the fuck?" he said to himself. She was too far gone to listen. Only Adolf heard him, but he didn't particularly give a shit at the moment. Why on earth would she decide to take a vacation, especially now? Or was it really a vacation? He didn't care. The only thing that concerned him was that it would be a convenient place to escape. Simply dissolve into the crowd. He had enough information to peddle off to somebody and he didn't care to whom. He'd cross that bridge when he came to it, then burn it behind him. Salvation was at hand. He quickly packed what little he had and that was it for the time being. All there was left to do was light a cigar and get drunk. And he was very good at that.

WASHINGTON, D.C.

Professor Lezlie Potts rolled his wheelchair into the Presidential Conference Room, curious as to what was afoot. The call for the meeting had been labeled as 'urgent', but no information regarding its nature was given over the telephone. It was an order, not a request. Potts was elated, anything for a break in the boredom that came along with being billeted in Washington DC was welcome. Considering that all he wanted to do is get back to Nellis and scrutinize the disk that he secretly had in his possession. The mere fact of its existence and being the only one that knew about it was a weight on his shoulders. And not being able to do anything about it made it worse.

The President was already seated waiting for him. This was highly uncommon. It was usually the other way around. For the President to allow so much time in her busy schedule as this meant it was of major importance. She didn't waste any time. "Good day Professor. We've finally received what we were hopefully waiting for," pausing for a reaction. There was none. She went on. "We received word from Nellis Air Force Base that General Exley called for you. It was recorded, so I'll spare you an explanation. She pressed the start button of the recorder beside her. Exley's voice was loud and clear.

"Lez, Bull Exley here. I found something you misplaced. I know it's yours, I gave it to you. There's a bunch of yahoos trying to take it from me. They won't get it. Listen, I'm throwing a little party down in New Orleans this week. Why don't we get together and I'll return it to you. Check in at Al Hirt's place and I'll find you. Have a good day."

The President smiled. "Eloquent. Isn't he? He takes no blame and doesn't implicate anyone. I'd trade the whole Joint Chiefs for him any day of the week."

Potts marveled at Exley's audacity. He talked like he was taking a walk in the park without a care in the world when in reality…

"He's a man of his word Madam President. I hope we can call off the dogs now that he's shown his true intentions."

"Yes. Well, there's still the matter of him 'borrowing' one of our latest model aircraft, but I think we can overlook any penalties once it's returned. Until then I really don't have a choice, legally, that is, but for now I can't publicly state that I've grown fond of that Old Rascal and hope he keeps leading our men in the field on a merry chase. What I can do is issue an order for the arrest of those who have been taking potshots at them. Although I'd have to deny it, I believe I know who they are."

Potts was already mentally at Nellis, working with the genuine artifact and the secret disc. He heard the President but his mind was elsewhere.

"There also."

"Ah, excuse me Madam. I was somewhere else. What did you say?" Potts did his best to hide his embarrassment. After all, she was the President of the United States.

"I said, since I think I know who they are I'm going there also."

"But you're the President!" Potts stammered.

"Oh can it Lezlie. I'm also a human being. Plus if it's who I think it is, I'm the only one who knows what they look like."

Potts looked for anything to the contrary, but there was nothing to be had. "You're the Boss," he surrendered.

"I have a body double. Every President has one, or more. And since everybody is going to be in costume, what's the difference? Actually, I love the idea. Jack and I deserve a vacation. What better than the Mardi Gras?" The President's enthusiasm was clear and Potts could see her mind was made up. So he dove in head first. "What are you going to wear?"

At that same moment on the other side of the Continental United States, the Bull, Jay-Boy and now Z, HT and Woody were flying formation three thousand feet above the Colorado state line. They really didn't need any extra heat for taking Clevelands' aircraft, but it seemed like a good idea at the time. When Reality set in, the Bull thought it prudent to return it ASAP, but not before he took care of the must/needs. They came in the form of Z, HT and the Bluebird and a few other necessary items.

After the Yorktown incident, the Bull earned Navy underground cult-hero status. Tom Hall, one of the surviving pilots, had gone on to become a Disney Studios executive. The Bull had done his best to keep tabs on his surviving pilots, especially the successful ones. He never knew when it might come in handy to call in a few 'markers', and he had done so a number of times with Tom Hall, and this one was going to be really good. "Hey Sea Hawk, how in the hell are you?" was the Bulls patented intro whenever he called him. This cut through the bullshit immediately. There were only a few left alive that knew his nickname.

"Oh hello you Old Rascal, what can you do me for?" was the automatic response.

The Bull explained the situation and put in his request. That was all it took to have a stretch limo waiting for them when they landed. J-Boy didn't really know with whom he was traveling so he was becoming rapidly impressed with his kidnapper. "Yall sure travel in stahle, suh," he remarked as they were whisked away to their destination. This time it was to the costume department of the Movie Studio itself, and they wasted no time in gathering a wardrobe for all, having a great time picking out who was to get what in the process. Exley thanked Hall and once again and they were on their way.

The next stop was Wood's where he found Z and HT. They were packed and ready and to the Bulls surprise, so was Woody. Not taking no for an answer, Woody pulled out his old pilot's uniform complete with pantyhose armband. It was bursting at the seams, but he could still get into it. The Bull was so impressed he couldn't help but give the go ahead. Besides, Woody already had his costume.

When they returned to the airport, it was the Bull's full intention to relieve J-Boy of duty. He didn't want the kid to get in any more trouble than he was in already. But J-Boy would have no part of it. "Ah have a workin' knowledge of Nahlans sir, high friends in places." It was an offer the Bull couldn't refuse, even though he wanted to leave J-Boy with the tilt-rotor aircraft right then and there. He decided against it. Although he didn't know at the time it was a monumental decision. They'd ditch the aircraft later.

During the flight the Bull made use of the time by making phone calls. The first was to the boys aboard the Flying Cloud to check in on their situation; they had made it through the Panama Canal with only a few minor bumps and bruises. This was due to the quality level of South American seamanship in the canal itself. They were currently in Veracruz stocking up on water and provisions and would be on the Mississippi by the day after tomorrow. Perfect. The next call was to Potts at Nellis. Had he known where Potts was, he would have called the President herself. Nevertheless, the message got through. The last call went to the fugitives.

PIKES PEAK

"The scenery disrupts the English language," quoted Mallory. "What?"

"It's a quote Teddy Roosevelt said about this place. I'm looking at Pikes Peak now. It's directly ahead." They had just gone through the florissant fossil beds where thirty five million years ago a large lake was filled with volcanic ash, which formed a Petrified Sequoia forest. "I'm looking at an eleven foot petrified tree stump as we speak."

"Okay, you're at florissant. Just ahead you'll want to turn South to Cripple Creek. We'll meet you there."

The trip from the Grand Canyon had gone smoothly with apparently no one following. They had to stop only once to put in oil due to a small drip in Townsend's 'patch job'. Mallory drove and had been keeping a constant vigil on the rear view mirror for anyone who might be in pursuit. So far so good, that is until he started talking on the satellite telephone which caused a momentary distraction.

That's all it took.

"Gotcha, we'll meet you there in… hold on."

Brown had been studying a topographical map and was waiting for this particular place in the road. It suited his purpose perfectly. There was a straightaway just behind the fugitives and a slight hillock ahead; just enough for the mercenaries to floor it and catch up after the fugitives went over the small hill. This way they could catch them without being spotted. While Mallory was on the phone, they went over the hill. By the time Brown reached the same hill, they were doing over a hundred mph. The fugitives were a quarter of a mile ahead.

"Bull, I think we've got… shit!" Mallory's rearview mirror disappeared in an explosion and a bullet hole surrounded by a spider web crack in the windshield. At the same time Dr. C, who had been riding shotgun howled as he was jolted forward. When he bounced back he was minus an ear. The passenger side became a shower of blood. "We're under fire! They've got us!"

Exley pondered the situation for about a total of a split second.

"Connor. Don't give up now! Floor it! Head for Pikes Peak and go up the toll road to the top. Don't argue, just do it!" The Bull bellowed like a Drill Sergeant. "We're almost there. We'll give them a little something to think about. Stay on the line and talk when you can. Meanwhile, get the hell out of there!" He looked at J-Boy "They are under fire. Let's go!" J-Boy didn't need to be told twice, he gave it all he could. Z and HT followed suit.

The mercenaries caught up in less than a minute, and Brown attempted to take out the driver. He missed, but could see he caught their attention. The red Cadillac that had been in the rear slowed down, but only for a moment. It picked up speed and shot around the Friendship Gulfstream.

Mallory's phone call, plus the Rolls-Royce trailer caused him to miss the mercenaries' approach. He knew for certain they'd all be dead if they stopped now, and Victoria was in the car. That's all it took. Although he failed to see the logic in going up the mountain, he did so without hesitation. The Bull must know something he didn't. Blind faith. After negotiating around the RV he put pedal to the metal. Loaf was in the other driver's seat and was already taking evasive maneuvers. The RV and the Van were knocking each other across the highway, the Van was losing due to the weight advantage. Then, all of a sudden, T-Boy popped his head out of the air vent on the rooftop. He couldn't fit in his whole body, so all he could do is calculate his aim. His head dropped back down inside and was replaced by his arm holding the shotgun. One blast in their general direction was all it took to discourage the mercenaries. They fell back behind out of range and kept firing until they hit their target and unfortunately for the fugitives it was T-Boy's arm holding the shotgun that was hit. T-Boy had bought enough time for the Red Shark to go into nitrous oxide overdrive, leaving them in the dust. He also distracted the mercenaries from shooting out the tires. At the last round of the ammo clip, Brown hit T-Boy's arm; causing him to drop the shotgun and take cover. Surfer Sue, who had been reloading for him turned instantly into a nurse. While Brown reloaded, Loaf floored the RV and put a considerable amount of distance between them.

Pikes Peak stands 14,110 ft and is called 'Colorado's Gateway to the Rockies.' It is also used for the 'Race for the Clouds'; an annual road race held every summer. Also called the 'Pikes Peak Auto Hill Climb', it is held on the United States Forestry Services' toll road which winds nineteen miles to the top. It is one of the most dangerous races in the world, complete with off-camber hairpin turns that with one mistake can send the race car and driver all the way back down to the bottom. The road itself is sometimes closed during the winter and this was one of those days. The Red Shark hit the toll gate at full speed ahead, sending the splintered gate flying in all directions. The RV was hot on its tail and the Van wasn't that far behind.

It didn't make any sense whatsoever to Brown why the fugitives had taken the road to the top. But he sure wasn't going to argue the point. It was a dead end and they surely would be caught. This didn't stop Brown from inflicting some damage though. It was target practice. He might as well have been in a shooting gallery. He kept on putting hole after hole into the rear end of the RV. He was actually having fun at the expense of those in front of him. The best part was that the road was going to dead end at the top with no turning area, so he would be able to torture and/or kill at will. He was happy for the first time in a long while.

Loaf, however, was failing to see the humor. With every 'thunk' in the back of his RV his mood wasn't getting any better. They've killed two of his toys already and this was the last. He could finagle more of course, but that just wasn't the point of the issue. The last straw came when they began shooting at the tires. A 'blow out' here could send them over the mountain to almost certain death. No thanks. He decided to do unto them before they did it to him. It wasn't the Golden Rule but it was as close as it was going to get. "T, set up the stove to mmmmm… half load. That should do the trick." T-Boy's eyes lit up. They were finally going to get to apply some of their 'tactical response' inventions to the test. He went to the rear bed and revealed to the others a door which he opened and set the gauge to five gallons.

"Ready." He responded.

"We'll wait for a good curve and send them on their merry way." Right then another shot came from the Van aimed at their tires. They were entering a medium sized curve. "Fuck it. Fire at will!" Loaf yelled like a U-Boat Commander just for show.

"Jawvohl, jowl, jahwool, yeah. Okay." Despite the danger, these two were poking fun at the situation.

Loaf's empty well of self control is what saved the mercenaries lives. Had he waited for a few more curves for higher elevation, they would have been killed for certain. It didn't however keep the Raiders' invention from being a complete success. The oil came out in one giant 'splat'. This caused a splash that sent the oil spreading in all directions at once. There was no getting around it even if they did have the time, which they didn't. The mercenaries' tires hit the puddle and instantly there was no traction to adhere to. It was as if they decided to drive over the edge. They weren't far enough up the mountain to have a straight drop, but the angle of descent was more than enough. They went over the side and there was no stopping, that is until they hit a boulder straight on. This flipped the van upside down, and down it went; gathering momentum like a sled. With each rock or rough spot they encountered, the roof caved in a little more. The closest thing it resembled at this point was a half of an accordion deflating with every bump. The frozen ground and melting snow didn't help much either. By the time they reached the bottom, the top half was completely folded in and there were no windows in sight. They were in a lockbox without a key. Aside from some cuts and bruises there was more damage to their egos than their physical condition. The muffled yelling and a howl was emanating from the inside until it came to an abrupt halt coinciding with the sound of gunshots. Brown had to vent his frustrations on somebody, so he did, which only served to make it worse; now they had another dead body to contend with.

If it wasn't for the Van careening upside down the hill, Cleveland might have driven right past. They had missed the chase and exchange of gunfire, but they came within view, only to see the Van strike the boulder and flip. On its descent it seemed to be shrinking but that didn't matter to Cleveland. What did however, was the two remaining vehicles heading up the mountain. Why they were heading towards a dead end was beyond him. It was a certainty that they would be boxed in with no way out. All the easier for him to get to the prize. They turned onto the toll road and with caution went up the hill. No need to hurry, he thought, they weren't going anywhere. Besides, he didn't want to wind up like the Van. As they went by the Van they could hear what seemed like arguing. The bullet hole he saw on its side would give them air to breathe, so he decided to deal with them later. The first order of business was to retrieve the Missing Link, and in doing so, vindicate his career. So involved with the situation on the ground was he, that he failed to notice the sound of aircraft above him.

After the brief elation of sending the Van to its just rewards, the fugitives were faced with two problems: The first being the other pair of vehicles heading towards them and the second being the condition of the Red Shark. The chase had blown the patch in the oil pan; the nitrous oxide saw to that. There was nothing they could do about it until they lost the Van and by then it was too late. Even the transfusion of some of the remaining oil from the Friendship Gulfstream's gizmo didn't do too much to help. The Red Shark was laboring and clearly in its last gasp. The fugitives were forced to take it slowly and stop at intervals to refill the oil. Meanwhile they could see whoever was pursuing them was gaining and closing the gap. By the time they reached the top the old Cadillac was at a crawl with smoke billowing out from under the hood. Mallory's driving visibility was zero, so he failed to see the searchlight that was situated at the top. In its death throes, the Red Shark plowed directly into the searchlight, a fitting end to the old Warhorse she was. Now all the fugitives could do is stand by helplessly and wait to be caught by the vehicles that were less than a mile away.

Cleveland couldn't figure out why the fugitives were taking it so slowly until he saw the smoke emanating from the hood of the Cadillac. So much the better. All that remained was to get up the road safely and that in itself was no easy task. When they hit the oil slick the first car almost followed the path of the Van. It slid sideways and came to a halt perched precariously above the Van's point of departure. If the Yosemite Rangers' trucks weren't equipped with winches they could have been stuck there permanently. To add to the confusion a goddamn seaplane of all things kept buzzing like a Kamikaze Pilot. What on Earth it was doing here they could not fathom, but at least it was keeping their attention away from the fugitives' laboring to reach the top. Finally they negotiated the oil slick and all there was left to do was gather the prize. Nothing could stop them now....

The mood was totally disconsolate at the top of Pikes Peak. Not only did they fail to elude their pursuers, but they killed their faithful vehicle in the process. The whole chase was for naught and who knows what kind of charges would be brought against them. Criminal property damage would certainly top what would probably be an endless list of trumped up violations. They were dead meat. Or so they thought.

Then out of nowhere came the Bluebird flapping its wings like they did on the Sea of Cortez. If this wasn't enough of a shock, much more so was the sight descending upon them. It was shaped like an airplane but was functioning like a helicopter. If there was any more room for astonishment, it was in the form of who jumped out of the aircraft to greet them.

"Hiya kids, miss me?" Exley said cheerfully.

A cheer rose from the fugitives but was quickly cut short.

"Listen. We don't have time for reunions. What I believe is General Cleveland is almost here, so load up the wounded and the ladies and we'll be on our way." Exley spoke in haste and the fugitives complied. As Slo Mo, Jackson, and Dr. C were helped to the odd aircraft by the womenfolk, the Bull strode over to his beloved Red Shark. A "tsk tsk" was all the time he had for a testimonial as he opened the trunk and took out the Missing Link. When he returned he quickly realized his mistake. The tilt-rotor aircraft was full and he needed more space. He walked over and grabbed Dr. C by the collar and yanked him out. "Sorry old chap, I don't even know who you are. Connor, jump in." Surfer Sue opted to take care of T-Boy which made enough room for Bloomfield. He turned to the remaining others, "Check into the Hotel Bouganvilla. It's adjacent to Louis Armstrong Park on St. Philip Street in the French Quarter. You drop the name J-Boy and they'll find room." J-Boy, in the pilot's seat tilted his hat in greeting. "Look for us at the Red Garter Saloon on

Bourbon Street." With that they were gone. Just when they were into the clouds Cleveland rounded the corner oblivious to what had just occurred.

Exley's timing was perfect. Cleveland was rounding the last curve that was out of view and by the time they reached the summit, the Raiders, Rangers and Surfer Sue were enjoying the scenery Pikes Peak had to offer. Their innocence was beyond repute. Cleveland rolled to a halt, imperiously walked up to the remainder of the outfit and announced confidently "By the authority of the United States Government you are hereby detained and required to hand over its property." The last part of his statement came out hollow after he noticed the missing personnel.

Rangers Souza and Townsend walked up to Cleveland. They were real 'official' with their uniforms all cleaned and pressed. They were reserved for such occasions as these. Cleveland realized they were dressed the same and all of his identification had been taken by Exley. His stature was shrinking with each passing second. Townsend spoke up first. "We have no idea what you're talking about."

"You know goddamn well what I'm talking about," Cleveland blustered, his composure rapidly receding. "Where are the others?"

"Oh. Them? They hitched a ride outta here," Souza replied smugly. "We were being attacked for some reason from those in that Van at the bottom of this mountain. It's them I think you should be detaining."

"Where is it?"

"What?"

"You know what I'm talking about!"

"I do?"

Cleveland could see this was going nowhere. He ordered a search that turned up nothing. Totally frustrated, he cried "You tell that Bull Exley I'll get him yet. I know where he is going."

"He did mention something about a gorilla suit."

That almost put Cleveland over the edge. Clearly he was getting nowhere with these people. Without further comment he ordered his troops back into their vehicles and headed back down the mountain. At least he could hassle whoever was in that Van.

But Brown had other ideas of his own. After seeing the bullet hole his gunshot made, he grabbed an automatic and riddled the side of the van a rectangular shape that with one easy kick allowed them a crawl space to freedom. After reaching the road, who should pull up but none other than Agents Fife and Persons. Brown and his mercenaries flagged them down just in time for the Agents to be facing down the barrels of their weapons. The only thing that saved the Agents' lives was the appearance of Cleveland in the distance. Brown quickly relieved them of their car and took off back the way they came. When they were out of sight they stopped to watch Cleveland's next move. Cleveland pulled up to the now stranded Agents completely bewildered.

"Agent Fife, what on Earth are you doing here?"

"Looking for you, actually." Was all Fife could think of to say. "Our vehicle was just taken by whoever was in that van. One of them looked vaguely familiar, although his face was disfigured." He let Cleveland figure out the rest.

Cleveland mentally saw his career crumbling to pieces. He knew exactly who Fife was talking about. And if Fife was looking for him, by whose orders? It didn't take much to figure that out. To save what little face he had left, he was forced to comply. "OK. Well, jump in and we'll take you to wherever you need to go." The cabs were full so Fife and Persons were forced to jump in the back. When they reached the turn-off they turned east in the direction of New Orleans. Cleveland was now convinced the Bull hadn't been lying. "Gorilla suit my ass," he muttered under his breath.

Brown waited just long enough to see the direction they took. He followed far back enough to escape detection. The Friendship Gulfstream, now with the Rolls-Royce trailer in tow, came down the mountain just in time to see both vehicles take off. This time the caravan was in reverse. There was no hurry because now the time and destination were known. Mardi Gras. Things could get fairly interesting.

CHAPTER 19

NEW ORLEANS, LOUISIANA. MARDI GRAS

To the millions of fortunates who have attended throughout the years, the Mardi Gras is generally known to be THE party of a lifetime: Held two weeks before Ash Wednesday in late February, it is a nonstop 24/7 round the clock celebration that lasts for two straight weeks. It is held in the honor of Conus, the god of Revelry and Rex, the King of Carnival and Monarch of Merriment; punctuated by nightly parades in which the whole town attends and legalized almost anything is in the streets making it hard to tell where the bars ended and the streets began. Everyone is there to have a good time. In which they do.

Although there is limited violence, each nightly parade includes a flotilla of Law Enforcement Vehicles that look more like a military riot squad than a police force, which is also met with cheers from the revelers as they know they are only there to keep the peace instead of enforce the laws. These parades also include a myriad of floats of every description, ridden by beautiful ladies in colorful costumes that throw bead necklaces and coins into the crowd as they pass by. Even the most inhibited soon find themselves diving for the baubles that are thrown, and there's more than plenty enough to go around. The parade is a signal for the start of each night's festivities and by the time it's over it's ready to start again, for two straight weeks. Absolutely everyone is ready to party which they do until all hours of the morning, evening, afternoon, dusk, dawn, all the above and more. Costumes are optional, although everyone decorates themselves in one form or another. But most people go all out. The more garish the better. This induces a more fun-loving attitude and facilitates a higher level of gregarious behavior, which coincides with the environment. The entire French Quarter is dedicated to one purpose and has one thing in common: fun.

The French Quarter itself is like going back in history. The decor is from the eighteenth to the nineteenth century and is rigidly adhered to, maintaining the flavor of the era. It's like taking a trip back in time. Located on the banks of the Mississippi, it is bordered by North Peters Street and Jackson Square, named after the then General Andrew Jackson who saved the town from the invading British. Paralleling North Peters and going inland are Decatur, Chartres, Bourbon, Burgundy, North Rampart, and Basin Streets respectively. Louis Armstrong Park on Basin Street serves as an informal border on the other edge of town. Running perpendicular to the Mississippi are Tulane Avenue, Canal, Iberville, and St. Louis Street, Orleans Avenue, and Esplanade Avenue. This is the meat of the French Quarter and is where most of the action of the Mardi Gras take place.

But not all…

"Massa cee wee no keemo peepole heeyah!" Mallory's blank expression gave away the fact that what he had just heard was totally unintelligible. The old colored gentleman from whom these words had come was dressed like a butler and was the first to receive the fugitives as they entered the Hotel Bouganvilla. "Mez Jewlines she gwine." From then on the old man went into an invective that was completely beyond recognition to Mallory's ears. As he stood there helplessly the others came up from behind equally as bewildered to the Front-Man's protestations. It seemed like complete gibberish. "Alright Melvin, it's only us," called out J-Boy from the rear of the group. He and the Bull had been gathering some of the belongings including the Missing Link from the taxis they had taken from the airport.

"Oh. Hello thea folks, welcome to the Bougainvillea." This time the man's words came out in semi-fluent English, a complete turnabout from his previous utterances. "Nice to see ya mistah J-Boy, it's been a hwhale." The old gentleman seemed like a different person.

In actuality the Bougainvillea wasn't situated next to Armstrong Park. It was tucked conveniently away down a dirt road amidst a grove of ancient Oak trees. And it really wasn't a hotel at all, but a reconditioned southern antebellum mansion complete with circular driveway and Gothic pillars that spread the whole length of the porch that fronted the building. It was obviously the pre-Civil War era that had survived the ravages of time.

"Ms. Juline has been expecting you." Melvin was about to continue but was interrupted by the appearance of the lady in question. She had entered from a side door that appeared to be just another panel on the wall. To guess her age would have been impossible. To the fugitives she appeared to be timeless. The only thing that adhered her to any time frame was the silver in her hair. Other than that, her cream colored skin was wrinkle free and flawless. But the most striking feature was her ebony black eyes that seemed to be out of proportion to her small body. They were wide set and fathomless that looked like they held the wisdom of the ages, which probably wasn't that far from the truth. Without a word she walked up to her new guests and looked them over one at a time. She first approached Victoria and broke into an immaculate white-toothed smile as she placed her hand gently on her belly. "Girl." she said appreciatively. Then she gave Mallory the once over. "Take good care." The others she approached and simply nodded affirmatively as if giving her seal of approval. But when she got to the Bull her eyes left his person and settled on the suitcase next to him. Her eyes widened and went back to the Bull, then to the suitcase and back again. She stuck her palms outward towards Exley and the Missing Link…Then after a few seconds of contemplation she nodded affirmatively as if they passed some kind of test. "You have plenty mojo in there, mister, and it's all good. Welcome." Then, as the grand finale to a show she approached J-Boy and said sternly, "I should put you over my knees like I used to do and give you a good likkin'. You stayed away much too long." She then broke into a smile that would melt a glacier and smothered him with kisses. Juline's personality could change in the blink of an eye.

Each of the Fugitives felt like they had been through an X-Ray machine, as if the old(?) lady could look straight into their soul. The fact that she was a voodoo queen was without question, and probably a mind reader to boot. After introductions that didn't seem necessary, they were led through the foyer and out towards the back. Their senses were assaulted by what seemed to be a dreamscape. The ancient jasmine trees were almost totally covered with honeysuckle vines and the aroma permeated the atmosphere. After the initial shock of its magnificence they were led towards what appeared to be what once had been slave quarters; a single line of small cottages that stretched the full length of one side of the back yard. Juline explained "These are usually reserved for bed and breakfast, but since you are with my boy J here, they're yours for as long as necessary." Without waiting for a reply, she gestured for Jackson and Slo Mo to follow her, which they did so without question. The rest headed for the cabins, then gasps of pleasure could be heard as each of them opened their doors. What appeared to be plain on the outside certainly wasn't the same within. Each cabin was complete with all the amenities including hot tubs in the washrooms. After everyone was comfortably settled in, the wounded returned with what looked like crushed leaves in place of their bandages, and the expressions on their faces were somewhat less stressed already.

"Auntie Juline is a 'doctor' of sorts," explained J-Boy. "Her poultices are legendary." Which was met without argument, the results apparent already.

Because they had the use of a high velocity aircraft, the Exley contingent arrived a day early. They left the tilt-rotor aircraft at Fort Polk with an explanation that General Cleveland would probably be picking it up soon. The mention of Cleveland's name was all it took. No further inquiries were necessary. HT and Z went on to the International Airport and refueled. Exley and company met them there, and they transferred all the luggage and boxes. Then they took off again in search of the boys on the Flying Cloud who were by this time dropping anchor on the Mississippi just outside the French Quarter. The Bluebird landed and tied up alongside the schooner and after they gained their 'land legs' again they made a beeline to the Red Garter Saloon to await the Bull.

It took some time for the Bull to show up and by the time that he did, the seafarers were well into their cups. As he approached they could see that he was visibly shaken. This brought their stage of inebriation down a notch, curious as to what could possibly cause this type of reaction in their Fearless Leader. It wasn't long before they found out. The Bull approached their table and after greetings were exchanged, the reason was explained.

"These," he pulled out the Satellite Globestar telephone, "are what saved our friends' lives." Then after a brief account of the Yosemite and Pikes Peak ordeal, the crew's curiosity was satisfied. "And my stupidity is the reason why they were almost killed. Somewhere along the line the lead suitcase sprung a leak that I didn't notice, giving our position away to anyone who might've been interested. I probably wouldn't have noticed it yet if it wasn't for the lady who is putting us up. She pointed it out while I was unpacking." The Bull explained how after they were shown to their cabins, Juline had come up to explain a "feeling" she had about the suitcase. She could tell that something very powerful was encased within but was wondering why some of its energy was spilling out into her home. "It was the damnedest thing, I didn't know what she was talking about. So I took a closer look and sure enough, one of the two latches was partially broken and the suitcase was open a miniscule fraction of an inch. I put a paperclip in the hinge and closed it up. She held up her hands and smiled, 'that's better,' and walked away. The Bull took a long pull of a frosty mug of beer that had just come for him. Then looked around at his listeners, "So in other words they have been monitoring our every move and most likely know exactly where we are at this moment. The leak is patched but the damage is already done and it's my own damn fault." The Bull finished his mug and ordered another. It was catch up time.

But the Bull, with his penchant for the unexpected, didn't wallow in self incrimination for too long. Instead, it filled him with a steely resolve. Captain Magic helped the process along. "Well, what's done is done and now it's fixed. So now we can deal with the present situation." He looked at the Bull, "Which is?"

The Bull looked at his friends appreciatively, then downed his second mug in one pull and ordered another. "Well, I know General Cleveland is hot on our trail. He has access to all of our satellites. And I believe the bastard responsible for the incidents in Guaymas and Yosemite are one and the same and whoever he is working for must have connections that penetrate very deep. Whoever they are must be formidable. And there is always Agents' Fife and Persons. Those we know about. There might be more." The Bull let this sink in and he threw down another mug. Then his eyes lit up. "But absolutely the first thing we must attend to…" Another mug came and went. "Is go to a wedding."

"He what?" bellowed General Cleveland furiously. His face was so red it looked as if it might explode right then and there on the spot. The orderly repeated the information regarding the tilt-rotor aircraft that arrived yesterday. Although it had been returned flawless, just the mention of Brigadier General Tyrone 'Bull' Exley Retired brought on what could have been mistaken as a seizure. He was about to demand why Exley hadn't been detained but decided against it. He had to calm down. After all, it wasn't the orderlies' fault, and Exley had shown his ID stating he was a Brigadier General. "That rascal Exley probably flashed it so fast that the orderly didn't catch the fact that he was retired." As he regained his composure he thought of the fact that at least Exley had told him the truth and he was where he said he was going to be. He had a vision of a gorilla and almost became apoplectic again. "Call the Chief of Police in New Orleans. I need room for my men and myself on one of their vehicles in the parade." The orderly saluted, about-faced and left as fast as his legs could march. "And bring us our uniforms!" Cleveland yelled after the retreating man. The orderly stopped again, turned around and saluted then almost fell over his feet trying to vacate the premises. This brought a small amount of satisfaction to the General. At least he was now back in his element and could order people around. While he was waiting for his uniform he made two calls. One to the President and the other to Violet. What a pair to draw to, he thought. Both were unavailable. This caused further stress but it didn't last long. On second thought he decided it was probably for the better. He could do things his way without obstruction. He actually smiled to himself for the first time in days. "I've got you now you bastard," he muttered to no one in particular.

At that moment agent Bernard Fife was strutting around like a peacock at the New Orleans Branch FBI office. Cleveland had left he and Persons there and headed on to Fort Polk. After showing his special Presidential papers he had been treated like royalty, unlike he usually had to deal with at his home office. A phone call to the President had allowed him to leave a message. The information he had gleaned from General Cleveland was sketchy. But if it was correct he had all the means at his disposal to call for an all-out manhunt; target, Tyrone 'Bull' Exley. But he wasn't ready for that quite yet. A small squad of agents would suffice for now. Agent Bernard Fife was desirous of all the accolades that would come with Exley's capture and retrieval of that object from Nellis. And at this point he wasn't about to share any of it. Besides, he was so full of himself by this time that failure was not even close to an option.

Brown, on the other hand, was only bent on destruction. Grabbing that fancy doo-dad was secondary. His primary function was to wreak havoc upon those who had ruined his life. Nothing else mattered. Once that he had surmised New Orleans was their destination, he contacted Violet via her private line. Much to his surprise she was there already, at the Hyatt in the Presidential Suite. He didn't fail to see the irony of that. She had booked him a room on another floor of course, and formal contact was strictly forbidden. At this point it didn't really matter. Let those who were vying for that peculiar object fight it out between themselves. He had another agenda.

"You are just another fucking hypocrite! I…" The Reverend Chuck T. Mansin slammed the Presidential Suite door on the rest of 'Violents' statement. He had heard and endured more than enough. And to think she would even consider he would wear a goddamn costume was ludicrous. He was a man of the cloth for Christ's sakes.

Violet, Adolf and the Reverend had taken her private jet to New Orleans that afternoon, checked into the Hyatt and it was then she produced these ridiculous costumes to actually be worn in public! First, she had given Adolf a cowboy suit. Great. Hitler posing as Roy fucking Rogers. She then broke out an ostentatious get-up that portrayed her as Queen Elizabeth or some kind of thing; as if she didn't have enough of a 'holier than thou' complex already. But the real capper was when she opened the box containing a red devil outfit complete with pitchfork, oversized horns and a tail shaped like a hard on. Had she actually thought he might find some sense of humor in the duality of it? It couldn't have been further from the truth. In reality he was at his wits end and the only thing he wanted to do was get the fuck out of there at the first possible opportune moment. But for now he couldn't get far because she held the purse strings, so he would have to bide his time and keep his eyes peeled for any form of an out. The devil costume however, drove him out the door. And he had enough chump-change to at least get a buzz on. With luck the old bitch would go into a stupor and leave him the hell alone. So, for the time being he decided to take a stroll down to the French Quarter and get good and fucked up before the opening parade started. Oh boy!

The Raiders, Rangers and Surfer Sue limped into town in the riddled Friendship Gulfstream the next morning a little worse for wear, but in one piece. In tow was the Rolls-Royce trailer and much to the Bull's surprise, the Red Shark. "I couldn't just leave her there after all she's done for us" was Townsend's explanation. An affirmative nod and a slap on the back was the Bull's response. T-Boy was quickly ushered away for one of Juline's poultices and the rest were shown to their cabins.

The backyard was a hive of activity. Once Juline got wind of a wedding, she immediately took over like the captain of a flagship. Her word was law. Her connections seemed endless as she plowed through the bureaucratic red tape like a hot knife through butter. Blood tests and licensing was taken care of by mid morning and the backyard quickly took shape as chairs, a pulpit and garlands of flowers materialized seemingly out of nowhere. She even managed to produce a band: Colonel Natural and The Jive Five. Melvin, the 'frontman', was also an Ordained Minister and by noon all loose ends were tied so the ceremony could take place.

The boxes that the Bluebird had brought were from the Hannibal Hamlin. After the Bull had contacted them, Z and HT flew down to Guaymas to pick them up plus extras for the Raiders, Dr. Bloomfield and the crew of The Flying Cloud.

Captain Magic and his crew were appropriately attired as pirates while the Raiders were given Confederate uniforms. Doc Bloomfield cut quite a figure as a southern gentleman riverboat gambler. And the ladies, goddesses in their own right, fit smartly into their southern belle outfits, complete with bustles, petticoats plus a low cut frontal assault made them a pleasure to observe. Victoria almost fainted when Juline brought her the wedding dress; a crochet crepe and white silk affair that was at least 200 years old and spotless. As she was swooning at the sight of it, Juline merely winked and smiled. Mallory was given a customary tuxedo except that it was also white, ancient, and spotless. "You aren't the first to wear these" was Juline's only remark. That fact was obvious, for when everyone began to assemble, it looked like they had all come through a time warp.

The only damper on the morning was when Juline found out about Morelli being the infamous Dr. C. He was immediately asked to leave the premises and not return, but not before Juline gave him an extra poultice for his ear. After all, she wasn't heartless. She also didn't give away the fact that she actually had tried his infamous 'concoction' with no results. Geno Morelli alias Dr. C had had enough anyway; rolling his vehicle, getting his ear shot off and being cold shouldered by most all the females made it easier for him to say goodbye.

When word got out courtesy of J-Boy, that Juline was having one of her infamous wedding celebrations, uninvited guests in all sorts of Mardi

Gras regalia began to show up. One didn't need an invitation to one of Juline's functions; all that attended were VIPs in their own mind, not exactly in the public eye, but more like an undercurrent of individuals that are the lifeblood of a city. Any city. In other words they fit right in. Victoria and Mallory's wedding held on the first day of Mardi Gras was going to be a pre-party function. And a good one at that.

By the time the ceremony itself was ready to take place it was mid-afternoon. Hundreds had shown up; all dressed in an array of getups. They were not of the 'High Society' realm, but were as J-Boy described them 'high friends in places'. In other words they were the behind the scenes elite that controlled the basic pulse that ran the city. The common denominator among them was that they were all outwardly friendly, but if one were to ever cross them or rub them the wrong way, a 'toll' could and probably would be extracted as the fugitives eventually would find out. Juline's dominion proved out to be all-encompassing. A buffet fit for Royalty appeared out of nowhere along with an open bar that had a deep well of anything anyone might want. The servers were clearly of Creole descent and many of them were a younger version of Juline herself. The Bull was about to make mention of this but J-Boy held up his hand with a 'don't ask' as if he was reading his mind. The band was one of New Orleans' finest downhome and dirty blues bands and the musicians themselves were well seasoned veterans. Juline's wizardry was made manifest in less than half a day.

The wedding was a singularly sobering affair, that was until the, "You may kiss the bride." Then like oncoming surf a low hum rose into a crescendo of cheers and applause. Now they had another real reason for celebration.

What little formality there was disappeared at the reception. Everyone was caught up in the moment, helped along with the music, the bar and the general congeniality that was extremely contagious. It was hard to tell where the reception left off and the Mardi Gras began. The Mallorys couldn't have wished for a finer celebration.

Towards the end of the afternoon the Bull and Juline took the newlyweds off to the side. Juline produced an envelope and passed it to the Mallorys. With a twinkle in her eye she explained "It took a little pull, but it's the Honeymoon Suite at Al Hirt's in the French Quarter. Apparently there's someone there of major importance but it's yours now." Tears welled in Victoria's eyes and all she could do is hug Juline. Mallory looked at the Bull who raised his eyebrows twice, both of them knowing who was of "major importance." Juline added "you can scat anytime you want. Just leave the wedding outfits. I use them from time to time." The newlyweds quickly complied, but when they tried to sneak out secretly, it was a total failure. They were pelted with rice from the time they left the front door. Awaiting them at the end of the walkway was Melvin the frontman turned Minister turned carriage driver atop a horse-drawn carriage that would take them to their destination. For the Mallorys it was a dream that really came true and one of the most memorable of their lives. And they both knew the best was yet to come.

For the people of 'major importance' it took some doing to escape the confines of the White House undetected. They took the secret passageway that previous politicals had used for their illicit affairs, the only problem being was that it wasn't wide enough for wheelchairs. Professor Potts made a go of it, but was eventually carried piggyback by Jack Brandt. At the end of the corridor they were met by a nondescript security vehicle with tinted windows; a limousine at this point would be too ostentatious. The loan car took them to Andrews Air Force Base where they boarded a small jet. Air Force One would have been a dead giveaway. By the time they reached New Orleans, out stepped Charlie Chaplin and Freddie the Freeloader and Professor Lezlie Potts who had morphed into Star Trek's Doctor Spock. Any resemblance to their previous identities had completely disappeared. They were whisked away by one of New Orleans' police cars, which was the only kind of vehicle that could make any headway through the traffic and crowds heading towards the French Quarter. At this point their timing had to be flawless. They had decided it best to get into the French Quarter during the opening parade, when most eyes were on the Floats and the beautiful women tossing goodies into the crowds. In this they were a complete success. Actually they might have been able to go as themselves and not be noticed, for there were quite a few 'President Brandts' in attendance already. Be that as it may, they made the correct decision because the last few blocks to their destination was closed to traffic; they were forced to go on foot. This was met with absolute delight to the usually surrounded President of the United States. Now they were just faces in the elbow-to-elbow crowds making their way to the beginning of this two week extravaganza. The only thing that saved them from being jostled towards the parade was Potts' wheelchair. Although inebriation was the order of the day, there was still a miniscule amount of common courtesy left for the trio to be allowed to go their way. After all, two clowns leading an aged Dr. Spock through the crowds was worthy of the attention. At their destination they were pleasantly surprised to be given just regular rooms instead of one that could draw any attention. The one that was previously reserved was now occupied by some newlyweds. So much the better. However, if they only would have inquired as to the identity of these newlyweds, all that was to follow might have been avoided.

The shooting star disappeared entirely, halfway across the night skies. As a matter of fact, to the lone observer, it disappeared directly overhead. He was what one might call a permanent fixture to Louis Armstrong Park. Most of his days were spent under a tree with a bottle as his companion, but on this particular afternoon he had managed to slip into Juline's festivity, only to wind up flat on his back in the Park staring up at the sky. Even though he was well on his way to oblivion, the star was peculiar enough to attract his attention. If that wasn't strange enough, what happened next he would attempt to explain for the rest of his days. A vibrating whirlwind seemed to descend into the trees behind him. Although it couldn't be seen, it did stir up the leaves on the ground. By the time the hallucination subsided he was as sober as he had been for as long as he could remember. Then, the air itself seemed to disappear and fold in on itself. A brilliant crack of dazzling bright light appeared, and through this crack, out-stepped two people dressed as aliens. After they were through, the crack of light disappeared as fast as it had come.

The observer, although in shock, was still loose enough to join in the fun. "Wow! That was something! 'Klaatu Barada Nictoe' guys! I'm called Dabo! Welcome to Earth. I'm here in peace." He held up one arm and spread his fingers in a 'V.' To Rawar and Oxomoxo, not knowing what any of this was about, returned the gesture. After a quick scan they deduced that this human was completely harmless and posed no threat whatsoever. The human repeated the gesture, turned and headed back to Juline's for another stiff one.

The Space Patrol was completely dumbfounded, no clue whatsoever. They knew their gift was somewhere in the vicinity, but the faint pulse had once again disappeared. But that wasn't the cause of their confusion. It was all the strangely attired humans wandering about aimlessly showing extremely extra outwardly friendliness. Never in their wildest dreams would they have been prepared for this. There were even some attempting to look like them? Some had even come up to them and said "nice costumes," whatever that meant. But the comment they had heard from that first exceedingly strange human they encountered, seemed to appease them. "Klaatu Barada Nictoe" made no sense whatsoever, but since it worked they kept repeating it every time they were approached. And what's more, none of them seemed surprised to see them. Even though this was extremely bizarre, they certainly weren't going to argue with it. They were free to roam this strange environment without complication. Locating those with the gift at this point seemed impossible. There was even a human walking around with the Budlites, and passing them out. When he got to them they happily accepted. The human said "two bucks." Not having any idea what this meant, they repeated "Klaatu Barada Nictoe" and the human seemed satisfied. The human repeated it back and moved on. Rawar and Oxomoxo looked at each other in total incomprehension, shrugged their shoulders in acceptance, then drank the Budlites. Maybe there was hope for this planet after all?

They had tracked their gift all the way across the United States, knowing they could retrieve it at any given moment. But curiosity had gotten the better of them. The violent ones they deduced, would go to any lengths to take it from the peaceful ones that currently had it in their possession; even to the point of taking the lives of their fellow human beings. The peaceful group was protecting it at the cost of risking their own lives. Why? It was definitely worthy of finding out. And now since these humans were so close to the next evolutionary step, it could quite possibly save their pet project from extinction. It was getting harder and harder for Rawar and Oxomoxo to keep out of the way and not step in. And after witnessing the past few days it was mutually agreed upon to go and find out for themselves; and possibly a direct confrontation could take place if, and only if, they could find the older one and take him away temporarily for some communication. That was not going to be very easy since everybody was pretending to be somebody else. Is this normal? How could they possibly imagine what their 'normal' was? This gathering they had fallen into was so different from anything they had encountered so far. That in itself was worth looking into. What they had seen up to this point gave them hope for the preservation of their rapidly decaying project. It was Crunch Time. The human Rawar had locked eyes with, might have some answers if they only could find him. At least it was going to be interesting doing so, especially since they were passing out Budlites for "Klaatu Barada Nictoe"; and all the players were gathering on this chessboard called the French Quarter.

    One of the things working in their favor was their ability to assimilate speech patterns. For Oxomoxo and Rawar the use of vocal cords wasn't necessary. Their telepathic-level communication allowed them to converse without words through thought transferral. Functioning together for so long was probably also a contributing factor. But even here on this planet, that particular talent was realized only by a precious few. Most everyone else was subjected to using their vocal cords. A peculiar habit of theirs was that the thoughts running through their minds and the words coming out of their mouths were more often than not contradictory. This didn't help them get any closer to that last crucial step or help in any way a form of communication. Curiouser and curiouser. Well, one thing was for sure is that they weren't going to get any answers here and now. Everyone seemed to be in total disarray, wandering about aimlessly with no sense of direction. And even stranger still, that seemed to be their priority. Then their bewilderment was compounded by the start of the Parade.

To big Stu McRobbie, the Chief of Police, the opening parade itself was having its own share of difficulties. First off, that prick General who was insisting he and his whole crew join the Police exhibition was being a complete nuisance. And he was ordering his people around like they were in the military. The next two weeks were hard enough without an asshole like this getting in their way. And what's worse is the General had enough clout to do it; his connections went all the way up. He had found out the hard way. There was no choice but to comply with their every wish. Then there was 'Conus, the God of Revelry', usually portrayed by Mayor Edwin Hudson's son Sparky. As was customary, Conus was to announce the beginning of the Parade, with his body painted head to toe in gold, then he was to blow a long thin horn; no easy feat in itself. Then he was to say something to the effect of "Let the parties begin". But somehow, this day Sparky had found his way to that Voodoo Witch Queen's home where she was having one of her weddings and got himself obliterated. If it wasn't for one of her 'concoctions', he'd probably be passed out cold already. There probably wasn't a legal substance in it, but at this point he wasn't going to ask any questions. Even so, they still had to help him up to the God of Revelry's pedestal to deliver his greetings atop the lead float.

Sparky himself was having no easy time of it. Once Juline spotted him at her party she cornered him and quickly deduced the situation. With the help of J-Boy and the Bull, they dragged him away from the open bar and threw him in the shower. After a cold dousing including ice cubes, Juline directed him to drink one of her 'teas' which appeared to have no immediate results whatsoever. She explained that it would take some time to counteract the volume of substances he had put into his system. Then she produced a packet that she stuffed into his pocket. She ordered Sparky to ingest this just before the start of the parade and it should do the trick. J-Boy escorted him to the staging area where he was painted gold and given his outfit. He was then more than less bodily carried to the Float and set upon his pedestal. The horn was thrust into his hand just as Juline's tea started taking effect. Unfortunately it wasn't enough: because instead of a clear note, the horn sounded like a bleating sheep. Mayor Hudson and Chief McRobbie could have strangled him right there on the spot. It was just then that Sparky remembered the packet Juline had given him. He asked for a glass of water claiming his lips were dry when in reality they were completely numb. He downed the contents of the packet and almost immediately felt a surge of energy coursing through his body. The bleating soon turned into clear notes as if someone else was blowing the horn. Hudson and McRobbie, not about to look a gift horse in the mouth, ordered the start of the Parade. Sparky/Conus almost lasted the whole tour. It wasn't until the last half block that he slumped over, out of gas. But the deed was done and Sparky had done a better job than expected. When the Float got back to the staging area he was completely gone. Juline and J-Boy came to the rescue and grabbed him before anyone could object, claiming they would nurse him back to health. He was taken back to Juline's and was force-fed another 'tea' that knocked him out completely for a whole day. By the time he came to, the aftereffects had evaporated and he felt almost normal, except for the fact that a whole day had disappeared. But by that time the household had its hands full.

When the Mardi Gras begins, it is an all out fun fest. Everyone is mutually dedicated to achieving altered states. Although every substance known to man is in play, the most widely used is alcohol. This is for two reasons. Firstly it's legal and secondly it's readily available. The bars fill up elbow to elbow and for those not interested in going inside there are street vendors and the bars have windows to the street to those wandering outside. An ingenious assortment of hip flasks are usually being shared by all. The order of the evening is to enjoy each other's company and go into the wee hours of the morning, get some rest if possible, then do the same thing the next day into the night for two straight weeks (?) or as long as one can handle it.

On the first night, everyone involved with the Missing Link was so caught up in the moment that it was temporarily forgotten. The Object itself was safely stashed at the Voodoo Witch Queens' home and nobody in their right mind, inebriated or not, would dare enter her sanctum without permission. The only near confrontation was when General Steve Cleveland was imperiously passing by in the Police Communication Center Vehicle. During the Parade, the Bull was standing at the curb on Basin Street when he passed by. Cleveland, who was not expecting to spot anyone, locked eyes with the Bull. If it wasn't for the Bull's phony Robert E. Lee beard, the General might have recognized him immediately. But the Bull, knowing Cleveland could do nothing about it, saluted him as he went by, catching his eye. Cleveland didn't put it together until it was too late. Infuriated, he watched the Bull melt into the crowd and disappear. The others in the police vehicle couldn't figure out why he became so hostile, muttering something about a 'fucking gorilla' amongst other choice colorful curse words. That was a close call, that is until as luck would have it…

The Reverend Chuck T. Mansin had been at it all day and was well past the state of coherency. He had been to so many bars he lost count. In most of them he had been bought drinks because his costume looked so much like who he really was. But the derogatory comments that went with them concerning the 'real' preacher got too much to take any longer. So halfway through the day he went to a novelty shop and purchased a rubber donkey's head. He chose this because the gap in the front was big enough to have a drink without having to take it off. He managed to meander all the way through the French Quarter until he wound up at one of the seedier joints called the Seven Seas adjacent to Jackson Square next to the Mississippi. In here he found obscurity and oblivion and he stayed there until his money ran out. He was now faced with the horrifying realization that he would have to go back and suck up to that old cunt until he could pilfer enough for his escape. At this point it didn't really matter because he was too far gone to give a shit. The only problem was he was all the way across town and he would have to subject himself to the masses to get there. On unsteady legs he began his trek. Much to his benefit he found he wasn't the only one in this condition; the streets were full of them. He bounced his way up Saint Phillip's Street, past Decatur, Chartres, and Bourbon. He was well on his way out. And it was on this corner that he ran head on into two clowns pushing a fucking wheelchair! He was about to formulate a meager apology when he locked eyes with 'Charlie Chaplin'. There was something about those eyes that stopped the words from leaving his mouth. When recognition set in, he had enough presence of mind to just heehaw like a donkey and pretend to be moving on. The 'clowns' were having a tough time of it negotiating the wheelchair through the masses, so they paid him no mind. As unlikely as it was, there was his old girlfriend, the fucking President, pushing her way through public unattended.

The shock of the confrontation had a sobering effect on the Reverend. His ever-ready opportunistic mind immediately kicked into gear. It was obvious that Beverly Brandt was not here in any official capacity, at least in the public eye, that is. Most likely she was involved in the same mess he was stuck in. But why was she so incognito? He decided to get a closer look. It wasn't that hard; they were making slow progress through the crowds with the wheelchair. And why the wheelchair? He crossed the street, got past them and made another pass. "Well I'll be goddamned" he said to himself. If it wasn't that weirdo scientist from Nellis disguised as Dr. Spock! That sealed it; this was information that was better than gold! This time when he passed them, he skirted around without being seen. It was time to follow. When he figured out their destination he turned around. It was time to sober up and consider his alternatives. He would peddle this information to the highest bidder, but not before he would get as much as he could. By the time he made it back to the Hyatt he was walking on air. When he reached the room, 'Violent' and Adolf were still out. On his bed was the Red Devil outfit. He decided he would wear it. It wasn't such a bad idea after all, he definitely fit the part.

Mr. Brown had no trouble playing The Invisible Man. His face required bandages anyway. He certainly wasn't in the mood to have fun, only to inflict harm. The hard part would be finding him. As fate would have it, while he went up one street the Confederates, Card Sharks, Pirates, and Southern Belles were going down another. He was having no luck whatsoever, which didn't do much to improve his mood. His only comfort was his concealed pistol with silencer; it was ready for action as was he. His hatred is what spurned him on, and it was the same hatred that alerted Rawar and Oxomoxo. His energy field was off the charts in negativity and the colors stuck out like a sore thumb. Although nothing would happen that night, they had his number. And he might lead them to who they were searching for, namely Tyrone 'Bull' Exley. Brown's negativity aura was so easy to spot they would have no trouble at all following him.

Brown quickly got sick of this futile search and all the happy people around him. Besides, his face hurt like hell. That, plus the fact that he was totally exhausted from the trip across the United States that had turned into a giant klusterfuk, he decided to turn in early. Tomorrow was another day; and with a little rest he would be more functional. While filtering his way through the crowds he crossed paths with Queen Elizabeth and Roy Rogers to whom he gave a slight nod and a thumbs up. Oh they recognized him all right, but ignored him anyway but not his signal. They looked so goddamed pathetic in their stupid outfits that he almost smiled. Then on top of it, he spotted that fucking hypocrite Preacher in the lobby of the hotel. He was walking with a sense of purpose. A follow up on that could prove to be useful, but not tonight. All he wanted to do is take his bandages off and fall into bed. It had been a long walk and a futile one at that. Exley was somewhere in this town and he would find him, kill him, and with a little luck inflict a little torture first. This time he actually did smile at just the thought of it. But the smile disappeared as quickly as it came because it hurt like fucking hell to do so.

'Undercover' Agents Bernard Fife and Persons might as well have had a pulsating neon sign stating 'cop' on themselves. They and their small force of FBI Agents were some of the only few that were not decorated in some form or another. Everyone avoided them like the plague. The only familiar face Fife saw that night was General Cleveland in the parade. The communications vehicle in which he was riding was lit up from the inside and it would have been real hard not to spot him. This made him think that maybe he and his Agents might require a little more subterfuge. So he decided they would all get costumes also. Heck, it might even be fun. He also chastised himself for not thinking of it in the first place. But then again he had been made fun of for so long that anything out of the ordinary was ammunition for his hecklers. And after all, this was the Mardi Gras. He was pondering what he should wear when he was jostled by a group of Confederates led by Robert E. Lee himself. Again he was so caught up with himself that he failed to notice the familiarity as they quickly marched by. But it did give him what he thought was a good idea. Being the patriot that he was here in the deep south, he decided to find uniforms of Union Blue. 'Save the Union' and all that. Sometimes Bernie amazed himself; what better way to show his patriotism than representing solidarity? Besides, the Civil War ended almost a hundred fifty years ago, didn't it? And surely there shouldn't be any grudges, (?) Plus, if he was lucky he would run into that Robert E. Lee again… If he only knew.

Juline's backyard the next morning was reminiscent of a Civil War battlefield. Bodies were strewn everywhere. Usually notorious for her privacy, this situation is reversed during Mardi Gras. There's really not much choice in the matter, curfew is non-existent and people rock until they drop, pick themselves up and do it again. People in the know call Juline's a sanctuary during this time. That plus the fact that her hangover concoctions are known to be the best around town. Nobody asks what's in them, they just know they work. Each morning Juline gets down to business and her home looks more like a depression era soup kitchen line. People also pay good money for them, if they have it, which sometimes they do. If not, it's a given they will pay when they have it, which is almost always the case because of the concoctions' miraculous capabilities. She sets up a cauldron the night before, lets the 'ingredaments', as she calls them, simmer all night long and distributes it on a first come first serve basis until it's gone. Even though the cauldron holds fifty gallons it is gone before noon, one ladle at a time. This morning however, she set some aside for her guests. They'd probably need it.

Her guests spent most of the morning licking their wounds. As first time Mardi Gras participants usually do. This is because they haven't yet learned to pace themselves for this two week marathon. The wedding reception had something to do with it also. The Bull was again first up, but even he went back to bed after taking his medicine. But not before a stranger caught his attention. He too was one of the first to arise and was claiming something about rushing air, dazzling light, and two aliens. Juline seemed to know him quite well and humored him. A glance at the Bull's attentiveness told her there might be something to do with this so she gave him a double ladle and asked him to come back later. When the rest of the fugitives learned of the Bull's repose, they did the same. That's when the rains came.

The rains turned out to be a week long deluge which only managed to hamper the festivities slightly. To some it was an improvement. Torrential horizontal sheets of water pounded down mercilessly while Revelers danced in the streets soaking wet. The only difference is things seemed to wrap up earlier, which gave everyone more time to recuperate for the next installment. For the fugitives it was a Godsend, because none of them realized how exhausted they really were. There hadn't been any time to think about it, so when the rain set in, so did they.

For the Bull, one could go as far as to say he went into hibernation, coming out only for meals and to check to see if any danger presented itself. Each time he found that all was well he grunted satisfactorily and went back into hibernation. No one questioned his actions because they felt the same way also. All except for the Old Coots, whose sailing was less strenuous. Besides, once they had made acquaintance with the Creole ladies, who in turn introduced them to their Relatives that were not in short supply and also fabulously beautiful, everyone had an escort. The fact that these ladies were related to Juline in some form or another didn't hurt either. The only other set of fugitives not in repose and rightfully so, were the newlyweds.

The first few days of their marriage was spent and room service bliss. When they arrived with Melvin as the driver, The old man went to the front desk with them and had a few words with the Concierge. After that they were given unlimited credit and the finest room in the house. Obviously the tentacles of Juline's empire spread everywhere. Once they reached the room, they didn't leave for days. They didn't have to; every amenity known to man and woman was brought to their room without asking. These included three sumptuous meals a day brought like clockwork, champagne on ice, and appetizers in between. At first they were baffled, but after a while they accepted it without question. Why not? It was fit for Royalty. This break however, gave them some time for reflection.

"Oh Connor," Victoria sighed complacently, "this has all been so surreal. What's going to happen when this is all over?"

Mallory smiled at his new bride. "Actually I'm looking forward to it. We can go back to spelunking the lava tube for starters. That is until you're too fat to fit in the cave."

He caught her off guard. Her only course of action was to pelt Mallory with the first thing available, pillows, until he pleaded for mercy. This wasn't before one busted open and the room was covered in feathers. The point of their conversation was lost, but not forgotten.

Halfway through the Mardi Gras, Cleveland was at his wit's end. He searched high and low for any sign of the fugitives. He turned up nothing. Was this some elaborate scheme on Exley's part to confound him even further? Yet he had seen him, or thought he did, on the very first night. At this point he wasn't even sure of that. On top of it, there had been no contact with President Brandt, and he was sure his cover was wearing mighty thin if not already blown. Shit, if Exley knew, why not Her? And then there was Violet and her lunatic henchmen; they had to be somewhere in the vicinity. It seemed all of them had dropped off the face of the planet, which wasn't such a bad idea, now that he thought of it. But he knew that was ridiculous even though it was appealing… And he had definitely worn out his welcome with Chief McRobbie and Mayor

Hudson. He couldn't blame them either; because of his lack of results. And the worst thing happened when he woke up in the middle of the night over nightmares about gorillas. He was sitting at a riverside cafe pondering this over chicory coffee and what the locals called 'beignets', a lightly deep fried powdered donut that he couldn't seem to get enough of. He didn't even know how to pronounce the damn things but they had been a comfort in this rain soaked week long fiasco. Totally disheartened, he was trying to decide his next move. He was just plain out of them. Then at his lowest ebb, it finally dawned on him. "If I can't beat 'em, I'll join 'em" he said to no one in particular, but it did catch the attention of a table full of pirates next to him. Even that was peculiar. He seemed to be running into them everywhere. He locked eyes with one of them who had real tattoos and a genuine pirate earring who merely smiled then went back to paying attention to his comrades. Shortly thereafter they abruptly got up and left. Cleveland was envious of the camaraderie of the easygoing group and he had noticed before that they had such a beautiful schooner docked off the banks of the Mississippi.

Back to his thoughts at hand, he decided to relieve his squad of their military uniforms, and get with the program. Hell, if everyone else is running around making asses of themselves, why not us? Hmmmm, maybe, just maybe, he might get a lucky break if he joined in on the fray. Too bad those pirates just left he thought. They would probably know where to get a decent costume. But unbeknownst to him, the Card Sharks had taken over trailing duty.

The only one apparently with any real desire to carry on with the program was Professor Lez Potts. But with each passing day it grew less and less, mainly because the President and her husband Jack were having so much fun and getting away with it. They were like two students ditching school. He realized he could start the ball rolling at any given moment, because earlier in the week he had spotted the Newlyweds during one of their few appearances in public, and they were directly on the floor above them. Besides, in all of his years he had certainly learned patience. And if the Mallorys were here, it was a good bet that so was the Bull and the Missing Link. Just before he started to become extremely up-tight over it all, the Sun broke through and brightened the spirits of everyone everywhere. What was a few more days he concluded. Actually, the only thing wearing thin on his nerves was the silly Spock outfit. But even Lezlie Potts was young once and the nature of this whole extravaganza was contagious.

With all this in mind he decided to give things a little… 'nudge'. So at the first opportune moment, which came shortly thereafter due to Jack Brandt's amorous behavior, he left his wheelchair and walked slowly to the elevator. Naturally it was going down when he wanted to go up, (courtesy of Murphy) so he had to wait. When it finally arrived it was empty. He ascended one floor and found the Honeymoon Suite occupied half of the whole floor; the other door was marked 'Private'. It didn't take a rocket scientist, even though he was one, to figure out its function. He tapped lightly on the Mallorys' door and said, "room service." He heard a female giggle behind the door, explaining that it would probably take a minute. When Victoria opened the door her jaw dropped. "I come in peace," announced Potts amicably. After the initial shock Victoria beckoned him inside.

"Connor, look who's here" said Victoria gleefully, which immediately made Potts feel comfortable for not intruding. Well, a little less, anyway.

"Great to see you Professor," exclaimed a surprised Mallory. "Is it time then?"

Potts explained the situation as he knew it, revealing who was with him and the Mallorys reciprocated. That was just before he was going to go into details he had a brite idea. "Professor, since your 'roommates' are on vacation, why don't we just bring you back to your room and take a little champagne with us? That way we'll only have to tell the story once. And have fun doing it. After all, it is our honeymoon."

Potts looked thoughtful for a moment then smiled, "I might get some flack for bringing you down unannounced, but considering the circumstances, I think it's a smart idea. Besides, what are they going to do? They're in a wonderful mood…" Potts made the universal gesture for bump and grind which was immediately understood by the Mallorys. They had been at it also.

After the introductions, President Brandt and Victoria were like two school girls at Prom Night. If one didn't know any better, they would have never guessed who they really were. Mallory's idea turned out to be a monumental shortcut. The champagne didn't hurt either. The lines of communication were established when they called the Bull via Globestar. His nonchalant response made them wonder if this had been the plan all along. Either/or, he would take the credit for it. Why not? It was working. Two bottles of champagne later, stories were swapped and friendship cemented between them all.

Potts was proud of his spur of the moment decision. It couldn't have gone off smoother even if planned. Everyone was so confident in their game plan that it was decided upon to wait until 'Fat Tuesday'; the last night of festivities to do the deed. Things were looking up, especially since all of the ordeals they'd thus far encountered. All the pieces were coming together, especially for a certain Preacher, who had been eavesdropping the whole time.

It was a very scary thought that the one with the most information at hand would turn out to be the Reverend Chuck T. Mansin. Instead of peddling it to the highest bidder, why not sell it to all of them? If he timed it right they could all dispose of each other, and he might just walk away with the Prize. This would require some fancy footwork on his part not to get caught in the process. Oh, but it was well worth it. Even if he didn't get the Missing Link itself, he would walk away the winner with hero status to boot. The Church of the Universal Brotherhood was now within reach, with him at the undisputed helm.

The Bull was also becoming fond of the little powdered donuts and Juline had the recipe for them, and downright everything else for that matter. And that wasn't all he was becoming fond of. This little lady was pushing buttons in places that hadn't been touched in a long time. Of all the times and places, why now? Furthermore, Julines straight forward approach let it be known that she had feelings of the same nature. At their age there was really no time to beat around the proverbial bush. If things weren't so heavily complicated, their relationship would have gone a step further a lot quicker. But they both understood that the matters at hand took precedence. This did not, however, stop their personalities from becoming an open book to read. By the end of the week-long rain it felt like they had already known each other for quite some time.

All the others had taken notice also. The Bull's usual no nonsense approach had softened, and Juline, usually the decision maker of her undercurrent empire, was actually considering someone else's opinion before issuing orders. And even though Connor and Victoria had just gotten hitched it was this pair that grabbed front-stage-center and rightfully so, for their extreme contrasts is what made them so complimentary.

On the afternoon of the second day, when Juline's concoction had begun the curing process, the Bull went to thank her again, plus ask about the person whom he had met that morning who presumably had seen the aliens. He had his guard up and expected to be the brunt of a few jokes, but he was amazed to find out she took it as seriously as he. It was then they started exchanging opinions and delving into each other's backgrounds. Much to their surprise they had a lot in common, even though they had taken completely different paths to reach their conclusions. From then on each afternoon was spent in conversation sharing ideas and relating stories from their past. Others would try to join in, but would soon find out that they were on a completely different level; both in communication and understanding.

"You know, I could get used to this," commented the Bull after inhaling a batch of her fresh beignets. He was sitting on her porch leaning back on two legs of his chair, his own legs stretched out over the balustrade. The first morning of Sunshine in a week made everything sparkle from the wetness from the many nights before. Everyone else was still asleep, and yet these two had been up for hours already. "It makes me wonder if there is ever an end to your bag of tricks," he added suspiciously.

"Get used to it mister, because it's the only way you are ever going to find out." It was a combination of a threat and promise; both equally appealing. She was clad in a simple cotton sundress that exposed her luxurious cream and coffee colored skin that had withstood the trials of time. And her glorious curves that until now had been well hidden made the sundress and in what was in it a work of art. "If you have any objections, you better scram while you can. My 'bag of tricks' can acquire any results I deem necessary." She had the knack for being well understood: and quickly.

The Bull stared at this ageless beauty for a full minute before replying, and with a straight face said "I'm sold."

They both erupted into laughter at the same time until they were interrupted by the Bull's phone. It was Mallory and the conversation that proceeded set their future, and the worlds, in motion.

When the conversation was over, the Bull announced, "That was the Newlyweds. They ran into some friends of mine. I'd like you to meet them. They are really nice people." His innocence was transparent especially to Juline.

"Really? You're not fooling me one bit Bull Exley. I'll read your mind if I have to…"

The Bull threw in the towel. Any cover he thought he might have had was blown. "Okay I give. I believe you have a right to know anyway. Let's go while everyone is still sleeping. I'll explain on the way." So he did.

And if it wasn't for the Reverend's desire to facilitate his greed, he might have spotted the Bull right there and then. But by the time the pair arrived, he was already down to his own particular path he had chosen. If this hasn't been the case, there would have been a completely different end to this tale.

The Space Patrol were completely taken by surprise. With all the seemingly pointless happenstance going on all around them, there was hardly a negative energy field in the whole bunch. The only other prolonged contact had been before, at Consortium gatherings and compared to those, this was not even close. And to make it sweeter they were basking in the realization that they propagated this one. But this was a week-long interaction. With the Inhabitants of what they called 'their baby'. And for some reason or another they were being treated like they were one of them; and that was as good as it gets.

Amidst all these people the two Aliens were as incognito as they needed to be. "I can't get over it. Just look at these people, they're almost all totally happy" cried out Rawar in the jostling crowd. They were both in the thick of it, chasing after beads and coins thrown by the ladies passing by. The ladies were being transported by the weirdest looking vehicles, thought Rawar.

"What? Oh yes, it's great." Things were just too loud for a prolonged response. Plus Oxomoxo was preoccupied with keeping an eye on Mr. Brown, whose negative energy field by this time had even gotten worse. "They're glad their rains stopped."

"So am I. Klaatu Barada Nikto" yelled Rawar. He was getting involved. Now I know what 'rain on your parade' means. Rawar took another long pull off his Budlite. He really was most definitely getting involved.

Oxomoxo was getting to the point of just plain ignoring his co-pilot. Brown was reaching a 'danger' level. He could see it, he could feel it. Brown's negative energy field was by this time sticking out like a sore thumb. "I'm glad I have my stunner" he yelled back but to no avail. Rawar was completely caught up in the action and he didn't want to 'rain on his parade' anyway.

When the Parade was over things calmed down, but not by much. It was however long enough to keep Brown from blowing his top. It could happen at any time and they both knew it. They just hoped to be around when he caught up with the older one that had their gift. It was obvious that Brown meant harm, and judging from his energy field, maybe even the taking of a life.

Not if they could help it.

Brown had been negative for the whole past week. Other than him, almost everyone else's energy fields' were in a much more positive aura. Although the Space Patrol had no idea what the reasoning was behind this, they certainly weren't going to argue the point. Not only had it been educational, but loads of fun at the same time. Their confidence in the

Human Race had taken a step in the right direction, and that in itself was moot. This had also contributed to the decisions regarding their new project. If they could hand-pick a select few to inhabit there, they could quite possibly do away with wars and whatnot, and the general negativity that went along with it. But that wasn't going to be easy and they weren't even close to getting there, yet. And after this week they had decided that this planet was well worth saving at all costs. The potential was limitless even if there were people like Mr. Brown. As before, their hopes for Planet Earth centered around the fugitives and quite possibly more, much more.

It was more like a truce than a meeting. And once again, the Reverend Chuck T. Mansin's hollow empire came crashing down once more because of it. He had first attempted to peddle his information to 'Violent', her deep pockets being the reasoning. But she in turn contacted both Cleveland and Brown before he could, thus eliminating the auction he had planned. She had seen through his flimsy front and decided to beat him to the punch before Mansin could get them bidding against each other. It really wasn't that hard because they thought alike. She didn't even hold it against him for giving it a try, yet. She also knew that to keep the upper hand on minds like these, she had to stoop lower and play dirtier; that, she was used to. But just to twist the knife, she didn't let on to Mansin until the meeting took place that they would work together instead of giving him the upper hand. He would give the information free and clear, if he wanted to live, that is...

On a ploy suggesting she had to get permission from the Trust, she bought time to contact Mr. Brown and General Cleveland. Mansin hadn't seen through her facade until it was too late and they were all sitting in the smoke filled room. Although they would have paid twice as much, the sum of a million dollars would be deposited in a separate account bearing Mansin's name. After this was verified, Mansin told them the whereabouts of the President and her husband who were with that strange professor from Nellis. As a bonus he included the Mallorys. Although they tried to squeeze him for more information there was none to give. Satisfied, they organized an around the clock surveillance to hopefully lead them to the Bull and the prize. Now that Mansin's usefulness was hanging by a thread, he was forced to take the initiative and take part in their activities. Even though he already had his cool million, he was in too deep to back out now. He was past the point of no return. There was nothing more to be gained with this alliance unless they walked away with the Missing Link, and then he would only be set up as their puppet in a new religious conglomerate with them holding the puppet strings. And the Reverend Chuck T. Mansin thought of himself as better than that. Besides, he was so thoroughly disgusted with these people by this time, any future alliance was out of the question. He had his money and was going to get the fuck out and live the rest of his days in obscurity on some south seas island with amenities only money could buy. But not until, he thought to himself smugly, he leveled the playing field.

"What's the method behind your madness this time?" Asked Captain Magic, eyeing the contents of the package he had just opened. When everyone had arrived, Exley gave each of them a package with instructions not to open them until told to do so. It was Monday afternoon, the day before Fat Tuesday and Exley had called for a meeting that included bringing said packages. When everyone had gathered he told them they could finally open these packages which satisfied their curiosity, only to be replaced by bewilderment. Each package contained identical gorilla suits. It was as if the French Quarter was to be inundated by an army of monkeys which was more than less the Bull's intent.

"It's mostly just to confuse our would-be pursuers." Exley went on to explain how he and J-Boy had gone to the studios to gather costumes. They weren't looking for them, but stumbled onto them by accident. When he added that he had told Cleveland to look for him in one of them, Exley's method of madness became crystal clear. "At first I thought it would be a good joke to play on our beloved General Cleveland; but after thinking about it, I figured what better way to confound the shit out of them." Exley stated it proudly as if he had planned the whole thing.

"Now let's get into character as they say." In a matter of minutes Juline's backyard turned into a gorilla convention with everyone hopping around doing their best imitation of their character. Between the "Oh oohs" and the "Ah ahhs", and pummeling each other, they fit the bill quite well.

After a little over an hour of 'monkey business' the Bull called everyone together. "Okay. Tonight's the night we have a little fun. With luck we might run into General Cleveland or anyone else that might be looking for us and lead them on a merry chase. There's enough of us to put them into a state of total confusion which is the desired effect because tomorrow, at the height of the celebration, we will return the Missing Link." The Bull's thoughts turned to the other-worldly pair he had crossed paths with, so he added, "Actually I'd love to return it to its rightful owners, but Professor Lezlie Potts will have to do." This brought quizzical looks from his listeners but he paid it no mind. To explain what he meant would only add more fuel to the fire and that fire was plenty hot enough already. And there was always the secret Disc. All things considered, he thought to himself, maybe the human race isn't quite ready for the gift that had been once been bestowed upon them. If only he could contact Rawar and Oxomoxo.

Cleveland's mind was a complete blank. After almost giving up on the notion of finding Exley in a gorilla outfit, his problem came back at him a hundred-fold, because it seemed to him that there were at least that many gorillas that had suddenly infested the streets of the French Quarter. And what was worse is that they all seemed to be taunting him. Naturally during the course of the festivities there had been a few to whom he had paid closer attention, but now there were so many of them that were giving him open stares and seemingly going out of their way to cross his path. Everywhere he turned there was another one. And if that wasn't enough, one or two of them seemed familiar. And there was absolutely nothing he could do about it. What could he do? Arrest them for impersonating a gorilla?

Fife wasn't having it much better. His brilliant idea of dressing in Union blue had backfired heavily; to the point of physical confrontation more than a few times. He had no idea how deep the sentiments still went, even a hundred and fifty years later, and he had paid the price dearly. He was covered from head to toe with bumps and bruises, had one black eye, and his troops were rife with deserters. But now they looked more like a band of battered and defeated Yankees, so they were treated more sparingly except for the boos and catcalls they had to endure day and night when out in public. The last straw came when they became surrounded in Jackson Square and forced into the Mississippi. Some of his troops simply swam away, while the rest huddled on the banks of the Big Muddy dripping wet and totally miserable. And now there were all these gorillas Cleveland warned him about. Agent Bernard Fife's delusions of grandeur were crumbling right before his horrified eyes.

Mr. Brown was the only one singularly focused, even if it was for no reason whatsoever. And this sudden influx of fucking monkeys seemed to have a profound effect on the competition. They were all situated within viewing distance; the Mallorys, the Brandts, and the Scientist. The General, he observed, was standing arms at his sides and mouth agape, amidst at least a half dozen of them gyrating and contorting as if it was some sort of personal joke. If it was, Cleveland was failing to see the humor. Then there was that stupid FBI Agent all dressed up in union blue of all things. What could possibly possess him to do something like that, he could not fathom. Whatever the reasoning, it certainly appeared to be working against them. And that, he concluded, was a big plus. Just when he was beginning to feel comfortable, here came that Preacher.

Once Mansin had made his decision with his pockets sufficiently lined, he decided to warn his old girlfriend and her allies of the impending doom. Earlier that afternoon, after reaching his conclusions, he shit-canned the ridiculous donkey's head, showered and shaved and laid out his last remaining evangelical outfit that he used to use for television performances. If he was going to be a turncoat, he was going to do so as the newly reformed Reverend Chuck T. Mansin going to the rescue of the President of the United States and maybe quite possibly remove some of the tarnish from his already blemished career. Whatever the outcome, he was going to be immaculate.

As he preened and brushed his snow white hair, he mentally conjured up an acceptance speech for being the hero of the day. After admiring himself for more than a few minutes and practicing profiles for the would-be cameras, he sat down for a few stiff belts of Southern Comfort and one of his few remaining Cuban cigars. Satisfied and well lit, he set out to make things right. But not before arousing the suspicions of 'Violent'.

There was no time to dress for the occasion and something about the Preacher didn't look good. She hadn't seen him this way since before the loony bin and the President's confession. On top of it she felt the need. As quickly as she could, she administered a light dose and set out to find the man in white. He wasn't that hard to follow dressed as he was; blinding white in a sea of colors. He was even being stopped for an occasional blessing which slowed his progress even further. It wasn't until then she determined that she should alert Mr. Brown.

But Brown had already spotted him. As did General Cleveland and Agent Fife. Brown would have taken him out right then and there if it wasn't for all the goddamn monkeys. The Preacher made it safely to the sanctuary of the President and there was nothing he could do about it. It didn't even matter to Brown anyway. Because the Preacher wasn't his primary target.

When Mallory opened the door, he was temporarily immobilized. It was an apparition from the past and the last thing he expected to see standing in the doorway. His initial shock alerted everyone else in the room and both were equally as surprised. Taking advantage of their temporary immobility, Mansin entered the room and shut the door behind him. Without wasting words he quickly explained their precarious situation. For the first time in a very long time the sincerity on his face left no room for doubt.

"You are all in danger. They are all outside and you should know by now what angle General Cleveland is really coming from and there's no telling what that Maniac Mr. Brown is capable of and there is this Violet..." Mansin spat that out in one breath.

"Save your breath Chuck, I'm all too aware of her." The President turned to the others, "It seems our timetable has been moved up for us. Connor, call General Exley and alert him of the situation. Jack, it looks like our vacation has been cut short. Pack it up." President Brandt was not one to beat around the bush. She addressed Victoria. "My dear, if you will look out for the Professor here, we will make immediate arrangements to leave safely. And you..." She looked Mansin directly in the eye, "Thank you, welcome back." Much to everyone's astonishment she reached up and planted a smooch on Mansin's cheek. Probably the most astonished was Mansin himself, disbelief clearly etched on his features. The President broke the spell. "Let's get this over with before anyone else gets hurt." She was being the President again. In ten minutes they were ready, when there was another knock on the door. They were greeted by a dozen gorillas and half more of Juline's 'nephews', the bulges in their coats testifying they were ready for anything. It was agreed upon that Mallory and the Preacher would hook up with the Bull and make arrangements for the transfer later that night. Juline's 'nephews' would stay with the President, her husband Jack, Victoria and Professor Potts. This way the Bull could keep watch on the Preacher and not worry about the womenfolk. With a little luck and lots of spontaneity, they were ready to roll.

Since anything goes during the Mardi Gras, nothing is out of the ordinary. Not even this: During the two weeks of the event, traffic is not permitted in the French Quarter. Subsequently the streets are packed with revellers. So, moving in any direction can be tricky. As the contingent of gorillas blazed a trail down Phillips Street, Cleveland and his military escort followed down one side and Fife and his soggy Union troops up the other. Brown and his mercenaries skipped another block and took St

Louis Street as to approach from the opposite side of Louis Armstrong Park. Violet had spotted him and followed, which made their negative energy fields easy to follow by the Space Patrol.

The Bull and J-Boy we're working on a route to take the next night when they received Mallory's call. J-Boy's knowledge of the inner workings of the French Quarter, the back alleys, and outlying Creole district proved to be irreplaceable. They could actually get from point A to point B without taking public byways and having to deal with the jostling crowds that by Fat Tuesday would have reached a frenzy. And considering the magnitude of the operation, it was a Godsend.

But Mallory's call changed all that. The Bull's niece and new nephew in law, the President, her husband, and Professor Potts were in danger because of his actions. Or so he thought. There was no time however for self-recrimination. The situation at hand saw to that. And the Bull wasn't the type to sit around and ponder, especially when the stakes were so high.

At that moment Juline came in and was appraised of the situation. One look at the concern on the Bull's face and she leapt into action. Seemingly out of nowhere, her little private army materialized, some out of panels in the wall and even more surprisingly out of the foliage that went around the perimeter of her estate. All were well equipped.

The Bull gave her a brief smile. "You don't fool around, do you? Have they been here the whole time?" Juline's answer came in a single nod and a smile. "J-boy, you and the Old Coots, the Raiders and Rangers get our friends. I'll tie things up around here. It looks like our little 'soiree' is going to be a day early."

By the time they got back to the Bouganvilla everything was almost ready. Brown and his mercenaries were hidden in the bush on the other side of the Park and Cleveland with his military squad on the other. Fife managed to get into another scuffle due to their blue uniforms, and the Space Patrol stayed back to observe what was going to happen next.

The Bull came up the dirt road to meet them dressed in his gorilla outfit. Not knowing what to expect, he at least wanted to keep his promise to General Cleveland. As they approached, the Bull scanned the area but the Preachers' white suit distracted him from doing a thorough job. The gorillas had been toying with Mallory, not saying a word just to keep him on his toes guessing as to who was who. His confused expression was quite clear on his face. It was then that the Bull decided to relieve his confusion, so he removed his gorilla head to greet him.

It was a big mistake.

All the attention was on the Bull. He slapped Mallory on the back and approached the Preacher to thank him and compliment him on his good deed.

General Cleveland, Mr. Brown and Fife all saw Exley at the same time. Fife was still dealing with the locals, and Cleveland, still with divided loyalties, was unsure of what to do next.

But not Mr. Brown. All his frustration, anger and unquenchable desire for vengeance drove him into action. He came out of the bush, weapon firing at full automatic.

Cleveland had caught Mr. Brown out of the corner of his eye and he yelled "Exley! Look out!" But it was too late.

Exley had just reached Reverend Mansin and was about to express his thanks, when Mansen's snowy white suit quickly became a blood splattered mess. So thick was the gunfire that Mansin didn't even have time to drop. It was like he was being shook like a rag doll with each increasing bloody bullet hole. It is also what saved the Bull's life, but not before going down with a line of bullet holes across his chest. Then the whole Park erupted in gunfire.

The mercenaries were well hidden and didn't make good targets. Cleveland's squad, however, did. Juline's 'nephews', not knowing who the guilty party was, started firing at Cleveland. Cleveland in turn was trying to ferret out the mercenaries and defend himself at the same time. All was chaos.

Juline came running up the road and it didn't take but a split second to ascertain that they were in deep shit. "Get to the house! J! Get my medical bag!" she yelled to her compatriots. She checked the Reverend's neck for a pulse. Nothing. Exley however, being the old warhorse that he was, was still breathing, but just barely. "J! Quickly!" she pleaded.

J-Boy ran at full speed back to the house with gunfire giong at full-tilt behind him. It took a little over a minute to find Juline's Medical Supplies and he bolted out the door to deliver the bag. What had before sounded like a full scale battle, had instantly turned into Cemetery quiet. J-Boy was stunned, but not enough to approach the Park carelessly. When he arrived he dropped the medical bag in shock. Strewn all over were bodies stationary as if dead. It was as if they had all been killed at once; until they all started moving. It was like they were coming-to after being knocked out. The fight was out of them. But that wasn't what he was shocked about. The Reverend Mansin lay dead in a pool of blood, his once immaculate white suit stained crimson. But most of all, his auntie Juline and General Tyrone 'Bull' Exley were not where they were supposed to be. They both had disappeared.

CHAPTER 20

THE FRENCH QUARTER

A full scale manhunt the next day turned up nothing. Mayor Hudson and Police Chief McRobbie used all the means at their disposal to no avail. Hospitals, Clinics and Doctor's offices were all scrutinized for the missing pair. Once word spread that Juline was missing, the New Orleans underworld made a valiant but futile attempt to find them. For a lady of Juline's social status they even worked together.

Nothing.

Those who had taken part in the park battle weren't any help either. To a man, all they could remember is exchanging gunfire one moment, then picking themselves off the ground the next. They all had no memory whatsoever of what had occurred. Brown had managed to slither away with Violet covering for him during the confusion of everyone's waking moments. Violet had arrived just in time to see everyone coming around from apparent unconsciousness. She grabbed Brown who had been wounded in the arm and motioned to the mercenaries to follow her during the confusion. They left one dead. Cleveland, trying to salvage what dignity he had left, picked himself up after coming-to and began organizing a search party and Fife joined him in a feeble attempt to save face. This also deflected any blame they might have incurred. They were, after all, representatives of the US Government. Throughout the day the mood changed from despondent to worry, fear, rage, frustration and back to despondency again. The once energetic search turned lethargic then sorrow as abject misery set in. A giant void remained unfilled as the magnitude of the loss became grim realization. By the late afternoon no one moved and Juline's backyard turned into what seemed to be a graveyard.

Captain Magic finally broke the spell. "Well, standing around here doesn't help; I'm sure they would have wanted us to complete the task we set out to accomplish. Otherwise, their disappearance would be for naught." The response was less than enthusiastic. There were a few nods of agreement, but no action was taken. Everyone was so used to the Bull's customary disposition in the face of adversity and Julines stoic yet motherly disposition and invulnerability, that the fuel of fire for action seemed almost completely doused. "Besides, if they were somehow here, what would they think of this reaction?" Captain Magic's statement caused a slight spark of response, so he pressed on a little further by raising his voice to almost a yell. "They would kick our asses into gear! That's what!!!"

Mallory joined in by interjecting "Could you imagine what they would do if they caught us moping around like this?"

Then Townsend added "It wouldn't be pretty, that's for sure." The comment actually brought on a few chuckles from the group.

Then Woody, who had been on the sidelines most of the time, added "I've seen this first hand a number of times." He then proceeded to relate some of their misadventures during his military career and slowly but surely they began to come out of their lethargy. He ended by telling the story about the party aboard the Yorktown, then displayed his Party Armband, which did the trick. Although the laughter was strained, it was still laughter after all.

Then it was Doctor Bloomfield's turn to speak up. He stood up and cleared his throat for effect. "Listen, we've come a long way, some more than others, to accomplish what we set out to do. The main thing is we're all in this together. Granted, we're all used to following the Bull's lead, but since now that he's not around, we should utilize this sorrow to strengthen our resolve. Both he and Juline wouldn't have it any other way. It was a pep talk and it was working. "What I think we should do here, is figure out what he would probably do to deliver the Missing Link. I for one believe he would attempt to throw confusion into our pursuers while having a good time doing it. And since we have only one night to go before it's all over, let's make them proud."

Bloomfield's speech broke the ice of an otherwise dismal afternoon. J-Boy produced the map they had been working on which was the basis for their tentative game plan. Mallory took it upon himself to notify his wife and the President, who by this time had struck up a schoolgirl type of relationship. The transfer would occur directly after the parade, when chaos reigns supreme. Getting the Missing Link to its destination would require a number of diversions, as to avoid a repeat performance like the night before. And in that department there were still plenty enough devil-may-care minds to take care of that. Soon ideas were flying back and forth and everyone became involved in the project that lay ahead. By the time it was over, everybody generally agreed that it was as close to an Exley-plan as they could get. Satisfied, the meeting broke up to suit up for the night's festivities.

The plan turned out to be a real piece of work. Juline's 'nephews' would now occupy gorilla suits, the only difference is that they would be fully armed to the teeth. The Raiders and the Rangers would revert back to their Hannibal Hamlin outfits; an assortment of Confederate Soldiers, and the Riverboat Gamblers. The Old Coots would be Pirates of course, since they fit the bill anyway. And the ladies would become the greatest diversion of all, naturally. Their numbers, reinforced by Juline's Creole 'nieces', made a formidable group of females indeed. They would all get decked out in the most alluring, attention grabbing and sexy outfits their modesty or lack thereof, would allow. And when it came down to that, the competition was on. They all agreed that if they were going to do it, they were committed to bring the entire French Quarter to its knees. And on Fat Tuesday, that was quite an undertaking. With reckless abandon they attacked their project wholeheartedly. The results would speak for themselves.

The Missing Link itself would be going with Mallory, Dr. Bloomfield, and J-boy who would be leading the way through the maze of the back alleys in the Creole District. Without J-boy's knowledge, the transfer wouldn't even have been feasible, or might not have been possible at all. Edwin 'Sparky' Hudson, who had by this time made a full recovery, made his contribution by absconding with three sets of full fledged Police Uniforms for them.

When the parade began and all was ready, Townsend and Melvin came into the backyard with stacks of suitcases, all similar to the one carrying the Missing Link. It was icing on the cake. After a unanimous applause, the pair took a bow. After all was said and done, so deep was their commitment that confidence reigned supreme.

Mallory made the call to the President. They were on their way.

Fat Tuesday is the culmination of a party endurance marathon that has lasted for two weeks. Only the strong and/or the oblivious survive, or the ones with the most stamina and those with enough common sense to pace themselves. Then of course there are those that resemble the walking dead or are just plain too fucked up to know when to stop. It is a celebration within a celebration for those who have made it thus far, coherent or not. This combination of gluttons for punishment and party animals is what set the stage for what was to come. It would be the coup de gras of the Mardi Gras, in more ways than one.

The general idea of the plan was diversionary tactics. And who but the gorgeous ladies could do a better job than them? Any normal red-blooded American male would be stopped in their tracks just by the mere sight of them. And that was exactly how they wanted it to be. As planned, they timed their entrance just as the last float in the parade was passing by, as to appear to be an extra addition to the final parade. It worked beautifully. As luck would have it, with a little help from Mayor Hudson and Chief McRobbie, General Cleveland and his military squad brought up the rear. Not only were all the eyes on the ladies, but they could also practice their feminine wiles on Cleveland and his group once the parade was over. Perfect. This would allow the Pirates, Confederates,

Card Sharks, and Gorillas to infiltrate the crowds relatively unnoticed. While the ladies were flirting gregariously with anyone and everyone, the Rebels were to seek out Agent Fife and his Union troops for yet another skirmish. The Card Sharks and Pirates would keep an eye on the ladies from a distance, just in case their flirtations were taken seriously. It didn't hurt that they all had invested personal interests either. The Gorillas were just plain out for blood, in the form of Mr. Brown and his mercenaries, because it was he they held responsible for Juline and the Bull's disappearance. Everyone had their set goals and if everything went according to plan, the exchange would take place without a hitch…

Fat chance on Fat Tuesday.

Mallory was more than a little spooked. Not only did he hold in his hands the possible fate of the world, but he and Doc Bloomfield were being led by J-Boy into a labyrinth of back alleys in the Creole District. Not only that, they were in Police get-ups. If anyone was just to say 'boo', he probably would have jumped out of his skin.

When the rest of their comrades set out for the center of town, J-Boy led them to the rear of Juline's backyard. There, behind a wall of vines was a well hidden door that appeared not to have been used for quite some time. As J-Boy produced a very old skeleton key he explained "This tunnel has been used a number of times to save quite a few lives, from the War of 1812, through the Civil War and on. We 'move things' through here still." He winked as he opened the door and surprisingly it opened easily without a sound as one might not expect from such a door as ancient as this. Inside were stairs leading downward. A kerosene lamp hung by a hook on the wall. The walls, Mallory noted, we're etched out of ancient stone and fit together amazingly well. J-Boy lit the lamp and motioned them inside. The tunnel appeared to go on forever. As if reading Mallory's mind, J-Boy explained: "This goes all the way to the Mississippi, but we're not going that far."

It was then that Mallory noticed J-Boys' speech. "What happened to your southern accent?" he queried.

"It goes away when I'm scared."

"Oh great, that's comforting." Mallory looked back at Bloomfield who merely shrugged his shoulders. Bloomfield was taking this better than the both of them he thought. Wonders never cease.

Another fifteen minutes later they came to a ladder. J-Boy motioned them upward with his forefinger to his lips for quiet. At the top was a trap door. Mallory carefully lifted it and when it was open he was looking down the twin barrels of a sawed-off shotgun, with the biggest ebony black man he had ever seen in his entire life, on the other end. Mallory gasped and almost fainted right then and there. "Gaylord, it's me, J-Boy Cripsin." He yelled from behind. The menacing look that accompanied this ebony behemoth immediately evaporated and was replaced by a mouthful of extra white smiling teeth. Mallory made a mental note to see if his undies were soiled, as he was lifted out of the tunnel by one hand of Gaylord's. Bloomfield followed, then J-Boy.

They were in a small courtyard with high walls that had torches burning on each corner. The air was thick with the scent of flowers and incense. Candles were spread out intermittently and crystals hung everywhere. Out from the doorway that was only shielded by long lines of beaded crystals stepped probably the most striking woman Mallory had ever seen. Dressed in various layers of see-through silks of different colors, the proportions of her lithe frame could be easily seen. They were stunning. Her lineage was indiscernible; the combination however was goddess material. With auburn red-brown curly hair and cream colored skin, it was easy to see she was part of some kind of combination, but her sky blue eyes and straight nose betrayed Caucasian and possibly American Indian ancestry included. In reality she was all the above and more. Her Asian lineage only appeared in her petite perfect body. And like Juline, she was ageless.

"Gentlemen, let me introduce Deena Jackson, direct descendant of the hero of 1812" announced J-Boy, somewhat amused. He had witnessed this reaction a number of times.

When she smiled Mallory felt his knees weaken, as did Dr. Harold Bloomfields'. They were both incapable of speech. Deena approached them and allowed them to kiss her hand, which they did so robotically and then she turned to J-Boy. "Any news about my cousin?" That it was Juline they were speaking of was obvious. J-Boy answered negatively and Deena nodded. "She's here somewhere, I can feel it." At this, J-Boy brightened. It was a given that she was a palm reader/fortune teller. "As well as her new beau." Before they could respond, the seer handed them three red armbands, curtsied and without another word retreated. It took Mallory a full minute to recover and when he did, he found his mouth still hanging open. Bloomfield didn't look much different.

"These will get us through town" explained J-Boy motioning to the armbands. "Without them..." He let the comment hang, the meaning obvious.

As they were led down one-lane paths and in between hedges, Mallory could feel rather than see many sets of eyes following their route. The roads looked more like back alleys and were wide enough for horse and carriage, but certainly not cars. There was no doubt in Mallory's and Bloomfield's minds that they were in the oldest part of the city in one of the oldest cities on the Continent. What unnerved them the most was the heavenly smells that assaulted their nostrils; from crawdads to chitlins to corn pone to southern fried chicken and boiled cabbage and every other downe-home recipe for that matter, filled the air. Even though they were on one of the scariest missions of their lives, they still found that they were salivating. Eerie or not, they would have gladly stopped for dinner.

When they finally reached the outskirts of the French Quarter, they were pleasantly surprised to find they had circumvented the busiest part of town and the chaos taking place there. The first sign of a paved road was at the far end of North Peters Street, where nobody in their right mind would dare to go without an invitation. If someone would have been traveling their way from the other direction, they would have turned around a few blocks earlier.

Finally a street light! And under it waited a couple of gorillas. Both Mallory and the good doctor breathed a sigh of relief. J-Boy just chuckled. This was not a new reaction. "Ah hope y'all enjoyed the toah" just to rub it in a little. Mallory was comforted by the fact that J-Boy's accent was back. He figured they might be out of danger.

Not!

Before the trio even reached them, the gorillas went down in a hail of muted gunfire. None of them could tell from which direction it had come. Of the few people out on the edge of town, the only ones anywhere near was an old lady dressed as Queen Elizabeth, her sidekick that looked totally out of place in a cowboy outfit and someone going as the Invisible Man. Surely it couldn't be them. But their opinions were shattered when the strange trio lifted Firearms with silencers and were pointed directly at them. J-Boy yanked them out of the light from a street lamp and back towards where they had come and the safety of the shadows. Before they had gone even a few steps, Gaylord stepped out of the darkness, shotgun in hand. Without a word they started trotting back towards Madame Deena's, J-Boy and Gaylord guarding the rear. When they reached the courtyard Deena was there to greet them, appearing to already know what had just happened. "I felt their presence and sent Gaylord to fetch you." She motioned to the trap door leading into the tunnel. "You go now. They will not follow."

J-Boy appraised Mallory and Doc Bloomfield. They were shaken but relatively in one piece. There was no time for hesitation; for they were on a time schedule and now they were running late. J-boy quickly explained: "Plan B. We go to the end and approach Jackson Square from the river side. It's closer anyway." Without waiting for an answer he slipped down the ladder and motioned them below. Clearly out of options, they complied.

It was solely by sheer luck that Mr. Brown, Violet and Adolf ran into the trio with the Missing Link. After the incident at Louis Armstrong Park, Brown's suspicions about anyone in a gorilla suit had reached its peak. Even though he was convinced he had hit Exley, there was still no proof. And at that time there had been so many other fucking gorillas around him there just had to be some form of connection. Then he was strafed in the arm and right after that everything went blank. The next thing he knew he was being dragged away by Adolf with a little help from her highness. The wound turned out to be just a puncture. The bullet had gone through the outer edge of his arm and he would be sore, but not enough to put him out of commission. When he had time to take inventory on what had transpired, he found that at one point there was a complete blank spot, where there was absolutely nothing he could remember. At all. Sure that was curious all right, but not enough to douse the fire of vengeance. And he was convinced that the gorillas were the key. So he decided to follow the two that had slipped away and that was when he recognized Mallory and Bloomfield stepping out of the shadows to meet them. And they had a suitcase. They still managed to slip away and nobody in their right mind would go in there after them. At least he knew that the Missing Link was on the move, Mallory and Bloomfield were dressed as cops and the gorillas still had something to do with this mess. He felt confident with this assessment until they ran into all the others carrying suitcases.

General Cleveland didn't know what to think. Before everything had gone blank he was sure he saw Exley go down with that preacher, but when he came-to only the Preacher was left sprawled on the ground. And somehow that asshole Brown had managed to slip away. Exley had disappeared and on top of that, now he and his squad were surrounded by beautiful women that seemed to be taking interest in only them. It smelled like Exley pure and simple. Then out of the corner of his eye he spotted Souza and Townsend dressed as pirates enjoying the show. And on top of that, they were standing with a bunch of goddamn gorillas carrying suitcases. By this time Cleveland had had so much of enough that he didn't even hesitate. He elbowed his way through the crowd of exquisite ladies and marched directly up to the Rangers. Before he could say a word Townsend and Souza stepped forward to meet him.

"Hiya General! Fancy meeting you here" exclaimed Souza as congenially as possible.

Cleveland looked behind them and he knew he was had. The bulges inside the gorilla's fur also confirmed that. There was no way he was going to become part of an incident like the night before. To save any face he might have had left, he imperiously demanded "On behalf of the

United States Government I demand to know what's going on here!" It was a meager attempt at best, but he had come a long way and it was clear he was running out of steam.

"Funny you should mention that, sir. As a matter of fact we are returning the Object to Professor Potts and your boss as we speak."

"My boss? What boss?"

"The First Lady sir. She is with him."

Cleveland paled considerably. Although this was one shock of many, it was the one he needed. Even though his sordid career had a tainted past at one time, he immediately realized where his true loyalties lie. Without hesitation he explained: "Listen, I don't particularly care what you think of me, but they are in extreme danger. I know what their pursuers look like and can point them out to you. Between us we might be able to prevent a disaster of major proportions. We have to protect them, now!" The pleading in Cleveland's voice left no doubt in the Rangers' minds he was speaking the truth.

Townsend and Souza looked at each other in unspoken communication, (not unlike Oxomoxo and Rawar actually), then back at Cleveland. The consequences were unspeakable. Townsend spoke first this time. "The exchange is taking place at Jackson Square, five blocks away. Let's move."

The ragtag army of Pirates, Gorillas and military personnel set a brisk pace through the crowds enjoying Fat Tuesday. More than a few were roughly pushed aside, but as they gathered momentum, the crowds began to part. They were on a mission to save the President of the United States and their close friends. Absolutely nothing was going to stop them now.

Fife surrendered on Bourbon Street. He'd had enough. As he and his depleted squad were surrounded by gorillas, Confederate soldiers and jeering crowds he saw the futility of his actions. Even when he produced his identification, it didn't do any good. It seemed that they already had his number. As they were being marched towards Jackson Square, their captors, sensing an emergency, immediately forgot about the situation at hand, leaving Fife standing there, forgotten. This was the last straw for Agent Bernard Fife. The roller coaster ride of the last few weeks of his career had taken its toll, and he wasn't about to give up now. He was going to see it through to the end. Left with no other choice, he took up pursuit.

Jackson Square itself takes up a full city block and has four entrances leading into a central courtyard. President Brandt arrived via St Philips Street from the French Quarter simultaneously with Mallory, J-Boy and Bloomfield coming from the opposite direction from the Mississippi. Violet, Mr. Brown and his mercenaries arrived immediately thereafter via Decatur Street only to be facing the ragtag army on the other side. Stand off? Oh yeah, four way kind. And nobody moved; to do so might cause a calamity beyond description.

The tension was so thick one could cut it with a knife. Everyone stood firmly immobilized as if their feet were glued to the ground. No one wanted to make the first move because to do so would cause a chain reaction beyond repair. Then, a most peculiar thing began to occur…

It was as if a tornado chose to touch down on the very spot they were standing. A circular wind enveloped all of Jackson Square and seemed to be emanating from the central courtyard. Most peculiar of all is that it appeared to be stationary and was not traveling in any direction except downward. There was a vibratory hum that could be felt instead of heard accompanying it. As if the sensation wasn't strange enough, the 'hum' emanated a numbing effect on the motor skills of those observing it. The winds subsided but the hum stayed constant. All those within range were effectively paralyzed, but their minds were clear.

Then, at what best could be described as an electrical power surge, a blinding white light in the shape of a doorway appeared. Space itself seemed to fold in as the hallucinatory door opened. All the observers received the shock of their lives.

Out stepped Rawar, Oxomoxo, Juline and Brigadier General Tyrone 'Bull' Exley not so Retired. What was even stranger still is that the Bull was unharmed even though there was a line of bullet holes across the chest of the gorilla get-up he was still wearing, and the most astonishing of all is that both he and Juline looked close to a half-century younger, as if like they were in the prime of their lives. This was totally beyond the realm of comprehension.

The Bull stepped forward, scanned the courtyard and appraised the situation. Even though no one could move, the look in everyone's eyes betrayed their astonishment. As if it were a walk in the park, the Bull strolled over to Mallory and Bloomfield and retrieved the suitcase. "My new friends want their 'Toy' back." He then walked over to where Potts was sitting and explained apologetically "Sorry Lez, we must return this to its rightful owners." He added a wink, not mentioning the disc. He nodded cheerfully to his friends and General Cleveland, then completely ignored Violet and Mr. Brown as if they didn't exist. Then with a voice that bespoke youth and vitality he addressed them all:

"Listen up. My new friends here have a message for you all." Then he walked over to the Space Patrol and presented the Missing Link back into their custody, and stood aside.

For less than a moment that seemed more like an eternity, Rawar and Oxomoxo looked them over. Here, in front of them was a microcosm of humanity, from base negativity to evolutional productivity, the range of energy fields were there. Then, by way of thought transferral instead of auditory speech, they addressed them all.

"To the inhabitants of this Planet, we bring you greetings from far beyond your imagination. You have been given the capability of being mutually beneficial to your kind. You still have this potential, yet not all of you choose to use it. Instead, you are ruining your Home, your Planet. Yet still you do nothing about it. Your limited understanding of harmony and equality keep you from reaching your potential. You, as we, are all related in this quest for evolution. Your unequivocal lusts for power over your fellow human beings is what limits you. You are all children of creation and you are far from alone. We gave you a gift that you are not yet capable of grasping, nor will you be; until you settle your petty differences. So now we must take it back lest you destroy yourselves in the process. Utilize this knowledge and we might return it to you. For you to even have the consciousness of this, is the greatest gift of creation. You must nurture and use it for the betterment of your fellow human beings. This crucial realization is left up to you. Do something about it!"

Whether it was a pep talk or an ass-chewing depends on one's point of view. Either/or, the telepathic communication reached into their inner being and was impossible to ignore. To punctuate the matter, Oxomoxo opened the suitcase and pulled out the Missing Link, pressed his finger on the pulsating light and twisted it, simultaneously saying: "We leave you with a parting gift."

The results were catastrophic for some and enlightening for others. The increased magnetic energy brought about results ranging from either self realization to ego death, depending on one's inner psyche. It produced a mental mirror image to one's inner soul, thus making or breaking their own personal makeup. It lasted only a few seconds, but altered their lives forever.

With that, Oxomoxo and Rawar stepped back into their doorway of light and the process was reversed. The winds increased and the hum decreased and then they were gone. Just like that.

As everyone's motor skills returned, the results were varied. From sheer ecstasy to abject misery and everywhere in between, they were all affected in one way or another, the results obvious.

In time, those capable of movement surrounded the Bull and Juline and smothered them with affection. Then came the questions, way too many to answer at once. The Bull raised his hands to gather everyone's attention. "In due time all your questions will be answered. Meanwhile, we have something to discuss with our new friends. The Bull looked up at the sky, "That I for one, and Juline, are going to take them up on, a chance to build a world as we see it to our liking. Obviously…" The Bull gestured to himself and Juline, "They have a lot of tricks up their sleeve to help us along our way." Then, with a twinkle in his eye, he made them an offer they wouldn't refuse.

EPILOGUE

Dr. Harold Bloomfield leaned back in his chair in his office atop Haleakala Crater and stared at the picture of himself and the Rangers with the Old Coots and tourists that had been taken at the beginning of this adventure. It seemed as if it had been taken a lifetime ago. In his hand was the latest edition of the Honolulu Advertiser. The headlines were in bold print and stated '!!!PRESIDENT VANISHES!!!' But that wasn't the news that amused him the most. At the bottom corner of the page was a small article titled 'Triangle takes one of Hawaii's Own'. The story goes on to tell the schooner Flying Cloud, owned by Maui's Randy Von Tempsky was found floating in the Bermuda Triangle empty of all personnel. Two days Later, the Schooner itself disappeared to add even more unanswerable questions to this mystery. Also reported missing with him are US Forestry Rangers Richard Townsend and Raymond Souza amongst others reported to have been seen leaving New Orleans for what looked like a party cruise. The schooner was reported to have been completely full of equal amounts of men and women, some from New Orleans itself. Lady Juline Jackson and many of her relatives were also reportedly on board. Their disappearance still remains a mystery.

"Well Bull, you've really done it this time." He said to himself. "And I'm going to miss you all, very much," he added. He was talking to no one in particular. As a matter of fact, his staff had been avoiding him ever since he returned. The fact that he looked thirty years younger probably had something to do with it.

It was now a week since Fat Tuesday and so much had happened. General Steve Cleveland and Agent Bernard Fife had quietly retired due to 'stress' from their assignments. The fate of Mr. Brown and Violet was unknown, but judging from their reaction at Jackson Square, they were most likely locked away in some type of loony bin for good. They had been transformed to what can best be described as Jello, their minds completely shot. The Reverend Charles T. Mansin was laid to rest in Louisiana. No one claimed his body. And then there were his friends.

After the Bull made the Space Patrol's offer clearer, almost everyone volunteered to go. They were actually going to be transported to the other side of the known galaxy to start a Planet of their own. A Garden of Eden with a whole bunch of Adams and Eves. And judging from the gorgeous ladies that were going, there would be a population explosion and pretty damned quick. Victoria's however, would be the first born in a Utopia that would certainly be of the finest quality. Plus they would have the Missing Link, along with some other 'surprises' that the Space Patrol was going to furnish. Only Bloomfield and Lezlie Potts declined to go, primarily because they both possessed the Discs' that could possibly save Planet Earth.

And then there was the Space Patrol. They appeared one more time at Juline's to appraise the candidates. Every one of them met their approval. The Bull admitted the existence of the Discs, and they allowed Bloomfield and Potts to keep them, knowing the Earth's metals could only take them so far. They actually seemed pleased.

And the Bull had one more trick up his sleeve. Apparently he had cut a deal with them. When they appeared, he produced for them a case of Budlites along with the recipe for making it. In return, Potts and Bloomfield were given the same 'treatment' that the Bull and Juline had received. Doc Bloomfield felt like a kid again and Potts was walking around for the first time in years, spry as a young buck. The Bull explained "They figured you would need more time with the Disks."

Then, they all just jumped aboard the Flying Cloud and sailed into their future. At the last minute the now ex-president and her husband joined them.

Bloomfield's reminiscing was interrupted by the telephone. He picked it up. "Bloomfield here."

"Harold, it's Lez Potts. I believe we have some things to talk about."

SPACE PATROL

The wormhole let them set their controls to auto-pilot, so they could kick back and relax for the first time in quite a while. Preparing spheres into habitable planets all the while keeping their eyes on their existing projects eventually can take its toll. They both enjoyed this break in the action, especially since they had a case of the Budlites along for the ride.

"So, Oxomoxo, where does this leave our bet?" Rawar carefully approached the subject they both had been contemplating since removing the schooner from earth. "Clearly it's not over yet."

Oxomoxo already had an answer. He'd had it ready for a while. "We have to let it ride, now that it has reached such a crucial stage. Unfortunately it might be too late. Let's examine the facts. First off, it's too crowded. Bar unforeseen circumstances, that's not going to change for the better. Secondly, they aren't taking care of their home the way they need to. Sucking their Planet dry for their antiquated energy source ends only in one way. What's worse, they know this and still keep doing it anyway. And there's even a hole in their atmosphere that they choose to ignore! If this doesn't change, Earth will certainly object. At this point, face it. There isn't much hope"

Rawar could see this was upsetting his co-pilot. He replied "It's not like it hasn't happened before, over and over, time and time again. Plus, we've already overstepped the boundaries we set for ourselves."

Oxomoxo brightened. "And, we managed to populate our New Project."

"Agreed. The bet stands. For now. There's no mess to clean up, and now we can take time to enjoy these Budlites. Maybe we should also try this 'Maui's Finest' Captain Magic gave us, hmmm?"

Oh Oh…

Pau.

Milton Keynes UK
Ingram Content Group UK Ltd.
UKHW022123030124
435425UK00018B/1206